Praise for *The Ganymede Club*

"*The Ganymede Club* does much to revive the best features of the SF juvenile mystery. . . . The character of Bat in particular is alone worth the price of admission."

—*Locus*

"A second yarn set in the medium-future, war-devastated solar system of *Cold as Ice,* with some characters in common. . . . Another intriguing and involving effort."

—*Kirkus Reviews*

Praise for *Georgia on My Mind and Other Places*

"*Georgia on My Mind and Other Places* showcases the work of a scientist with a fine literary sense. The title story deservedly won the Hugo and Nebula Awards last year."

—The Denver *Post*

"Sheffield is generally known as a hard SF writer, and many of his stories are about science. But in this lively, well-written collection, he does not limit himself to stories or themes that John W. Campbell would have bought for *Analog* twenty-five years ago."

—*The Washington Post Book World*

Tor Books by Charles Sheffield

THE GANYMEDE CLUB

CHARLES SHEFFIELD

A TOM DOHERTY ASSOCIATES BOOK ▪ NEW YORK

This is a work of fiction. All the characters and events portrayed in this book are either products of the author's imagination or are used fictitously.

THE GANYMEDE CLUB

Cover art by Berkey

A Tor Book
Published by Tom Doherty Associates, Inc.
175 Fifth Avenue
New York, N.Y. 10010

Tor Books on the World Wide Web:
http://www.tor.com

Tor® is a registered trademark of Tom Doherty Associates, Inc.

ISBN: 0-812-54460-9
Library of Congress Card Catalog Number: 95-23538

First edition: December 1995
First mass market edition: October 1996

Printed in the United States of America

0 9 8 7 6 5 4 3 2 1

TO JOE AND ED,
MY LONGTIME PARTNERS IN CRIME

SOLAR SYSTEM DEVELOPMENT PRIOR TO THE GREAT WAR

2012   First manned trip to Mars.

2020   First Mars colony; smart probes leave on solar system Grand Tour.

2029   First Belt mines and colonies.

2030   Von Neumanns released on Ganymede.

2032   First human exploration of the Saturn system.

2038   Solar studies research station on Mercury.

2040   Second human exploration of Saturn system; smart probes leave for moons of Uranus.

2044   Ceres and Pallas colonies achieve self-sufficiency.

2046   Venus terraforming effort aborted; first Venus station.

2048   Third Saturn exploration team; Von Neumanns released on Titan.

2050   Rapid development of Jovian moons Ganymede and Callisto; research station on Europa.

2053   Belt declares independence; major frictions between Earth and former Belt colonies.

2054   Disappearance of fourth Saturn exploration team.

2055   Earth population tops ten billion; Mars population tops ten million.

2057   Research station proposed for Oberon.

2060   Armageddon Defense Line installed on Luna; Luna population reaches seven million.

2061   Fifth Saturn exploration team.

2062	*Belt population tops one hundred million; colonies on Ceres, Pallas, Vesta, Juno, Hidalgo, and twenty-seven smaller planetoids.*
2066	*Sixth Saturn exploration team; Ganymede/Callisto population reaches eighty million.*
2067	*The Great War.*

1

Saturn System: 2032 A.D.

After fourteen months in space and ten weeks of irritation, the culprit had at last been discovered: Jason Cayuga was scraping clean the underplate of the air scrubber, while Athene Rios stood ready to bolt the cover back in position when he was done.

"I signed up for hardship and I signed up for danger." Cayuga spoke between vigorous sweeps of the scraper. "But I didn't sign up for *this*." He lifted the tool to his prominent nose, wrinkled his face in disgust, and transferred another film of blue-white mold into a sealed container. "Phew! What a stink. We should get medals."

"Where do you think it came from? We've made a dozen stops in the past six months." Small, dark, and delicate-featured, Athene Rios looked like what she was, a Spanish princess. She swore that in her own twenty-three years and in the hundreds of years of her known ancestors, no one of the Rios line had ever been called on to deal with what was, in essence, a plumbing problem. But on board the *Marklake* royal descent meant nothing. She and Jason Cayuga were the junior crew members, which meant they were automatically given the dull and unpleasant jobs.

"Came from? We brought it with us." Cayuga glanced

across to the little port, where the Sun was visible as a tiny disk of yellow brilliance. Earth itself was too small and distant to be seen, but each member of the crew knew just where to look. "The big mystery is why it waited ten months to start growing in here. It's a home-planet mold, though; no doubt about it. Munzer keeps talking contamination, but she's off the wall. You've seen the places we've been. The chance that a life form could survive on any of them is a flat zero."

"That's not what you said before when we left Earth."

"Course it isn't. I wanted to come, didn't I, same as you? If we'd said we thought there wasn't a chance in a billion that there could be life anywhere in the Saturn system, you'd still be in Madrid and I'd be sitting on my butt in Calgary. But extraterrestrial life is like danger. You say you're ready and waiting for it when you sign up, but you sure as hell don't *expect* it."

He had finished his efforts with the scraper, and now he was carefully sealing the cylindrical container. The foul-smelling mold would be stored away in the ship's hold along with the samples collected in the Saturn system: rock shavings and regolith from Enceladus, dirty ice crystals from the inner rings, probe returns from Titan's atmosphere, and the mysterious obsidian needles that Costas had found on the surface of Tethys. They would remain sealed in the hold for another two years, until the *Marklake* returned to Earth orbit.

"You can still hope for it, though," said Athene. "Alien life, I mean—not danger. Move your bulk, Jason." She was easing her way past Cayuga. The *Marklake*'s equipment room was scarcely big enough for two people, but it offered more privacy than the ship's cramped crew quarters. "What do you think?" She was leaning close and dropping her voice to an unnecessary whisper, at the same time as she swabbed the scrubber plate with a strong disinfectant.

"Jing-li said that you or I might get the next one. Think she'll stick to her word?"

"I don't see why not." Jason Cayuga's bark of laughter held more disgust than humor. "No one else is going to be fighting for it. Think of it this way: Costas will go down in history as the first person to set foot on Tethys. Jing-li was the first human on Mimas and Rhea; Dahlquist the first on Dione. Those are all major satellites, and one day they'll be as important for colonies as Mars or the Jovian moons. Von Neumanns will be working them all within twenty years, the way they are on Ganymede. But how many centuries before they work Helene? If ever. Who cares about the place?"

"I do. If you don't want Helene, I'll take it."

"Be my guest, dear." Cayuga watched as Rios slid the cover plate back into position. "Who's interested in colonizing something only thirty kilometers across? If Helene weren't at a libration point, it wouldn't even have a name." He turned, easing his broad shoulders through the hatch that led back to the main crew quarters. "You can have my whole share of Helene exploration," he said, without turning his head. "Me, I'll hold out for something decent sized. Maybe I'll get lucky and snag Hyperion or Iapetus."

It had sounded good at the time. Five days later, Jason Cayuga was regretting his generosity. The *Marklake* was approaching Helene, the little satellite that occupied the L-4 point of the Saturn-Dione system. Athene had been at the high-magnitude scope every spare moment of the past two days, ever since Captain Betty Jing-li had agreed that she would make the first landing on Helene.

Athene was becoming more and more excited. Jason could see why, even without benefit of the hi-mag scope. As the *Marklake* drifted steadily closer, it was clear that Helene was different from the other fragments of broken rock that the unmanned scout probes had reported a thousand times in the Jupiter and Saturn systems.

This planetoid was grainy and speckled, like a chalky egg covered with grains of black powder. It was also smoothly round, rather than jagged. There was no way that Helene's gravitational field could be strong enough to enforce such symmetry. The body must have been formed by the steady accumulation of small particles and dust that over the millennia had sintered themselves into an approximate sphere. But then Helene should appear more uniform in color. It ought not to possess that grainy texture.

Athene was puzzled more by the appearance than the shape. "I don't see how you could make a surface look like this," she said. She was squinting into the scope's main viewer. "Meteorite impact won't do it, and accretion won't do it, either. It's not cratered, and it's not smooth and even. It's *pitted*. I can see little holes all over it. It looks crumbly and porous. Like it's been nibbled by worms."

"What do you mean, *nibbled*? Mind if I take a peek?" Simone Munzer had silently entered the forward observatory without Athene's being aware of it. Now, although she asked the question as a formality, Munzer did not hesitate to push Athene away from the scope. As the expedition's anomalist she had the right to take over whenever any crew member hinted at something inexplicable.

Athene glared at Simone's angular profile, while Jason tried to appear sympathetic but was not too successful. He was sure that Athene had exaggerated what she was seeing, just so that he would think he was about to miss something special. On the other hand, if by some miracle Helene did contain something unique, Jason would have given away to Athene Rios much more than he had ever intended.

"I see what you mean." Simone Munzer was making delicate adjustments to the scope's focus. "They *do* look like holes, and the whole surface is peppered with them.

Ten to twenty meters across. But the sun angle's wrong to see down inside." She glanced up briefly at Athene and Jason. "One of you bring Captain Jing-li up from the cabin, would you? She has to take a peek at this for herself."

They both went. Athene was seething. "You know what's going to happen, don't you?" she said. She was half a step in front of Jason in the narrow corridor, barreling along, with her black eyes glaring at nothing. "That bitch, she's going to say that Helene appears *anomalous;* therefore it might be dangerous. Then she'll tell Jing-li that because it might be dangerous, Munzer has to go there herself. She's been drooling for a first landing ever since Tethys."

"I'm sure you're right." Jason knew that he would be just as angry as Athene if it had happened to him, but he hoped he would hide it better. She was still young. It had taken him all his twenty-eight years to learn that it never paid to show your emotions, least of all when you were angry.

"I wouldn't panic yet, though," he went on. "Simone wanted to replace Luke Costas as soon as he found the obsidian needles on Tethys, because she said we had no explanation for them. But Jing-li didn't go for that. She probably won't go for this, either. Cool off, Athene—or you'll blow your own chances."

He said the last words in an undertone that only she could hear. She was sliding the door to the main cabin, and as it opened, Jason could see that four other crew members were sitting in there. The two engineers, Roald Dahlquist and Luke Costas, were playing chess and talking. Hamilton Polk, primary physician and assistant anomalist, was, as usual, leaning back with his eyes closed, apparently sleeping but probably listening—no one was ever sure. Captain Betty Jing-li, who was at the far end of the table doodling on a computer pad, looked up inquiringly at the new arrivals.

"I wondered if it's too soon to suit up for Helene." Athene slowed her pace as she came into the cabin.

"That's up to you." Jing-li nodded at the clock on the cabin wall. "It's still a couple of hours before we'll be in matching orbit and at transfer distance."

"I know. But I'd like to be ready well ahead of time."

"Sure." Jing-li stared at Jason. "Not you, Cayuga. Just Rios. You passed up the chance of going to Helene in favor of another target."

"I know."

"If you want to suit up, though, you can serve as Rios's emergency standby."

"Thank you. I will."

Jason sounded suitably ungrateful. Betty Jing-li was not doing him any favors, because standby was one job that everyone on board had learned to hate. In each of the twenty-nine target encounters in the Saturn system, one of the crew had been forced to sit in a suit for periods ranging from five hours to sixty hours, waiting for an emergency signal from the landing party that never came.

Athene and Jason headed on through the cabin, skirting the long table. Opposite Jing-li, Athene paused. "Simone is up front using the scopes to take a look at Helene. She asked if you would join her there."

"She's seen something?" Betty Jing-li was rising to her feet.

"Nothing special. I saw it first, and I think Simone's overreacting. The surface may be porous and a little softer than usual; that's all. But with Helene's low surface gravity I expect no problem landing there." Athene spoke casually and carried on without waiting for Jing-li's reaction, passing into the corridor that led aft to the sleeping quarters and the exit locks.

"What do you think?" she asked, as soon as there was no chance of being heard in the main cabin. "Did you see her face?"

"Yes." Jason had deliberately remained a few steps behind. "She didn't look worried, and now she's expecting a pitch from Simone. Pretty good damage control. Don't worry, you'll go to Helene. And I'll sit in my damned suit for a day or two, playing with myself and waiting for you to come back. I should have sided with Simone. Then *you'd* have been acting as emergency standby to her. You owe me, Rios."

"Not necessarily." Athene was lifting down her suit and Jason's, and beginning the standard thirty-six-point check: air, filters (dual), heat, insulation, temperature, communication, nutrition, elimination (dual), medication, attitude control (triple), position jets (dual), joints (thirteen), seals (four), and suit condition displays (three).

"You may luck out," she said, when at last the check was satisfactorily completed. "You just have to hope that I'll run into trouble." She smirked at him. "Then you'll be the one who gets to play the hero and come to my rescue."

"Sure." Jason's voice showed that he gave the event the same low probability of occurring that she did. "I'll be waiting. But I won't hold my breath."

Close-up, Helene displayed more surface irregularity. The smooth ovoid visible from a distance became a wilderness of rocks that ranged in size from gravel and pebbles to white boulders taller than a human. The holes in the surface were less variable. None was narrower than a couple of meters, and none wider than twenty.

Athene had made her approach with due caution, while the *Marklake* hovered two kilometers away. Her suit video saw exactly what she saw and returned its images in real time to both the ship's central data files and Jason Cayuga's in-suit monitor. In spite of Simone Munzer's warnings there was nothing to suggest any cause for alarm.

Expedition protocol required that the landing itself be made with appropriate ceremony. Athene handled it by the book: "Recognizing the historic nature of this first human contact with another world, I, Athene Linda Rios, crew member of the Earth exploration vessel *Marklake,* on this fifteenth day of April, 2032, set foot on Helene, moon of Saturn, at fifteen hours and twenty minutes standard solar . . ."

Impatient as she was, she forced herself not to hurry through her final sentences. As she spoke she was inspecting the body below her. The planetoid turned slowly on its axis, with a period of seventy-eight hours, and solar illumination at the landing point was close to optimum for surface inspection. The sunlight was weak, one ninetieth of its intensity on Earth or the Moon, but it easily was enough for her to make out horizontal striations within the holes. She was itching for a closer look at the one nearest her. Nothing remotely like this had been encountered before in the Jupiter or Saturn systems, and although the Belt's mining colonies were notoriously secretive in dealing with the rest of the system, not a rumor of such banded holes had come from any of their many worlds.

". . . will be added to the shared resources of the Inner and Outer Solar System," she concluded. And then, without a pause: "Captain Jing-li, I request permission to explore the surface and structure of Helene."

"I oppose any notion of investigating the interior structure." Simone Munzer's voice, jarringly loud in her suit, cut in before Jing-li could reply. "I have been given no time to evaluate the records obtained so far. There is no urgency for such exploration. The surface of Helene is qualitatively different from any previously known, and the interior may present unknown hazards."

"It may." Betty Jing-li sounded calm as ever. "But chances are, it won't. May I remind you, Dr. Munzer, that the *Marklake* is, after all, an *exploration* vessel. We are fourteen months and a billion kilometers from home, and acceptance of a certain level of risk and a reasonable urgency in completing our mission are expected of us. Rios, you are authorized to proceed."

"Thank you, Captain."

"With suitable caution."

"Yes, Captain."

Athene was already moving. Jason found himself looking, through her telemetry feed, down a long narrowing tunnel illuminated by sunlight for its first thirty or forty meters.

"You can see the banding on the tunnel walls clearly now," said Athene's voice. "It's the sort of strata you might expect on a planet with sedimentary rocks, but of course that's out of the question here. I wonder if we're seeing the effects of zone melting and refreezing. The field is only a few thousandths of a standard gravity, but it might be enough. Of course, we still have to explain the source of heat for successive thawing. And the proportion of volatiles would have to be high. All right, I'm starting my descent. I'll be taking samples as I go."

The sunlight was gradually fading, direct illumination replaced by down-scattered light from the tunnel walls. The width narrowed steadily and then seemed to hold constant at about four meters. Soon the range data showed Athene at close to three hundred meters down. Still there was no sign of an end to the shaft. The descent continued in dead silence for another thirty seconds.

"I'm beginning to wonder if this thing goes right the way through to the other side," Athene said at last. She sounded different—breathless, slightly nervous, oddly distorted. The only illumination came from the lights in her suit. "No, it doesn't! The tunnel ends down there, with a different sort of formation. Strange. It looks like there's a milky layer of something across the end of it. See?"

Except that Jason didn't. The image in his suit monitor had been deteriorating for the past minute. Now it was a dim and grainy picture that flickered and faded as he watched.

He began, "I can't see what's—"

"No further, Rios." Jing-li cut in. "We're losing your signal. We shouldn't be having a problem at that depth, but we are. I want you to start back up again—now."

"Right. But I'm not getting . . ." The distortion was much worse: ". . . the over . . . up to the walls . . . coming . . ."

A long pause. Then, ". . . touch it . . ."

Faint crackling, like static—nothing more. Jason found himself unable to breathe. Captain Jing-li's voice, close and calm, cut in again: "I'm taking the *Marklake* to within two hundred meters. We'll be in position three minutes from now. Cayuga, what is your status?"

"I'm ready."

"Suit checked and sealed?"

"Yes."

"When I give the word, you head for the surface where Rios landed. Take a cable with you. Go into the hole, get her, come right back. Go slow. And no matter what you find, don't investigate. If you get stuck, signal along the cable. If you don't see her in the tunnel, come back. Costas and Munzer, into suits in case we need you. Dr. Polk, stand by for possible medical emergency."

Jason stood at the lock, waiting for the go-ahead from Captain Jing-li. It took forever to come. He was shivering in his temperature-controlled suit. He did not feel excited at the prospect of a major discovery. He did feel scared.

The cable attached to Jason's suit could stand a load of hundreds of tons, but it was light and perfectly flexible. He was scarcely aware of it as he drifted toward the waiting bulk of Helene. The Sun, off behind his right shoulder, seemed a remote and ineffectual spark of light. Saturn loomed as a half-disk to the left, the rings a thin bright line across the planet's equator. But it was Helene, the little

planetoid that he had dismissed five days ago as insignificant, that now seemed to fill the sky. The pocked surface
was fast approaching. The pinprick hole for which he was
heading became a dark violet shaft, leading to unknown
depths.

"Go into the hole, get her, come right back," he had been
told.

If only he could.

"Go slow"—that was the hardest order to obey.

Jason took a deep breath and entered the tunnel. The
light level dropped abruptly. His suit imagers compen-
sated at once, and he could see far ahead. He peered down.
There, no more than a few hundred meters away—he
gasped with relief—he saw a familiar shape. Reflected
light was gleaming from a white suit.

Athene.

"She's here," he said loudly. "Right in front of me. I can
go down and get her."

He heard the sudden buzz of conversation in his radio
link, and realized for the first time that no one had spoken
since he left the *Marklake.*

In the same moment he realized that Athene had remained silent, though he was right above her and must be
outlined against the sunlit shaft. She ought to be able to see
him. Also, the arms and legs of the suited figure were not
moving, except that the whole figure was rising slowly up
through the shaft. He felt overwhelmed by the implications.

Although his mind was stunned, he found that his body
knew exactly what to do: He dropped farther, steadily and
surely. In half a minute he was at her side. He saw, far
below, the odd milky surface that she had talked about.
There was no time to worry about that now. He attached a
grapnel to her, then jetted the two of them gently up to the
surface and toward the *Marklake.*

"Polk to the air lock, if you please," he said, surprised

at the calm tone of his own voice. "Dahlquist, prepare the emergency treatment facility. We have a medical problem."

And pray it was no more than that.

The *Marklake* loomed ahead. Jason used the grapnel to pull Athene close and move her in front of him into the lock. Her suit felt stiff and unbending, as though the body inside was already frozen to a final rigor. He peered in through the visor. Her face was pale, in places almost silvery. A trick of the sunlight, weak but at the same time harsh?

No time for a second look. He was in the air lock, cycling it at maximum speed. And Hamilton Polk was there, taking Athene's body from him, dismissing Jason with a casual, "Get your suit off. Then come back here."

Jason wanted to ask a question—*the* question—but he could not, because Jing-li and Munzer and Costas were hustling in, all talking, crowding him out. He went to the next cabin, stripped out of his suit at record speed, and squeezed back in through the door. He was just in time to hear Polk say, "A breach of suit integrity, can't say how it happened. Slits and tears, lots of them—see, here and here and here." Polk pointed to the suit's chest, arms, and upper legs. Athene's helmet was off, revealing her face—silent and pale and with faint, silvery blotches on her cheeks.

"We'll have to check every one of the suits," Polk went on. "They could all have the same potential problem."

Jason's question seemed unnecessary now. He had to ask it, anyway: "Is she dead?"

"I'm afraid she is." Simone Munzer had been standing next to Jing-li, and now she turned to him. He was glad to see that there was no trace of "I told you so" in her manner. "I'm sorry, Jason."

"But it's most peculiar," added Polk. The physician was bending low, peering at Athene's face. "Dead and already cooling. Yet it doesn't seem like a case of asphyxiation, which is what the suit punctures would suggest. Fascinating. Did you see anything strange, Cayuga, while you were in the interior?"

It had all happened too quickly, and Jason had been totally focused on what had to be done to rescue Athene. He shook his head.

"Of course, it may have nothing to do with her visit to Helene." Polk began to release the wrist seals on Athene's suit.

"We must prove that, one way or the other." Simone Munzer turned to Jing-li. "It's not like a normal ship fatality, where the body can go into sealed storage and await investigation until our return to Earth orbit."

"I agree." Jing-li's face was grim. The warning from the ship's anomalist—that Athene Rios should not explore the interior of Helene—was already in the ship's record. The official investigation would be unpleasant for Captain Betty Jing-li. "Dr. Polk, please prepare for and proceed with an autopsy."

"Already getting ready for it." The physician, unlocking Athene's ankle seals, seemed fully awake and enjoying himself for the first time in months. "But I'll need an assistant."

Athene had been his designated backup for medical emergencies.

"Of course." Jing-li turned to Luke Costas. "We will follow the usual—"

"If you please," Jason cut in. "I would like to help."

You interrupted a captain's order at your own peril, and Jason knew it. But Jing-li merely stepped closer, studied his face, and nodded.

"Very well. I understand. The autopsy will not be pleasant, they never are. If you have problems handling it—or yourself—tell me and I will arrange relief. Dr. Polk, please proceed. Dr. Munzer, I need to meet separately with you."

At her nod, Luke Costas turned and left the room. Jing-li and Simone Munzer followed, while Polk dispassionately watched them go.

"Wouldn't mind hearing that conversation," he said.

Jason believed him. Hamilton Polk disliked both women. He resented Captain Jing-li because she, a non-doctor, could give him orders, and he hated Simone Munzer because she ignored all his suggestions as assistant anomalist. She was also willing to challenge Jing-li where he dared not.

"What do you want me to do?" Jason didn't care to get into the middle of Polk's shipboard animosities.

"Finish getting Rios out of her suit. I'll go and prepare for the autopsy. When you're done, put the suit in a sealed container, then bring both it and Rios to the med center. We can't work here."

Polk's tone made Jason very glad that he had asked to be involved. As far as the doctor was concerned, Athene's body was no more than a piece of dead meat, to be examined with curiosity but no sympathy. Jason would treat her with proper reverence.

He waited until Polk had gone; then he began. With the helmet off and the suit's seals released, it was simple to open the front completely and ease the body free. He had to take hold of her hands and feet to do so. Athene had been barearmed and barelegged within the suit. Lifting her, he noticed that the odd body stiffness he had felt when he had removed her from the shaft on Helene was no longer present. Her flesh was soft and smooth, and much warmer than he had expected from Polk's comment. Her eyes were closed, her face calm. He wanted to believe that her death had been as easy and painless as her expression suggested.

He paused. There were silvery patches on her thighs and upper arms, and also on her hands. They were far more pronounced than those on her face. After a few moments he unzipped the front of her one-piece garment. It felt like an intrusion when he opened her clothing to examine her bare chest.

More patches, and brighter. He ran his fingers along a big one on her lower rib cage, and found it slick to the touch. He knew Athene's body well. There had been nothing like this, as recently as twenty-four hours ago.

Contamination.

He had not believed it until this moment, but suddenly he was sure of it. Simone Munzer had been right to warn, for something in the interior of the planetoid had entered Athene's body and killed her.

He had to get the corpse into a sealed container and report what he had found. But his fingertips were still on Athene's chest. Before he could remove them he felt a tremor, a movement.

Jason jerked his hand away. The bare chest was moving, the first faint tremble slowing and strengthening to a regular up-and-down motion. She was breathing. A thin wisp of vapor was creeping like a pale-blue tendril from her right nostril.

"Athene!"

He reached out again, wanting to help, not sure what to do. Her eyelids were flickering. As he watched, they opened. She was trying to lift her head.

He put his hand forward, intending to assist her. At the same moment he felt a wave of heat sweep over him. It began in his fingertips and spread rapidly through his whole body. With it came a tremendous feeling of strength and well-being.

But with it also came dizziness. He found himself unable to breathe. As the cabin around him began to fade, he saw that Athene was sitting up, turning in his direction. Her eyes were bright and unblinking. The last thing that Jason saw was the streak of silvery skin creeping along the back of his own outstretched hand.

2

Mars: 2063 A.D.

A sales pitch was always the same; it hadn't changed in five thousand years. First the salesman—though this one happened to be a saleswoman—told you all the advantages: the spectacular view—from eighty kilometers up you could see the whole lower city and, beyond it, the broad curve of the planet; the amazingly generous amount of floor space, enough for a dozen people to live in comfort; the unique privacy, with no one but you living on the whole floor section; and the astonishingly low cost.

And finally, the inevitable kicker: ". . . last one left, going fast, showing to three other people later today."

Julius Szabo listened, nodded, and evaluated her performance: not bad for a beginner. But he had been in the game back when she was kicking her shapely little legs in the air and crying for a change of diaper—and he had played on a field a hell of a lot tougher than real estate.

"I just don't know, Ms. Diver." He rubbed at his nose, put on his bewildered, worried look, and cut in when she was well into her windup and just five seconds before she was ready to state an inflated price. "It's very nice, but I can already tell that this place is way too rich for my blood. I'm retired, you know. I'm looking for something in the three-eighty range, and I can't possibly go more than four-twenty. Four-thirty, maybe, absolute tops."

Gracie Diver stared at him with her mouth open and her luscious pink tongue showing. She was a lovely piece of work. Twenty years ago—make that ten—hell, if he were just back on Earth.

Down, boy. Remember your official age: He had made his own instinctive assessment, inverting every one of the variables. Eighty kilometers up, you were well outside the thin wisps of Martian atmosphere. Damn it, you were *in space*—hard vacuum right outside the windows. The spectacular view (a 740-kilometer outlook in every direction over the arid Martian surface) was enough to terrify anyone with even a trace of acrophobia. Privacy was guaranteed by the fact that the lift tubes took forever to get you up so high. And the generous floor space and low price were sure signs that they could hardly give the place away.

But for Julius, each of those drawbacks happened to be a virtue. He had done his analysis and had quoted Gracie Diver a figure he estimated at just two percent higher than the minimum she was allowed to accept on the rental. He had cut it close not because of the price—he could afford a hundred times as much and never notice—but from sheer ingrained habit. He told himself he would have to watch out for that. He had altered his appearance, aging himself enough to fool anyone, and he was already thinking of himself as Julius; but personal foibles and vanities were hard to recognize in yourself, let alone change. And that could be fatal.

"Four hundred and thirty?" She hid her disappointment well, and she didn't even deign to mention his lower figures. Maybe young Gracie had a bright future, after all. "I'll have to check with the office, of course, because that's far less than I'm allowed to—"

"Would you do that?" The knife could cut both ways, and he had been wielding it long before she was born.

"You see, if I don't take this place, I'm supposed to see another property later today, and I'll be pushed to make the appointment schedule, what with all the time we took to get up here." Julius turned toward the window. "While you call your boss, why don't I wander around and take a look at the view? I've never lived anywhere so high up, I'm not sure what it feels like. And what with today's news, all those tough words from the Belt, I'm not sure Mars is the best place at all. Sometimes I think we'd be a lot safer out in the Jupiter system, on Ganymede or Callisto."

"I'll tell you what." At once she was right in front of him, smiling guilelessly up into his eyes and holding her remote-entry unit out toward him. "Why don't we fill out your application and transfer it in, right now? My office can evaluate it as it arrives, and we'll have a go/no-go decision in just a few minutes. Then we can both go on to our next appointments."

Good girl, he thought. Don't waste time thinking of profits you might have made. Take what you can get, tie it down, and go on to the next one.

Julius reached out and patted Gracie on her bare upper arm. It was a friendly touch; even—steady, man; act your age—a paternal touch. He felt a real affection for her. If she ever wanted to move into a different line of business . . .

He cut that thought off early. "Let's do just what you suggest. You know, you're a good saleswoman, Gracie. And in a couple more years you're going to be a lot better."

Seeing the blush of pleasure on fair young cheeks was worth the extra one percent he was sure he could have squeezed out of her on the rental price.

Julius Szabo, who used to be Danny Clay, had pondered the problem for twenty years. You could run Earth's highest-stakes gambling operation. You could have a genius for rapid calculation and a memory for numbers and statistics that guaranteed your own success. You could accumulate more wealth than your modest tastes would let you spend in a hundred lifetimes.

What you could not do was get away. You were bound to the system by a thousand shackles, and you knew too much about too many people ever to be allowed to leave. In fact, a quarter century of observation suggested only one way out. Some young upstart would covet the top spot, as you had coveted it yourself. You would guard against that as best you could, and your own long experience would help. You watched for "accidents"—aircar or lift-tube failures, a Hecate spider in a flower bouquet, shower faucets that turned instantly from warm water to superheated steam, idiopathic diseases uniquely tailored to your own body chemistry, even things as simple as stray bullets and natural food poisons. Those had all been used on others, and they could just as well be tried against you. You'd be on the lookout—of course you would—but there was a basic rule of life: The one that got you would be a surprise, the one you had not thought of.

Your talents allowed you to calculate the chances of your own death from natural causes. They were depressingly low, odds unacceptable to any self-respecting professional gambler. Throw in what Danny saw as the high probability that before the decade was out, there would be a no-holds-barred war with the Belt, and your survival chances dropped so close to zero you couldn't calculate them.

So, you had to find another approach. And the only one that he could think of called for lots of planning and a long lead time.

When Danny Clay died early in his fifty-second year, in a vacation boating accident on Lake Baikal, Julius Szabo had already been officially "alive" for six years on Mars. He was a sprightly eighty-three-year-old bachelor with no surviving siblings. His bank credit, as a successful retired actuary and statistician, was substantial. It was less than a fiftieth of what Danny left behind in his estate, but so what? *You can't take it with you.* Danny/Julius was smart enough not to try. Given the infighting, legal and illegal, that would be going on for his territory and possessions in Mexico City, no one would be able to estimate his wealth at the time of his death to within even ten percent of the total. A two percent skim would be perfectly safe.

He would be safe, too, provided that he made the separation complete. It had to be mental as well as physical. Julius told himself—morning and midday and evening—that he was *not* that other man, whatever his name was. He did not even know such a person. Danny Clay—who was that? If the mental block was to be effective, it had to be total. But it wasn't easy.

He moved into his new home on the eightieth-kilometer level in the Space Fountain pyramid, a huge ziggurat that stretched for another eight kilometers above him. He furnished the open vastness of the apartment in a spare, drab style that would have disgusted Danny Clay, who had had decadent casino/bordello tastes for plush red velvet and gold-framed mirrors. He provided a change-of-address notice to the Mars Society of Actuarial Consultants; placed a discreet sign, "Dr. Julius Szabo, MMSAC (Ret.)," in the building directory; and settled in to watch sunrise and sunset through the planet's thin apology for an atmosphere. He was prepared for several happy decades of a new and more relaxed life.

Danny had been thorough. Julius was fully certified and a genuine actuary, totally at home with and fascinated by the probabilities that governed human life expectancy. It was actually not far from the gambling life, except that vagaries of human heredity and environment took the place of a hand of cards or the spin of a roulette wheel.

However, despite his genuine interest in statistics, Julius Szabo had, according to his own society statement of actuarial capability, long ago retired. He did not advertise his services. He did not seek clients. So it was astonishing and disturbing to receive a call when he had been established in his new home for one and a half Martian years.

"Dr. Szabo?" The woman peering at him from the screen had bright violet-blue eyes embedded—that was the impression, jewels in jet—in a shiny black face surrounded by a halo of frizzy black hair.

"Indeed, yes." Those dazzling eyes carried Julius back a full twenty years. He resisted the temptation to add, "my dear." The biggest danger in becoming a courtly, white-bearded gentleman was in overdoing it to the point of caricature. "I am Julius Szabo."

"And I'm Neely Rinker. I need the services of an actuary. Can I come and see you? Today?"

She didn't look or sound like anyone from the Organization. Of course, if she were any good she wouldn't. And if she were their agent, he would learn nothing by refusing to see her, while such a refusal could turn any vague suspicions to certainty. If he did see her, of course, there was a danger that she might try to dispose of him on the spot; but if he were lucky and skillful, he might learn something to protect himself. At the very least, he might gain some time. If everything went wrong, he had one other escape hole, but it was a dubious and frightening long shot, relying upon an emerging (and illegal) Belt technology that most people did not know existed. If he made it through the day, he would check that he was fully paid up for the service.

Odds, odds, everything in the world was odds. You could calculate and calculate, but after all was said and done, you still had to throw the dice. Julius nodded. "If you wish to see me, then of course I will be happy to meet with you."

"Right away?"

"If you so desire. However, to avoid any possible misunderstanding at the outset, I want to be sure that you realize that I am retired, and have been for some years."

"But you still have a mortality computer, don't you?"

"I do. And of course I am still a member in good standing of the MSAC."

"I'll be right up. I'm in the building, but I'm down at ground level."

"My fees—"

"Will not be an issue. I have plenty of money."

She vanished, leaving Julius to his own thoughts. First, in the world of his own past, only a fool ever claimed to have lots of money. Second, Neely Rinker sounded oddly tense, while a professional from that same past world would never reveal tension. Third, if she thought she would "be right up," she was an optimist. The fastest lift tube needed half an hour to ascend eighty kilometers. Julius had ample time for preparations.

He made sure that his weapons were unobtrusive and ready. With one movement of finger against thumb, he could apply force to stun or even kill anyone, anywhere in the apartment, from half a dozen different directions. When he had finished that review he called his special service and confirmed that they were on-line for a possible emergency. Finally, he forced himself to sit down in an easy chair in his study. Thus far, Neely Rinker had the feel of a genuine client. It would be curious if she were. Julius smiled. It was the rueful smile of a man who, for the first time in his whole life, was perhaps about to make money by legal means.

Half an hour was an absolute minimum to get up from the ground level. He told himself that and tried to relax, as forty minutes passed and no one arrived. The final ring of the bell was both a release of tension and a new heightening of it. He pressed the door control before he could have second thoughts.

She entered quickly, in a swirl of violet-blue cape that

matched her bright eyes. She glanced around nervously as she entered. In person she was more striking than he had realized. The screen could not begin to capture the glow of total health, nor the beauty of perfect dark skin. Julius told himself, not for the first time, that total solitude wasn't working. He might pretend to eighty-three, but his hormones said otherwise.

One thing at a time. He led her along the broad corridor that ran from the lift tubes to his usual living quarters, walking carefully behind her and studying her tall, slim figure. No sign of concealed weapons—but then, if they were visible they would not be concealed. He ushered her into his study and indicated a seat across from his. So long as she was sitting there, he could destroy her instantly in a dozen different ways.

He sat down by the computer console and smiled at her. "Now, before you tell me just why you are here, satisfy my curiosity. How did you come to choose me, of all the actuaries in Oberth City? I feel sure that we have never met, for I would surely not have forgotten so beautiful a young woman."

"No. We've never met. I just consulted the directory."

"And picked my name? But how, Ms. Rinker? It could not have been alphabetical."

"No. It wasn't. I used a different criterion." Neely Rinker cast another swift glance around the room. She licked her lips and leaned forward. "I consulted the directory, as I said, for actuaries. And I picked the one with a current active license who has done the *least* work as a consultant for the past five Mars years. That is you."

After all his efforts to blend perfectly into the background, he had made himself conspicuous after all. Julius marveled at the irony of it, at the same time as he resolved to do something as soon as Neely Rinker was gone. He would change his society status from active member to associate member, on the grounds of increasing age.

But she was continuing, with an earnest and pained intensity: "I didn't want someone with a busy practice, people wandering in and out of the office all the time. And I told you that money was not an issue. It is not. I will pay you well, and more than well. But I ask something in return. I need your promise that you will never talk about this meeting."

"That will be no problem, Ms. Rinker." Except, why did she want such a promise? "Although actuaries are seldom the recipients of the system's most exciting secrets, it is our general practice to respect client confidentiality."

"Good. I want you to tell me my life expectancy. Actually, I want to know two life expectancies. I assume you can calculate that."

"Indeed, I can." Julius reached over to the computer and pulled the entry unit onto his knee. Neely Rinker's request suddenly made a lot more sense. She was planning some kind of long-term relationship, and she wanted to know if she was likely to outlive her partner.

"A life expectancy," he went on, "is exactly what a mortality computer is designed to provide. However, I assume that you realize that what you will get is no more than a *probability?* It answers the question, given a very large number of individuals just like you: What is the *average* life of all those people? It promises nothing about *you* in particular, or indeed any specific person."

"I understand that."

"Very well. And a life expectancy depends on many more things than the age of a person." He rubbed at his nose—an old habit, damn it, that he somehow had to break—and went on, "So, Ms. Rinker, if you do not mind giving me the answers to a rather large number of questions—some of which, I'm afraid, must be quite personal . . ."

When she nodded, he began. The first few variables

were so standardized that he expected no problems: name, personal ID number—

"No."

Julius looked up. "I beg your pardon? All I need—"

"No. I can't tell you my personal ID number."

"But really, my dear Ms. Rinker, this is just to save you time and money. I need your ID number to pull from the data files the most general information about you. Nothing personal. Just things like your place of birth, age, height, weight—"

"I will give all of those to you directly. Please go on."

Julius shook his head in pretended bewilderment. Actually, he ought to be the last person to complain if Neely Rinker—surely an assumed name—chose to hide her true identity. That made two of them. But what was she hiding? He might find out in due course. He already had one piece of information that she had probably never intended to give him: that she was not from Mars. If she were, she would have said she picked the actuary who had done "the least work as a consultant for the past five years," rather than "for the past five *Mars* years."

He went on. Age (thirty-one), height (one-point-eight meters), weight (sixty kilos), education, profession, health profile from infancy, personality profile, children (none), long-term liaisons (none), parents' and grandparents' health history, health profile of siblings, food preferences, use of stimulants, sleep needs, sexual preferences and habits.

Julius paused. This was the place where people often became coy.

Neely Rinker described the strength of her sexual needs and the frequency of their fulfillment, including her tastes for and extensive experience with vaginal, oral, and anal sex. She spoke calmly, fully, and clearly, without batting an eye. Julius felt that the answer was affecting him a lot more than her.

But the very next question was: "Current residence?"

And she was hesitating, biting her full purple-black lower lip. "You really need to know that?"

"Certainly, or I would not be asking. Low-gravity environments induce calcium loss. High-gravity environments impose excessive cardiovascular load. Nonstandard atmospheres change blood ionic balance. Deep habitats often introduce a high level of ambient radioactivity. Need I continue?"

"I guess not." Neely Rinker drew in a long breath. "All right, I'll tell you. I live on Ganymede. In Moira Cavern, forty kilometers below the Hebe access point."

Julius nodded and entered the data into the computer. His deduction had been confirmed. After all the secrecy, it was nothing even to raise an eyebrow. Ganymede was by far the most populous of the Jovian satellites, even though the hot prospects for development today were on Callisto and, as soon as the Von Neumanns got through with their work, on Titan. Ganymede was a safe, settled, and well-regulated environment. If the Earth-Belt situation deteriorated further, he might even head for Ganymede himself.

He went on, working his way through the second-order variables: hobbies and recreations, religious beliefs, phobias, dream patterns, ambitions. When he had everything, he paused.

"That's it. Unless there is something else that you think may be significant, and want to tell me about? Remember, a mortality computer can't do better than the data fed into it."

She stared back, the beautiful dark face as expressionless as an obsidian mask. "Nothing else, Dr. Szabo."

"Very well." Julius performed the run. The results came back without even a request for backup data. "According to what you have given me, your future life expectancy is one hundred and nineteen years. I assume that you would like a printed and signed statement confirming the input and output?"

"That is not necessary. A hundred and nineteen? All right, now I want to do the second case."

Julius nodded. "I might add that one hundred and nineteen is rather good. The average life expectancy for all females of your age is ninety-two years. But now, I wonder if we will in fact be able to run the other case that you need. Unless you can provide equally complete input data for your proposed partner—or for whoever that other person might be—"

"That won't be a problem." But suddenly she was restless, unwilling to proceed, standing up from her chair and walking across to the window. She showed none of the fear of open spaces that a Ganymede cavern dweller typically showed, but leaned against the thick transparent plastic to watch the setting sun strike the silvered sides of buildings, thirty or forty kilometers away. The ziggurat's next level was a full half-kilometer down, and beyond Oberth City the naked red plain stretched far and wide.

"How old are you?" she asked suddenly. "How old are you *really?*" She spat out the question without warning, as she turned back to face Julius.

The temptation was to destroy her instantly, annihilate her where she stood. She knew—she must know, to ask such a thing. But if she *knew,* why did she ask?

He forced himself to smile and to ask in reply: "Now why do you want such an uninteresting piece of information? However, it is no secret. I am eighty-three years old. May I inquire as to the reason for your question? And what do you mean, how old am I *really?*"

"Because you *look* old, but you don't *seem* it." She came close to him, her jeweled amethyst eyes staring into his. Strong young hands gripped his thin arms, specially treated to reduce their natural muscle fiber. "There's something about you, the way you look, the way you look at *me*. You don't act like an old man."

Bad news. So much for safety and security. Julius felt his smile freeze on his face. "But I am old, my dear," he said gently. "Maybe it is you. Maybe there is something about you that makes me wish that I were not old, that I could be young again."

If she treated it as a geriatric come-on and grabbed him, he would do his bit or die trying. Close-up, she smelled delicious. Mostly, though, he was just trying for a change of subject.

He got one.

"That's a very charming compliment." And then, before he could speak, she asked, "Have you lived on Mars your whole life?" Her question again unsettled him before he could gain his mental balance. He had just enough self-possession to make the quick calculation.

"Hardly. Ms. Rinker, the first Mars colony was not established until forty-three years ago."

She was staring at him with what seemed to be genuine astonishment. Didn't young people know *any* history any more?

"At the time," he went on, "I was already forty years old. Like everyone else in the solar system, I was living on Earth. I came to Mars at the age of fifty-two."

This last statement was, as it happened, absolutely true. But one more wild question and he would lose control.

And here it came.

"What does it feel like, being old?" Neely Rinker was standing closer, gazing into his eyes. "I can read about aging, and I can think about it, but I can't *feel* it."

"Age is—shall we say?—not an unmixed blessing." Julius caught his breath and tried to smile again. "Your bones ache, your senses dim, you sleep fitfully, your desires exceed your energies. Everyone wants to live a long time. But no one would choose to be old."

"That's what I needed to hear." Again, there came the tangential change of subject. She released her grasp on his arms and headed back to her chair. "Thank you, Dr. Szabo. What you just said is exactly what I had to know. I'm sorry, I've been wasting your time. When you are ready, I want to do the second calculation."

"But the profile—are you sure that you can provide me with all the inputs?"

"I already did. They are the same as before."

"Your own parameters?" Julius was calm again, back with something he knew how to handle. "My dear, although the mortality computer works to provide us with probabilities, there is no indeterminacy or random element in its calculations. With the same profile, you will obtain exactly the same answer as before."

"I understand that. I want to change just one of the assumptions. Suppose that everything about me is the same, except that I won't die of disease, or of general degeneration due to old age. Suppose that the only way I can die is from some kind of accident. What would my life expectancy be then?"

"There is no way that the mortality computer can answer such a question. It does not contain suitable tables, or appropriate computational procedures." But even as Julius Szabo spoke, Danny Clay came chiming in. It wasn't a question for an actuary, but it was a natural for someone who could handle probability calculations in his sleep.

Assume that the only way to die was from an accident. Suppose that the chance of *avoiding* such a fatal accident was a constant, P, the same every year. Start with a large population—say, a million people. Then the number living at the end of the first year would be a million times P. During the second year, of those remaining, a fraction of P would avoid dying by accident, so at the end of the second year, a million times P^2 would be left. Keep going: in the third year, a million times P^3; in the fourth . . .

"Dr. Szabo?"

"I'm sorry, Ms. Rinker." Julius came back down. He wondered, for the thousandth time, what the young Danny Clay might have become if he had not been forced to claw his way to adulthood in a city desensitized and brutalized by its ruling gangs. Then he denied, for the thousandth time, that he had ever in his life known a person called Danny Clay. "I was saying, the mortality computer cannot provide an answer. It is not designed to do so. But I can do it. I can easily work it out for you from first principles, from the known risks that you will die of different forms of accidents. However, it may take me a minute or two."

"I can wait."

Even if Neely Rinker had said she was leaving at once and had no further interest in the answer, Julius would not have been able to resist doing the calculation. The only hard step was to determine her risk of accidental death. He had to retrieve part of the mortality computer's data, and allow for all possible accidental causes. He found that there was one chance in 2,935 that Neely Rinker—assuming she had not lied about her habitat and lifestyle—would die from an accident in the next year.

Then it was easy. Take the individual terms of the P series, weight them by the year number, and calculate the sum of the whole series to infinity. The answer was surprisingly simple. Her life expectancy was just the reciprocal of the chance that she would die during one year. In other words, a disease-free and aging-free Neely Rinker would live, on average, for 2,935 years.

Julius stared at his answer with a mixture of pleasure and annoyance. Pleasure, that the answer had come so quickly and cleanly. Annoyance, because the result had no meaning in the real world. The oldest validated age in the solar system was one hundred and fifty-seven Earth years.

He looked up, to find Neely Rinker displaying her own

mixture of emotions, a combination of worry and anticipation.

"Well." She moved to look over his shoulder at what he
had written. Since it consisted of one number and three for-
mulas, he doubted that it could provide her with much satisfaction.

"I have the answer to the question that you asked," he
said. "But it is not a useful one."

"What does it show?"

"If you did not die of disease, or aging, but only from
an accident—that means 'accident' in the general sense,
including murder and suicide—then you could expect to
live for almost three thousand years. To be specific, you
could expect to live for another two thousand nine hundred
and thirty-five years."

She didn't snort, she didn't scowl, she didn't laugh at
him with mocking disbelief. She stared at the starscape beyond the window, and he could not even guess what she
saw there.

"Thank you, Dr. Szabo." She reached into the pocket of
her pantsuit, pulled out a fistful of money, and handed it
to him without looking. "You have been very helpful.
Now, I have to be going."

She was heading out of the study, striding down the
long corridor. Julius hurried along behind. "I don't think
I should be taking your money." He tried to keep up, but
she was moving far too fast for his artificially aged legs.
"I shouldn't be paid for what I did with that calculation,"
he called out, as the entrance to one of the lift tubes opened
and she stepped toward it. "It was just a meaningless exercise."

"Thanks again, Dr. Szabo." She turned, waved, and
dropped out of sight. The lift-tube entrance closed.

Julius was left with his mouth open. The only residual
traces of Neely Rinker were a hint of her light and pleas-

ant perfume and the wad of money in his left hand. He stared at it.

Cash—*no one* paid in cash, unless they were engaged in gambling, blackmail, or a political payoff. Cash was easy to make, and as a result it was easy to counterfeit. He had been handling fake money, good and bad copies, for thirty years. The bills in his hand were garishly colored, of improbably high denominations, and bore, across the top, the words *Ganymede Interior Trading Company*.

Neely Rinker had come, Neely Rinker had gone. She was surely not from the Organization. But from the look of it she might have stiffed Julius Szabo.

He could employ a lift-tube container to deposit the notes in his account, and learn in a day or so whether they were a legitimate form of Outer System currency. If they were not, their deposit was likely to arouse a good deal of unwelcome attention. Or he could make a descent to a bank level himself, and have an answer within the next hour.

It would be impossible to think of anything else for a while. He might as well admit that, and waste a little more of an already wasted day.

Julius opened his mortality computer and hid all but two of the bills within its largely empty interior. He returned to the lift tubes and rode one down, not to the nearest bank at the seventy-kilometer mark, but all the way down, until he was below ground level. And when he got there he headed not for the financial section, but over to the sprawling open kilometer of a multilevel shopping mall.

The food stores offered selections from everywhere in the system. He chose a vending machine on a lower level and inserted one of his two notes. The machine was smart enough to make change or detect a counterfeit, but not to question why a customer would pay with a note big enough to purchase a thousand items.

The machine swallowed the note and hummed softly to itself for a few seconds. The money apparently passed its rigorous inspection, because a bottle came sliding down along the rack to where Julius could reach it, along with a stack of change. He took the bottle and placed it, unopened, in a disposal bin. The money he stuffed into his pocket; then he started back toward the bank of lift tubes.

He was halfway there when he became aware of a cluster of a dozen people in the broad mallway on his left, with many more converging to swell their number.

None of his business. Safety lay in avoiding all forms of anomaly. But on the ground there, that flash of color within the cluster . . . He somehow found himself walking with the rest, standing at the edge of the crowd.

"From there." Heads around Julius were craning up, following the arm of the woman speaker in front of them. Far above and right overhead, a stone balustrade reached out in a long rising arc to connect two of the mall's upper levels. "That's where it must have come from. A loose piece. I wouldn't like to be the one in charge of maintenance."

Instinctively, the people around Julius backed up a few steps, afraid that something else might fall at any second. He moved in the other direction, closer to the huddled shape on the ground. It lay sprawled with one arm reaching out in front, as though pointing accusingly at the rounded, red-stained stone on the ground ahead. The cape of violet-blue covered her like a shroud. It was not enough to hide the deformed and crushed skull, or the mat of bloodied hair.

Julius backed away. In his old life he had seen violent death so often that it did not sicken him in the way that it might affect most others. What he felt was more of a sense of hysterical improbability.

Less than an hour ago, he and Neely Rinker had been talking of lives that might extend for almost three thousand years. But death cared nothing for probabilities. Death had arrived in the tiniest fraction of the time calculated as the life expectancy (one hour, or one twenty-six millionth of that time, said his mental calculator). In the real world, statistics made statements about *averages* and were useless in predicting individual events.

But were statistics the issue here? Julius had a sudden sense of his own vulnerability. Neely Rinker had refused to tell him her personal ID number. She had sworn him to secrecy, without giving him any idea why. She had traveled all the way from Ganymede, where mortality computers were as available as they were on Mars. Had someone else followed close behind her? Someone to whom Neely's secret was even more important?

Julius headed straight for home. He waited until a lift tube with no other passengers was available. He was nervous through every second of the ascent, waiting for an unprecedented power failure that would drop him to his death. He did not begin to relax until he was once more safely in his apartment with all his defenses primed.

Even then, he found it impossible to eat. He made himself a strong drink, went to sit by the window, and mocked his own weakness. Almost certainly, Neely Rinker's death had been a stupid accident; but even if it were not, they had been after *her,* not Julius Szabo or Danny Clay. She had picked his name almost at random from the directory. Probably no one else knew she had visited him. He could even argue that from his point of view, her death was a benefit. All knowledge of the visit had been destroyed at the moment when Neely Rinker's skull was flattened.

He felt an urge to call his special service, but for what? He had nothing to tell them.

It was long past sunset, far past the hour when he usually went to bed. Julius felt no desire for sleep. He made himself another drink, stronger than the first, and returned to sit by the long window.

The stars were as bright as always, undimmed at this altitude by even a trace of atmosphere. Phobos was visible as a fast-moving silvery point, sweeping from west to east across the Martian sky. He stared at it. Trouble, if it came, would derive from his own past, not from Neely Rinker's. He was just as safe now—or as unsafe—as he had been at this hour yesterday. The odds had not changed. The only thing different was his own mental attitude.

He frowned out at the night, pulled abruptly from his reverie. Something had happened. What?

It took a few moments to see it, to realize that what he had noticed was an *absence* of something. Phobos was no longer visible. But it could not have disappeared so quickly beyond the horizon.

As he watched, it winked back into view. Something had briefly occulted the little moon, some object between him and Phobos. There was no natural body that could have come between them, so it must have been an aircraft. But that implied a craft of such immense size that it could shield Phobos for at least five full seconds. No aircraft was that big—Phobos vanished again, then, just as quickly, reappeared—or that mobile.

Unless—

Julius leaned forward. Unless it was *close*. And under active control.

In the final half-second he saw it: a flattened and spinning, star-occulting shape that hung briefly to adjust its position, then rushed toward the window. He had no time to move. He saw the impact of the remotely piloted vehicle, and watched inch-thick, shatterproof plastic stretch and bow inward.

The wall was tough, designed to withstand heat, cold, and air pressure, but not a scything force of many tons per square centimeter. The spinning blade cut through the window and exploded as it did so. A five-meter section of plastic vanished.

Julius was not hurt by the explosion, but the outward burst of air took him with it. He was suddenly in a hard vacuum, falling, falling, falling. The air was bursting out of his lungs as he struggled to orient himself. He saw, far off, the lights of distant buildings.

No fear of hitting them. He was dropping vertically, a full half kilometer to the flat roof of the next building level. The impact would certainly kill him, unless he died first of lack of oxygen.

How long? His flair for calculation, functioning even now, fed him the answer. Half a kilometer drop in Mars gravity with no air resistance—he would hit after falling for sixteen and three-quarter seconds. He would still be alive and conscious at the moment of impact. He must do everything that he could to land feetfirst and try to save his skull with its metal protective mesh. That would not, however, save the rest of his body. He would hit at sixty meters a second, fast enough to smash every bone.

As air and blood frothed into ice spray from his ruptured lungs, Julius managed to reach his belt and key in the signal to Special Services. For what it was worth, they guaranteed their arrival within fifteen minutes anywhere on Mars.

He was falling, faster and faster. The roof was no more than fifty meters away. He had time for one final moment of revelation. He had still been right in one way. The odds of his old game had not changed. But the arrival of Neely Rinker had thrust him into a totally different game—one which Julius Szabo, who had once been Danny Clay, had never learned.

And he would never be able to answer Neely's question: *What does it feel like, being old?*

3

Ganymede: 2066 A.D.

There's no place like Ganymede. It has volatiles in abundance, ammonia and methane and water. In fact, fully half of Ganymede is water or water-ice—pure and potable—more than anywhere else in the solar system. Its surface gravity is just right, a pleasant and healthful one-seventh of Earth's field. Put all these things together, and they make Ganymede the perfect world, a paradise, the jewel of the Jovian system.

There's no place like Ganymede. All the Ganymede publicity and press releases tell you so.

Conner Preston looked around him and was unpersuaded.

He was far from his home on Ceres, shipped out for a one-year assignment that his boss had described as "broadening." Conner thought of it another way: A year in the Jovian system was one more bridge to be crossed on the way to the top of Ceres Broadcasting, the system's top news agency.

But it wasn't going to be an easy year. He was standing on the highest interior level, just a hundred meters below Ganymede's surface, and even here the noise was loud enough to rattle your teeth. He wondered what the Von

Neumanns could possibly be doing so close to open space. The damned things had been at it on Ganymede for almost forty years. It made sense that they might still be active deep in the interior, because Ganymede was *big,* the biggest moon in the solar system, larger than the planet Mercury. It represented a huge amount of real estate that had to be shaped and developed. But surely work on the outer layers should have been finished years ago.

Maybe it would have made more sense to leave the Moon uninhabited until the Von Neumanns were all done, instead of people rushing in to colonize at the earliest possible moment. Humans had needs: air, warmth, water, food. The Von Neumanns required none of these. So far as they were concerned, humans were nothing but a nuisance.

One of the bigger Von Neumanns, the size of a small dog, came trundling by Conner while that thought was still in his head. It was holding a vibratory borer, whose subsonics and ultrasonics would powder the hardest rock. If it chose to turn that damned thing on, anywhere within thirty meters . . .

He was tempted to ask what it thought it was doing, up here so far from interior construction, but he knew that would be a waste of time. The self-replicating machines were dim. They were just smart enough to do their jobs, respect the presence of humans, and reproduce themselves from local materials; and not one bit smarter. Humans had learned, the hard way, Fishel's Law and Epitaph: *Smart is dumb. It is unwise to build too much intelligence into a self-replicating machine.* That applied as much on Ganymede as it did in the Belt or anywhere else.

Conner sighed. He could escape from the noise if he were willing to take the next step, and head out onto the actual surface. He had been putting that off.

It wasn't that he disliked suits. He had worn them for jaunts around the Belt since he was three years old. But

Ceres and Pallas and Vesta didn't have Jupiter looming over them, a mere million kilometers away and apparently ready to drop onto your head.

It couldn't, of course. Ganymede's orbit was totally stable. But Jupiter could do something almost as bad. It could bombard you with an endless sleet of high-energy protons, gathered from the solar wind, accelerated by Jupiter's magnetic field, and delivered as a murderous hail onto Ganymede's frozen surface.

The Ganymede suits with their woven-in threads of high-temperature superconductors took care of that. The charged particles followed the magnetic-field lines, harmlessly around and past the suit's surface. Conner, inside, would be safe and snug.

But how could he be sure? How would he know that the suit hadn't quietly failed, leaving him to cook where he stood?

He wouldn't know—better admit it. Conner glanced at his watch. It was time to go. Death before dishonor. Except that Ceres Broadcasting seemed to provide assignments where there was a good chance of both. He checked his suit again and walked across to the elevator that would give him the hundred-meter boost to the surface.

The shuttle craft was waiting for him when he got there. Within five minutes he was lifting off and heading toward the ship of the Sixth Saturn Exploration Team, nine hundred kilometers above him in its orbit around Ganymede.

Conner felt that he was flying clear of danger. He did not realize that he would have been far safer standing on the surface of Ganymede in a suspect suit.

The journey out took half an hour. Conner had time to review his notes and to admit to himself an important truth: Ceres Broadcasting was not to blame for bringing him up here from the Ganymede interior. He was.

There had been a briefing the previous day by a member of the Sixth Saturn Exploration Team, far below in the interior levels. It had been more than adequate for most reporters, answering in full each of the few questions that were asked. The invitation to visit the ship itself, made by team deputy leader Alicia Rios, sounded like a pure formality. It was clear from her manner that she did not expect anyone to take her up on it, with its implied uncomfortable and time-consuming trip to orbit.

And no one else had. Conner was not quite sure why he was going himself. The only thing that he could think of was the contrast with the *First* Saturn Exploration Team, the party of ten people that had set out from Earth, thirty-five years ago, for humanity's original contact with the Saturnian moons. Conner was a nut about background checks. Before yesterday's briefing he had reviewed every file that he could find about that earlier expedition. He had studied interviews held with the first team's members before they left, and had watched videos of them exploring the Saturn system. On the face of it, the resemblance between the first and the latest expedition was surprising. But underneath there lay a basic difference that Conner found hard to put his finger on. Maybe that was the real reason he was here.

There were a couple of obvious differences, but those he could discount. This time only three people would be going, rather than the original ten. That represented progress in both ship automation and robot construction. One person could fly the new ship, and if necessary the computer and automatic pilot could handle anything short of a major emergency without human presence. There had also been big improvements in ship construction since the *Marklake* had left Earth in 2030. Conner had noted in the early video records how cramped the quarters of the first expedition had been. Now, approaching the *Weland,* he saw before him as large and, presumably, as spacious a vessel as any used by the Belt nomads. The main engines were Diabelli Omnivores, which could use as fusion fuel any of the lighter elements up to neon. He looked at those with special interest. They were banned from use in the Belt (although there were unconfirmed rumors that the Omnivores were undergoing secret development there as weapons). But with their use, the *Weland* would be able to live off the land anywhere from Mercury to Pluto.

The three members of the Saturn expedition were waiting for Conner when he passed through the *Weland*'s lock, removed his suit, and drifted through into the first of the three main cabins. One of them was Alicia Rios, whom he had met the previous day. The other two he recognized by name and appearance from the briefing materials: Jeffrey Cayuga, the expedition's leader, was a grey-haired man in his forties, and Lenny Costas was the big, slow-moving, and apparently slow-thinking engineer.

"Welcome aboard, Mr. Preston." Cayuga's words and smile were cordial enough. His tone and his eyes were something else—cool, measured, and guarded.

"Thank you." Conner did his best not to stare.

"I understand that you would like a tour of the ship?"

Cayuga's question made sense. What else could Conner get here, that he could not have obtained at yesterday's briefing? At Conner's nod Cayuga went on, "Then I suggest we begin aft. Unless you have questions before we start?"

"I'd like to ask as we go. But I do have one for you now. The three of you are all relatives of team members on the *first* Saturn system expedition. How did that happen?"

Did he imagine it, or was there in fact a change in Cayuga's expression, a glimpse of something new behind the eyes?

But he was answering smoothly enough, turning to lead the way so that Conner could no longer see his face: "Call it an obsession, Mr. Preston, one that we all three share. Saturn exploration has been a family affair with us for three generations. My great-uncle, Jason Cayuga, together with Luke Costas and Athene Rios, flew on the first, second, third, and fourth Saturn expeditions. They died as they would have chosen to die: exploring. But after their disappearance, as you might imagine, we felt an obligation to try to learn what had happened. The three of us were on the fifth Saturn expedition."

"But you never found them." Conner turned his head quickly. Alicia Rios and Lenny Costas were following close behind, watching him intently.

"Unfortunately, no. But here we are." Cayuga was opening the door to the engine room and waving him through. Conner went ahead, a little nervous, although he knew that the Diabelli Omnivores were completely powered down. He found himself facing a half-dozen blue cylinders, each about three meters across. These were the hearts of the Omnivores, where the actual fusion reactions took place. He found even their appearance unsettling.

"Never a trace of anyone," Cayuga went on, "although we searched for several months. There had been a final signal, indicating that they were heading for Titan to check the progress of the Von Neumanns left there by the second expedition. It is possible that they lost control of the ship and plunged into the Titan atmosphere. If that happened and everyone died, the Von Neumanns would of course have employed their remains."

From his voice there was no way to know that he was talking about the fate of one of his own close relatives. Conner compared Jeffrey Cayuga, standing before him, with his recollection of the video images he had seen of the uncle, Jason Cayuga. It was easy to see a physical resemblance: Both men were tall and pale and had full lips and prominent noses. The nephew's dark beard made further comparison difficult, but even without it there was no way that anyone would mistake one for the other. Jason had always had a smile, answering even the rudest or most stupid question during media interviews in a light-hearted, laughing voice. He looked like a great man to party with. Whereas Jeffrey . . .

A real cold fish, cold and pale as Alicia Rios. Lenny Costas, with his hunched shoulders and expressionless eyes, seemed no better. Maybe that was what they needed to tolerate the lonely journeys to the undeveloped reaches of Saturn and beyond.

But Cayuga was a cold fish that Conner had better pay attention to, because now he was over by the Omnivores, patting one of the bulbous cylinders with a pale, hairless hand.

"As you probably know, the Omnivores are able to op- erate in five different modes, depending on what is easily available." Cayuga beckoned Conner closer. "The fusion takes place right here, inside this section. We can burn hy- drogen to form helium, with an internal temperature as low as ten million degrees. If hydrogen is not available, the Omnivores can fuse helium to make carbon, but that needs at least a hundred million degrees before it becomes effi- cient. In mode three, carbon will burn to oxygen, neon, and magnesium, starting at about six hundred million degrees. Then we have mode four, neon burning once we get above a billion. And finally, if necessary we can fuse oxygen to silicon and then to iron. But those reactions don't really cut in until the Omnivores reach an interior operating tem- perature of at least one and a half billion degrees."

One and a half billion. Conner stared at the bulbous cylinders of the Omnivores with a new mixture of horror and respect. That was scores of times hotter than the cen- ter of the Sun itself. No wonder they were banned for Belt use and could be turned into weapons.

And if one of these Omnivores went wrong, in its hottest mode? The crew of the *Weland* would never know it. They might as well be sitting in the middle of a supernova.

"Are they *safe?*" The question popped out before he could stop it, but Cayuga did not seem to mind. He was even smiling, in a distant sort of way.

"Safe compared to what, Mr. Preston? Residence aboard the *Weland* is far safer, in my opinion, than residence today either on Earth or Mars, or in the Belt."

"You really think there is going to be a war?"

"Don't you?"

It was the question of the hour. On the one hand, Conner argued that the economic bickering between Earth and the Belt had gone on for as long as he could remember, and that was a full twenty years. But there was no doubt that recent exchanges were more rancorous.

"I believe that Earth deserves to be taught a lesson." Conner was parroting standard Belt politics, and felt uncomfortable doing it. "But I don't see how that can happen. I mean, there are eleven billion of them, and only a hundred million of us. And anyway, Earth has the Armageddon defense line, and it's supposed to be impenetrable. They drain a ridiculous share of our resources to support their population bloat, but I don't think there can be a war."

"Many people disagree," Alicia Rios said. "The rate of immigration from Earth and Belt to the Jovian system has tripled in the past four years. I gather that you yourself are a recent arrival."

"I was *sent* here. It's part of my job."

True enough. But Conner knew that it was not the whole story. He might claim that the stint on Ganymede was cruel and unusual punishment; but here, far from the threats and the posturing of Earth, Mars, and Ceres, he certainly felt a lot more secure.

Jeffrey Cayuga was staring at him as though he could read Preston's thoughts. "As I said a moment ago, the *Weland* and Saturn exploration is safe compared to *what?*

Nature is less of a threat than human actions. Our expedition team, cruising the moons of Saturn, will be subjected to less danger than your friends and relations on Ceres. I am not sure that even Ganymede and Callisto will be safe if a full-scale war breaks out."

"But you plan to come back here, when the expedition returns."

"That is not quite true." Cayuga nodded to Alicia Rios and Lenny Costas and they turned, leading the way from the engine room.

"We will return to Ganymede," he went on, "if it seems completely safe to do so. But I do not live here. I make my home on Lysithea, one of the minor satellites of Jupiter. It is almost twelve million kilometers out, and it is rather small—just thirty-five kilometers in diameter. But it offers privacy. And it is, above all, safe."

He stared at Conner Preston and spoke the final word with peculiar intensity. *Safe.* It made Conner feel physically uncomfortable. Suddenly he felt anything but safe. He was eager to leave the *Weland,* and the company of Jeffrey Cayuga, as soon as possible.

When the shuttle carrying Conner Preston was on its way back to the surface of Ganymede, the three members of the Sixth Saturn Exploration Team convened in the ship's main cabin.

"Opinions?" Cayuga was at one of the scopes, watching the descending shuttle.

"I do not think that we have a problem." Lenny Costas had not spoken more than two words to Conner Preston, but his pale, cautious eyes had watched him closely every second that he had been aboard. "He knows nothing. I believe that he suspects nothing."

"You are too easily persuaded. Why then did he bother to come here?"

"Sniffing and scouting. He is a reporter. That is his job."

"Maybe." Cayuga, still using the scope, did not look around. "Alicia?"

"I don't like it. As a reporter, he gets places. It is possible that he was on Mars, three years ago."

"Even if he were, it is unlikely that he met Neely."

"But not inconceivable. They could have talked, before we were able to put the trace on her. I say, why take the risk? It is better to be rid of him, and be safe."

"I do not disagree with you." Cayuga was still at the scope. The shuttle with Conner on board was finally making its landing on the surface of Ganymede. "But the timing is inconvenient. Our review of progress on Helene is overdue. The others are already there. We should not delay our departure."

"We can use Jinx Barker. He did a good job for us on Mars. He's a professional, he's reliable, and he's discreet."

"He appears to be. But let us not forget that he is no more than a hired hand. He is not one of the Club. We must be careful."

"Of course. Why not make this a test case? We will be away for at least eight months. We tell Jinx what we want him to do about Conner Preston. When we get back we check that he did a good, quiet job. No matter what happens, there will be nothing to tie Preston to the Club. And we will all be a billion kilometers away."

"Lenny?"

Costas nodded. "I doubt Preston knows anything, but after listening to Alicia, I have to agree with her. It's just possible Conner Preston picked up some information from Neely. No point in taking the risk. I say, let Jinx handle it."

"Then we three are all in agreement. We will inform the other Club members when we arrive at Helene. Alicia, you will need to brief Jinx Barker in person."

"I know. I'll go down and do it today."

"Tell him to take his time, to find out as much about

Conner Preston as he can, and report to us when we return."

"Suppose he decides that Preston has no connection at all with Neely?"

"He will still do his job, and dispose of Preston. Those must be his instructions. We cannot have someone who is not a Club member assessing risk on our behalf."

"Suppose there *is* a connection? Suppose Jinx finds out too much about Neely?"

"Then we must make another decision. It could be membership. He might make an excellent recruit."

"I'm sure he would." Alicia was smiling.

"No." Costas shook his big, shaggy head. "I don't like that at all. Don't forget that Neely was once considered a prime candidate for Club membership."

"A valid point." Cayuga turned off the scope. The screen turned dark, and the image of Conner Preston's shuttle blinked out of existence. "Caution is always the best policy. However, it does not affect our decision regarding Conner Preston. It is a pity that we took time explaining the ship to him. That is favorable publicity that will probably never be used."

4

EARTH: 2067 A.D.

Ten miles from the Corpus Christi spaceport, above-ground progress became impossible. Lola Belman took one last look at the sea of vehicles ahead as the bus driver made its assessment of all route loadings, computed probable delays, and ramped down into the tunnel net.

"Where are we going? What's happening?"

Spook, sitting at Lola's side near the front, was more annoyed than alarmed. To a ten-year-old, anything new was interesting. For all he knew, the spaceport access route was always crowded. But Lola had told him that they would see hundreds of spacecraft on the ground as soon as they got near enough, and now he felt cheated. The thin plume of lifting ships, taking off under laser boost, had been visible from fifty miles away as violet jets in the late-afternoon sky; but by now the novelty of that had faded.

"It's nothing. Just a traffic jam."

Lola said it, but she didn't believe it. Jaime and Theresa Belman might pretend that everything was normal, that the family trip to Ganymede was a vacation they had been planning for a long time. At ten their son was young enough to accept the story. Lola, at twenty-two, knew better. She wasn't much interested in news broadcasts, but at the moment they were hard to ignore. Everyone seemed to be making boring speeches: accusations of skullduggery, frantic boasts of Earth's military might, mockery of Belt threats and weapons—and warnings to civilians to prepare for possible attack.

After a few days of that, the speeches were just noise in your ears. But this—clogged roads and tunnels, nervous passengers, checkpoints tended by men in uniform—was different. It seemed like history, a video reconstruction of ancient times. This was the sort of thing that had happened a hundred or two hundred years ago, but not now.

Most significant, her parents had suffered a sudden and unexplained change of mind. Instead of all four of them leaving Earth for Ganymede in one week's time, she and Spook had to leave *today,* without adequate time to pack, without visiting grandparents, without the farewell party for friends. The explanation—that cheap tickets were available—had been enough for Spook. He couldn't wait to be off into space. To Lola, though, her parents' statement was no more credible than the political speeches of the past month. Her mother and father wouldn't even listen to her plea: that she would rather stay and travel with them. She and Spook had been hustled onto the bus with maximum speed and minimum dignity.

They were slowing down now, creeping along at a walking pace. Finally the bus halted completely.

"The spaceport terminals are one-point-two kilometers ahead," said the driver. "Unfortunately, the tunnels beyond this point are presently impassable for vehicular traffic. Passengers must proceed the rest of the way on foot. There will be signs to direct you to your flights."

The whole bus filled at once with a hubbub of protest.

"What about our luggage? Will it be loaded automatically?"

"We were supposed to meet our group at the drop-off point. Are there signs for that?"

"I have four cases with me, and they're *heavy.* How am I supposed to carry them?"

"A kilometer? You stupid machine, I can't walk a kilometer. I need wheelchair assistance. I can't walk more than a few steps."

That came from an old man who had been sitting just behind Lola and Spook. He seemed to have no trouble at all walking as he hurried forward and began to hammer on the blue cylinder of the driver's control unit with his black walking stick.

Lola grabbed her brother's hand. "Come on. We've had all the help from the driver we're going to get."

"But our luggage—"

"Can look after itself. Either it gets on the same ship as us, or it gets on the next one." *I hope.* Lola felt she should be crossing her fingers. "We can't worry about it now. *Come on.*"

Even on foot, progress along the tunnel was slow. Vehicles were everywhere, some empty, some still containing passengers conducting hopeless arguments with the automated driver units. The lighting was poor. It had never been intended for anything more than vehicles, whose controls had no need for any sort of illumination.

Lola followed the signs for Gate 53, still holding tight to her brother's hand. She knew he was supersmart, but when the mood took him he could be a super-smart-ass. He wasn't called Spook for nothing. If he exercised his famous skill at disappearing and made them miss their flight, it would somehow become *her* fault. Her parents would never forgive her.

Less than half a kilometer to go. Would they emerge above ground, or would the tunnel lead them right to the Gate's lower level? That was Lola's main worry when, without warning, all the lights went out. The darkness around her filled with curses and nervous moans. At the same moment she lost her grip on Spook's sweaty palm.

"Augustus Belman! Stay where you are and don't move."

"Don't you *ever* call me that! I'm *Spook*. And I'm *not* moving." His voice, right next to her, was high-pitched and indignant. "Where d'you think I could go? I can't see a frigging thing!"

"No cussing!" He sounded perfectly normal—and the lights, thank God, were flickering back on. Not as bright as before, but enough to see by.

"Let's go, Spook—as fast as we can."

Something far more serious than a lighting failure was going on. Lola felt a tremor—the ground vibrating beneath her feet. A current of air swept through the tunnel from behind, and it was filled with fine dust that, for a few seconds, had everyone coughing and choking.

Forward movement was becoming more difficult. She had told Spook they must travel fast, but some people seemed to have given up. They were lying down or sitting, leaning against the tunnel walls. It was necessary to step over legs and bodies. Trying not to tread on them, Lola also had to keep an eye open for the routing signs that blinked occasionally to life.

Gate 55. Gate 57. The signs were there. Had they somehow missed Gate 53? With enormous relief, Lola saw the sign they wanted over to their left. Its light was out, but she could make out the arrow pointing to an escalator.

An escalator that seemed to lead up forever into darkness—and that was not working. Lola pushed Spook ahead of her, clutching the back of his shirt. The steps were clogged with people, some doubled over and panting for breath, a few others standing hopelessly waiting for the escalator to return to life and carry them upward.

Spook stopped, making her bump into him. "Sis, what's *happening* here?"

She didn't have the breath to answer, even if she could. The ship they were supposed to be on departed at 7:00 P.M.

It was now five forty-five, and she dared not even guess at the turmoil and delays they were likely to encounter at the gate.

"Keep going." The end of the escalator was finally in sight. Gate transit and security were just beyond. Ominously, the area was almost deserted. A solitary woman in transit blue stood at a security checkpoint, directing angry and baffled passengers.

"Flight 670 already left." She hardly glanced at Lola's outstretched tickets. "I know it shouldn't have, but we're not running on the usual schedules."

"What's happening?"

"Go along the tunnel there and up the other escalator— that one's working." She ignored Lola's question. "Hurry. Another flight is ready to leave. It's full, but we'll squeeze you on board."

"Our bags—," protested Spook.

"—will be fine." Lola grabbed his hand again. "Let's go." She dragged him toward the tunnel, and was rewarded with a grateful smile and a wave from the transit official.

The tunnel was long and curved to the right. It led to a rising stair. At the upper end Lola saw the purple of the night sky. She ran up the rising escalator, eager to be above ground again. Just before they reached the top, the opening ahead filled with a flash of pale orange. As they emerged onto a wide spaceport launchpad, Lola expected to hear the explosion. There was no sound, only another flicker in the sky like a far-off sheet lightning, and then, from one of the other pads, the *whoosh* of a laser launch.

"Go on." A man in blue was waving them toward the stubby ship that stood on their pad. He showed no interest in tickets or any form of identification. "Run. You'll be the last. Lift in two minutes."

It was sunset, with the last glimmer of light on the western horizon. As Lola and Spook ran along the ramp to the entry hatch above the ship's engine and pusher pad, the silver of the ship's curved side had an orange-yellow glimmer. Lola turned her head. She saw a lightning flash, high in the sky behind them, which, as she watched, blossomed into a rosette of crimson and white. And then the ramp cover was over them, and they were being hustled aboard.

Every passenger seat seemed to be taken, but a man wearing the grey uniform of Lunar Service gestured to them to sit down next to him on an attendant's foldaway bench. It was a space designed for only one person, and Lola and Spook could barely fit. She wriggled her hips, trying to avoid the seat arm. She had been to space before, and she knew how uncomfortable even a couple of gees of acceleration could be.

The hatch was closing. This was the time for a flight attendant to stand up and give them the usual three-minute lecture about safety procedures, exit points, and the use of belts, hatches, and free-fall barf bags.

But not today. Before Lola could fasten or even find her belt, a powerful vibration filled the cabin. The seat swiveled so that they were lying on their backs. She was pressed hard into the cushions. She heard Spook's grunt of protest. He was wedged in between her and the bony lunar serviceman.

"What's happening?" It was Lola's turn to ask that question.

"We're taking off." The man was almost too casual, and she noticed he was wearing the chevrons and crossed bars of the Lunar Defense League. She saw the name tag on his pocket: *Audie Coline*. "In a bit of a hurry," he went on. "Don't worry, though, we're perfectly safe."

"But *those*." Lola knew quite well that they were taking off—that's not what her question meant, and he must have known. One of the ship's small circular ports was on his left, and she lifted a lead-filled arm to point. Another rosette was blooming in the sky, on the northern horizon. Off to the west, the sun had reappeared as the ship lifted higher.

"Nothing to get excited about." Coline was answering her but he was turning to look at Spook, managing a grin that was turned oddly lopsided by the ship's acceleration. "The spaceports are operating on an emergency basis, and as you saw for yourselves they're totally screwed up. Heads should roll down there, because we've been expecting something like this for quite a while. We should have been ready. It's the Belt government's idea of a show of force, letting us know what they could do if they really tried. They've sent a bunch of probes into cislunar space."

"They're attacking Earth?" Lola was suddenly terrified, not for herself and Spook, but for the parents they had left behind.

"No. The probes have dummy warheads. The Belt wants to make the point that since they can beat our deep radar detection system, Earth and Mars should meet their economic demands. But the point they've actually made is quite different. See that?"

He gestured at the port next to him, apparently unaffected by the acceleration. The ship was curving off toward the east, already into the last minute of its laser-boost launch. Farther east and high above them, another bright blossom of light was growing. Beyond it the Moon was visible in its thin crescent phase.

"The Belt has just learned that the Armageddon Defense Line up there can pick off anything they send into cislunar space, without hardly trying. Wish I'd been on Luna to help. You can't see it without a scope, but we're targeting their probes and blowing them up."

"All of them?" Lola remembered the frightening ground vibration and failed lighting. "Something hit while we were in the tunnel on the way to the spaceport."

"Quite true." Coline seemed delighted. "The Armageddon line knocks off everything the Belt sends with no trouble at all—but some clown on Earth couldn't resist having a go with the ground-based spaceport perimeter defense. That equipment is half a century old, and it's never been used. They should have known it wouldn't work. And it didn't. One of the hi-vee projectors blew up when it was discharged. You felt it, and I saw it. *And* the power draw knocked out half the electricity supply lines. Thank goodness, the laser launchers are on independent power lines, or we'd still be sitting there." He laughed. "Anyway, all the damage to Earth today has been *self-inflicted.* Maybe from now on they'll leave it to professionals."

As he spoke, the laser boosters on the ground finished their work. The ship was suddenly in free fall, moving more than fast enough to take it into orbit.

"Where are you two heading?" The lunar serviceman had reached across both Spook and Lola with his long arm, making sure that even without their belts they were in no danger of floating across the cabin.

"To Ganymede. Our parents are coming out next week to join us." Lola felt a huge sense of relief. Her worries about Jaime and Theresa Belman had all been unnecessary. "We're taking our vacation there."

"So you'll make your ship transfer when we get to geosynch. That's a couple more hours. Looks like the excitement's all over." He nodded at the port. "By the time we arrive at geosynch everything should be all quiet again."

The flicker of lights had ended. Bright, steady stars were replacing the blooming deep-space explosions.

"I only went to Ganymede once," Coline said, "and I didn't care for it." The slight vibration and the return of partial gravity showed that the ship's own engines were working, lifting them to a higher orbit. Attendants were beginning to move from seat to seat, helping passengers who had thrown up during the free-fall phase. Suddenly it felt like a normal flight. "The natives there are rock rats," he went on, "all of 'em, they don't see the sky more than once a year but they don't seem to miss it. Any idea what you're going to do when you get there?"

"I want to try the Puzzle Network. Ganymede is supposed to have some real hot-shot juniors." Spook had been quiet so far—a first for him, in Lola's experience. But then he had never been to space before. She knew that feeling. During free fall he must have wondered what his stomach was doing.

"Bit young for that, aren't you?" Audie Coline spoke to Spook but winked at Lola, with an expression that said he was more interested in her than he was in her brother. "What are you, ten, eleven?"

"But he's a genius." Lola grinned back. "He'll tell you so himself."

"Quit that!" Spook, wedged between the other two, sat straighter and stuck out his chin. "I've seen the Ganymede problem sets. They're tough, but I can handle them."

"Hardest in the system, I've heard. And the best, if you believe their publicity. But they say they're best in everything." Coline sniffed. "Listen to the Jovian moons, and you'd think Earth, Luna, and Mars are washed up and nothing but old history." He casually reached over and fastened a belt across Lola and Spook. " 'How I spent my Ganymede vacation.' I aced the Puzzle Network. What about you, miss? Any idea what you'll be doing?"

Lola hesitated. She knew what she wanted to do, but was she willing to admit it? Even her parents did not know, but the images had been locked in since the time of her earliest memories: Uncle Wilber, grinning at nothing, frightened of everything, forever on the brink of self-destruction. And his madness had been an *unnecessary* madness.

"I want to check out the schools," Lola said at last. "I've

heard that they have a reputation for—for being good at what I'm interested in."

"And what might that be?"

She had to say it now: "I want to train as a haldane."

That certainly got his attention. "A *haldane?*" he said. "Do you, indeed. Well, remind me to be careful what I say to *you* from now on."

It seemed to be the universal reaction—and Audie Coline was being kind. The usual comments were much harsher: "Only someone who is crazy to start with wants to work with crazy people." Or: "You want to be a haldane? How long have you been off your head?" She had better learn to get used to it, or change her career plans.

"But I might not make it." Lola could see the Earth's dark bulk, with the Moon on the horizon beyond it. The ship must have turned on its axis during the ascent. "It's supposed to be really tough. I'll need another five years of training, even if I pass the rest of the entry tests. And after that—"

She paused. A bright spark of blue light had appeared, not on the Moon's illuminated crescent, but over on the other limb where the disk was supposed to be dark.

"After that?" prompted Coline.

Lola did not reply. She pointed. Two more flecks of flame had sprung into view, close to the first one. Even as she watched, there were others. The Moon was suddenly ablaze, a line of flame spreading rapidly across its dark face like a windblown fire.

Audie Coline had turned casually to follow Lola's gesture. He jerked upright, pushing Spook to one side. "The line!" he exclaimed. "My God, this is impossible. That's the Armageddon defense line!"

His tone and the horror on his face said a lot more to Lola than his words. The scene behind him told even more. The Moon was on fire. A great swath on the lunar surface was burning with the ghastly blue light of nuclear fusion. In the foreground, a matching spark glowed suddenly on Earth's nightside. It was followed by another two, both in the Northern Hemisphere. They grew rapidly, ever brighter. A dozen others appeared—a score, a hundred. The atmosphere itself was beginning to glow in orange-red streaks.

"Is it?" asked Spook.

Lola did not answer—did not want to answer. Because it *was*. It was war, the unthinkable war between Earth and the Belt that everyone had talked about forever, but that no one had believed could really happen. The Moon was on fire, Earth was on fire. The world was ending.

She and Spook might have a chance to escape. Ganymede was not involved in the Earth/Belt dispute, so a ship heading for Ganymede might be spared. But Mother and Father . . . , they were down there, on the flaming ruin that a few minutes ago had been the peaceful Earth.

She reached out and grasped Spook's hand, hard enough to hurt him. Her mother's instructions had been specific: *"Until we arrive, you're in charge. Look after Spook. Don't let him get into trouble."*

He was in trouble. They were all in trouble. Earth and the Moon and the Belt and Mars, now and for years or decades to come. But that did not relieve her of her responsibility.

She was in charge.

Lola stared at Spook's frightened face, and past it to the flaming sky outside the port. She felt the last of her childhood disappear, bleeding away into the harsh emptiness beyond the ship.

THE SOLAR SYSTEM
BEFORE AND AFTER
THE GREAT WAR
(2067 A.D.)

PREWAR

Mercury: *Research station for solar studies, occasional science staff.*

Venus: *Three surface domes, plus research stations and an experimental biosphere: investigations into meteorology, planetology, ecosystems. Permanent staff.*

Earth: *Population eleven billion.*

Luna: *Population seven million, plus automated factories.*

Mars: *Self-sufficient colony, population seventeen million.*

Asteroid Belt: *Self-sufficient colonies on Ceres, Pallas, Vesta, Juno, Hidalgo, and twenty-seven smaller planetoids. Total population one hundred and seven million.*

Jupiter: *Interdependent colonies on Ganymede and Callisto, research stations on Europa and Io, unmanned collection vessels in Jovian atmosphere; combined population, Jovian system: eighty-three million.*

Saturn: *Ganymede-based exploring parties to rings and all major moons. Von Neumanns working on Dione and Titan. No colonies.*

Uranus: *Smart probes to all major moons; research station proposed for Oberon. No colonies.*

POSTWAR

Mercury: *Research station lost, no survivors.*

Venus: *Surface domes lost, no survivors.*

Earth: *Population two billion in Southern Hemisphere and tropics; Northern Hemisphere uninhabitable.*

Luna: *Population zero, no production capability.*

Mars: *Population eight million, self-sufficiency maintained.*

Asteroid Belt: *Colonies on Ceres, Pallas, Juno. Population nine million, no longer self-sufficient.*

Jupiter: *Relatively unaffected, except by rapid prewar immigration. Interdependent colonies on Ganymede and Callisto, research stations on Europa and Io, unmanned collection vessels in Jovian atmosphere; combined population, Jovian system: eighty-seven million.*

Saturn: *Unaffected by war. Ganymede-based exploring parties to rings and all major moons. Von Neumanns working on Dione and Titan. No colonies.*

Uranus: *Unaffected by war. Smart probes to all major moons, research station proposed for Oberon. No colonies.*

5

Ganymede: 2072 A.D.

The Great War was over. It ended just four months after it had begun, in a final cataclysm that shattered the solar system and reshaped it into a new form. Its aftermath would reverberate down the centuries. It was the war to end wars.

Except that wars still went on. This particular one was fought without armies, without hardware, without bloodshed, without reinforcements or mercy or remorse. Its warriors would probably never meet. They were unlikely to know their adversaries' real names, since the Puzzle Network permitted—and encouraged—anonymity.

But the Masters of the Net did not need names. They knew each other very well, at the profound mental level where battles were engaged.

Bat, just two years in the Masters' division, was learning fast. He had advanced to the point where he could recognize a puzzle designed by Claudius, a five-time champion, as surely as if she (he was convinced that Claudius was a woman) had signed her name. She took a unique delight in misdirection, layer after layer of it. Four weeks earlier, Bat had set his own trap, hoping to exploit that misdirection and turn it into a weakness. He was convinced that he had caught her—until she sent back the correct solution, with an added note, "Old age and treachery will defeat youth and skill. Keep trying."

He would. Most of the other Masters fell far short of Claudius, and all of them had their own strange quirks. He would recognize Attoboy, Simple Simon, Gaslight Tattoo, Pack Rat, James the Rose, and Sneak Attack, no matter where or how they appeared, or under what name.

But the Puzzle Network could still offer surprises. One was appearing now, filling his display with four complicated three-dimensional sets of interlocking donuts. The accompanying text read, "Specify connectivity: simply connected or multiply connected?" It was signed *Ghost Boy*.

The name was unfamiliar, but that meant nothing. Claudius, when she was in an unusually vicious mood, was likely to sign on as *Xantippe*. Bat normally signed on as *Megachirops*, but presented his word puzzles as *Thersites*. The puzzle, not the name, was the thing, the only thing; and this one was a major oddity. The structures were so clearly multiply connected that no one with any self-respect would offer this as a problem at the Masters' level. That suggested two things: First, the puzzle was not what it seemed; and second, a new and distinctive personality had been added to the game.

Rule number one of the Puzzle Network: *Use all of the information available to you.* Rule number two: *There is no such thing as cheating.* Bat had his own Rule number three: *Know thy enemy.* He had a trick that he suspected might be his alone.

First, he checked the response time for Ghost Boy's net access. As he had hoped, it was only a few milliseconds. Therefore, Ghost Boy was somewhere on Ganymede, rather than being an off-world entry. Bat knew the style of the dozen Ganymede Masters. It was unthinkable that Ghost Boy could emerge as a new Master, without years of experience on the Puzzle Network.

And that led to only one possible conclusion: Ghost Boy had been in the net for some time, but he had been promoted recently to the Senior League.

Bat took the next logical step. He did what no self-respecting Master would ever do. He went slumming, dropping down to the Journeyman level in the network and scanning back in time over the past two years.

No sign of Ghost Boy as either a proposer or solver of any puzzles. Which left only the Journeyman puzzles themselves, hundreds and hundreds of them.

Sorting through them was going to take some time. Bat raided his own Bat Cave sweetmeat hoard for orange jujubes, peppermint bonbons, and chocolates, returned to his terminal, and settled happily down to work. It was the middle of the night. No one was going to disturb him. Given a good puzzle like this, with its promise of yet another puzzle if he solved it, the idea of boredom or fatigue was unthinkable.

Five hours later, he had it. A dozen Journeyman puzzles involved odd topological elements similar to those of Ghost Boy's problem. They were hard to solve, and it was even more difficult to imagine how someone of the Journeyman class had managed to dream them up in the first place. But each puzzle had been proposed by a player named *The Snark,* and the most recent came three months ago.

Obviously, The Snark and Ghost Boy were one and the same. He had changed his name when he moved to the Masters' level. And just as obviously, the earlier puzzles were going to tell Bat enough about the workings of Ghost Boy's mind to solve the most recent one.

But not easily. It was another two hours before Bat groaned, raised his eyes to stare at the ceiling, and whispered a single word: "Dimensionality!"

The Snark was devising his puzzles in spaces of a higher

dimension, the fourth or fifth or higher, and then project-ing down to three dimensions. The way to solve them was to reverse the process, imagining Ghost Boy's sets of in-terlocking figures as cross sections of some higher-dimensional structure.

It still wasn't easy to solve this latest one, but now it was possible. Bat stared at nothing until he was sure that the entire puzzle construct, viewed in four dimensions, had no holes or reentry features. Finally, he wrote that the puzzle was "simply connected in 4-D," signed his solution *Megachirops,* and sent it off.

He didn't expect a reply. For one thing, it was many hours into the standard Ganymede sleep cycle; for another, Puzzle Network protocol did not call for answers.

It was a shock for him to find a message popping into his display area, just a couple of minutes later. It read: "Hey! You're not supposed to solve me that fast!" And then, an even bigger surprise, a smiling face appeared above the message.

"Hi," the face said. "I'm Ghost Boy."

"So I deduced." There was a silence, while Bat stared in astonishment at the display. It was not a surprise to find that a Master on the Puzzle Network was young—the men-tal agility of youth was an asset—but this was ridiculous. Ghost Boy was a *kid.* He was thin and gawky, with freck-les and a big nose, and he had no sign of facial hair. He looked even younger than Bat! And Bat knew that he him-self was a rare prodigy.

"My name's Spook Belman," Ghost Boy said. "You see how it goes, I'm *Ghost Boy* now and I used to be *The Snark.*"

Didn't Belman know anything at all about Puzzle Net-work manners? He was not only intruding, but also *ex-plaining.* Bat tried to make allowances for the gaucherie of a newcomer. "I know," he said. "I caught both allusions from your name, thank you."

"Well?" The kid's grin faded, and he frowned. "Aren't you going to return the compliment?"

"What compliment?"

"Your name. Tell me your real name. And turn on the visuals, so I can take a look at you."

Unbelievable. "I prefer not to."

"Well, you're a real sourpuss, aren't you." Spook Belman glared out from the display. "I guessed you were pretty young, from your style, and I thought maybe the two of us could get together and compare notes on the old fogies. But you sound like one of the old fogies yourself. That puzzle I set was supposed to stop anyone on the Network for a few days. Seems I was wrong, about it and about you. How old are you, anyway?"

"My age is of no possible concern to you." Bat paused. He never met with anyone if he could avoid it, but this was one of the rare moments when he might question his choice of lifestyle. He added grudgingly, "I am sixteen years old."

"So I was right! But you sound like you're sixteen going on a thousand. I'm sure you don't care to know it, but I'm fifteen." Spook Belman was still doing his best to be friendly, but it sounded like an uphill fight. "Look, I had another reason for connecting to you. I was going to do this anyway, even if you hadn't solved my puzzle. I wanted to ask: How come your puzzles involve the war so often?"

He had said the magic word. Bat had been all set to break the connection. Now he said slowly, "It is a special interest of mine—"

"Mine too!"

"—since I believe that it will prove to be the defining event for our century, and for many centuries to come."

"But you lot weren't even *in* it." Spook waved his arm around, including in "you lot" the whole of Ganymede. "You were so far away, how could you possibly know what went on? Did you live in the Inner System before the war started?"

"Certainly not." Bat quivered at the prospect. The thought of an open sky gave him the willies. He would not, without coercion, venture so high as even the outer levels of Ganymede. "There are more rational ways of obtaining information, without blundering around all over the solar system. Only a fool would choose to visit Earth or Mars—still less, choose to live there, even before their destruction."

"You think so, do you?" Spook sneered out of the display. Bat had touched some exposed nerve, and Spook's conciliatory manner was discarded. "Well, that just shows how little you know. I was going to give you some real good stuff about the war, material no one else out here on Ganymede has ever seen or knows exists. *Firsthand* experience. But you think you know everything. You don't want to meet, you don't want to be seen." He paused, as though he were making some difficult decision. "I'll tell you what I'm going to do. I'm going to send you something, a couple of extracts from a data file. You take a look at them, Megachirops, or whatever your real name is. And if after you've seen them, you decide maybe you *don't* know all about everything, then *you* can give *me* a call."

Abruptly, he was gone, his frowning visage fading from the display. Bat puffed out his full cheeks. So much for Ghost Boy.

Good riddance. He surely didn't know anything about the war that Bat had not already discovered for himself. He couldn't possibly. Bat had drained every source of information on Earth, the Moon, Mars, and the Belt, in addition to tapping whatever was available on Ganymede and Callisto. There was nothing more to be found in any of the data banks.

But suppose that Ghost Boy, against all the odds, had managed to locate something that was *not* in the banks . . .

The rest of Ganymede was waking up. Bat was expected to go places and do things. Like studying. But he could not resist.

He queried his access unit. Sure enough, a new file was being transferred to his personal directory. A big one, calling for the use of full derived reality. Bat summoned the file, and calmed himself as he waited for the environment to establish itself.

Against the standard blandishments of men or women, he believed himself invulnerable. There were, however, other forms of beguilement and seduction.

As elsewhere in life, in derived reality you got what you paid for. Bat had experienced a dozen different environments through the Puzzle Network. In the cheapest of them, only the people felt real (and sometimes not even they did). The rest of the surroundings were grainy and poorly defined, as though you could push your fist right through the furniture. The perspective was usually off, providing lopsided doors and walls. Sometimes you would find a dark patch, where part of the field of view had been omitted entirely from the synthesis.

At the other end of the scale, the best environments were completely self-consistent and perfectly scaled. There was a feeling of *solidity,* a palpable quality to the surroundings that justified the term "derived reality." The synthesizers of such high-quality environments were professionals, and they were good.

But they were never this good.

This was *real,* as real as dinner.

Bat was hurrying along a dark-walled tunnel, dragging someone with him. People were everywhere. Most of them were moving forward, but some sat slumped wearily against the walls. The light was dim and flickering, the air thick and hot and filled with a fine powder that made his eyes water. The ground shook beneath his feet.

His body felt most peculiar. It was terribly heavy, dragged down by a powerful gravitational field. It was also unnaturally shaped. There were organs, interior and exterior, which had no right to be there. He was in a *female* body, which was towing along behind her a small boy, not much more than half her size.

Before he could adapt to that strangeness, the whole environment changed. The woman was no longer underground in a high-gravity world. She was now in free fall. There was no danger that she would float away, because she was wedged in between the same small boy and the hard arm of a seat. Beyond the boy sat a big man, and beyond him, through a viewport, Bat recognized a familiar image. It was Earth's Moon, visible through the ship's port, in the crescent phase—the face of the Moon as seen from Earth, as it had been *before* the war. Most of that face was dark, but on the illuminated limb he recognized the patterns of dark, smooth *maria* and cratered uplands.

And then it changed again.

A bright spark of blue light appeared. It was followed at once by another, then another. A burning line was etching itself into the Moon's shadowed disk.

Bat, himself and yet not himself, felt the hair bristle on the back of his head. He knew exactly what he and his alter ego were seeing. That was the Armageddon Defense Line, exploding along its whole length like a line of firecrackers, as it was attacked by the fusion fires of modified Diabelli Omnivores. He was witnessing the very moment of the Belt's first attack, when the conflict changed from a war of words to a war of deadly weapons. Within the next few minutes, the whole Northern Hemisphere of Earth, together with its nine billion people, would die.

He had read about this a hundred times. But this time he was *here,* in person, an eyewitness. He waited, as the field of view turned, to take in the broad face of Earth, no more than a few thousand kilometers away. A first bright spark glowed on its nightside, grew . . .

And vanished, together with everything else. The data file had ended, derived reality was gone, and Bat was sitting in his chair staring expectantly at nothing.

He ground his teeth in frustration. Spook Belman had done this *deliberately;* Bat knew it. Spook had more, he must have, but he had cut off the file at the very moment when he knew it was most interesting to Bat.

The irritation and the mystery did not end there. A person might be present at the event, as Spook Belman claimed to have been present. He might even record it. But no recording could capture the sensory detail that Bat had just experienced. And it was sensory detail as experienced not by Spook Belman, but by a *woman.*

Ghost Boy had some other trick up his sleeve, some way of turning experience into derived reality.

Bat admitted the galling truth: Belman had found his weak spot—Bat's overwhelming curiosity. To satisfy that, he would have to call Spook back and reveal his own identity. It felt like groveling. It *was* groveling. He could imagine Spook now, sitting there complacently waiting for Bat's capitulation.

Bat reached out for the communication pad, then drew back. The temptation was terrible, but he would not give Spook Belman an easy victory. He would resist as long as he possibly could—and hope that before he weakened, Spook would again call him.

There was no way for Bat to divine that Ghost Boy, still sitting at the other end of the communication line, was feeling far from complacent. In fact, Spook was facing up to the consequences of his own rash action, and he did not like what he saw. When his sister found out what he had shown Megachirops . . .

He had let his pride and anger get the better of him. In sending those data files to Megachirops, he had guaranteed that he would soon be in more trouble than he cared to think about.

6

The sign in the entrance lobby was printed in bold white letters on a red background. It read: YOU ARE IN THE OFFICE OF LOLA BELMAN, LICENSED HALDANE. IF YOU THINK THAT YOU CAN BE HELPED, THEN YOU PROBABLY DON'T BELONG HERE.

The young man who fidgeted in the only chair had been staring at the sign for the past five minutes. Lola, observing him through a small pane of one-way glass, ran a final physical-response correlation, checked the drug levels in her own body, and decided that the time had come. If she didn't get started soon, she would need a booster. She closed the panel and turned her office over to Fourth-Level Fax response. It would handle most things and interrupt the session only for a real emergency.

She went through to the outer office and addressed the visitor for the first time. "Bryce Sonnenberg? I am Lola Belman. You can come with me now."

She read him as apprehensive, but not excessively so—nothing like some of the wretched mental messes who had shivered their way in to see Lola in the past ten months. In fact, most people would pass Bryce Sonnenberg on the street without giving him a second look.

She didn't assign significance to that. External appearances proved nothing. And he had come an awfully long way for a consultation.

"Sit down." Lola smiled and gestured to an easy chair covered in dark-brown suede. "Right there, if you please."

A lot of work had gone into that chair. It was designed to look normal, adjust to any angle, and feel comfortable, but a fortune in psychometric equipment sat concealed within it. The data outputs that came from its back, arms, and seat went into permanent records, while a quick-look version was provided directly to Lola's implant. She was already scanning for extreme values in Sonnenberg's physical parameters. She found nothing. He was a little uneasy, but nothing more.

Unfortunately, that was not necessarily a good sign. The hardest cases were the ones of most subtle deviation.

"I know you've spoken with my fax," said Lola. "And of course I have that record. But if you don't mind I want to go back to the very beginning. I'd like to ask who you are, what you know about me, and who suggested that I might be able to help you."

He seemed suitably doubtful. The sign in the lobby was not kidding. Anyone who came to see Lola Belman, or any other haldane, had exhausted the conventional channels of treatment.

"I'm Bryce Sonnenberg," he replied after a few silent moments. "Though of course you know that already."

"I do. But say anything you like, repeat anything you like." Whatever he said would make little difference. The real message was delivered by the psychometric monitors and models. Lola felt the powerful psychotropic drugs awakening within her, like a giant stirring from sleep. She was coming to the critical point, the very edge of stability, the place where a haldane must operate.

Sonnenberg was nodding, relaxing. "I am twenty-four years old. I was born in the Belt, on Hidalgo, but when I was only three, my mother moved us out to Callisto. I don't know who my father was." He paused and glanced doubtfully at Lola. She confirmed her first impression. Even with the worried frown on his forehead and the uncertainty in his dark eyes, Bryce Sonnenberg was handsome. It made her aware of the fact that she was only three years older than he was—and that she had been a licensed haldane for less than one year.

She nodded. "Go on."

"Do you want me to talk about that kind of thing?"

"Anything you like. For the first quarter hour, it won't make much difference. We'll be calibrating the equipment."

"Right. Anyway, my mother, Miriam, is a Von Neumann designer, doing the advanced models that fine-tune the cavern biological balance after main excavation is all finished. I didn't realize, until I was eighteen years old, how good she is at her job, but in her own specialty she's top dog on the totem pole. When I was a kid I had more little Von Neumanns as friends than I did children. Our apartment was full of them. Sure you want to hear all this?"

"It's exactly what I want to hear. Go on; you're doing fine."

"Three years ago, when I reached twenty-one, mother told me that the Von Neumanns could handle the rest of the work on Callisto by themselves. She wanted to head farther out to where the work was more challenging, to Uranus or beyond. The habitat construction on Oberon was just getting started, she said. Did I want to go along? I wasn't sure, but I said I'd think about it. I did that while she was wrapping up her work. Finally she was all done, and ten months ago she was ready to go.

"So then it was up to me. I'd been changing my mind from one week to the next, but when the time came I decided I didn't want to leave Callisto. I was doing something

I enjoyed, and I wanted to keep on doing it for at least a couple more years.

"But then, just four months after she left, I started to have . . . well, problems." He paused, and shook his head. "I guess you know."

Uneasiness, and much more pronounced. It was time for Lola to show a little of her hand.

"As a matter of fact, I do know. But not in the way you think. Some idiot has been putting nonsense into your head." Lola allowed a little irritation to show through. "Forget all the simple-minded rubbish you've heard about an Oedipus complex. That was discredited centuries ago. Your problems, whatever they are, have nothing to do with your mother leaving."

"Are you reading my mind?" He was frowning, grimacing. "I've heard it said that a haldane can read people's minds, but I didn't believe it."

Now he was truly uneasy, Lola sighed to herself. It was always the case—you had to blow away the misconceptions and half-truths before you could even begin.

She shook her head. "I said I know, and I do, but not the way you think I know. You're confusing haldane technique with witchcraft." She slowed her speech by a calculated amount. "Despite what you may have heard, I don't have a cat and a broomstick. I don't have a cauldron, or a third nipple, or warts and a crystal ball. What I do have is a computer, a mass of telemetry equipment, and six years of special training and experience. I also, like every licensed haldane, have an M.D. and a doctorate in statistics. With the help of the equipment and some fancy nonlinear models, I will *usually* be able to deduce what you are thinking. If I can't, I don't deserve to stay in business. But one thing you can believe for sure: I can't read your mind, or anybody else's."

He stopped his grimacing, and his core body temperature edged up one-tenth of a degree. That was a good sign. He believed her, and now he was feeling a bit of a fool for swallowing the common rumors about haldanes.

"I'm sorry." Lola dropped her voice in pitch and volume. "I interrupted when you were just about to describe your problem."

" 'Problem' may be the wrong word for it." Relieved, Sonnenberg moved away from the question of what Lola could and could not do. "What's been happening to me sounds as though it ought to be a standard medical question, but it's not. I'm a mathematician. I specialize in number theory. Most of the time it's fascinating, but it's also very intense. Sometimes, after a week or two of concentrated work on a problem, I think my skull is going to crack open. Then I have to get away from the pure head work and run wild. That's why I started space racing as a hobby. Nothing spectacular. Just ion drives within the Jupiter system. Ever tried that, or seen it done?"

It was Lola's turn to grimace. "I haven't left Ganymede since I got here. I haven't been up near the surface for at least three years."

"Then you'll have to take my word for it. Low-thrust racing sounds easy, because the acceleration of the scooters is limited to a fraction of a gee—the absolute opposite of hot-rodding. But it's not easy at all. We pick up our speed and improve our times using gravity swing-by maneuvers, and that means skimming in so close to the moons that you can reach out and touch the peaks. We have no backup equipment, and flight computers are forbidden. Everything depends on your own judgment and mental calculations. Screw up, and you lose. Screw up at the wrong time, and you die. I've had friends smash into mountains. It's really exciting, but it's not something you try unless you're absolutely alert."

Or even then. Lola merely nodded, and monitored the telemetry. He was not scared by his hobby, just exhilarated.

Bryce Sonnenberg did not fit the image of the ivory-tower mathematician. He was a risk taker. He was also something that she could not yet define.

"I used to race every week," he went on. "Then one day, when we were still at the takeoff part of the race, I had a blackout. One moment I was sitting in the scooter, waiting for the starter's signal. Next thing I knew all the other scooters were out of sight. I hadn't moved. The starter light was blinking on my panel. I didn't know how long it had been like that, but later I learned that I had lost at least three minutes. The other competitors assumed that I had suffered a power failure, so they just took off without me.

"That was the first time. Since then I've been losing chunks of time, anything from one minute to ten. I never know when or why the next blackout is coming. Obviously, I've had to give up space scooters. A one-second blink at swing-by point could kill me."

What he was saying was a disappointment to Lola. She switched her implant to the standby mode and held up her hand before he could continue. "I agree that you have a problem, and you do need treatment. But it's not a job for a haldane. What you have is a physiological difficulty. I can give you the names of people with the right equipment and qualifications, and they can explore the physical side of what's been happening to you."

"You could, but it wouldn't be worth it." He was staring at her in mild reproach. "You didn't let me finish. First, I've been to a dozen medical specialists, the best ones on Callisto. They all agree that it's *not* a neurological problem. Not, in fact, a physical problem at all. Because there's another bit of information that I didn't get to. I black out, and when I wake up I have no idea what happened; but *afterwards,* when I lie down to sleep, I start to *remember* things. Things that feel as though they happened to me while I was unconscious."

"If you remember things, then you weren't unconscious."

"I'd agree with that, if what I remembered had anything to do with reality." He stared at Lola, openly troubled. "But the things that I remember never happened to me. They *feel* like memories, but they happen in places I've never been to in my whole life."

"For example?" Lola stared back at him, careful to conceal her surprise and satisfaction.

How about that? It looked like there was a job for a haldane here after all.

Visions. Distorted perceptions of space. Time inversions and time loops. Out-of-body experiences. They had been reported parts of the human condition for thousands of years, but surely they were much older. The religious experience had been present from the dawn of recorded history. Ten thousand years ago, the seer, in his ecstasy, foretold the distant future. The keeper of the temple felt himself rise into the sky, and saw the world below, no bigger than the palm of his hand. The sacrificial virgin felt within her the presence of the living god.

The early psychologists grappled with the bases of sensation and memory, struggling for an understanding using the inadequate tools at their disposal. They performed their long couch sessions and pronounced their exorcisms, invoking The Word according to Freud and Jung. They called on their magic potions, norepinephrine and dopamine and serotonin. They applied their mind-blistering philters, of imipramine and fluoxetine and Thorazine and chlorpromazine.

Sometimes the patient was even helped. But the mystery of the human mind remained untouched, until nonlinear statistical analysis, combined with telemetry, pulse probes, and powerful bespoke medications for both doctor and patient, brought the haldanes onto the scene.

Lola never mocked her primitive predecessors. The early psychotherapists had been like chemists before Dalton and Lavoisier, like astronomers before Kepler and Newton. They did their best to make sense of a bewildering variety of facts, but they had lacked the basic tool for the job: a general theory that would underpin everything, and make a coherent whole from a wilderness of single instances.

Whenever Lola was tempted to self-pity—recalling the loss of her parents in the war, or the first miserable years for her and Spook on Ganymede, or even the trauma of the haldane's training—she reminded herself that in other ways she had been lucky. She was fortunate to have been born at exactly the right time, just after the breakthrough.

It was still hard work. The training of a licensed haldane had a rigor and intensity that made the standard physician's apprenticeship seem casual and lightweight. In addition to their medical training and their knowledge of the effects and side effects of every psychotropic drug, Lola and her associates had to understand their computer tools, know their programs down to the last bit. Their ability to construct and validate neural network analogues had to be as good as any worker's in the field.

But it paid off. The physical mechanisms that underlay visions, déjà vu, time slips, and other-life memories had at last been dissected, defined, and captured in quantitative models.

No wonder that all religions had hated the haldanes when they first appeared in the 2050s. No wonder that preachers and demagogues still hated them.

But no one could discredit them. Prayers and politics might work, or they might not. A haldane's therapy did work, indisputably. Now the pendulum had swung too far the other way. A haldane's powers were overstated, to include direct mind reading and mind control.

Lola and the other haldanes knew that was not true.

They knew the limits of what they could do. They also knew they had powers that no one but a haldane could comprehend.

Powers, and problems. You could not probe into another's troubled mind and remain untouched. When the haldane's ranks were thinned, it was almost never because one of them had chosen another field. It was usually a slide off the edge into madness, to a depth where not even a haldane could reach.

Lola had enough preliminary information. The instruments were calibrated. It was time for Sonnenberg's first interaction session.

"We'll keep this short today." She already had his chair extended to form a couch. He was lying down, the sensor cups in position over his eyes. "I'm going to put you into a trance state with stimulated recall. I'll know, from your eye movements and eye-lens muscle contractions, the direction that you're looking and how far away an object is. I'll take a cortical scan from the part of the brain that handles visual and auditory memories. I'll also know your emotional response to anything that you see and hear. But I won't actually hear and see what you see. That's why I want you to talk whenever you can, as a running commentary on everything. Understood?"

"I'll babble until you tell me to shut up."

"That's what I want. Now, just to get a feel for things and see how well we work together, I'm going to tap a memory that we certainly know is real. We'll take one of your recent space scooter races. Tell me when you're ready."

"Anytime." He was relaxed, reassured by Lola's casual confidence. At the same time, and appropriately, she was becoming more tense. Calibration was the easy part. Her real task lay ahead.

"Here we go then." Lola gave the computer the command to initiate transfer. "Remember, the more you say the easier it makes my job."

She had placed her own seat into an inclined position. With the sensor cups in place over her own eyes, she waited. She had not lied to Bryce Sonnenberg. What she had told him was literally true. She could not see what he saw, hear what he heard, or read his mind.

But that did not mean she would be without visual and auditory inputs. Her computer would take everything that came from Sonnenberg, feed the data as inputs to its own models, and present the computed output to Lola's implants—as sounds and pictures. Sonnenberg's words, whatever they were, would not come directly to Lola. They would be taken by the computer, merged with other signals tapped from his cerebral cortex, and used to generate a derived reality. The result could be anything from a muddled blur to crisp, realistic scenes; everything depended on Bryce Sonnenberg's powers of detailed recollection, the sophistication of the computer programs, and Lola's haldane wizardry. The computer could only do so much. Lola had to fuse her own prior experience and imagination with the computer's data feed.

There was one more stage in the process. Whatever she experienced would be read out in turn, to provide a record of the whole experience in derived-reality format. If necessary, another haldane could review that and give a second opinion.

Data transfer began. Within the first two seconds, Lola knew that he was going to be a great subject. After a brief flicker of false grey images, she found her hands grasping two knurled levers. Her feet were pressed together and secured by wraparound pedals. The vision centers of her brain assured her that she was sitting within a cramped little bubble, facing a hundred dials, while wrapped all around her was a transparent cover.

And beyond that cover, clear as anything that she had

ever seen in her life, a mountain of grey ice and mottled black rock was rushing toward her. She was heading for impact with its left-hand edge, a sharp line that splintered the weak sunlight. Her hands and feet seemed frozen in position. At the last moment, when she was convinced that there was no way to avoid smashing into a stark and jagged rock face, she saw that the ship was arrowing into a narrow cleft.

Her hands and feet shifted to make a tiny thrust adjustment. The ship squeezed through, scraping-close to the wall. Lola saw a flashing blur of rock and ice. Then they were clear. There were stars ahead, and the ship was moving even faster than before.

Lola hit the disconnect and felt the emotional jar of the return from derived reality. Her hands and feet still clutched the controls of a ghost scooter, while her eyes saw the walls of her own office. She lay back and took a slow, deep breath. It was all very well to tell your brain that you *knew* you were experiencing no more than a standard—and highly successful—haldane interface, one that promised well for Bryce Sonnenberg's future. But a haldane coupling was intimate, more intimate than sex. Your heart and stomach and hindbrain didn't buy your forebrain's argument.

"That was great!" Bryce Sonnenberg was boosted to euphoria by the stimulated memory. The computer link was subsiding in a fading flicker of grey ghost images. "We couldn't have cut it closer. You see now why I love space scooting. Did you get anything?"

"You might say that." Lola silently ordered her pulse to return to normal. "I certainly know why I never go near the surface of Ganymede. And you do that for *pleasure!*"

"I used to, until the blackouts started. And if you can cure me, I'll do it again."

"You'll be cured." Lola sat up and removed the sensor

cups. "I'm sure I'll be able to help you. You have first-rate visual recall, as good as I've ever met. Of course, your blackout dreams won't be as clear and detailed as that."

"They feel that way to me."

"I'm sure they do. One famous haldane precursor, a man called Havelock Ellis, put it perfectly. He said, 'Dreams are real while they last. Can we say more of life?' No, Bryce, don't sit up yet!" He was reaching for the sensor cups on his eyes. "Stay just where you are. That last episode was so vivid, I want to try one more. I'm going to take one of your blackout sequences, and make a comparison. How long since you had one?"

"Just after I arrived from Callisto. Two days ago. It's a scene that keeps coming back again and again."

"Fine. We'll use that one."

Lola reached out to the computer console by her left hand. She started the search sequence, lay back, and replaced the sensors on her own eyes. "Don't be disappointed if we don't get much," she added as the grey flicker of images began again. "False memories are tricky things, and this is our first session. We've done well to get this far."

She was speaking as much to herself as to Bryce. An opening session often did not go much beyond calibration, but in this case she was going on because she was fascinated. Sonnenberg did not fit any textbook pattern of mental illness. In fact, the more that she saw of him, the less ill he seemed.

Was that his sickness, that he *imagined* himself to have a problem where there was none? That was the least satisfying answer. Far more interesting was the possibility of some new form of mental illness, one not recorded in the long history of psychotherapy. That was unlikely, but could it be the case?

She was asking herself that question as the computer again achieved synthesis.

Free fall.

Not in an orbiting ship, or floating outside it in a space-suit.

Free fall, real fall, toward a planetary surface. As the world spun around her, Lola caught a glimpse of a panorama of buildings. She was dropping toward them, gaining speed, falling vertically past the dark bulk of a great tower on her left-hand side.

She was not wearing a suit. And she was not on Earth. This was hard vacuum. The fog of ice crystals in front of her face was her own breath and blood, spouting out of agonized lungs.

Her motion steadied, so that she was dropping feetfirst. Now she could see where her trajectory would take her—to the roof of a lower level of the building on her left. The impact would kill her, no doubt about it, but incredibly some part of her brain was able to remain aloof. As oxygen starvation made the world before her dim and blur, she was calculating: three more seconds to impact; velocity, forty-nine meters a second.

Two seconds, fifty-two meters a second. One second. Terminal velocity, sixty meters a second. No chance of survival.

She looked down. The black flatness of the roof rushed up to meet her . . .

. . . and the computer disconnect took place.

Lola was left gasping, gulping in air to the depths of her lungs. Unbelievably, she was *alive*. The panorama of brightly lit buildings was disintegrating into streaks of flickering grey. She was in her own office.

And not before time. She sat up, shaking all over, and ripped the telemetry contacts from her temples, the sensor cups away from her eyes. It hadn't been a dream sequence; it had been gritty, hard-edged reality. She forced herself to her feet, convinced that Bryce Sonnenberg would need her help.

He was sitting sideways on the patient's chair, one sensor cup in each hand. Lola stared at him, unable to speak. He was the one who nodded, walked over to her side, and said, "You got it, didn't you? I can tell you did. It's not so bad for me, you see, I've been through it before. But you should have seen me the first time."

"Where is it? Where were you?"

He helped Lola to stand up. "I told you, I don't know. That's one of the scary parts. It seems like somewhere absolutely real and familiar, but wherever it is, I know I've never been there."

"Have you ever been to Earth? Or Mars?"

"Never." He released her hands. "You may not believe this, but I feel better now. You actually *felt* it, didn't you, even though you say you can't read minds? You know what it's like."

"I know what it's like." Lola struggled for control and managed a thin smile. "I'm not going to thank you for that."

"There are other places, too. Not as bad as that. Some of them I kind of like, the ones where I'm the boss and doing something clever. Out in the Belt, some of them. We hit the worst one first. Want to see the others?"

"I will, in due course." Lola sat down again. "But not today. We're done. I'm done."

"What's next?"

"I review your data, see if I missed anything. Then we have another session. Can you come back in three days? Midday, local time."

"Sure." Bryce Sonnenberg moved toward the door of the office. At the threshold he paused. "I know it's too early to ask, but do you really think you'll be able to help me?"

He was right—in principle, it was too early to say. But Lola was getting the clearest images she had ever seen. Bizarre information was difficult to interpret, but it was a lot better than no information at all.

"I'm sure I can help. Just don't expect instant miracles. It's a slow process." She waved good-bye, but she took little notice of his departure because she suddenly had been struck by two oddities at once.

First, he had said that some of his false memories were "out in the Belt." How could he know what the Belt was like, if he had left it for Callisto at the age of three?

Second—and more directly disturbing to Lola—she had been all set to transfer Sonnenberg's records to her general case files when she noticed the access record. It indicated that an access had been made on the previous day, when she had certainly not been using the system. The implication was as clear as if it had been written as a message on the screen: Someone else had been snooping around in her haldane file of stored experiences.

Someone. Lola swore to herself. She didn't have to go far to know who that someone was, someone who seemed unable to stay out of anything, even Lola's private case records.

When she got her hands on Spook she was going to wring his scrawny neck.

7

"Look after Spook. Don't let him get into trouble."

Lola had never forgotten her mother's plea. She had done her best to honor it, to look after him, to make sure he was well cared for. And she had done well.

In fact, in the eyes of at least one person she had done far too well.

Spook was fifteen years old, certainly not a kid any more. Surely he was entitled to a bit of breathing space.

On the other hand . . .

He looked at Lola, standing at the entrance to his private domain, and knew he was in deep trouble. She wouldn't normally charge into his den without giving at least a few minutes' warning.

"All right." Lola ignored the new setting, Spook's careful reconstruction of the sky as seen by a high-gee probe in one of the local comet clusters of the Kuiper Belt. "You've really done it this time. Those are absolutely private files you've dabbled in. Haldane files. *Patient* files. Do you realize what would happen if a patient learned that someone who wasn't a haldane had been poking around in them?"

"I've not been poking around." There was a time to tell

the truth, but this wasn't it. "I just copied one small file."

"Copying one is as bad as if you copied all of them. Unless a patient gives permission, *nobody* except a haldane is supposed to see anything."

"Suppose it wasn't a patient's file?"

That stopped her, as it was designed to do. She glared at him. "The only things in that directory—"

"Not true. I didn't touch a patient's file. And I wasn't trying to peek, not really. I summoned your directory by accident—I'm a Belman, too, you know, and you didn't protect properly with a unique ID. Once I had it I couldn't help noticing a file in there. It was called 'Wartime Memories.' And your name was on it."

"You rotten little geek." Lola flopped down into a seat opposite Spook. "That's *personal* material, from a session that another haldane ran on me as part of my final training. Those are *my* war memories!"

"I know." Spook managed to think tricky and look apologetic. "But I wasn't after anything creepy and personal—you know I'm not interested in that sort of stuff, 'specially in you. What I hoped to get—what I got—was *this.*"

His fingers stabbed the console on the arm of his chair. The den environment changed. The comet cluster disappeared, and in its place was Earth's Moon. Wan and glaring with pale-blue light, it hovered over them. The Armageddon Defense Line formed a livid scar across its face.

"I saw that," he went on. "And I had to have it. See, I *remember* it, but the whole time when we were leaving Earth is like a muddle in my head. Your file was like being there *in person,* all over again. I wish you'd probe me, the way you were probed."

"Never!" Lola told herself that her violent reaction was appropriate: No one fifteen years old should be exposed to haldane sessions except in a medical emergency.

Another part of her mind told her what an awful hypocrite she was. She had been itching to sit Spook down in that special chair since the day she finished formal training. Thanks to the haldane sessions, she had some idea what the loss of Earth, friends, and parents had done to her, at age twenty-two. What must it have done to poor Spook, at ten years old? What was it doing to him *now,* at fifteen?

She remembered her own adolescence, filled with fears and wants and nameless worries over the nature of sanity, especially her own (according to haldane training, no one became a haldane completely by choice). Spook didn't admit to any worries at all—least of all, to Lola—but surely he had some. And he had no mother or father, infinitely understanding, to discuss things with. He had only a sister preoccupied with her own problems . . .

"Well, all right." Spook had seen the change in Lola's mood, from anger to something else. He didn't know what she was thinking now, but he wanted her to go on with it. He had done one other thing with part of the "Wartime Memories" record, something he didn't want his sister to discover before he was good and ready to tell her. "I know you won't let me be probed. But I don't see any harm if I see something through you that I already saw for myself, in person."

"Maybe." Lola sighed. Her anger had gone, replaced by the usual dull worry. Was she doing what her mother had asked? Was she doing enough? She could not ignore Spook's obsession with the war, but was that abnormal when the destruction of the Inner System was probably the main interest of every teenage boy who lived in or on the Jupiter moons? "Promise me you won't dig any more into my directory, without asking me first. And promise me that you'll *never* try to get into the locked patient files."

"I promise." It was an easy commitment to offer. Spook had taken a quick peek at some of the haldane stuff, out of sheer curiosity—the keys were easy to crack, for any Puzzle Network devotee. But he was quite willing never to look again. Someday, Lola would learn just how little interest he had in soggy emotional experiences. He held up crossed fingers. "Honest. Fingers cross my heart."

"And don't go into *my* files, either."

"I won't." That should have satisfied her, but still she was sitting there frowning. And not at him, but at nothing. "I mean it, sis. Don't you believe me?"

"I want to ask your opinion on something. Your sort of thing." She had gone off at right angles, in another direction completely.

Which was fine with Spook. "Ask away."

"I want to see if you come up with the same conclusion as I did. Think of it as one of your puzzles. You have an object, and it's free-falling under gravity. It's going to hit some hard surface. Three seconds before impact, it's traveling at forty-nine meters a second. Two seconds before impact, at fifty-two meters a second. And when it hits, it will be traveling at sixty meters a second. All right?"

"Go on."

"Right. Where in the solar system is this happening?"

Spook looked at her in disgust. For someone who now operated at the Masters' level in the Puzzle Network, the question was like an insult. "Is it important? And there's no tricks?"

"It might be really important. And no tricks, it's a straight question."

"Then it's Mars or Mercury, close to the surface." His shrug showed his disdain for the simplicity of the question. "I mean, from what you said, the object is accelerating at about eleven meters in three seconds. That's three and two-thirds meters per second per second. The only two bodies in the solar system with anything like that value for surface gravity are Mars and Mercury. Neither one has enough atmosphere to change the answer, either."

"I decided the same thing. But which is it, Mars or Mercury?"

"Not enough information to distinguish between them. I assume that your numbers have been rounded off. Mercury's surface gravity is 3.57 meters per second squared, Mars's ranges from 3.56 at the equator to 3.76 at the poles. It could be either one. Does it matter which?"

"It might. I don't see how it could, though. He's never been to either one."

"He? Hey, I thought we were discussing a falling *object.*"

"I can't tell you any more."

"But you know more."

"Why do you think that?"

"Sis, don't play dumb with me. You said, 'It's going to hit some *hard surface.*' How do you know that? And then you say, *'He's* never been to either one.' You have things you're not telling me."

"Things I can't tell you."

"You can't tell me anything personal, if it's from one of your patients." Spook was seeing a glimmer of hope, a possible way to extricate himself from his own rash act with Lola's file. "But couldn't you sanitize it, and then show me? I mean, take away anything that would let me know who the person is, but let me see the record for myself. Maybe I could figure out where the person is, and what's going on."

"How?"

"I can't tell you that, can I, if I don't see it for myself? There might be all sorts of subtle clues in a visual record." Now was the time to make the stretch. "In fact, even if I couldn't give you a precise location, I bet that someone else could, someone who's been around the system more. This would be just the sort of thing to throw at the Puzzle Network."

Not a smart move. He had gone too far, and the steam

was coming out of Lola's ears. Spook backed off fast.

"Not the *whole* Puzzle Network, of course, I didn't mean that. But I'd like to help, and it would really make things easier if I had somebody else to bounce ideas off of. And you're busy, you don't have time to spend on this."

"Forget it. I'm not *that* busy, and I never will be."

"But I have more spare time than you do. One other person, then? Just one. That's all I would really need to work with me."

Spook crossed his fingers again—but, this time, out of sight—while Lola hesitated.

"Who is this other person?" she said at last. Lola didn't want Spook to know it, but she was feeling a terrible need to show that she cared about him, that she trusted him.

"He's one of the top Puzzle Network people." What else did Spook know? He had some idea how the other's mind worked on problems, but that was not going to impress Lola. "He calls himself *Megachirops.*"

"That's his real name?"

"No. Hardly anybody on the Puzzle Network uses his or her own name. I certainly don't. *Megachirops* is taken from *Megachiroptera*. That's the name of the Order of Great Bats."

"I hope that tells you more than it tells me. What's his real name?"

A good question. "I'm not sure he'd want me to tell you that."

"Well, *he'd* better be prepared to tell me that. *In person.* I'm willing to make a heavily edited version of the record for the two of you to work with, but I want to meet him. Soon. You arrange for us all to have dinner. All right?"

"No problem."

Spook stared at the ceiling, where the war display had continued and Earth's Northern Hemisphere was dying under a silent rain of radioactive dust. Now all he had to do was persuade the reclusive Megachirops—who had so far shown no interest in meeting anyone, not even a soul mate from the Puzzle Network—that he would enjoy nothing better than a cozy dinner with Lola and Spook Belman.

"No problem" was right. No problem for Lola.

8

Five years after the end of the war, traffic within the solar system was at last creeping back to planned schedules. With regular traffic came systemwide traffic monitoring, but there was one major difference: Before the war, the transportation nerve center had been on Earth; now and for the foreseeable future, it was on Ganymede. The populated Southern Hemisphere of Earth was too busy struggling for its own survival to control or direct anything anywhere.

The deep space radars of Ganymede and Callisto had readily picked up the silvery exploration vessel when it appeared on their perimeter. Its trajectory suggested an origin farther out, almost certainly in the Saturn system, but the computers were not sure.

Transport computer talked to ship's computer, and made the confirmation. This was the explorer ship *Weland,* returning with the Seventh Saturn Expedition to its home base on Lysithea after two months away.

At that point the Ganymede dispatch computer lost interest. Lysithea was far from Jupiter's main moons and off the beaten track for all major transport routes. The probability of conflict with other trajectories or competition for docking resources was zero. The *Weland* was turned loose, free to determine its own rendezvous. It moved on toward Lysithea under minimal power, the Diabelli Omnivores barely sustaining their fusion reactions.

The ship would not dock on the outer surface of the planetoid. No human facilities were there, or ever likely to be. The surface communications and control stations were staffed entirely by machines, designed to operate with an ambient temperature that never went higher than seventy-five degrees above absolute zero.

These machines did not merely tolerate the cold. They depended on it. Their components would fail if the temperature ever rose as high as the boiling point of nitrogen, a "hot" seventy-seven Kelvin. In the event of a supersized solar flare or other anomalous heat, the machines would estivate, tunneling down through the volatiles of Lysithea's surface like crabs into sand, until they reached a colder level a few tens of meters beneath.

Lysithea was all right for machines, but what about humans? Three hundred years earlier, people would have argued that any form of life was unthinkable on anything as cold and small as Lysithea. A hundred years ago, "unthinkable" might have changed to "undesirable." Today, a machine could tolerate—even be programed to relish—surface conditions on Lysithea. A human could survive on the surface with special equipment. But why would one choose to, when the interior was cool, quiet, and safe?

The *Weland* eased up to the landing circle on the icy shield of Lysithea's surface and entered a broad entry shaft that slanted steeply down through rock mixed with a slush of nitrogen and methane. The ship descended nine kilometers vertically, until it finally docked on the three-hundred-meter metal globe of the central habitat.

Jeffrey Cayuga and Alicia Rios, suitless, emerged into an icy vacuum and moved to the entrance of the air-filled and heated interior. A monitor confirmed their identities by half a dozen tests before it permitted them to enter.

Lenny Costas was waiting for them within. A stranger would have remarked on the musty and unpleasant odor that permeated the habitation bubble. Neither Costas nor the newcomers seemed to notice it.

"I arrived here two days ago." Costas spoke in his usual dry monotone. "There have been no significant problems during your absence. I will bring one small oddity to your attention in due course. I assume that the trip went according to plan?"

"Construction continues on schedule. Three more months, and it will be complete." Cayuga moved on past Costas, drifting through the habitat toward the main lounge and message center. He offered no form of ritual greeting, any more than the other had said a word of welcome. "There was one small complication, which is why we arrive one day later than our original return date. We saw evidence that a smart probe recently performed a Helene flyby. However, when we investigated further we decided that it was not necessary to send a message here."

Costas froze. "A probe. That is surprising and disturbing."

"It is not as bad as it sounds." Cayuga was at the computer console. "We determined that there have been no recent lease-monitoring probes sent to the Saturn system. The trajectory of this one indicates that it was launched decades ago, before the First Expedition. My guess is that there was some flaw in its navigation program. It traveled way out, beyond the Kuiper Belt, and finally swung back toward Sol. Helene was no more than a target of opportunity for its return journey. We confirmed that the probe did not penetrate or explore the Helene interior. I doubt if any analysis facilities on Earth or Mars are in a position to accept its findings, whatever they may be. However, this proves that our decision to make Helene modifications as inconspicuous as possible was a wise one. We also need to make sure that no anomalies have been reported locally."

"I feel sure that they have not. I talked to Polk and Dahlquist yesterday, and everything is perfectly normal on Ganymede." But Costas offered no objection when Alicia Rios joined Cayuga, and they shunted a large fraction of Lysithea's computing facilities to augment the standard search routines.

Within a few seconds the first results were appearing. They did not constitute a real-time message analysis, since although the communications net of the Jovian system was under scrutiny—constant and automated—by the Lysithean monitors, its message load was too vast and variable to permit instant analysis. However, within twenty-four hours any chosen subject could be queried.

In this case there was no need to wait. *Helene,* the tiny moon of Saturn in its libration point orbit with Dione, was a permanent key word for query in the Lysithean computers. Any mention, for any reason, would have been flagged.

The three watched impassively as a scant handful of references were played out.

"Good enough," said Cayuga at last. "Reports and standard catalogs for natural bodies within the solar system. No mention of a probe flying close to Helene. You said that you had an anomaly of your own to report?"

" 'Anomaly' may be too strong a word." Costas took over the panel. "Polk came across this four days ago. It was generated by the search routine that we have been using for singular events related to life and death. This record was part of a data transfer taking place on Ganymede."

"Open line?"

"No. It was on one of the closed pathways that we have been able to tap. One of the oddities is that the transfer destination wiped itself automatically from the records. Someone has gone to great trouble to make sure that no one can track them to their physical location. That's another reason why Polk believes this may be significant. I am skeptical. In view of your impending return I decided to wait before taking action. Get ready. Any second now you will enter derived reality."

The warning was necessary. The sequence began at once, as a disconcerting fall through space. Cayuga and Rios found themselves accelerating toward a dark surface. A ghostly clock, overlaid on the scene but not part of it, was ticking away the seconds. Lights, steady but dim, shone far off toward a distant horizon. The drop continued for hundreds of meters, until the surface beneath resolved to the flat roof of a building, marked by skylights and antennas. Their body position had steadied so that they fell feetfirst. They could see where the landing would occur, on a dark flat area of smooth metal. Down, down, down, faster and faster, moments from final impact.

And then, without warning, the sequence ended.

"I don't see why this was worth noting." Cayuga remained impassive. "Where is the rest of it?"

"You've experienced the whole thing. For some unknown reason, that file has been cropped. It lacks subject identifiers. That's why I think it is no more than a clever simulation."

"Rios?" Cayuga turned to her. "You are the specialist."

"It is not a simulation." Alicia Rios shook her dark head and gave the instruction to repeat the last few seconds of the record.

"Definitely not," she went on, as the sequence again ran its course to the final dizzying moment of the fall. "Too much detail for a straight simulation. That's the real thing. Some person experienced that fall—and it didn't kill them. It should have. I am not sure that any one of us would survive it. And someone else was able to tap the person's memory record. This is a haldane product, it has to be."

Cayuga nodded. "I'm beginning to see what Polk is making a fuss about. A haldane product would explain the use of the closed pathway, but it doesn't account for the big problem: survival."

"I agree. Any normal human who experienced that fall must have died on impact." Alicia Rios turned to Lenny Costas. "What do you say to that?"

"It may not be a real-time sequence. Maybe it was a fall in a low-gee environment, speeded up."

"Not unless the clock overlay was false. Time was passing at a standard rate."

"Even if we can produce an explanation for everything, I still agree with Polk." Cayuga requested the header-record descriptors. "It is something to be taken seriously. We must have answers to some basic questions. Who is this? Where did it happen? When did it happen?"

"Polk says he can answer one of those," said Lenny Costas. "If that is a real-time sequence, and if the clock is right, then the motion indicates a fall on either Mars or Mercury. And there are no large buildings on Mercury. So it is Mars."

"Mars again." Cayuga was scrolling through the header record, frame by frame. "I thought we were finished with Mars when we disposed of Neely, and then for sure when Barker got rid of that reporter. But perhaps not. Maybe someone else managed to become a Club member, and we don't even know about it." He paused, freezing the frame display. "Look at this. We may not have a subject identifier, but at least we know who initiated the transfer. Here is the name. Spook Belman. Rios, would you—"

"I know." Alicia was already making a query of the general data files. "He's here, in the open census file. Spook Belman, of Ganymede. But he's just a child. He's only fifteen years old. He is in the custody of . . . ah!"

"Of who?"

"Of a woman identified as his sister, Lola Belman." Alicia paused. "She is in the file, too. And Lola Belman is shown as a licensed haldane."

Members of the Ganymede Club did not "argue" with each other, according to the usual meaning of that word. They held discussions, they examined problems, and they considered alternatives. In this case, it seemed to Lenny Costas that there was little to decide.

"It is simple," he said. He had queried the census bank for more information on Lola and Spook Belman, and had been studying the return. "Their mother and father died on Earth in the first Belt attack. All their other near relatives died in the war. No one in the Jovian system is close to them. If we take care of them, nice and quietly, that will be that. And since they are already on Ganymede, it makes matters easier. Another little job for Jinx Barker?"

Alicia Rios and Jeffrey Cayuga exchanged glances. During their two-month journey to the Saturn system and back, Lenny Costas had been the subject of discussion many times. He would carry out instructions to the letter, and no one was more zealous in safeguarding the interests of the Club. But there was a point at which single-mindedness and lack of imagination became dangerous. And he seemed, to both of them, to be getting worse. Alicia often compared Costas with Jinx Barker, to the former's disadvantage.

"We could ask Barker to serve as you suggest," Cayuga said quietly. "But it doesn't address the real problem. Whoever had the fall on Mars, we know it wasn't Lola or Spook Belman. Their records show that neither of them has ever been there. Disposing of them won't tell us who it was."

"It's worse than that," Rios added. "Without the Belmans, we have nothing. They are our only lead to what we really want."

"So what do we do?" Costas frowned in perplexity.

"Someone has to meet with Lola and Spook Belman and

get to know them personally," replied Cayuga. "Find out what they know, learn how they know it."

"Me?" Costas said the word reluctantly.

"Not you. Definitely not you. I don't want a Club member exposed to a haldane, under any circumstances. We have too much to lose. I think your first suggestion was better, but with a variation." Cayuga turned to Alicia Rios. "You have assured me that Jinx Barker has superior talents as a male companion."

"He does. He is the complete professional, as lover or as assassin *par excellence.*"

"Although of course no one with experience of the latter function is available to report on his prowess. Do you have first-hand experience of the former?"

"Trust me."

"Very good. Tell him that if he performs well in the first role, he will almost certainly be asked to perform later in the second, and with the same individual. That may pique his curiosity. And tell him that he will be amply rewarded, financially and possibly in other ways. I think it is time to consider again the notion of Jinx Barker as a Club member. Do not of course say anything to him about that."

"Naturally. I think we have learned a lot since Neely. But I must say that in Barker's case this is not before time."

"Remember that you have the most to lose, Rios. He is your protégé, and he would be your responsibility. You know the Club rules. Warn him to be extremely careful on this assignment. After all, Lola Belman—"

"Is a haldane." Alicia was smiling, cold and confident. She stood up. "I am well aware of that, Cayuga. Do not worry. I will make sure that Jinx is fully briefed. If I know him, that challenge will merely add to his enjoyment of the new assignment."

9

The five years from ten to fifteen are like half a lifetime. Spook, with no friends or relatives other than a sister who alternated between preoccupied and overprotective, found himself with lots of leisure time. He had spent much of it wandering alone through the interior of Ganymede. By his fifteenth birthday, he reckoned he knew as well as anyone alive the moon's labyrinth of cross-connecting tunnels and shafts and chambers, constantly enlarged on the lowest levels by the hands, scoops, picks, drills, and explosives of the tireless Von Neumanns. The connectivity and complexity were astonishing, but it was not beyond the grasp of someone at home with the topology of knotted four- and five-space.

Even so, there were many regions unfamiliar to Spook. That was not surprising, because Ganymede was after all a whole world, whose habitats, diversity reserves, sea farms, hydroponic gardens, and experimental biospheres occupied interior layers that in total would one day exceed the land area of Earth.

Not only that, some parts of Ganymede were *boring*.

Spook was approaching one of those now, a bit of *Ganymedea incognita,* a level only seven kilometers below the surface but previously bypassed on his travels because it showed on the computer maps as a dull agricultural-research area. And the maps did not lie. Spook skirted a field of gigantic orange flowers—each one facing the direction of the bright overhead light—and wondered what they would do if and when the second light in the chamber's high ceiling was turned on. The plants were clearly phototropic. Would they suffer some form of vegetable schizophrenia, trying to face two ways at once? Would they need treatment from some vegetable-haldane version of his sister?

At the far edge of the field, he asked himself a more sensible question: Had he screwed up? The directions he had been given had seemed so clear and unambiguous that he had disdained to bring a written copy. But did anyone really live here, at the end of the dark, dirty, and deserted corridor at whose open end he now found himself?

If anyone did, they must be just ahead, beyond the great yellow door that marked the tunnel's blind end. Spook hurried forward, banged on one of the panels, and waited.

Nothing. After a second blow without response he tentatively pushed the door. It opened silently inward on lubricated hinges.

Spook entered, and found himself in paradise. The room he had walked into was an odd shape, no more than four meters high and three wide, but stretching back in the gloom for at least thirty. The central aisle was made still narrower by the materials stacked along both side walls.

And what materials.

Close to Spook, close enough to touch, stood a Seeker. It was not a scale model of the smart weapon that had been the Belt's deadliest contribution to the war, but the real thing. The brain must have been thoroughly lobotomized, otherwise Spook would be dead—but he felt his skin crawl when the blunt head swiveled and the five ruby lenses turned to survey him.

Just beyond the Seeker crouched the mesh cage of a Purcell invertor. The war-crimes tribunal had declared its use by the Belt colonies as an abomination and a crime against humanity. But Megachirops, on the Puzzle Network, had pointed out to Spook that winners, not losers, staffed the war tribunals. And the Belt had certainly lost. What weapons had Earth and Mars used, when Seekers and Purcell invertors could not provide a Belt victory?

An alternate point of view had come to Spook from an unlikely source. It was Lola, hearing the winners-and-losers argument, who had said, "Sure. Winners write history. But suppose that the Belt leaders really *were* monsters."

"I'm surprised to hear you say that. I thought you haldanes claimed to cure all nut cases."

She had shuddered at the final phrase, but had only said mildly, "If we did, brother dear, wouldn't I have done better with you? Anyway, you're missing the point. It's the same nonsense that ruined psychiatry and made its practitioners a laughingstock a century ago. You see, there really *are* bad guys in the world. You think Hitler and Stalin and Attila the Hun could have been *cured?* Well, if you do you are dead wrong. They weren't misunderstood, they weren't sick, they weren't victims; they were *evil*—and incurable. A haldane's job is to look at people and determine the difference, those who can be helped and those who are beyond saving. Some men, sad to say, are just plain and simple *bad.*"

"There are bad women, too."

"Sorry, I didn't mean to suggest there aren't. When it comes to refined torture, we have you outclassed. Men who were wounded in old Earth combat weren't afraid of the enemy men. But they prayed to die before the women got to them with their skinning knives and slow fires."

Spook had preferred not to pursue that particular line of thought. But now, pushing aside the memory, he felt a strange urge to climb the invertor's spidery frame and enter the glittering cage.

Was it this sort of irrational impulse that lured men to go to war? It was hard to believe that the invertor could do what the tribunal claimed. One hour inside, and the deepest emotional bases of a human were supposed to reverse polarity. Best friends became bitter enemies, lovers were haters, heterosexuals became homosexuals, old loyalties dissolved and vanished. Spook had no lover, no enemies, and few loyalties. How could it possibly change *him* in any way that mattered? An undertow of curiosity tempted him to find out.

The next item standing along the wall drew him on and dissolved the temptation—or, replaced it with another. It seemed no more than a simple chair, with restraining metal bands for head, arms, and legs. Spook recognized it from image files as a Tolkov Stimulator. That was wartime technology from Mars, "friendly" technology, according to its description, but illegal for use in anything but extreme need. It raised the intelligence of a subject exposed to it—if that subject was strong or lucky enough to live through the treatment. The survival rate was rumored to be three percent.

And beyond the Stimulator, those silvery cubes that were stacked head high . . .

Belatedly, Spook came to his senses. He had not come all this way to wallow in a pool of war artifacts. He was here on serious business; but it seemed he had come to a deserted museum.

"Is anybody home?" he called into the darkness at the end of the long room. "I'm Ghost Boy—Spook Belman. Are you there?"

A bass grunt, almost a snort, came from behind a partition: "We made an appointment to meet at a precise time, here in my preferred abode. It would be perplexing, would it not, should I then fail to be present?"

A black-garbed figure came around the edge of the partition, moving lightly and easily despite his size. Spook guessed that the body in its too-tight clothing massed at least four hundred pounds. The head that protruded from the dark robe was as black, round, and smooth as a cannonball.

"I am, of course, Megachirops, the Great Bat." An expression of distaste twisted his fat face. "However, to the intrusive Ganymede census, I am officially known as Rustum Battachariya. Welcome, Spook Belman, to my Bat Cave."

"This stuff"—Spook waved a dazed arm—"is all this *yours?*"

"It is my hobby." Bat still wore the suspicious expression of a bad-tempered baby. "What of it?"

"Why, it's—it's—" Spook stared all around, searching for the right word. The more he looked, the more he saw. Finally, he gave up, and said, "It's just *fantastic.*"

"Indeed? To refined tastes, the cave in truth has some small appeal." But Bat's gratification showed through the offhand words. He was trying not to smile, and failing. "Few are invited here," he went on. "And fewer are so perceptive."

"Especially old people, I bet. Old people act as though the war never happened."

"They seek to banish it from existence by ignoring its reality."

"You must be *rich.*"

"Not at all." Bat flourished pudgy fingers at the wall. "Everything you see was available for the taking. Free. It is all deemed useless, 'war surplus' goods that no one else wants."

"Your parents let you have as many war mementos as you like?"

"The question does not arise. Since my fifteenth birthday, my parents and I have—by mutual consent—seen little of each other. Their idea of a 'normal' existence is not compatible with mine. I refer in particular to their ideas on diet. They are macrobiotic vegetarians, and they were in my opinion actively engaged in starving me to death." Bat eyed Spook's skinny form. "Are you hungry?" He obviously didn't know Spook.

"I'm famished."

"So am I. Let us remedy that." Bat led the way around the partition, into a kitchen that doubled as a communications center. Terminals and displays filled the right-hand wall. An elaborate range occupied the whole back of the room, with a long table and four chairs set in front of it. One of them was an enormous padded black seat that would have swallowed Spook up into its depths. Bat sat down on it and gestured to the covered pot that was waiting on the table. "Goulash. A specialty of the house. Help yourself."

Spook lifted the lid and his respect for Megachirops went up another notch. The steaming tureen held enough food for a dozen people, and it smelled great. Not only that, but when they began to eat Bat turned out to be one of those rare individuals with enough sense not to talk while he was doing it. There was a long period of contented silence, until at last Spook sighed, stared sadly at his empty bowl, and said, "I'm stuffed. Pity. Did you cook that?"

"Of course."

"Invite me anytime." And, at Bat's snort, "Well, sometime. But I guess we ought to get down to business. I wanted to ask, did you take a look at the file I sent you?"

"I did indeed." Bat placed the lid on the heavy pot, licked the back of his spoon regretfully, and leaned back. He gestured to the end wall, where a display region stood waiting. "Of course, that file raises more questions than it answers. Someone has been through it and edited it with a heavy hand."

"Not my doing and not my fault. My sister Lola did it. She wouldn't let me send it to you otherwise."

"I would welcome the opportunity to explore the original. But even this, with all its defects, was not without interest. I assume that there is no dispute as to the *place?*"

"Mars."

"Of necessity. The strength of the gravitational field indicates either Mars or Mercury, while the more distant horizon and the presence of numerous buildings eliminates the latter possibility. There is a major problem, of course, in that whoever experienced such a fall could not have survived it. However, did you also note another small anomaly?"

"I thought I did. I wanted an independent opinion."

"Which I am certainly in a position to provide. It is Mars, yes. But *today's* Mars, no. The size of the buildings points to Oberth City. But Oberth City as it existed *before* the war, before it was flattened to rubble."

"That's just what I thought."

"So the file came from a memory at least five years old, from someone who was on Mars before the war. I assume that we still agree?"

"Yes. But there's another problem. According to Lola, the person that the memory came from was *never on Mars.*"

"Then, at the risk of appearing obtuse"—Bat's tone suggested that such a risk was not to be taken seriously—"since this person is apparently available to your sister, why does she not opt for the simple solution and *ask* for an explanation?"

"She can't. You see, he doesn't know himself. That's why he came to her for treatment—"

Spook paused. As usual, he had said much more than he was supposed to. Until Lola met Bat in person and was convinced of his discretion, she had insisted that not one word be said about the subject of the memory file. Not even his sex, and certainly nothing of his background on Mars or anywhere else.

"Look," Spook went on, "I think there's a fine puzzle

here—as tough and as interesting as anything on the Puzzle Network. But my hands are tied. Any additional information has to come from my sister. In person."

"You mean, I will be obliged to *meet* her?" Bat's puckered lips looked as if he had been sucking a lemon slice.

"Sure. Have a meal with her. It won't be as good as you gave me—or as much—but it will be all right. Her food's really not bad. She's all right, too. Even if she is a haldane."

As soon as Spook said it, that sounded like another tactical error. He knew Lola, and she was easy enough to get on with; but he also realized how most people felt about encountering a haldane.

Fortunately, Rustum Battachariya did not seem the slightest bit worried. He was sighing, rising from the broad black stool, and pulling up the black cowl of his robe to cover his head. "It is no wonder," he said thoughtfully, moving away from the table and along the narrow room toward the exit, "that I choose to frequent the Puzzle Network, where all acceptable problems are soluble by knowledge and logic alone. Every other interesting enigma appears to be accompanied by some irritating encumbrance. In this case . . ."

Spook, following close behind, had no trouble finishing Bat's sentence. In this case, the irritating encumbrance was Lola.

He had enjoyed enormously his visit to the Bat Cave, and after a shaky start he felt that he and Great Bat/Megachirops were getting along well. On the other hand, Spook and his sister failed to agree on many things.

He stared at the cowled, cannonball head and vast black-clad back in front of him, and wondered. Human relationships were definitely not his specialty; but he couldn't help speculating on Lola's reaction to Rustum Battachariya.

Bat knew the Ganymede interior even better than Spook. When Spook explained the path he had taken to reach the

Bat Cave, Bat listened carefully, nodded, and said, "Passable, but not optimal. There are three points at which your journey could have been slightly shorter in time, although longer in distance. I will demonstrate as we proceed."

Spook hid his irritation. He told himself that Bat was a full year older, and anyway he had spent his whole life on Ganymede. He felt a lot better when he also learned that transportation systems, inside Ganymede and outside it, were more than a minor interest for Bat. They were the source of his livelihood.

"And, contrary to popular opinion, they are not boring at all," Bat assured Spook as he led him down a dizzying spiral chute that was barely wide enough for his bulk. It was a shortcut that could not have been used in travel to the Bat Cave, because in that direction it rose at a steep angle along its whole twisted length. "You would probably find the study of the transport system quite rewarding, although your natural method of attack on problems does appear to be geometrical and topological, rather than algebraic. I suspect there may be unexplored virtues in that, which at some time you and I should pursue. However, theorists define the transportation problems of the solar system as a nonlinear optimization subject to constraints. While that may be true, you will never make any money with that approach. What you need are what I have: gimmicks—special tricks of my own, rather like your device of regarding the space we live in as a projection of a space of higher dimension."

"So people come to you, and they ask for a cheaper way to shift goods and passengers?"

"The choice of the first verb is debatable." They were out of the chute and moving side by side. Bat turned to glower sideways past his hood at Spook. "They 'come to me,' in a general sense. However, lacking your importuning intrusiveness, they never see me *in person*. They communicate via standard electronic channels."

"But how do they know that you even exist?" Spook was halfway certain that Bat objected to his presence a good deal less than he pretended. Everybody liked to have somebody to show off to now and again.

Bat shrugged, a rippling movement that went from shoulders to hips. "I can do no more than conjecture that it is by word of mouth. But I recently achieved a certain amount of off-world notoriety when I was able to employ my knowledge of control mechanisms to divert an unpiloted cargo vessel with a shipment of helium-three from a collision orbit with Europa."

"I thought you never went anywhere near the surface."

"No more did I. There are key entry points to every ship's guidance computer system. That is true whether the vessel is bearing a crew or not. I merely linked in from the Bat Cave, performed two minor onboard program patches, and monitored the result in real time to be sure that I had achieved the desired result."

"And it worked?"

"Of course."

"So who paid you? The owners?"

"No one paid me. In fact, I could not reveal what I had done. It would have been judged an unauthorized and illegal tampering with a ship's controls."

"But that's ridiculous! You saved a ship, and you prevented Europan contamination."

"In the eyes of a standard bureaucrat, such considerations are of little weight. However, certain knowledgeable individuals who know my style were able to deduce what had probably happened. One of them even called to congratulate me."

"What did you do?"

"I declined to talk to her. Naturally. But such things have a way of spreading. I have received numerous requests for assistance with difficult cargo schedules in the past half year."

Spook didn't ask the question he wanted to ask: How do I get in on this good stuff? He thought he knew the answer: slowly. Anybody who hoped to work with Bat would have to show that he was of the same mental caliber. Spook hoped that he was. A few hours ago he would have bet on it. Now he was not so sure.

It was a question he had pondered since he was barely more than an infant. You went through your whole life being smarter than anybody else around, convinced that most of the time you were dealing with people who couldn't think any better than chimps. Then one day you met somebody as smart or smarter than you. What did you do then?

Fortunately, this might not be all one-sided. There had been hints that Bat took Spook seriously, since although he could follow what Spook did in N-space analysis he apparently didn't find it second nature, the way that Spook did. There was hope. In any case, the issue didn't have to be settled at once.

In fact, it could not be, because already they were arriving at Lola's office quarters. It was late, but with luck she would still be around. Spook knew that she seldom left early.

At the entrance he took one more look at Bat, trying to see him through his sister's eyes. It was not too encouraging. Inside, Bat might well be a genius. Outside was another matter.

Spook saw a huge black-garbed figure, whose tight, ill-fitting clothes and flowing, open robe made him seem almost as wide as he was high. He was pouting his lips and frowning horribly, presumably aware that in another minute or two he would have to meet yet another human being—two in one day.

And now that they were standing still, Spook could detect a definite and unpleasant odor.

That was one other thing about shunning human companions. You didn't have to wash often, or worry about smelling your best.

It was too late to back out. They had already knocked on the outer door. In any case, Spook couldn't see Bat taking kindly to the suggestion that he go away and return after taking a bath.

He led the way in.

Lola was sitting at her desk, doing nothing, her eyes slightly wild and a little bit out of focus. Half an hour earlier she had finished another haldane session with Bryce Sonnenberg. It took a while to come down, even when, unlike today, she felt perfectly normal afterward. That was one of the reasons that she tended to stay late at her office. She didn't like to be seen in public (or even in private) while the psychotropic drugs were rattling around inside her brain.

Today she did not feel normal at all. Today she felt like the Grand Panjandrum himself, with the little round button at the top and the gunpowder running out of the heels of his boots. Very peculiar.

She heard a noise and looked up. With a slight effort, she managed to remove the blur from the scene and realized that what she was seeing was familiar. She was seeing Spook. He was staring bug-eyed at her, already starting to back out, muttering, "Sorry. We'll come catch you later."

"No, no, it's fine. I've been expecting you. In fact . . ."

Lola peered at what was standing behind Spook, and wondered if the drugs were having a new and powerful effect on her.

Could they? . . . it must be her imagination. *That* was the Grand Panjandrum, a gigantic, scowling figure, his clothes as black as his face except for the places where, on the front of the too-small shirt that failed to conceal his navel and billowing belly, liberal streaks of grease and gravy provided evidence of his last meal. Or maybe his last but six. There seemed to be more than one food stain there.

"Lola." Spook's voice came from far, far away. "This is Megachirops, also known as Rustum Battachariya when he is not in Master mode on the Puzzle Network. But he would prefer us to call him Bat. He is the one I told you about. The one I said I wanted to-to-"—Spook paused self-consciously—"to help on the you-know-what."

That hit Lola like a brain quake. She came down from Fuzzland with an awful crash, to glare at Spook and the object that he had dragged in behind him. "The you-know-what. Are you by any chance referring to my *case?* The one we have been talking about in strictest secrecy? Because if you are—"

She knew what was happening but she could not stop it. The drugs were pure magic, capable of achieving miraculous results. Unfortunately, when they dropped you, they dropped you all the way. That wasn't Lola talking, not the real Lola. Spook knew that; he would make allowances.

But Megachirops/Rustum Battachariya/Bat wouldn't. So far he had not spoken one word. Lola tried to smile at him, with ghastly results. She felt her face twisting like a crumpled sheet. She opened her mouth to attempt a conventional greeting and heard a deep musical voice saying, "Hello, I hope that I am not intruding."

She had not spoken. And certainly that was not Spook. Lola gaped at Bat. How did he do that? He had talked to her without moving his lips. In the same moment she realized that another person had appeared at the entrance of her office.

"I'm sorry," he said. "But the outer door was open."

He was a tall, solidly built man in his mid-thirties, dressed in faded clothes that did not quite match. His face had the same casual, slightly rumpled look as his clothing. He was smiling, but it was the smile of a man who has the feeling that he has committed some sort of social blunder and is not sure what.

"Are you all right?" he asked, and took a step forward into the office.

It was obvious that he was talking to Lola, rather than the other two. She straightened her back and made a mighty effort.

"Sorry. I'm a bit tired, that's all. It's been a long work-day."

That had come out all right. She still had the feeling that her features were crawling out of control, all over her face, but no one else seemed to notice. Spook was looking at the newcomer with obvious relief, while Bat glared at everyone with equal distaste.

"I know how that feels." The man nodded, as though about to leave, then seemed to change his mind and took another step forward. "I wouldn't have come in like this at all, uninvited, but I'm moving into the office three down along the corridor. It seems as though it's been empty for a while, and there's no power. I can't find a maintenance machine. I wondered if you might know where the control box is."

She had no idea. But before she could answer, Spook was in there first. "Bad time, Sis," he said. "You're obviously busy, and I'm sorry we interrupted. We'll see you and talk about this later."

He gave Bat an urgent glance. The two of them headed rapidly for the door without another word to Lola. On the way out Spook nodded to the stranger and said, "Wall panel. End of the hall, above the air-supply duct—power and computing services. I'll get it as we go."

"Thanks." The man watched them leave, then turned to Lola with a perplexed shrug. "I guess that's that. Quick service. But I think I drove them away."

"No." Lola sighed. "I did that. I shouldn't talk to anybody for at least an hour after I finish a session."

"Session?"

"You didn't see the sign as you came in?"

"I didn't look. I came where I heard voices."

"Just as well. Half the people who come into the outer office never make it past the sign." Lola settled back again into her chair. She was feeling a lot better. "I'm a haldane."

"Are you, now." He didn't show any of the usual reactions—no nervousness or distrust. In fact, he came forward to stand at the other side of the desk and grinned down at her as though she had just made a joke. "Well, I guess I ought to be careful what I say to you. But I never learned how to do that." He held out a long-fingered hand with neatly trimmed nails. "Since it seems we're going to be neighbors, we should introduce ourselves."

"I'm Lola Belman." She took his outstretched hand. It was warm and felt more muscular than it looked. "I'm pleased to meet you."

"Conner Preston." Rather than releasing her, he put his other hand on top of hers and gave a little squeeze. "I'm pleased, too. Let's see if we can both stay pleased."

10

Lola was in bed. Alone, and not asleep.

She had been lying there for over an hour, reluctant to use a sleep inducer. Reluctant because, although she needed rest, she wanted to review the events of the past day. Too much had been happening in too short a time.

The morning and early afternoon had been perfectly normal, a quiet day in her office with one unproductive patient who was responding poorly to treatment. Then Bryce Sonnenberg had appeared in the late afternoon, unscheduled, complaining of new problems.

"Another blackout," he said, "right around lunch time. Big one. Ten minutes."

"With different memories?" Lola, the residue of psychotropic drugs still in her system, would have preferred to postpone the meeting. But he seemed truly troubled.

"Different and *weird,* and then at the end, some of the old memories. The oddest thing is that I remember the new stuff as though it happened a long time ago, but somehow I was *older* then than I am now."

Lola could not resist. This just might be the key that they were missing. "Do you have time to stay a while? Good.

Sit down. I want to try a session while all this is completely fresh in your memory."

More drugs, until she felt herself poised delicately on the edge. Bryce, in the chair, more nervous than usual, his face suddenly far older than his twenty-four years—the telemetry calibration—the sleeping giant, stirring within her. And then, suddenly, the synthesis.

Thick, perfumed air, and a heavy but familiar gravity field. (Lola knew, deep down, that she was on Earth.) Loud, cheerful music. Everyone in brightly colored clothes. It was a party, and yet more than a party. He was strolling along a line of long tables, not looking at anything yet seeing everything. At one of the tables he paused.

"That's the one," said the tiny earphone. "The woman in blue."

"Got a name for her?"

"Her credit note gave the name as Dulcie Iver. Could be fake, but I don't think so."

"Right. I'm going to take a look." He stepped forward, filled with a tension that was pure pleasure.

"Good luck," the voice said. "She's still winning, not all that big, but too steady. She's way outside the odds. I've been working on this for two hours, and I've not come up with a thing."

"Keep the cameras going, Sid."

He waited and watched in silence for a few minutes. The woman was dark-haired and pale in complexion, maybe twenty-five years old. Her pale-blue dress was short, low-cut front and back, and sleeveless. Her legs and arms were bare, with smooth skin as white as chalk. She wore no jewelry, carried no purse, and her shoes were simple dark-blue flats. She had slipped them off, and every few seconds her toes wiggled and clenched as though responding to some unreadable emotion.

"You sure you scanned for implants, Sid?"

"Of course." The voice in his ear was reproachful.

"What you think I am? Implants and telemetry and calculator. She's clean."

"Just wanted to be sure." Even with Sid's reassurance, he made his own careful assessment, seeking evidence of scars on the fine skin or bulges within the clothing. As he did so he felt a sudden stab of lust, strong enough to surprise him.

He turned his attention to the terminal and screen in front of the woman. Dulcie Iver was playing Delphi, a group game, with nineteen other members. Another round was under way, and bets were already being made.

He knew the game well—he ought to, he was one of its designers. Delphi was popular, but the house take was big, an average of eighteen percent. A clever player, by taking advantage of the pattern of betting, could change the odds so that an eighteen percent loss was converted to a two percent gain—at the expense of the other members of the group. Dulcie Iver, for the past two hours, had made an average profit of eleven percent. As Sid had pointed out, she was way outside the reasonable statistical variation provided by the game's random element.

But Sid's value lay in his reliability, not his intellect. In this business, you didn't want too many people too smart.

The clock was ticking down, and only twenty seconds were left in which to lay bets. Dulcie Iver sat with her fingers poised over her board. She was studying the display, but so far she was not in the game.

Ten seconds. A flurry of activity, as a dozen bets were made in two seconds. Still her fingers did not move, but her toes began to wiggle and clench. At the last moment, with no more than two seconds to go before the cutoff, she stabbed at the board in front of her, placing five bets before the board went blank. There was a tiny pause, as the electronic selector took its input from quantum fluctuations—totally random and totally unpredictable. Then the winning selection appeared on the main display.

Eleven members had lost, four of them heavily. Five others had broken even, or chosen not to make a bet. Three players showed small gains. And Dulcie Iver had come out ahead, with a profit of thirteen percent on her bet. She did not respond in any way to her success. Once more she was sitting back in her chair, fingers and toes still.

He went for three more rounds, watching and calculating furiously until he was absolutely sure. Then he said, "Don't worry about her, Sid. She's clean. I'll take care of this."

He moved forward and touched her on the shoulder. "Miss Iver? Could I have a word with you?"

She turned, taking in his casual dress and absence of ID. "I don't think I know you."

"Not yet." He smiled at her. "I'm with the management, as you probably guessed. A private word, if you don't mind."

After a moment she slipped her shoes on and stood up. She was tall, almost as tall as he. She followed him without speaking—no comment, no question. He nodded his private approval. Smart woman. I bet you think you know what this is about, but you give nothing away until you're sure.

He took her to the small office, high up on the wall of the gaming chamber. It looked out over the whole room through its wall of one-way glass, adding direct observation to the ranks of monitors that allowed the activity to be seen from every angle. He gestured to a seat.

"I won't waste your time or mine, Ms. Iver. I know what you're doing."

Still she did not speak.

"But I want to be sure that I know how," he went on. "Would you like to tell me how you operate?"

"I don't know what you mean."

"Miss Iver, please. Let us not insult each other's intelligence. If you insist, I will tell you how you operate. When

you play Delphi, *you have one minute in which to place your initial bet. Then when you have seen what everyone else has bet, you have a chance to bet again. The first bets that are placed change the odds, but you only have ten seconds to use that fact in the second round. Lots of players don't bother, or at least they don't take real advantage of the first-round bets. The few who do we call second-level players. They are the ones who will go home a winner most of the time. Agreed?"*

"Probably. But I'm not a second-level player."

"I agree completely. You, Ms. Iver, are a rarity that I have not seen for a long time. You are a *third-level player. You place your own bet in those final brief seconds when all the second bets are complete. True?"*

"What if it is?" She had dazzling violet-blue eyes, startling with such black hair and white skin. She was staring at him stone-faced, still giving away nothing. "Everything that you have said is within the Delphi *rules."*

"It is not against the rules of Delphi, *nor is it against house rules—though it disconcerts my staff considerably.* Delphi, *you see, was carefully designed. The calculations required to operate at the third level are more than can be done in the time available. Even with a computational aid, the interval is too short to enter the data and then use the result. And you have no such aid."*

"You seem to have just proved that I am not a third-level player."

"I do, don't I? But I want to suggest another answer. You are what in another age would have been termed a 'lightning calculator,' a person with the ability to perform feats of memory and rapid mental calculation that most people would consider impossible."*

At last, he saw a reaction. Her blue eyes were frightened, and her lower lip was quivering. "You can't prove any of that."

He reached out and patted her hand. "My dear Ms.

Iver—may I call you Dulcie?—you do not understand. I am not seeking proof. I did not bring you here to accuse or punish you. I wanted to congratulate you and to admire your talent. And to offer a proposition."

"Ah." Her expression became contemptuous. "I've been getting those since I was fourteen."

"Not that sort of proposition, Dulcie." (Not yet, at any rate.) "I mean a business *proposition. Come and work here, with me."*

"You mean as an employee, in this place? Why should I? I can make more money playing Delphi."

"You can. Unless—or rather, until—you are black-balled here and in the other gaming rooms. But I don't think you are telling me the truth. Your gains have not been large. Also, I watched you. You don't play for money. You play for the thrill, the excitement of beating the system. I know that thrill, all too well."

"How can you? You sit on the house side, you make the system. There's no way you can lose."

"Do you think I always sat up here, in this room, rather than down at the tables? How do you think I was able to recognize third-level play so quickly? If you want proof, come back with me to the gaming floor, and let me convince you that at least one other person in the world is capable of third-level Delphi play."

"You are—"

"Of course I am. It takes one to know one." He reached out his hand. This time she grasped it in both of hers, and smiled at him in a way that sent tingles up his back.

"I never met another. I never thought I would." She laughed like a child. "We should compare what we can do."

"You show me yours and I'll show you mine?" He thought it might be too soon to say that, but all it did was make her smile more broadly. "And there is something that is even more fun than playing the games. I'm referring to

designing *them, creating something that offers scope for
all skills from blind betting to your own level of play. Are
you interested in working with me on that? I can make you
an attractive offer. And I can assure you, there is no one
else with talents remotely like yours in this establishment.*"

"I am interested. Very interested." The excitement on
her face brought back memories of his own younger days.
"But you have to tell me more about everything, and
everybody here. I don't even know your name. Who are
you?"

"My name?" He paused. Why was there a reluctance
to tell her? "My name is—"

Don't say it, don't say it. That was the past. You are not
that man any more.

*The deep mental block came into play, shattering real-
ity. He was falling again, falling as he had fallen many
times, falling on a dark airless world—lungs gasping out
a final bloodied froth of breath—falling until the solid roof
below rushed up to put an end to everything . . .*

And Lola, breaking out of the haldane synthesis with a
second shock that rivaled the first one in its sickening intensity, knew that with Bryce Sonnenberg she was out of
her depth. Memories of Mars, and now memories of Earth,
when according to his own statements and all his records,
he had never been to either planet. If those were false
memories, how many more of the things that he had told
her might be untrue?

She had to learn more about his past if she were to help
him, and she could not rely on him to provide that information. To make progress, she herself must have independent help.

Lola tossed and turned in her bed. She had known that she
needed assistance even before the most recent session with
Sonnenberg; today had merely provided a confirmation.

But when possible help had come along, she had rejected it, and for all the wrong reasons.

She remembered, ruefully, what she had told Spook a hundred times: *Don't judge people by appearances.* That was exactly what she herself had done when Bat had lumbered onto the scene. Thinking back, she felt sure that he had formed no better impression of her than she had of him. He had not spoken one word from the time Spook dragged him in to the time he dragged him out again. And he had scowled at her throughout the brief meeting.

But Spook insisted that Bat was a genius, someone who as Megachirops operated at the highest Masters' level on the Puzzle Network. He had shown her some of Bat's problems and solutions, and Lola acknowledged that the mind that came up with those possessed a subtlety and a deviousness far beyond what she would ever be able to achieve, plus an uncanny skill at handling large data bases.

Unfortunately those were skills that she had rejected, out of hand, because of a fat body and a few food stains.

She turned over in bed and looked at the clock. It was the middle of Ganymede's sleep period, a time when everyone sensible was asleep. But if she didn't do something, she was not likely to join that group.

Lola rose, pulled on a grey, one-piece suit, and walked along the dim-lit hall that led to Spook's rooms. He had chosen a separate part of the living quarters, as far away as he could get from where Lola lived. There was a message in that choice: Spook liked privacy. But in this case she didn't intend to do more than leave him a note on the door of his bedroom.

She opened the outer door quietly and slipped inside. She had expected all to be dark, but as her eyes adjusted to the gloom, she could see a faint light showing under the closed study door. Lola shook her head. Everyone *sensible* was asleep at this hour. She ought to have known that category would not include Spook.

She tapped gently, waited a second, and went in. Spook was there, peering into the display volume at a bloated cylinder with six convoluted and reentrant legs that sprouted from and reattached to its body. At Spook's side, arms folded like a judgmental Buddha, stood Rustum Battachariya.

Lola hadn't expected Bat still to be here, but actually it might make her job simpler. Before she could get to that, though, she had to fulfill her duty as a responsible surrogate parent.

"You shouldn't be up at this hour." She glared at both of them, the scrawny Spook and the Great Bat, and realized for the first time how young Bat was. Certainly no more than sixteen or seventeen. His huge size made you think he must be old, but his face had the innocent, unlined, and peaceful countenance of a baby. "Both of you should be asleep in bed."

"The late hour, I am afraid, is my fault." Bat spoke to her for the first time. "I pleaded with Ghost Boy—Spook—for instruction as to a certain geometrical construction technique."

"No, it's *not* your fault. You don't know the house rules." She pointed her forefinger at Spook. "He certainly does. What are you doing up so late?"

"Hey, it's no big deal." Spook was more annoyed than defensive. "I'm up as late as this nearly every night. The only reason you don't know it is you're always in bed, snoring your head off. A better question is, what are *you* doing up so late?"

"I couldn't sleep." Lola sat down on the one free chair in the cluttered workroom and told herself that she was making the right decision, improbable as it seemed. "I threw the two of you out earlier today, and I shouldn't have."

Spook shrugged. "That's all right. We could have done

nothing if we'd stayed. I explained to Bat that you were stoned out of your skull."

"You might have found a better way to put it." She turned to Bat. "I want to apologize. I had just finished an intense drug-augmented session with a patient. I am a haldane."

"So Ghost Boy informed me. However, that does not call for an apology."

Lola decided that Bat might or might not be a genius, but he was without doubt an irritating smartass. "I'm not apologizing for that. I'm *proud* to be a haldane, but it takes time for the sensitizing drugs to lose their effect. I was at a low point when you arrived, that's why I was rude."

"You came here in the middle of the night just to say you're sorry?" Spook whistled. "Well, that's a first."

Spook, genius or not, was no less a smartass. Were they deliberately trying to annoy her?

"I came here to tell you that I have changed my mind. If Bat is interested in helping, I'll let you review the full files on—my patient." Still she found it hard to say his name. "On Bryce Sonnenberg. I'll tell you what he told me, but I'm wondering if his recollections are reliable. You know your way around the data banks. How would you like to make an independent check on Sonnenberg's history, right from the day that he was born?"

She thought there might be hesitation—it sounded to her like a grind—but Spook answered at once, "Great! Can we bring in other members of the Puzzle Network?"

"Definitely *not*. You two, and only you two. You work in strict confidence, and the unedited files never leave my office. All right? And I want to know about anything you find, just as soon as you find it."

Spook was looking at Bat. The fat cheeks puffed out for a moment in thought; then the cannonball head nodded. "Acceptable. We will of course need appropriate access."

"I'll provide that to you." Lola saw they were staring at

her expectantly. "You don't mean *now,* do you?"

"As good a time as any." Spook waved her toward the terminal in the corner. "Do it, Lola. Some of us don't like to sleep our lives away."

Fifteen minutes later Lola was back in her bed, wondering if she had made the right decision. Spook and his new friend had waited until she provided the file access codes, and then they had pointedly ignored her. They didn't come right out and say that her presence was superfluous, but they went off into a strange form of communication, all terse and incomprehensible references to data-bank pointers and legal index modifiers that excluded her totally.

She settled down to sleep, telling herself that that was the whole point of asking Spook and Bat to help. If she could do what they were doing, then she would not need them. And while she slept, they would be working on the problem.

Probably working all night long. Lola had the impression that Bat regarded sleep as an option, something you might choose to do but could manage very well without.

Not her, though. If she didn't get seven or eight hours, she was good for nothing the following day.

A day which would soon be here. She realized that she would have to get up in four hours. And still she felt wide awake.

Now it was not Bryce Sonnenberg and his problems that filled her mind, but the newcomer who had dropped into her office when Spook and Bat were there. Conner Preston had come by to ask one simple question, and stayed on after they left to ask another.

"It's an imposition, I know." The confused, little-boy-lost look was out of place on a strongly built man in his middle thirties, but it was charming. "You see, I only just got here today."

"What do you need?" Lola remembered her own total confusion when she had first arrived on Ganymede. "Don't apologize. When you're a newcomer this place seems like a labyrinth."

"It does. Actually, I've been here before, but not to this part." He moved forward as though intending to occupy the seat opposite her, glanced at the busy desk, and straightened self-consciously. "I'm sorry, I'm interrupting your work."

"I think I've enjoyed as much work as I can stand. I'm wiped out. An interruption would be nice." Lola waved to him to sit down. "You said you have a question?"

"Well, only a pretty basic one. My food unit isn't working yet because the power was off, and I've had nothing to eat since this morning. I was wondering if you could tell me how to get to a public restaurant."

"You're in a bad place for it. This is all industrial and residential. You have to go four levels away. I can give you directions, but it's quite a distance."

"That's all right. I've got plenty of time. Just tell me where to go. Unless . . ." He hesitated, and would not look at her.

Lola smiled inside. You didn't think of becoming a haldane unless you already possessed a talent for reading people, and Conner Preston's body language was unmistakable. But she was not going to help him out. (Only the brave deserve the fair.)

"Unless—" His eyes, brown and beseeching, turned to hers. "Unless I could talk you into joining me; then you could show me instead of telling. Of course, if you have already had your evening meal . . ."

"I haven't. And I am hungry." She stood up. "Come on. I know a great place, and on the way you'll see a bit more of the inside of Ganymede. If it's been a while since you were here, you may not even recognize the place. It changes fast."

Strolling along corridors and standing on slideways, she learned more about Conner Preston. He was a senior news reporter, posted to Ganymede for a special one-year assignment. He had last been here six years earlier, one year before the war, when he was still a junior reporter.

Then came the first surprise: He was not from Earth or Mars, as she had assumed. He worked for United Broadcasting, and he had come from the Belt.

"I didn't know United Broadcasting even *existed* any more," Lola said. "I mean, I thought that the whole of Ceres and Pallas and Vesta—" She paused. She might be on the brink of a big social gaffe.

"Don't exist, either?" Conner Preston, uneasy in personal relationships, took that in his stride. "You won't offend me if you say it, because it comes close to being true. People think Earth suffered most in the war, and so they did in terms of sheer numbers. Nine billion dead, that's a horrifying total. But if you think percentages, the Belt got hammered worst. When the war began we had thirty populated asteroids and a self-sufficient economy. We led the system in some areas of technology. By the time that we surrendered, all we had were colonies on Ceres, Pallas, and Juno. We were down to nine million people, from a hundred and seven million—less than ten percent survival. I'm the only survivor of my whole family. And afterwards we lost another million and a half to starvation and cold, because we weren't self-sufficient any more. We barely are today. We have to import food, and our data banks are still total chaos."

Lola resisted the temptation to ask, "And what did *you* do during the war?" Had he been involved in the attack on Earth? Polite Ganymede dwellers, themselves remote from all the conflict, did not ask such personal questions of the combatants of either side. But Lola could not help thinking it. Strip away Conner Preston's casual manner, and beneath it she sensed a man who was always alert for trouble. They had reached the restaurant and were settling in at their table, and Lola noticed how carefully he inspected everything around him—the room, the automatic servers, and the place settings—and how precisely he placed his own eating utensils. That was another contrast to his casual clothing and easygoing manner. It might be the result of wartime experience, but possibly it was a simple by-product of a Belt upbringing and restricted living quarters. The Belt was often thought of as wide-open space, with many millions of kilometers between the major planetoids, but the habitats on most of them were cramped. The Von Neumanns had not touched the smaller worlds before the war began. Now it was anyone's guess as to how long it would be until they could start work in the Belt again.

"I'm sorry, Lola." Conner Preston had noticed her silence. "I've been talking too much about myself. That's boring."

"You didn't bore me at all. You just got me thinking about the war. I lost my whole family, too."

"I'm really sorry to hear that. So you are alone here."

"Yes. Except of course for Spook. You met him today."

"The thin one. He's your brother? I mean, he couldn't possibly be your son."

"He could—just. He's fifteen, and I'm twenty-seven. We were the lucky ones; we made it away from Earth just in time. The Armageddon Defense Line was on fire as we rose to orbit."

"Really? I've only heard third-hand reports before. You probably don't want to talk about that, but I'd really like to hear what happened."

"I don't mind."

Conner Preston was astonishingly easy to talk to. Once Lola had started, she found it hard to stop. Under casual prompting from him, she found thoughts and feelings coming to the surface that she had hidden away for years. He was a first-rate listener, perhaps as a result of his work in the media. She normally despised media people—all show and no substance—but it wasn't the time to say so. And maybe there were exceptions. She talked on and on, moving forward and backward in time, from leaving Earth as a would-be haldane, then to her training, and back again to the first bewildering months on Ganymede, and at last to her final graduation and current practice.

"So you decided that you wanted to be a haldane long before you left Earth," he said, when the serving machine had forced a break in the conversation by clearing the table. "I never met a haldane before. We don't have them, you know, in the Belt. You're supposed to be intimidating. Haldanes know everything, even what a person is thinking. But you don't feel threatening. I'd love to hear more about being a haldane, and a lot more about you. Not tonight, though. I have to travel up to the top level and check that the rest of my luggage has arrived. I hope the power is on by now in my office."

"Spook would have been to see us if he'd had problems."

"So I owe the whole Belman family."

"No, Conner. I owe you." Lola rose from the table. She had just realized how much she had said to him, and how much she had enjoyed doing it. "You let me babble on at you for hours. That was nice of you."

"That's what I'm here for."

"No. That's what *I'm* supposed to be here for. Nothing of what I've said has any interest to a news reporter."

"It does to this reporter. But don't misunderstand me, I wouldn't dream of using anything that you say to me." They were leaving the restaurant, and at the exit he took her hands in his. "You have no idea what a good time this has been. It's the most pleasant evening I've had since I don't know when. Goodnight, Lola."

He smiled, turned, and headed quickly for the elevators that would take him to the upper levels. Lola, watching him go, felt some of the easy, warm feeling inside her fading away.

It was a perfectly reasonable way for the evening to end, but it wasn't what she wanted. He had implied that he would like to know her better; then he had failed to follow up on it. When he left he had said not one word about the possibility of their meeting again.

Why did that annoy her so? You didn't have to be a haldane to make a good guess.

She started for home, knowing that Conner Preston was going to be on her mind for the rest of the evening. As she walked, vague other thoughts roamed the margins of her consciousness. She had been through two haldane sessions within twenty-four hours, and traces of the drugs were still active in her system. But even without drugs, a trained haldane possessed a sensitivity to nuances of personality that no one else would ever read.

Conner Preston was bright, easygoing, and charming. He was also intriguing and personally interesting to Lola, in a way that few men had ever been. He seemed equally interested in her. But with all that . . .

Some deep-rooted analytical faculty was at work inside her head. She sensed anomalies in Conner Preston. She itched to interact with him when psychotropic drugs were active in both of them, when she as a haldane could explore his inner workings. At the very least she would like to hear him under hypnosis.

She had no possible way to fulfill these urges. By all objective standards Conner was healthy, happy, and not remotely in need of a haldane's service. But the idea kept nagging at her. She had already sensed, although it was not yet late in the evening, that an uneasy and thought-filled night might lie ahead.

11

The General Assembly had set the ground rules in the 2040s, when the Organization of Outer Planets that the assembly represented was little more than a fledgling body: *No individual, or group of individuals, may own real estate assets lying permanently within the domain of the Organization of Outer Planets.*

No matter that "permanently" was a poorly defined term, in a solar system whose long-term chaotic nature had been recognized by everyone but the legislators. If and when there was a change in the planetary configuration from Jupiter to Persephone, the law would change with it. Meanwhile, no one but the government of the outer planets could own any part of the surface or the interior of a planet, a ring structure, or a major or minor moon.

Comets, passing through the outer-planet region, were up for grabs. You were free to mine one for volatiles—if you could snag it.

And, of course, you could *lease* property.

The negotiators for the General Assembly drove a hard bargain. Even in the 2040s, when the Von Neumanns had been at work on Ganymede and Callisto for only a decade, and the human inhabitants were no more than a handful of supervisors, the future potential of these worlds was recognized. You could not get a cheap lease, and you could not get a long lease. On Europa, the protected waterworld of the Jovian system, you could not get a lease at all. The only permits available were for research work.

What about sulfur-spitting Io; or little Amalthea, buffeted by Jupiter's intense radiation storms; or the small and barren outer satellites? Those were another matter. No one had ever applied for a development permit on Io, where even the hardiest Von Neumanns had so far proved unable to replicate and could barely even survive. But should you happen to want a lease there, or on Leda, Himalia, Elara, or Ananke, or on one of the other frozen chips of rock in orbit many millions of kilometers from the mother planet—well, in that case have we got a deal for you.

But you would have to be crazy to ask.

The negotiators, at that time still based on Earth, were astonished when they were approached by a small and exclusive group known as the Ganymede Club. The Club's representatives inquired about leases on Lysithea, a frigid mountain of rock that circled twelve million kilometers from Jupiter. Is it available?

It certainly is. No one else had ever made so much as an inquiry. How much of Lysithea do you wish to lease?

The whole satellite.

No problem. And how long a lease are you talking about?

The General Assembly team heard the answer and chuckled up their sleeves. A good chunk of change now, for thousand-year future rights to a small piece of nothing; the Ganymede Club members must have more money than sense.

When the same Club representatives went on to inquire about an additional lease for Helene, the General Assembly team changed its mind: The Ganymede Club members didn't have more money than sense—they had no sense at all. If Lysithea was worth nothing, then Helene was worth a negative amount. It was a major pain even to reach that tiny world in its far-off libration-point orbit in the Saturn system. But if that's what the Ganymede Club wanted . . .

The negotiators were all set to write the deal when a junior Club member pointed out one irritating detail. Some wild-eyed crank in the General Assembly, convinced that the Saturn system was going to become the promised land of the twenty-second century, had insisted on adding a supplemental condition—no lease for a Saturn moon could run for more than thirty years.

The team swore, apologized to the Club representatives, and drafted a new agreement. When it was ready they asked if a few of the Club members would like to come to the ceremonial signing. It seemed only right that the Club should get *something* for its money, even if it was no more than a free drink and a group video.

The offer was politely declined. The Ganymede Club, it was pointed out, was not merely exclusive; it was also reclusive. Signature would be performed by proxy. The Organization of Outer Planets agreed. They took the lease fees; held the signing party by themselves, handed over the figurative keys to Lysithea and Helene, and put a note in the tickler file to think about the leases again in 2074. Then they forgot about both worlds. They were sure that no development of Lysithea would take place for centuries, perhaps not ever.

A flyby of the planetoid twenty-eight years later would have confirmed their opinion. But a visit to the interior would have astonished them. Where Jeffrey Cayuga was sitting, in the main control room at the center of the habitation bubble, he could review all the little world's communication and defense systems. They were considerable. The array of antennas on the surface station provided continuous contact with every world in the Jovian system.

The forty-second signal travel time was a small price to pay for a high level of privacy.

The antennas of the communications system were visible from space. The defenses were not. They had been designed and installed by armament specialists from the Belt, all of whom had died in the final spasm of the war. Cayuga had not been responsible for that but he did not grieve for their passing. The discretion of the designers was now assured forever.

Beam and projectile weapons resided in a dozen hidden pits carved into Lysithea's surface. They could be activated in a second from where Cayuga was sitting. If the attack was too much for them, another option had been provided. Half a dozen small but high-acceleration vessels sat in their own concealed caverns, well away from the weapons. They were ready for liftoff at all times. Cayuga could leave his seat in the control center, throw himself into a high-gee ascent shaft, and within a couple of minutes be away into space using any one of the escape ships.

There was enough escape capacity for the whole Ganymede Club, but that was a gross design overkill. The other Club members preferred to live on Ganymede or Callisto and visit Lysithea and the Saturn system only occasionally. Cayuga was the exception. Lysithea was his home. He did not travel unless there was good reason to do so.

That would shortly be the case. He was alone on Lysithea making final travel plans. Normally his life was not so solitary. Partners selected by Alicia Rios were imported regularly from Ganymede. Each one was strawberry blond, leggy, energetic, and terminally unimaginative. Each was treated well and offered every consideration on Lysithea. Each was convinced that her relationship with Cayuga was different from that of any predecessor. Each one was sure that she was winning his heart in a special way. And each one, after no more than three months on Lysithca, found herself heading back to Ganymede, laden with gifts but left in no doubt that she would not be returning to share Cayuga's bed and company.

If anyone had asked her about the internal workings, computer facilities, or fortifications of Lysithea, she would have had no idea what the person was talking about. She could give only the vaguest description of where she had been—to many Jovians, anything beyond Callisto was nowhere. Most likely, she would do no better than explain that the place itself was pretty neat, but it had a moldy smell and Cayuga needed better cleaning machines.

Cayuga's most recent companion had departed two weeks ago. His outbound trajectory had finally been approved by the outer-planet transportation board. He would travel a constant acceleration path to the Saturn system, with a final destination stated as Rhea, the fifth, and second largest, of the major Saturnian moons. Movement beyond that point would be Cayuga's own affair, not controlled or monitored by the central authority.

He confirmed the trajectory and notified the board that there would actually be two people traveling outbound on the *Weland:* Jeffrey Cayuga himself and a nephew who had shipped in to Lysithea from the Belt. The round-trip signal delay was something he was accustomed to. He waited patiently until the confirming return message came from Abacus, the artificial world circling Callisto, where the central Jovian computer complex was located. Finally he switched to a Ganymede connection, private and coded against tapping or outside interference.

Again, he had to wait. Ganymede was occulted by the mass of Jupiter itself when the call went through, and it was not worth using a relay station. He sat through the few minutes of delay until line-of-sight communication could be established. Patience in communications was necessary for anyone who chose to live as far away from the inner moons as Lysithea. At last Alicia Rios popped into view in the display volume.

"I thought you would be calling round about now," she said at once. She was staring hard, presumably at the screen, which would normally have been showing an image of Cayuga. "Why no picture?"

"I must be leaving soon. I am closer than I thought to the change, and it would be disastrous if anyone were to see me."

"Isn't this a maximum security line?"

"Naturally. But visual signals have such high redundancy that unscrambling is not impossible. Audio alone is better for transmission from this end. Can you summarize the current situation? I am eager for a report before I leave."

"Sure. Things are going very well. I saw Jinx this morning, and he's already made contact with Lola Belman. He says in another week or two he'll have her eating out of his hand. She's twenty-seven years old and definitely heterosexual. Jinx describes her as the sort of intellectual who likes to think she's in control, but she'll go overboard when her juices start flowing. Her last affair was eleven months ago with one of her haldane instructors. He judges that she's more than ready for another. Certainly, she was starved for company. She wanted to talk his ear off."

"Maybe. And to listen. Let us never forget that she is a haldane. What did *he* tell *her?*"

"Nothing that could possibly point in our direction. Or even in his. Relax, Cayuga. For this job he's using a different persona. So far as Lola Belman is concerned, he's not Jinx Barker—he's Conner Preston, visiting for a while from the Belt and in need of some kind-hearted person to show him life on Ganymede." Alicia laughed. "A nice touch, don't you think?"

Cayuga's delay in replying was due to more than signal travel time. "I don't like that," he said at last. "He's overconfident, trying to be too clever."

"Don't blame Jinx. The Conner Preston idea was mine.

And you are the one who insisted that no matter what happened, Lola Belman must not be able to trace anything back to us."

"I also don't want her suspicious. She's a *haldane,* Rios. I can't make that point too strongly. And Jinx Barker is lying to her."

"What man doesn't, when he's interested in a woman? Lola Belman isn't some twelve-year-old virgin. She's been around. She'll expect him to embellish a bit if he's interested in her. And it works both ways. I doubt if she's being totally honest with him. It's all part of the game."

"This is not a game, Rios. I seem to have trouble persuading you of that. Next time that you talk with Barker, I want you to emphasize once again his real objective. The seduction of Lola Belman is no more than the means to an end. That end is our understanding of the data file showing a person falling to his death on Mars, and our assurance that the event is unrelated to the Ganymede Club. If Barker can achieve that result more quickly and safely by other means—persuasion, or bribery, or torture, of Lola Belman or some other—then he should do so."

"You mean her brother, Spook Belman? Jinx has already ruled him out as a source. He and somebody called Battachariya were around when Jinx met Lola, but the other one's a kid, too, big and fat but only sixteen years old."

"I am not worried by the presence of children. Neither would I put any trust in what they say. I am thinking of the possible use of one of Lola Belman's patients."

"That's something that so far she hasn't talked about. She won't even say who her patients are. That's why Jinx and I think that bed will work best. You can't beat pillow talk. And don't worry about it going the other way. Jinx is a real professional, he won't tell her a thing. Anything else I need to know before you head out?"

"Only that my will is now signed, and I have deposited it in the central files on Ganymede. My entire estate is bequeathed to my nephew, Joss Cayuga. The *Weland* is scheduled to leave for the Saturn system tomorrow. It will make a visit to our usual destination, but that is not on the flight plan. The *Weland* will return to Ganymede in five weeks' time."

"So I'll see you then."

"Not exactly."

"You know what I mean, Cayuga." Alicia Rios smiled. "I'll see Joss, if you prefer to put it that way. And don't worry. By then Jinx Barker will have results. I have every confidence in him. *Bon voyage.*"

Her image disappeared, leaving Jeffrey Cayuga staring thoughtfully at the blank display region. After a few seconds he keyed in another destination. The high-gain antenna on the surface of Lysithea turned slowly, to lock onto Callisto. That connection took a little more time to establish. The ancient, cratered moon surface was more difficult to work with than Ganymede, and the population of both humans and service machines was far less. The communication system was primitive by Ganymede standards. When Lenny Costas's pitted, impassive face finally appeared in the display volume, the engineer's image wavered and wobbled for a few seconds before it stabilized.

"Who is that?" Like Alicia Rios, Costas was peering at his own blank display region.

"This is Cayuga, audio only."

"I thought you were on your way."

"I will be. Very soon. But I have just concluded a disturbing conversation with Alicia Rios. I would like to summarize and hear your opinion."

Costas listened in silence as Cayuga spoke, and at the end he grunted and shook his head. "No surprise to me, any of that. I told you a long time ago that Rios is too close to Jinx Barker. She puts over-much trust in him, tells him too many things she doesn't need to. My bet is he knows a lot more about the Club than we think. She acts as though he is a member, but he isn't, and if I have any say in it he never will be. That Conner Preston stunt was just plain dumb. All Lola Belman would have to do is meet somebody who remembers the *real* Conner Preston, and she could be led straight to Jinx Barker and Alicia Rios. And maybe to us. What do you want me to do?"

"For the moment, nothing active. Just keep a quiet eye on them. Get Polk and Dahlquist and Munzer to help you. Go to Ganymede yourself if you have to. When I return the five of us will get together and reassess things. Then we may have to act."

"It will be a pleasure."

"I wouldn't bet on that, Costas. Don't underestimate Jinx Barker. Whatever else he is, he's a professional. He'll handle you and Polk and Dahlquist together without raising a sweat."

"No, he won't." Costas smiled for the first time. "Not one of us would ever be stupid enough to get near him— we have too much to lose. But there are other ways. It raises a good question: Who do you hire to kill an assassin?"

"You'll have five weeks to think about that while I'm away. And don't forget that our actions might have to include Alicia Rios as well as Jinx Barker. She seems to be showing dangerously bad judgment. Form your own impression, and we'll talk about this as soon as I get back." Cayuga studied the image of Lenny Costas for a few more seconds.

"I think the time is getting close for you, too," Cayuga said as he gave the command to break the connection. "You'll have to make a trip in the near future. Another year, and not even makeup will be able to disguise the changes."

12

Spook was running along a long, spiraling corridor, in a dream-dark world. He could see clearly, more clearly than usual, but everything was muted tones of charcoal and grey. The air was chokingly thick and hot, and as he ran, an acrid smoke swirled from a jagged crack in the ceiling ahead. It made his eyes water and his lungs burn. He could still run, but it was the flight of nightmares. Although he was on a path that turned steadily upward, his feet made so little contact with the floor that no amount of effort would increase his speed.

The ground beneath him suddenly twisted and heaved, throwing him off balance so that he banged painfully against the tunnel wall and collapsed to his knees. From that position he stared at the way ahead. It seemed lit by random flashes of light. He knew that they were reflections, that the light actually came from behind him. And they were closer every moment, each lightning flash accompanied by a hot breath on his back. He had to keep running.

He rose, the knots of muscles in his calves and thighs bunching and flexing to bring him to a standing position. Instead of standing, he found that he was propelled high

*into the air. When at last he came down again, he stood
for a moment, swaying. He felt terribly weak, as though he
had eaten nothing for days.*

Run. And then eat.

*No. Run, and drink, and then eat. Thirst and smoke had
desiccated his throat so much that he could not swallow,
could barely breathe. Could do nothing more than yearn
to fall to the floor and rest.*

*He paused, ready to give way to the temptation. As he
did so, he saw a dark object close to the wall of the tunnel. It was another human. A woman, lying face down and
not moving. Someone had taken the option of surrender-
ing to fatigue and bad air—and death.*

*He started forward again, along the curving tunnel that
never ended. Hope and escape, if they lay anywhere, were
in that direction, up toward the surface.*

*He had been wrong. It could not be run, and drink, and
eat.*

*It must be run, and run, and run. That was the rule, for
the whole of the world, forever and ever . . .*

It ended without warning. In a millisecond, Spook was
hurled out of derived reality. He found that he was gasping, weeping, gulping in air to the utmost depths of his
lungs. The tunnel had vanished. Another world was appearing in a kaleidoscope of bright colors. The computer
had broken the link.

And not before time. Spook sat up, ripped the telemetry contacts from his temples and neck, and looked around.
He was in Lola's clinic. Bat, sitting six feet away in a chair
three sizes too small for him, was watching calmly.

"The sequence is finished?" he asked. "Excellent. Now
we can compare notes. What did you make of it?"

Spook fought back the butterflies in his stomach. He and
Bat had been jousting like this for two days, each unwilling to admit to any weakness. He was not going to give in

now. He allowed himself one more deep breath before he tried to speak.

"I can't tell you what it is. But I can tell you what it *isn't*. That's not Earth—the gravity field is all wrong. And I don't believe that it's Mars, either."

"Agreed. Not Earth, or Mars, or Ganymede. There was insufficient gravitational field in that sequence for any of them."

"Callisto?"

"No again. The Callistan field is only about half of what we experience here on Ganymede, but that is still far too much."

"Where then?"

They sat staring at each other. Bat's great moon face had the calm rapture of the Puzzle Master facing a new challenge.

"I will state an opinion," he said at last. "Although I admit at the outset that it introduces more questions than it answers. I believe that the low gravity indicates a sequence occurring somewhere in the Belt. In view of the well-developed tunnel structure, it was clearly one of the colonized worlds. Beyond that we cannot go. We have no direct indications of body size or mass, other than that it is smaller than any of the inhabited planets or major satellites."

"That's great." Spook had been thinking the same thing, but was not keen to propose it. "You realize what that implies? We've already had Bryce Sonnenberg in sequences on Earth and Mars, two places where he says he's never been. Now we want him remembering the Belt, too—which he insists he left twenty-one years ago, when he was three years old. He sure wasn't three years old in this sequence."

"That is not perhaps the worst problem. Let us adopt, as a working hypothesis, that the *place* is in fact somewhere in the Belt. Then we must consider the *time.*"

"That's easy." Spook had his own unpleasant memories to help him. "If it's the Belt, then that sequence happened just five years ago. That's when Earth and Mars were doing their best to smash the Belt worlds to pieces."

"And conversely. Regrettably, both were succeeding. I agree, this sequence could only have taken place during the war."

"No matter when it happened, it's the same problem all over again. First, Sonnenberg had a sequence on prewar Mars that he could not possibly have survived. Then he had an *earlier* sequence on Earth, but he was *older* than he was on Mars. Now he dies in the Belt during the war, but according to Sonnenberg, in this memory he was *younger* than he was on either Earth or Mars. It's screwy."

"We are not sure that he died in the Belt experience." Bat, who had been sitting totally immobile, lifted a judicial finger. "Permit me to point out the logical difference. In the case of Mars, death seemed both imminent and inescapable. By contrast, in this case Sonnenberg was in a difficult situation but he was actively seeking to escape from it. Perhaps he did escape."

"What do you mean, *perhaps?*" Spook waved his hand toward the other office. "He must have escaped. He was in there this morning, having another haldane session."

"If you could somehow persuade your sister to let us talk to him directly about what we are doing—"

"Forget it, Bat. She'll get up on her high horse again and talk about her sacred duty as a haldane. I've been through it a hundred times and got nowhere. Anyway, she says it wouldn't do any good if we did talk to Sonnenberg. He has these blackouts and weird memories, but he has no more idea what's happening to him than we do."

"He has less. He does not have Puzzle Network experience, which hones the talent for assembling a whole from a miscellany of small fragments. You and I both possess such invaluable experience. Let us accept that Sonnenberg—for the time being—is inaccessible to us. That leaves only one alternative."

"What's that?"

"We must get down to real work." Bat sighed—a sigh of satisfaction more than frustration—and stood up. "We must attack the data banks."

A name, Bryce Sonnenberg, and a family history. Bat had often started in the Puzzle Network with a lot less.

He had returned as soon as possible to the Bat Cave, where conditions were more favorable for sustained thought. To say that he disliked Spook, once he had taken the big step and reluctantly agreed to meet him, would be quite untrue. He enjoyed the intellectual interaction, and they shared many interests.

What he found hard to take was the jittering, the furious nervous energy and the hyperactive disposition. Spook was only a few centimeters shorter than Bat and could match him course for course at the dinner table, but he massed only one-fourth as much. He was as thin as a stick, with biceps no bigger than his Adam's apple. After spending the day together, Bat understood why. Spook burned off all his calories, buzzing around the room and never sitting still.

Whereas Bat, like any rational person, preferred to do what he was planning to do now: Sit, sift, compare, and think.

He made sure that ample snacks were available, put on his favorite cowled robe, seated himself at the terminal, and went visiting. First stop: the general census files.

One of the basic rules of the Puzzle Network was also the simplest: *Nothing is what it seems.* And as a corollary of that: *Don't believe anything that you are told, check it for yourself.*

Bat made the most basic check of all. Was there such a person as Bryce Sonnenberg?

There was. According to the census file, he was twenty-four years old. He lived on Callisto. His occupation showed as mathematician, specializing in nonpolynomial algorithms. His hobby was low-gee space-scooter competition.

At that point, any resemblance between the census files and the history that Sonnenberg had given to Lola Belman ended.

After an initial moment of disbelief—could this be another Bryce Sonnenberg?—Bat set out to chart the differences.

CENSUS FILE	LOLA BELMAN'S RECORDS
Birthplace, Belt, otherwise unspecified.	Birthplace, Hidalgo.
Arrived Callisto five years ago, at the end of the war.	Arrived Callisto twenty-one years ago.
Miriam Sonnenberg, mother, employed on Ceres in Von Neumann design.	Miriam Sonnenberg, mother, employed on Callisto in Von Neumann design.
Mother in Belt, presumed to have died in war.	Mother on Oberon, still alive.
Father in Belt, presumed to have died in war.	Father unknown.

Which data set to believe? The census file, or what Lola Belman had been told by Bryce Sonnenberg? Mother worked on Ceres, or Callisto—or neither?

The census data and Lola Belman's records were alike in this: They depended totally on what was told to them.

Bat didn't have that limitation. *Don't believe anything you are told.*

He moved up a level in the data base and inquired as to the sources of the census entries. As he had feared, he met the Wall: *Requested data unavailable.*

The distributed-information network for the solar system had been designed in the 2020s. The Unity was a wonderful and logical construct, one of humanity's shining and most perfect creations. Within the Unity every data bank was smoothly interlocked. A query might bounce from Ganymede to Earth to Mars to Pallas, but the user would neither know nor care. The answer would come eventually, if it were stored anywhere, because every data element was accessible from anywhere. Each bank could service or call for data from any other, efficiently, economically, and logically.

There was one default assumption: The human race was presumed to be equally logical. Unfortunately, the Great War was not the act of a logical species.

The Wall had been thrown up hastily after the war, when it became obvious that the Unity had collapsed to a wilderness of isolated data sources, informational ganglia without a central nervous system. A user, wandering the system, would be turned back by the Wall whenever a destination data bank no longer existed.

The Wall was intended to save time and effort. Why encourage a user to search for something, when no one knew where it might be or if it still existed? On Earth, Mars, Moon, or in the Belt, a trillion facts had dissolved to a swirl of random electrons. The Wall was telling Bat and a billion other users to forget it—their search would be a waste of time. It was protecting them all from an uncharted Sargasso Sea of lost and derelict data sets.

But Bat had been here before. He had built up, within his head, his own map of that sea. The Luna data base had gone completely and forever. It was a waste of time even looking there. Earth had a reduced service capacity, but the basic data were there—if you could find them. Mars was a mess, but a team was working on it and little by little it was coming back on-line.

All the leading Belt colonies had been hit hard in the war. The Ceres data bank was gone, except for a few skimpy index files stored in backup form on Ganymede—index files that pointed, like ghostly fingers, to phantom data no longer existing on Ceres. The situation for Vesta was even worse. There were no files, pristine or backup, of any kind. Data banks on Pallas had been purged by the warlords of the Belt, just before they killed themselves rather than surrender to Earth. The record of bloody deeds that those banks had contained could only be conjectured.

Hidalgo, the planetoid that Bat was interested in, was one of the lesser Belt worlds. Its defenses had proved totally inadequate and its human population had been annihilated in a single raid. The basic computer system apparently still existed together with its census files, but it was in isolation. The Wall insisted that the data were not linked to any access node that Bat could reach. Also, Hidalgo itself was still under military embargo. Some highly unpleasant experiments had been conducted there before or during the war, and the surviving results could not be allowed to escape.

At that point, anyone but a masochist would have given up. Bat did not think of it. He had tools in his bag of tricks that no one else even suspected. A ten-minute pause for refueling: cheese, dried fruit, and walnuts, all grown or synthesized by the service machines on the agricultural level, within walking distance of the Bat Cave; and then Bat took the next step.

From his program directory he summoned one of his own routines, *Mellifera*. Its program data area had been left empty. He prepared the instructions to fill that void with great care. It would be galling to fail because of some minor coding error, although in human terms the basic message was simple: *Seek access to the Hidalgo data base*. Bat made ten thousand copies of the completed version of Mellifera, provided a different system entry point for each one, and released them into the Ganymede network.

Mellifera was not very smart, no more intelligent than the honeybee after which it had been named. Like the individual bees of a hive, each module would quest far and wide through the interconnected data banks of the solar system. If one of them found what it was looking for, it would return at once to the "hive" of Bat's computer, bearing with it the sequence of steps that it had taken on the way.

Once he saw that sequence, Bat would decide what to do next. What he could not specify in advance was how long the search should take. Movement within the Ganymede data banks would be very fast, but he felt sure that his answer did not lie there. The myriad copies of Mellifera would need to leap out into space as tight bundles of digital signals, beamed to every node in the solar system. That would be done at light-speed, but at the present time Earth was—how far away? Bat leaned back and thought for a moment; the orbital ephemerides of the planets and major moons were something that he kept in his head, since they were basic to efficient solar system transportation. Earth was 828 million kilometers away from Ganymede. Round-trip travel time would be a little more than an hour and a half. Assume that there would be a need to bounce around quite a bit, to the Belt and inner planets and back, and the Mellifera units would not be returning for quite a while.

It was time to try something different. Bat turned to consideration of the Hidalgo data base, together with the Sonnenberg "memory" that he and Spook had reviewed earlier. It suggested a new train of thought. Bat adjusted the cowled hood on his shaved head and pulled his robe tighter. He closed his eyes and became totally immobile.

A stranger entering the Bat Cave would have judged him asleep. A physician, examining the pattern of his brain waves, would have disagreed but been unable to describe accurately the mental state. Bat had entered the dreamlike trance where thinking blended the workings of conscious and unconscious mind.

Suppose that both the census files and Lola Belman's records were partially correct. Suppose that Bryce Sonnenberg had been born twenty-four years ago on Hidalgo, just as he had told Lola, but he had come to Callisto only five years ago. Suppose that until then, he had remained on Hidalgo, or on another of the Belt worlds. He had managed to escape during the war, but in the prewar period he had been doing—what?

Bat was sure that he was a genius, smarter than anyone he knew, but he still admitted to a teenager's ghoulish fascination with some things—like the Belt's prewar activities. The subterranean levels of the information highways rang with talk of strange experiments performed on human subjects, horrors far beyond the mild perversities of the Purcell invertor or the Tolkov stimulator.

There was the gene splicing of human and great ape, rumored to be the basis for the organic smart warheads of the Belt's Seeker missiles. No ship had ever escaped from a Seeker, once it had recognized its target. No captured Seeker complete with its brain had ever been released for inspection.

The Seeker neural network could be grown using elementary techniques that were well within the grasp of anyone who chose to perform such work. Far more difficult and outré were the blends of vertebrate and invertebrate DNA performed on Geneva. Reputedly, that work had produced spiderman warriors, amazingly strong and resilient but uncontrollable even by their makers. The Belt's own fusion weapons had been turned on Geneva, vaporizing the inhabited layers of that little world.

Bat's own personal nightmare was the brain corer. This was more than rumor—it had been reported by cleanup squads, cautiously exploring the battered Belt worlds. What they found had been placed in data files that would remain locked for a century. Sometimes Bat wished that he had not taken those ciphers as a personal challenge. He had cracked the codes and been rewarded with dreadful images, of men and women without heads, lumbering like sightless automata along the hidden corridors of the Belt worlds. An augmented spinal cord was enough to offer control of basic body functions. The cored brains, complete with optic nerves, floated naked and alive within transparent jars of nutrient solutions. The attached eyeballs at the ends of their stalks of nerve tissue gazed at the inaccessible world beyond the vats. Delicate traceries of conducting fiber entered the vats and tapped the silent thoughts.

That was the worst part of all. The brains, awake twenty-four hours a day, knew what had happened to them. They begged constantly for release.

It did not help to know that although the work had been done in the Belt, financial support had come from somewhere in the inner system. The cleanup squads had wept, cursed God and man, and provided the mercy stroke before anyone could send orders to do otherwise. The naked brains blessed their killers as they died.

Bat shuddered and returned to normal consciousness. Was that the milieu from which Bryce Sonnenberg had derived—not before the war, but at the end of it? Suppose his "memories" were a cover for a more sinister past.

Bat dropped the idea almost immediately. He had allowed the recollection of Belt atrocities to derange him temporarily. If Sonnenberg were an escaped war criminal in hiding, the last thing he would do was allow a haldane to probe his mind.

There was a more rational alternative. Suppose that Sonnenberg had been not a perpetrator of Belt war crimes, but a *victim*. The technology that developed the Purcell invertor was certainly capable of filling a mind with wild memories, or of inserting a false past. Perhaps it was Bryce Sonnenberg's true past, welling up now from the depths of his mind in random and uncontrolled flashes. Lola Belman's work might be hastening the recollection process.

Except that could not be true, either. Sonnenberg seemed to have memories from multiple individuals, including memories of someone's certain death.

The false-past idea was untenable. And yet . . .

The workings of the subconscious were, by definition, inaccessible to the usual thought processes. Bat hated that. At the same time, he had learned never to ignore his own irrational hunches. They often turned out to be right—and intelligible after the fact in logical terms.

He felt that he was close to the truth but was unable to see it. He tried his usual trick. He put the problem to the back of his mind, and turned to another subject. A search for Sonnenberg's mother would certainly prove productive one way or another. If she were alive and working on Oberon, it should be trivial to find her, regardless of the name she was using. Oberon was one of the "big two" moons of Uranus, but it was still a shrimp by Jupiter system standards, only a fortieth the volume of Ganymede. The number of Von Neumann designers there could hardly run to double figures. If she were not on Oberon, it would be one more reason to question Bryce Sonnenberg's reliability.

Bat was constructing the query when an attention light flashed on his console. A Mellifera probe had returned, and it was indicating success. The first one back usually found the shortest path to the data destination, but Bat made himself wait in delicious anticipation for another five minutes, until four more were in the hive.

Access to the Hidalgo data base could be found—where?

Bat examined the node sequences determined by the Mellifera modules, at first with delight and then with dismay. All five questing programs agreed that a copy of the Hidalgo data files was kept on Callisto. But incredibly, the files were not on-line. In order to examine them, it would be necessary to go to Callisto in person.

That confirmed Bat's worst suspicions of Callisto, a hick world with a total IQ less than Bat's own. What sort of morons kept data bases without access?

He felt his frustration grow. Callisto was where Sonnenberg had supposedly made his home after he left Hidalgo. All investigation paths seemed to lead there. In solar system terms Callisto was almost in Bat's own backyard—just the next moon out from Ganymede. As far as he was concerned, it might as well have been in a different galaxy. He never ventured as far as the surface of Ganymede, and the prospect of going beyond it appalled him.

His irritation lasted for only a second or two. Another Puzzle Network dictum: *Every well-posed problem has a solution.* In this case Bat realized that the solution was obvious: Spook Belman.

Spook loved the idea of charging off all over Ganymede, grubbing into old files and examining tattered war relics. He had more energy than sense. Surely he would view the prospect of a trip to Callisto with great enthusiasm.

Bat reached for the phone. It was the middle of the Ganymede night—but what better time to be sure that Spook was home, alone, and available to talk?

13

The cartographers of the solar system had pegged Helene as a dead, quiet rock fragment of little interest to anyone. Probably it had once been a comet, swinging in close to the Sun and then far out again, until on one approach it had come too close to Saturn and been captured by the planet's gravitational field. That had happened millions of years ago, long enough for Helene to find its way to L-4, a low point in the Saturn/Dione gravity-potential well. It remained there still, in stable orbit. The little world's low density was consistent with a captured comet, most of whose volatiles had survived the approaches to the Sun and were still trapped inside it.

That capture by Saturn was the end point of Helene's history. The worldlet was known to be quiet, dead, and dull. The Ganymede Club, the group of apparent eccentrics who had taken a lease on Helene in the 2040s, had done nothing in thirty years to change its external appearance or reported status. But the cartographers would have received a big surprise if they had been able to pay a visit to the interior.

A dozen concealed shafts had been sunk into one side of the little moon. Below the surface plates that concealed them, a group of special-purpose Von Neumanns was constantly at work. They were installing drive units whose dilute exhausts were designed to be indistinguishable in composition from the solar wind. Around the drive shafts, but well separated from them, stood the original Helene tunnels. Numerous and interconnected, they produced a deep interior riddled with holes, like a great chunk of termite-infested wood. At the surface those tunnels were dark and frozen, but spreading across their mouths, a few hundred meters down, were thin membranes of a white rubbery material. It remained tough and flexible, although the local temperature was hundreds of degrees below freezing.

Jeffrey Cayuga had parked the *Weland* in contact with the surface of Helene. It was held there by superconducting magnets. Only a huge force would wrench it free.

He descended the closest tunnel, dropping steadily until he came to the membrane. It was not necessary to slice through it. A tug detached part of the tunnel wall and made a slit wide enough for him to slide past. He was still wearing his suit. Once on the other side of the membrane, he unlocked the seals and lifted his helmet.

The head that emerged was hairless, with sagging cheeks cratered and fissured by deep lines in pockmarked and withered skin. As the helmet came off in a puff of freezing air, Cayuga gasped and shivered. His body drifted slowly forward and down.

The interior below the membrane was forty degrees warmer than above, but its cold, hard vacuum would kill an unprotected human within a couple of minutes.

Cayuga indeed seemed to be dying. His eyes were wide open and his rigid body went floating helplessly toward the tunnel wall. That wall was no longer a featureless crust of rock. It was pleated and striated, and within the numerous cracks and pouches lurked a pale blue phosphorescence. As soon as Cayuga's body touched the wall, glowing strands of blue reached out from the crannies to envelop him.

Then there was no movement for four days, until at last a cloud of blue-white vapor puffed without warning from the corpse's open mouth. Staring eyes blinked, slowly and then faster. The broad chest shivered. A few seconds later Cayuga's hands began to twitch and clench and moved up to place his helmet back into position. There was a clicking of seals. The suit began to fill with air.

Cayuga sneezed, once and then twice more. There was another long pause, until his suited figure began to move upward. Out again on the frozen surface of Helene, he began his inspection. He visited each of the drive installations, determining how close they were to completion. Another two days passed before he was ready to return to the waiting ship.

An hour later, the *Weland* left. Helene became once more the silent and unpopulated world known to the solar system's official cartographers.

Lola was at an all-time, rock-bottom low.

The day had started with the sort of patient that she wanted to kick around the office. It was a man, twenty years older than she, who said he needed a haldane's help because his life was "unfulfilled" and his talents were not appreciated. Before the end of the first session, Lola, without the aid of any psychotropic drugs, knew exactly what he was: he was a lazy, incompetent, greedy whiner who all his life had taken from anyone who would give—family, lovers, government, and former friends. Now he was expecting to take her time and was clearly not proposing to pay for it.

When she suggested, after listening to his maundering complaints for most of the morning, that she couldn't do a damn thing for him because he was the cause of his own problems, he became furious. She hadn't heard the last of this, he said, as he stormed out. Bitch—he was going to report her. She would lose her haldane license.

That was the beginning. Then came news that the next patient would not be arriving for his second session, because he had committed suicide. The person who called Lola clearly blamed her for that. He asked her, bitingly, if she had billed the dead man for "previous services."

She had, she replied, and she had not been paid a cent. It was pretty clear that she would not be.

The whole experience did not make a person ecstatic to be a haldane. You might perform miracles occasionally, but people expected them of haldanes all the time.

Which brought her to Bryce Sonnenberg and her third appointment of the day. They previously had been through a long, intense session that had left both of them exhausted and soaked in sweat. The difference was that after it, Bryce could go away and recuperate, while Lola must sit in her office and live through the whole thing a second time, and then maybe a third time, to see if she had missed anything.

She was already feeling tired, but she called up the background files for Bryce's sessions in case she needed them during the review. That led to another irritation. She had set up file protection so that no data could be changed, and so that if anyone else asked for one of those files, she would know about it. Someone had. The flags showed that someone had been in the system since her previous session, four days ago.

Spook. It had to be. She always locked her office doors, inner and outer, but he could get in from their connecting apartment. He had been told the ground rules under which he and Bat must operate, and he was ignoring them.

She tried to call him, tried everywhere he was likely to be, to tell him in person what she thought of him. No good. He had vanished without a trace. He must have known that she would come after him and he had gone on a walkabout, rambling the byways of Ganymede, where he knew that Lola would never be able to follow.

Well, his escape was only temporary. He'd be back sometime, looking for food, like the greedy pig that he was. Then he would get it—and she was not referring to food.

Lola slipped off her shoes, removed her stockings, loosened her belt, and took the slides from her long brown hair. She was grimly settling down to review the day's work with Bryce Sonnenberg when the inner office door behind her opened. She was more annoyed than worried. Nobody but Spook came in without knocking on the outer door.

She swung round in her chair. "You revolting little crawler!" she started. She found herself staring at the surprised face of Conner Preston. "Oh. I'm sorry. I thought—"

"That I was your brother," said Preston. "I know. I'm quite familiar with the way that siblings talk to each other."

"You should have knocked."

"I did knock. And I called. Your line was perpetually busy."

"I was trying to find Spook."

"To tell him what you thought of him? I'm sorry, I'm interrupting, aren't I?"

"No, you're not." Lola glared at the file on her display. She didn't want to go through that harrowing session with Bryce Sonnenberg all over again. It could wait until tomorrow. So could her fight with Spook. What she needed tonight was a meal, a drink, and an hour or two of relaxation. She turned back to Conner Preston. "What do you want?"

"It depends what mood you're in. If you're feeling as grim and bitchy as you sound, nothing. On the other hand—" He held up two small gilt cards. "Today is the fortieth anniversary of the first human expedition leaving Earth orbit for the exploration of Saturn. It's a small and exclusive party, no riffraff. Unless of course you happen

to be media, who are all riffraff, as you were kind enough
to point out to me the other night. But we have to be invited, scum that we are, because if we don't report it, an
event didn't happen."

"I'm not media."

"This card and badge says you are, if I say you are. If
you say you are, too, who's going to argue? Want to
come?"

"Like this?" Lola pushed her hair back from her face and
glanced down at her bare feet.

"You look just fine to me." He sounded as though he
meant it, too. "But I'm willing to give you fifteen minutes."

"Ten. Just wait here." Lola hurried from the office to the
apartment and into her bedroom. Haldanes were the ones
who were supposed to read minds, but Conner Preston
might as well have been reading hers. A party was exactly
what she wanted. Make that *needed*—she had been working too hard for too long.

She did an instant change to a dark-blue formal outfit
that she knew suited her coloring, decided to keep her hair
down, and was ready to go in nine minutes. That gave her
enough time to confirm that Spook was not back and post
a threatening note on his door: *"You'd better have a good
explanation or you're a dead jerk."* That was weak, but
she didn't have time for anything fancy.

When she returned to the office, Conner was sitting in
her chair, lolling back and staring idly at the screen. "You
look absolutely wonderful," he said, as he turned. "Don't
you have to store this away before we leave?" He nodded
at the display.

"It's already filed." She moved to his side. "But it ought
not to be left where people can see it—he's one of my patients. He might not care, but I do. Not that anyone could
get in here to see it anyway."

Conner showed no great interest, but he deliberately
turned his head away as she gave the command to clear

the file from memory and from the display.

"He must be really rich," he said. "Every media type I know could do to be worked over by a haldane, but we're all too poor."

"That doesn't stop some people. I had a man in just this morning who expected free treatment." Lola led the way out, carefully locking the doors. It had surely been Spook sneaking around in her files, but just in case she didn't want to make it easy for anyone else. "As for you needing a haldane, you seem fine. I don't know what you think I might do for you."

"I'd find something." There was a hint in his voice that said his remark was intended to be taken two ways, and he tucked her arm in his as he led the way along the corridor. She noticed how at ease he now seemed in Ganymede gravity, and how confidently he navigated the system of elevators, escalators, dropchutes, and slideways.

"Necessary professional skill," he said when she remarked on it. "They send me somewhere and expect me to hit the ground running. I have to be in a particular place at the right time, and it's no good saying that I got lost on the way there. Give me another few weeks and I'll take you places you've never been before."

He was already doing that. They had traveled three or four kilometers on a top-speed slideway, to a development beyond Moira Cavern that Lola knew only by reputation. It was First Family country, just a few levels down from the frozen Ganymede surface where the Von Neumanns had created the first habitats. The lifestyle here was now unimaginably different from that of those primitive early days, and the modern decor reeked of wealth. However, money alone was not enough to get you living space in this section. You needed to prove that your family presence on Ganymede went back to the 2030s, when the original settlers had arrived.

"We're going to get thrown out, you know," Lola said,

as she noticed ahead of them the biggest pair of doors that she had ever seen, painted in white and gold. "As soon as I open my mouth, they'll realize I have an Earth accent. They'll ask me when I arrived on Ganymede, and that will be it."

"Not a chance." Conner Preston led the way confidently forward, and the doors swung open. "You're not here as a guest or as an equal. You're here as *media*. You don't speak, you listen and record. You don't expect to be admired—or even to admire, because your opinions don't count. Think of us the way they do, as flesh-and-blood service machines, or some sort of invisible vermin. Then you'll be fine. Come on, let's go in."

A small party, he had said. But Conner's idea of "small" was not the same as Lola's. There had to be a couple of hundred people inside, in one lofty chamber almost as high as it was wide. Small knots of people were standing talking to each other, while others formed lines at two great tables that ran down the middle of the room. Lola saw them look at her and Conner Preston, register the gilt media badges, and ostentatiously continue their conversations. If they gave the occasional sideways glance, it was only to make sure that their presence was being noted.

Conner was right. Media people were here to observe rather than to be observed. Lola walked forward to the tables, where a dozen serving machines were rapidly filling orders. The food on other people's plates looked absolutely wonderful. She was starting to give her own order when Conner laid his hand on her arm.

"What's wrong?" She paused. After a few seconds of programed waiting, the machine turned away to serve another woman in a dark-blue dress (similar in color, Lola noticed, to her own, and far more expensive).

"This table is the special food," Conner said softly. "It's for the regular guests. Media food will be at the back."

"Oh. I'm sorry." Lola was beginning to move away

from the table when she caught the look on his face—and realized that two people no more than twenty feet away were wearing gilt badges and holding drinks and loaded plates of food. "Conner Preston, you are *rotten.*"

"I am, aren't I?" He took her arm again and led her back to the table. "You don't know much about media people. If my friends didn't have a shot at the best food and drink, they'd never come to parties like this. It's one of the job perks. Order anything you like—or, better still, sit down at the side table there and let me order for you. I know the best stuff at events like this, things that plebs like us never normally get to taste or even to see. I'll bring you your food, and while we're eating, I'll point out the high and mighty."

"Government people?"

"Not tonight. The top dogs here are people whose families had something to do with the original Saturn expedition of 2032. They may look the same as the rest, but they're not."

Lola sat down as directed and allowed herself to relax for what felt like the first time in years. Maybe it was. Since the day that she and Spook had left Earth, she had been required to make every decision, major and minor. It was such a pleasure to let her mind float free and, for just one night, allow someone else to take over worrying about everything.

He returned with too much food, then went back to bring them two carafes of wine. While he talked, she ate a great deal, drank even more, and listened in silence. It was wonderful; he didn't expect her to say anything, only to follow his little gestures so that she knew which people he was talking about.

"That's one of them," Conner said softly with his mouth close to her ear—though there was so much noise in the room now that he could have shouted. "He's a descendant of the original Saturn team. His name is Ignatz Dahlquist, and his great-uncle was an engineer on the *Marklake.* " He was indicating a pale, thin-faced man in his early twenties. "He's talking to another one, Lenny Costas. A relative of Luke Costas, the *Marklake*'s chief engineer. And see her?"

Lola followed his gesture and found herself looking at a small, dark-haired woman about forty years old, with delicate features and a slim, elegant body.

"She's beautiful. I wish I looked like that." The wine was getting to her; she could feel its warmth in her belly.

"You look a lot better than that, Lola Belman. But don't distract me. That's Alicia Rios. One of her aunts was on the first expedition."

A cat may look at a king. But it seemed to Lola that Alicia Rios was staring right back at her, showing more than casual interest. In fact, the woman began walking toward them. She slowed as she came up to their table and looked down. Lola, seated, found herself gazing up into cool, dark eyes. For a long silent moment it seemed as though Alicia Rios were going to speak; then she nodded and moved on past.

"There." Conner Preston was grinning in satisfaction. "Your presence has been noted by the biggest top dog here tonight, and you didn't get kicked out the way you thought you would. Alicia Rios's aunt was Athene Rios, second in command on the *Marklake* and reporting only to Jason Cayuga himself."

Lola remembered those names from long-ago lessons back on Earth. "Doesn't Cayuga have any descendants? Everyone else seems to."

"He does. Jeffrey Cayuga is related to Jason Cayuga. Jeffrey doesn't live on Ganymede, but I feel sure he would have been here tonight anyway, except that he's away on another trip to the Saturn system. I lose count, I don't know if it's the sixth or the seventh one. A lot of the family members have remained involved with Saturn system exploration and development."

Lola saw that once again Alicia Rios was staring at them. She was relieved when someone else whom Conner Preston had already pointed out to her—Lenny Costas, was it?—walked over to Rios and diverted her attention. He was a slow-moving man with grey hair and a granular, pitted face, and he was frowning and shaking that big grey head at Alicia Rios. For a moment both of them glanced in Lola's direction; then, rather to her relief, they turned away.

"I told you." Conner Preston had noticed what was happening. "Even if they realize that you're not one of the regular media crowd—they see the same faces over and over again—they don't care who you are. Relax. You'd get thrown out if you started a fight, but not otherwise."

She didn't need his advice. He didn't realize it, but even if she did get thrown out she wouldn't much care. She had enjoyed enormously the food, drink, and conversation that she had been craving earlier in the evening. She was feeling better than she had felt in months.

In fact, if anyone were going to be thrown out there were better candidates than Lola. She was not the only one drinking, and the party was warming up. The conversations at the tables on either side were becoming louder and more argumentative. A fat woman bursting out of her skin and a tight purple dress was holding forth in a penetrating nasal voice that was impossible to ignore.

"Of course, the first Saturn expedition started out from Earth," she said. "But only because it had to. In those days people on Earth thought they owned everything. We would never agree to that sort of thing now. You notice that as soon as we could break free of Earth oppression, the later Saturn expeditions all started from Ganymede."

"What's she talking about?" Lola hissed at Conner Preston. "Earth oppression? That's total nonsense. Forty years ago an expedition *had* to start from Earth—nowhere else had the resources to support one. Even Mars was barely self-sufficient."

"Do you think she knows any history—or would care if she did? What she's saying is in fashion at the moment." Conner nodded toward the next table. "See?—the rest of them agree with her."

"If you ask me," the woman was continuing, "the war was a blessing in disguise. It moved the center of power of the solar system from Earth out here to Jupiter, where it rightfully belongs, and at the same time it solved Earth's population problem. Earth was monstrously overpopulated before the war, you know. I don't know why the Inner System would never admit it, but it's quite obvious."

"Conner." Lola gripped his arm and started to stand up. "I can't believe this. That idiot is talking about the war as if it was a *good thing.* Doesn't she realize that it killed nine billion people? Nine billion!"

"I know." Conner Preston rose with Lola and took hold of her hand and arm. He began to move her firmly away from the other table. "Ignore her. When you have someone as stupid as that, does it matter what she knows or says? She never had an original thought in her life. All she's doing is mouthing popular Ganymede opinion. Not many people will come right out and say it, but a lot of them are thinking it. Earth bashing is in. Anyway, I think it's time we were going. You've seen everyone worth seeing, and from this point on the party will just run downhill."

"She shouldn't be allowed to talk like that!" But Lola allowed him to steer her toward the exit. She didn't want to hear more stupid talk. "Where are we going now?"

"Unless you have a better idea, we're going home."

"Whatever you say." She saw that they were not the only ones thinking of leaving; others were crowding ahead of them and pushing against them as they approached the great double doors. She held tightly to his arm. "Whatever you say. You're in charge."

In charge. Now *there* was a strange notion: that someone else would decide where you should go next and what you would do. Like being a child all over again, back safe on Earth, hanging on to mother's hand. Strange. But nice.

Lola allowed herself to be led through a maze of chambers and corridors. She didn't know where she was going and she felt a little bit clumsy and awkward. It didn't matter. Conner was in charge, he was completely self-confident, and he had coordination enough for both of them.

It was inevitable that he would lead her safely back to her own apartment, and perfectly natural that when she fumbled with the lock, he would take over and let them in. The only odd moment came when they had moved together into her bedroom, and he paused.

"What's wrong?" She slipped off her shoes and sat down on the bed.

"Are you fertile?"

"Not today."

"Then nothing's wrong." He sat down next to her, and ran his fingers gently along her forearm. "I just like a clear division of responsibilities."

Lovemaking had not been on Lola's wish list for the evening, but within the next two minutes she knew that it should have been. He felt, smelled, and moved exactly right. When he whispered in her ear, "You know, I've been thinking about doing this since the first moment I saw you in your office," she had no doubt that it was true.

She did not know if he was a good media reporter; but she was soon sure beyond question that Conner Preston was a wonderful lover.

"Every job seems strange unless it's your own job. For instance, I can't begin to imagine what it's like being a haldane."

They were lying close. All the lights were off and he was playing with her hair, coiling a long lock around his forefinger. Lola was feeling warm and sleepy and utterly relaxed. She had been telling him how rare it was for her to meet a media person, and asking him what his job was like.

"I mean," Conner went on, "don't you find it hard to keep your patients sorted out in your head? If it was me I'm sure their emotional problems would all get mixed up inside me."

"Mental problems are unique, usually nothing like each other. You don't mix them up, any more than you have trouble distinguishing your friends. And I don't take many patients. The legal limit is twenty-four people at any one time, but most haldanes prefer to deal with a lot less."

"How many do you have?"

"At the moment?" Lola would have to count, and she didn't feel like doing it. "I guess it's thirteen or fourteen. But a couple are at the end of their treatment, and three— I should say two—are new."

The memory of the patient who had committed suicide just that morning came like a sudden cramp in her midriff.

"What's wrong?" He had felt her movement.

"Nothing you can do anything about. Nothing anybody can." But Lola found herself talking about what had happened, while Conner listened in sympathetic silence and gently stroked her cheek and neck.

"You couldn't help him?" he said, at last.

"He wouldn't let me try. I knew he had awful problems, but he wouldn't agree to any session using drugs and telemetry. He was too afraid of what I might find out. I couldn't make him understand that no matter what I found out—and haldanes hear some terrible things—I wouldn't judge him or tell anyone. He only came to me because his boy friend forced him to, but I was useless. Worse than useless. He was scared of me *because* I'm a haldane."

"I'm sure he was. Don't you realize how intimidating it

is to meet somebody and find out she's a haldane? I mean, I was lucky. I breezed into your office without reading your sign, and I reacted to you before I had any idea what you did for a living. Otherwise—well, I probably wouldn't be doing this."

"Which would be a pity. Don't stop. Right now I'm a woman first and a haldane last."

"You know what I mean. But it makes me wonder about your clients. I don't mean what's wrong with them, or what you do for them—that's none of my business, and I know you can't talk about it anyway. I wonder what it is that makes someone seem right for haldane treatment. You say you have fourteen patients—"

"Thirteen now."

"Thirteen. And that their problems are all unique. The sign in your office says that anyone who thinks he can be helped shouldn't come to you. But everyone I know, deep down, thinks they're crazy. So who comes, and how do they know to come to you?"

"They come to me when nothing else works. Other than that, they're all different. And they're all difficult."

With his warm, steady hands touching her body and his breath on her cheek, Lola found it easy to say things that she had never said before. How being a haldane was in some ways as she had expected it to be before she qualified, yet still a total surprise. How being a haldane was often rewarding, but never simple. How the psychotropic drugs, when she was in their grasp, made her own sense of reality weaker than that of any of her patients, and left her, when she emerged from their spell, adrift in a dream world and wondering about her own sanity. How people found intimacy with a haldane impossible, because they were afraid that too much of their inner self would be laid wide open and bare.

Just as Lola, at this very moment, felt wide open and bare. The difference was that this was not in the least frightening. It was thrilling. She trailed off at last into silence, because once again his body was stirring against hers.

Her last thought, before she gave up thinking, was an odd one. If Spook had come home before Conner Preston entered her office, none of this would have happened. When she saw Spook in the morning, she ought to thank him for staying away.

Alcohol was supposed to be a depressant, but after drinking too much Lola always found it hard to sleep properly. She would drop off easily enough, then waken much too soon. Sure enough, four hours after she and Conner had drifted away into satisfied sleep, she found herself lying wide awake and staring into darkness.

She turned on the little bedside lamp. He was sleeping naked by her side, his well-muscled body curled toward her. His knees were slightly raised and one arm shielded his head.

She studied his peaceful face. He looked quite innocent. But was he?

For most of the previous evening her critical faculties had been firmly turned off. But her memory had not. Now she could recall events and analyze them logically, rather than reacting to them with pure emotion. She was puzzled by what the rational side of her brain was telling her. Turn things any way she chose, and she could not deny that Conner had asked far too many questions about her job as a haldane. Or rather, and more peculiar, he had asked about her *patients*. That was where his focus had been. Who came to her, why did they come to her? Every question but one: What are their names? He must have realized that she would stop short of telling him that, no matter how carefully he phrased the question.

She gazed down at him, wishing that they were in her office and he was in the patient's chair. Her fondness for him was not less—maybe more. She had her own suspicion about what might be happening. He had told her during their first dinner together that there were no haldanes in the Belt—a fact of which she was already well aware. But that did not mean there was no interest in haldanes in the Belt.

He was here on Ganymede on a press assignment. It was more than plausible that he had been told to prepare a dirt-digging piece about haldanes—that would be the media preference, something that confirmed the general public paranoia. Maybe Conner had even chosen the location of his office to be near a haldane.

He had met Lola, according to plan. But then the unexpected had arrived: He had found her attractive—very much so, if tonight's physical responses were anything to go by. At that point, more personal factors had taken over. He had realized that he could not get what he wanted from Lola, and still hope to remain close to her.

Her patients, though, were another matter. If they chose to talk to the media about their experiences—for money—that was up to them. Lola would not mind. She had no professional "secrets" that they might expose. In fact, all that Conner would hear, if he did manage to contact one of her patients, was exactly what she had been telling him about being a haldane.

He rolled his head a little on the pillow, and she looked down at him fondly. So he was playing a game with her. Well, two could do that. Everyone said "haldane" and thought drugs and telemetry, but there were other weapons in the arsenal. She would employ those, when he was drifting off to sleep or in a dream cycle. Then she would learn exactly what his assignment was. And then, when he least expected it, she would spring it on him.

Lola switched off the light and settled down, turning her back and snuggling close to Conner so that she fitted all along the curve of his body and legs. The wine she had drunk was still in her system, and she was not sure that she would be able to go to sleep again. She was sure of one thing, though. If you were going to lie awake all night, you couldn't find a more pleasant environment to do it in.

And there was always the possibility of a nice morning surprise.

14

It was all very well for Bat to propose that Spook dash off for a quick look at the off-line Hidalgo data base tucked away on Callisto, and while he was at it check on Bryce Sonnenberg's background. Spook loved the idea of going. But Bat, in a way that Spook was beginning to find typical, ignored or brushed off the practical problems.

"I see no problems." Bat, a gigantic ebony Buddha on his Bat Cave chair, was at his most snooty and infuriating.

Spook paced the length of the Bat Cave, aware how much Bat disliked him moving around all the time. "That's because you're not looking for them. Try these two. First, I need a ticket to get to Callisto. And one to bring me back, I guess, unless I decide to stay there forever."

"Trivially easy, and not worthy of the name of 'problem.' Have I not assured you that I am more knowledgeable concerning outer system transportation than any other person, living or dead? You will have the tickets that you need, to leave and to return, whenever you decide to go."

"*Legal* tickets?"

"Legal beyond dispute. Not only do I have favors owed to me by all the major transporters, I also have accumulated travel credits sufficient for a hundred such trips."

"You've not been using them yourself?" But Spook said it only to annoy, and went on at once, "I mentioned the tickets first, but that's not the worst problem. It's Lola. What am I supposed to tell Lola?"

"What can you tell her, that will persuade her to allow you to make the trip?"

"It doesn't matter what I say. I'm grounded for the next two weeks, because she says I've been into her haldane data base."

"A vile calumny, I am sure."

"Well . . . sort of. Actually, I have been in there. Just a little. Not as much as she says, though. But that's not the point. The point is, she'll say no, regardless. She won't let me go."

"Then the matter becomes very simple." Bat gave a magisterial sniff. "You are permitting personal emotions to impede your mental processes. Were this part of a problem on the Puzzle Network, you would have reached the solution instantly. There is a solution, and from what you have told me it is the only clean and logical answer. No matter what you tell your sister, you say, she will not permit you to go to Callisto. Therefore . . ."

"Therefore, I go and don't tell her? Bat, she'll skin me."

"Possibly. But only upon your return. Do you really desire to go?"

"I can't wait."

"Then we will now obtain your tickets." Bat swiveled his chair, so that he was facing his communications console. "It is something I learned long ago in dealing with my own parents, that absolution is always easier to obtain than permission." He paused, as though obliged by honesty to make his next remark but reluctant to do so. "That, of course, was before they threw me out of the house."

Spook had escaped from Earth and come to Ganymede at the impressionable age of ten. He had never visited Callisto—the next moon out in the Jovian system—so his ideas about that world had been largely shaped by what he heard on Ganymede.

It was not complimentary. Callisto was almost as big as Ganymede, but in spite of—or because of—that, Ganymede treated Callisto with the disdain of an older sister for a younger one. A not very attractive sister, at that. Ganymedeans spoke disparagingly of the pockmarked face of Callisto—all ancient craters—and of the too-low gravity field, indicative of an interior that was low in valuable metals and high in water ice. While Ganymede was home to a thriving civilization and the power center of the outer system, Callisto was regarded as a coarse and backward frontier world.

Spook, after half a day on Callisto, decided that everything he had been told was true. This was a primitive world of risks and roughness and rapid change. The surprise was how much he liked it. Bat might be happy sitting in a hole in the ground for the rest of his life, but Spook for the first time knew what he wanted to do with his. He wanted to spend his days out on the edge, where things were new and wild and exciting.

He had left Ganymede at short notice and with no time for preparation. When he arrived he didn't know his way around the changing interior of Callisto. It didn't matter. He asked his way, and was cheerfully directed by busy men and women toward the central data facility. He passed through steaming caverns with their scattered lakes of melting ice, the future home of sea farms, enough to provide protein to the whole Jovian system. He took hair-raising rides along slideways at speeds that would never be allowed on Ganymede. He ate a meal in the ultimate fast-food cafeteria, where the dishes came by on conveyor belts and you had to grab what you wanted and eat it before the next course passed. He sat on a curved metal plate like a great pie dish and took an endless and heart-stopping drop down an unlit tube—twenty kilometers of free fall—until at last his raft was electromagnetically slowed for the landing.

No busybody human or machine stopped him to ask what he was doing or where he was going. Anyone he spoke to took his presence for granted. Best of all, no one seemed to care how old he was. Apparently a Callistan at fifteen was regarded as an adult and given full freedom and responsibilities.

Spook had decided to tackle the Hidalgan data base before he worried about checking on Bryce Sonnenberg's presence on Callisto. It sounded like the more interesting job, and one better suited to his computer talents. Unfortunately the data facility, when he at last reached it, looked like the central trash heap of the universe. It seemed that Callistans did not place information storage and retrieval high on their list of priorities. Spook had expected problems because he would have to learn a different access technology. He found a more serious problem: For the records that he was seeking, there was no access technology at all.

He knew now why the Hidalgo data base was not available on-line. It was supposedly somewhere in a monstrous chamber, whose door read: "Miscellaneous files and records." Everything was kept in individual boxes and cartons and cabinets, covered with dust, and with only the most rudimentary descriptions on their outsides—*handwritten* descriptions, in many cases, without any computer-readable codes anywhere in sight.

There was no other person in the room and no computer assistance. Without a choice, Spook began what looked like a hopeless job. He had to find the data file that he wanted, in a disorganized mass of a million other files. Only after the first hour did he realize that there was in fact an organizing principle, even if by his standards it was a crazy one: The files were stored in the order in which they had been *received,* rather than the order in which they had originally been created. Putting it another way, they had been hauled in and dumped. What was already there was just shunted a little farther down the room.

It was not much, but it was something that he could work with. Hidalgo had not been settled until 2051. Since the planetoid had been totally wiped out in the war, the transfer of records to Callisto must have taken place no later than 2067. He needed to work only within that sixteen-year window.

Spook marked out the temporal boundaries in terms of floor space. He estimated that his search was now reduced to five thousand possible storage containers. In Bat's words, trivially easy and not worthy of the name "problem." Unless you had to do it yourself.

Five hours later, covered with dust and with a tongue that felt like a piece of dry sandpaper, Spook held in his hands a brown container about the size of a shoebox. Within it, if the scrawl on one end could be believed, lay the long-sought Hidalgo data base. He blew off the dust, sneezed, and lifted the lid. He found himself staring at a blue cylinder the size of his forefinger. Not much to look at, but enough storage in principle for billions of data records.

It might be what he wanted—if only he could find a piece of clunky old equipment able to read it. Spook had never seen that kind of storage device before, and he doubted that it was because it was too modern.

He slipped the blue cylinder into his pocket and headed for the exit. There was no security. He could have walked out with anything he liked—a good measure of the value that the Callistans placed on any of the data in the chamber.

Why didn't they junk the whole mess? He could think of only one reason: They were being paid by Ganymede to store it, where space was cheaper—but not paid enough, apparently, to make them maintain it properly.

Wandering around looking for signs of life, Spook had one other thought. Given the degree of informality that seemed to be typical of Callisto, Bryce Sonnenberg could have arrived here any time at all, and nobody would have noticed.

The first man he came to, a bearded worker in a dirty blue overall, stared at the cylinder when Spook produced it. The man said, "Somewhere around here, or nowhere. This is where all the oddball reading machines are kept. Did you try the lunatic asylum?"

Not a promising suggestion. Spook learned after another couple of questions that "lunatic asylum" had to be interpreted literally. It was the place where all lunar records and equipment were held in protective safe keeping, until such time as Earth's moon was again populated by humans. The equipment, naturally, was all prewar technology.

He found his way there after only one false start. A thousand data-input devices lined the walls of the room that he finally came to, but most of them could be ruled out after a brief inspection. The little blue cylinder had a series of narrow flanges and grooves along its side, and it required a precise mate.

Spook's main worry was in finding the right hardware. Once he had that he had absolute confidence, as a Master of the Puzzle Network, in his ability to mesh with any software system in existence. Two hours of rummaging located the equipment he needed. It was a battered metal canister that looked as though it had barely survived the lunar wartime attacks, but it worked. The software interface was a lot trickier than he had anticipated. Another hour of work was needed before the data cylinder finally yielded and came on line. Spook began to transfer its contents to more accessible high-speed storage. Five more minutes, and he was reading through a list of index files.

That was when he decided that it was time to gloat. Although the little cylinder contained ninety-three billion records, some farsighted Hidalgan information specialist had provided a front-end query program. Spook could ask keyword questions, and the program would then do all the work.

Bryce Sonnenberg. It was the obvious first query.

And here came data. *Bryce Sonnenberg, resident of Hidalgo.*

All right!

And yet not all right. Spook frowned at the display. According to this, Bryce Sonnenberg had been born on Earth in 2049, and had arrived on Hidalgo only in 2067. That would make him twenty-nine years old today—five years older than he said he was, but not impossible.

What *was* impossible was the rest of it. According to the records, Bryce Sonnenberg was dead. He had died of a massive brain hemorrhage, just two years after he arrived on Hidalgo. There was no suspicion that it was anything other than natural causes. A postmortem had revealed the congenital malformation of a thin-walled brain artery, one that could have ruptured at any age. He had collapsed and been pronounced dead during routine exercise in one of the Hidalgan sports facilities.

Spook leaned back and glared at the offending display. He was a rational person, with no time for the logically ridiculous. And Bryce Sonnenberg, as recently as yesterday, had been sitting in a haldane session with Lola.

Solution: there must be several different Bryce Sonnenbergs. Spook had located the wrong one.

Fifteen minutes' more work disposed of that idea. The Hidalgan data base held one, and only one, Bryce Sonnenberg. More than that, the physical description given in this file was a look-alike to what was in Lola's record: Height, weight, eye color, hair color, build—they were all the same.

Time for some serious thought. Spook made a copy of the whole data file onto an output record that he was sure he would be able to read back on Ganymede, pocketed that wafer-thin output card together with the original blue cylinder, and headed again for the Callistan data graveyard. The chance that anyone else would want to look at the Hidalgan records was close to zero, but some things were sacred. You didn't destroy data sources.

On the way he bounced around other ideas. Bryce Sonnenberg had come to Lola because he was having strange memory problems. Spook had seen the records on some of them and agreed that they were very peculiar. Wasn't it more likely that Bryce hadn't actually died of a brain hemorrhage, but had *almost* died? Brain injuries were notoriously weird things. After a big one you were quite likely to lose a large fraction of your memories and then find them slowly seeping back.

Except that these were memories that Bryce Sonnenberg could not possibly have had. Memories of an *older* man than Bryce was now. And the record, without ambiguity, insisted that he had not just been injured. He had *died*.

It was time to call in reinforcements. Half the charm of Puzzle Network problems was that you solved them strictly alone, with no help from anyone. On the other hand, Spook knew from experience that puzzles were solved an order of magnitude more quickly when two people worked on them together.

He sent a short message to Bat: *Data located but facts present major puzzle*.

If that didn't have Megachirops panting for more, nothing would.

Well, Bat deserved to suffer. Spook still had the more disagreeable part of his task on Callisto ahead of him. He had to see what he could learn directly about Bryce Sonnenberg.

It was just as well that Spook did not know the results of the latest Sonnenberg session. Lola, hardened to the worst that human nature could produce, was having problems facing it again. But she had to make the review, just in case she had missed something the first time through.

She summoned up her resolve and commanded the computer to take her once again to derived reality.

The ceiling above the bed was breaking down, crumbling before his eyes. He knew that he must stay here in this room, that he was not ready. In a few more months he might go outside occasionally, but the full treatment must go on for at least another two years.

He had been warned of the effects of interrupting the protocol of drugs and indoctrination. But now the floor was breaking, too, revealing nothing beneath him but a long fall into darkness.

He could not bear the idea of another fall, even in low gravity. He remembered the last one, the long drop through vacuum, with its sudden and violent end, and it terrified him. Anything was better than that.

He balanced on the narrow support beams of the floor, staggered across them to the door, and pushed it open.

He emerged into a chamber of horrors. Doors were opening, all along the corridor. From them staggered half a dozen pale figures. The nearest was a woman—or had once been a woman. Her skull bone ended at her eyebrows, revealing the pink and grey of naked brain tissue. A mass of thin, white neural fibers, still attached to a heavy metal circlet around her head, sprouted like sparse and unnatural hair.

The woman was screaming—in pain or fear, he could not tell which. She was clutching the top of her head, still trying to hold the circlet in position, when she was sud-

denly thrust out of the way by a running man. She went headfirst into the wall. Blood and brain tissue splashed out around the metal circlet like a gory crown. The woman fell and did not move.

He crouched against the wall. The others were all running at him, heading away from wreaths of white smoke that spread along the sloping corridor. But "running" was the wrong word. They were hobbling, reeling, staggering, like hopeless zombies. He saw that everyone had something unnatural about the head—shaven skulls, split skulls, deformed skulls, no skulls.

He straightened as the last of them passed. He might feel bad, but compared with them, he was in perfect health. If they could try to escape, so could he.

And he realized something that they apparently did not. Escape, if it lay anywhere, did not lie downward. It lay upward, toward and through the clouds of choking smoke.

The white pall was thicker near the broken ceiling of the corridor. He dropped to his hands and knees and began to crawl in the opposite direction from the zombie crew, heading away from them along the gentle upward gradient. They had been right, though, to be afraid of the smoke. It was poisonous. His lungs began to burn. Much more of this would kill him.

But so would returning the way that he had come. Some part of his brain, functioning clearly, despite the pain and terror, made its calculations. He kept going. If he died, it would be while crawling forward and upward.

And maybe he would live. He had cheated death before—why not again?

You could never beat the odds. That was an unalterable law. But you could always try to place your bet where the odds were most favorable.

Lola wondered if there were such a thing as too much empathy. She was feeling the pain, not only of Bryce Sonnenberg but of all the human deformities in the smoke-wreathed corridor.

She was also beginning to doubt her own abilities to help him. His memories were so wild and so diverse it was hard to believe that they had all actually happened. Yet she had never heard of a case where anyone under the influence of psychotropic drugs could lie to a haldane.

She was alone in her office, peering at the log of her sessions with Sonnenberg. When the door opened behind her, she did not look up or turn around. She did not need to. Conner Preston had an absolutely uncanny knack of dropping in on her when she was feeling at her most depressed.

He came up behind her, dropped his hands onto her shoulders, and began to knead the tight muscles at the base of her neck. "Looks like hard work to me. Do you know what you're doing?"

"Sometimes. Haldanes aren't infallible, you know—not like media people."

"Same problem child?" He was leaning over her, peering at the records.

"He's not a child." Normally she would have cleared the display instantly, but with Conner it was different. She knew that he was interested in Bryce Sonnenberg and his records—hardly surprising, since she fretted over the case constantly. Even if she did not talk about it, Conner was smart enough to know what was eating her. She also suspected that Conner knew Bryce's identity perfectly well, though she never mentioned his name.

"He's far from being a child," she went on. "He's twenty-four years old, and sometimes I feel he's a lot older."

"Twenty-four, and not a child. And you're twenty-seven. Are you trying to tell me that he's the competition?"

"You have no competition, and you know it." Lola leaned back and let his strong, probing fingers work away at her tension. "If you want to hear about my real problem child, I'll tell you."

"Spook? I thought you said you'd heard from him."

"I did. He's on Callisto. He didn't say what he's doing there, and he didn't say when he's coming back. I'll murder him next time I see him."

"Don't say that word—you'll make me think you mean it." His hands were still on her neck, but their touch had changed. Conner was making a circle with his hands, all the way around her throat, then running his fingers up to touch the sensitive skin below her ears and play with her earlobes. "It's too late for you to be working, Madam Haldane. Aren't you ready to take a break?"

"Don't you think of anything else?"

"I try not to. Sometimes my work gets in the way." He was lifting Lola to her feet and turning her to face him. "Before dinner, or after?"

"Would you consider both?" She moved willingly against him, reaching around to rub the muscles of his back and rib cage. It made her feel almost guilty, the pleasure that she took in his touch and in touching him. What she was planning to do to him—had already started to do—ought to make her feel much more guilty. It didn't because it was all a game, part of the fun of lovemaking.

Haldanes aren't infallible, she thought, but we can still do some pretty amazing things that we don't talk about. *Without* using drugs.

Hypnotic blocks and spoken keys were the least of them. She could hardly wait to see Conner's face when she discovered what he was up to, and told him all about it.

Computers were easy. People were hard. Spook had thought about his own epitaph and decided how it should read: *Here lies Spook Belman. He was interested in ideas, things, and people, in that order.*

But sometimes you had no choice except to deal with people. Here he was, heading for the place on Callisto that, according to Lola's files, Bryce Sonnenberg came from. He had no idea what to do next. The central address system provided an exact location on Callisto, but it didn't say one thing about the nature of the place itself.

Spook sought inspiration in his surroundings as he was carried the final few hundred meters. This didn't look like the approach to any residential area, even by Callisto's modest standards. The walls on either side were feature-less—bare metal and plastic. At the end of the tunnel stood two massive doors, and in front of them was a funny-look-ing little house. Odder yet, inside that house he could see a guard—not a machine, but an actual human in a dark-green uniform.

He wandered along the last fifty meters, staring at the great doors. There were no handles on them and no way to see how they might be opened.

"What do you want?" The guard was leaning out over a half-door that came only up to his waist.

"Nothing." Spook studied the man. He was maybe ten years older than Spook, with dark round eyes and a dou-ble chin.

"Go away then."

Spook nodded, but it seemed to him that anybody who had to stand all day in a guardhouse doing nothing must be out of his mind with boredom. And probably not all that smart. Instead of obeying, Spook pointed at the doors. "What's inside there?"

"None of your business."

"It looks like a prison."

"Well, it isn't." The uniformed guard gave Spook a su-perior smile. "So now you can go away."

"I'm not doing any harm." Spook gaped again at the doors. "If it's not a prison in there, what is it then?"

"None of your business." And then, when Spook still showed no sign of leaving, "Look, what are you doing here?"

"Nothing." Spook shrugged. "I just came along this way and I wondered—why the big doors?"

The guard studied Spook's earnest, gawky face and his pipe-stem arms and legs. The temptation was too much. "It's worse than a prison," he said slowly. "Much worse. If you knew what was inside there, your flesh would creep."

"Dead people?" Spook moved two paces closer.

"Worse than that." The guard leaned confidentially over the half-door. "You want to know what's in there? Well, I'll tell you. You know about the war?"

That was like asking Spook if he knew his own name. He controlled himself, and nodded. "Uh-huh."

"Well, during the war the Belt colonies were hit worse than anywhere else. Nearly everybody got killed. A few people escaped on ships, only most of 'em were in terrible shape. See, the Belt had been doing *experiments*, experiments on humans. When people out here in the Jupiter system saw what was coming in on some of the ships, they set up a special refugee camp. And that's what this is."

"That all?" Spook snorted. "I don't think that's scary, just some stupid refugee camp for Belters."

"Ah, that's because you've never seen 'em. I have. I've seen 'em arrive." The guard lowered his voice. "People that weren't people at all. People missing bits of them. Others all stretched out, arms over here and legs over there, just connected together by bundles of neural fibers. Some of them were brain-shocked so bad they had no idea who they were or where they were, and they'd wander round 'til they starved to death if no one took care of them. Those doors, see, they're not to stop *you* getting *in*—they're to stop the things inside getting *out.*"

The guard straightened up. In the distance behind Spook

there was the hum of an electric motor. He turned and saw a runabout car approaching with a single passenger.

"Now you know," the guard said. "So scat."

"I thought you said the doors aren't to keep me out. So why can't I go in?"

"The doors keep them *in* and they keep *you* out. Now get out of here."

The guard was stepping forward to give a smart salute. Spook saw a woman wearing a dark-green uniform with gold on the lapels. She nodded to the guard as the car passed. The big doors were opening automatically.

"You're letting *her* in," Spook complained.

"Well, I have to, don't I?" The guard stepped back into the little gatehouse and sat down. "Even if I didn't, she has her own gate controller. That's Dr. Isobel Dusby. She runs the whole place, goes anywhere anytime. You don't, though. So scoot. I got work to do."

There was no sign of it, but Spook sensed that he would not be offered any more information. He gave it one last try. "Does this place have a name?"

"Of course it does. It's the Isobel Busby Sanctuary for War Victims." The guard was on his feet again, and again Spook heard from behind him the hum of an electric car.

"And I'll tell you one last time," the guard went on, brusque finality in his voice. The arrival of two bosses in a row was making him nervous. "This whole thing is none of your business. So get yourself right out of here, sharpish, before I come over there and do something about it."

15

A competent man does not merely follow his instructions; he leads them.

Jinx had heard through Alicia that she and Cayuga saw no threat at all in Spook Belman or Rustum Battachariya. They were mere children in an adult situation, and they could be no more than a distraction from the real problem.

Jinx was not so sure. With the information that he had, his job was probably finished, but he had seen the light of intelligence in two sets of young eyes. At the first opportunity he had, almost by reflex, tapped into Spook's data line and the access codes to the Bat Cave. He would be notified in real time whenever there was a conversation between Spook and Bat.

Which, according to the tiny signal processor in Jinx's left ear, was happening right now. He eased away from Lola's sleeping body, sat up in the gloom, and reached for his watch.

It was much later than he expected. Something strange happened to him when he was with Lola. After they made love, he lost hours and hours in dream-filled sleep. He didn't remember those dreams when he woke up, but he felt tired and uncomfortable.

He slipped into his clothes and rapidly wrote on her console, *Sorry, I had to go—work beckons. See you tomorrow. Love you, Conner.*

He locked Lola's door as he left. His office, with its tape recorder and scrambled circuit decoder, was just along the corridor. By the time that Jinx reached it, Spook's call had been completed and Bat was on the line.

A Bat who sounded none too pleased.

"You realize," he was saying, "that a more irritating message than the one that you sent from Callisto could scarcely be devised."

"I didn't want to send information over an open line."

"You certainly succeeded. Would it now be too much to ask what you discovered on Callisto?"

Bat, with Jinx as an interested but silent listener, heard Spook's summary of his two days away with no more than an occasional grunt. "Isobel Busby," Bat said at last, "and the Busby Sanctuary for War Victims. Hmph."

"Yeah. But I couldn't get in there, and I didn't get to talk to Busby."

"I am not sure that it would help if you had. I assume that you recognized the name?"

"Sure I did. You think I'm some kind of idiot? Don't answer that. Isobel Busby is in Bryce Sonnenberg's files, one of the doctors who recommended that he come to Ganymede and seek the assistance of a haldane."

"Precisely. So, even without access to the Busby Sanctuary or to its eponymous head, I believe that we are in a position to make a reasonable reconstruction of events. We can also pinpoint, much more clearly than before, the central mystery."

"Agreed. That's why I came right back. You want to take first shot?"

"Certainly. Bryce Sonnenberg has not been on Callisto for the past twenty-one years, as he stated to Lola Belman. In fact, he was on Hidalgo at the outbreak of hostilities between the Belt and the Inner System. When Hidalgo was destroyed by Earth forces, Sonnenberg was one of the lucky few who managed to make his way to an escape vessel. He reached the Jovian system five years ago as a refugee, much as you did. However, he did not arrive mentally and physically intact. The degree of his injuries can only be conjectured, although today he appears to be in excellent physical condition. We may therefore reasonably assume that, whether his problems were initiated during his years on Hidalgo or during his escape, upon arrival in the Jovian system his difficulties were psychological—as indeed they are today. It is not impossible that the Busby Sanctuary deliberately sought to provide him with a whole new personality, complete with memories designed to bypass the trauma of his wartime experiences."

"I don't believe that. If Isobel Busby *created* those memories, why would she send him here for Lola to find out what's going on?"

"Agreed. I merely said that it is not impossible that the Sanctuary performed that role. Our objective at the moment is just that: to rule out the impossible. However, let us postulate that it is far more likely that Sonnenberg's problems, in whole or in part, result from experiences suffered before he arrived on Callisto. If we accept that, it brings us at once to the central mystery."

"Yeah. The *other* Bryce Sonnenberg. The one who died on Hidalgo of a burst artery in the brain."

"Precisely. Observe, in this whole affair, how frequently death enters. We have a vision of death on Mars. We have two visions of death, or probable death, on Hidalgo. We have a Bryce Sonnenberg—of whose mother, by the way, there is no sign in the Oberon data base—born on Earth in 2043, arrived on Hidalgo in '63, and dead there in '65. He has never been to Mars. Then we have *our* Bryce Sonnenberg. He also states that he has never been to Mars. His memories, if in fact they are true memories, are totally inconsistent with those of a man who, like the other Bryce Sonnenberg, reportedly left Earth for the last time when he was twenty years old. Most intriguing."

"You can call it that if you like. What next?"

"I must settle down for some serious thinking. And you?"

"I guess as soon as it's morning, I go and see Lola and she beats me up. She doesn't know I'm back yet, but as soon as she finds out, I'm dead meat."

"Ah. In dealing with the opposite sex, I believe it necessary to bear in mind the old question: Are they less logical than they seem, or do they seem less logical than they are?"

"I don't know the answer."

"The answer is, it is an ill-posed question. Both answers are impossible."

"Well, thanks for nothing. That's a real help."

"It would be unwise for you to regard me as an expert on anything involving family relationships." Bat gave a rueful sniff. "Enough of that. We must talk again later, and see where our separate cerebrations have led us."

The line went dead, leaving Jinx sitting thoughtful in the darkness. He had heard everything. Although some of it remained a mystery, he had enough. He placed his own call.

There was a three-minute delay, even though the call signal did not have to leave Ganymede. He waited patiently until at last a sleepy voice came onto the line. "Hello. Alicia Rios speaking."

"This is Jinx Barker."

"And this is the middle of the night. Damn it, Jinx, I was sound asleep."

"I'm sorry. I thought you would like to hear this at once."

"Go on, then. I'm awake now."

"I will be brief. As you know, I have established the desired relationship with Lola Belman. The subject of concern to you turns out to be one of her patients, just as we suspected. His name is Bryce Sonnenberg. I have reviewed his records. I have also had limited discussions regarding him with Lola Belman, and monitored conversations between Spook Belman and Rustum Battachariya concerning an investigation of Sonnenberg's background. I conclude that although Sonnenberg's personal history contains some oddities and inconsistencies, there is no chance whatsoever that he spent time on Mars during the period of interest to you."

"Excellent." Alicia was suddenly awake and energetic. "You've done a first-rate job, Jinx. I'll pass the word along. It may take a few days. He's not back yet."

"There is no hurry, but I do need instructions from you as to how to proceed. If my work here is finished, and I am simply to conclude my relationship with Lola Belman, I can do so on the pretext of returning to the Belt. However, we had talked of . . . the other option."

"I know. Let me get back to you on that. For the moment, just keep on as you are. Good job, Jinx."

As Alicia Rios terminated the call, Jinx Barker sat for a few seconds longer in the darkness. He was tingling all over, more alive than he had felt for weeks. The very thought was enough to start the adrenaline flowing. Making love to Lola Belman certainly gave pleasure, but it could not compete with the preferred and ultimate form of personal interaction.

He went swiftly and silently back to her apartment, unlocked the door, and moved to cancel the message that he had left on her console. As he removed his shirt and pants, he stared down at her. She had turned over in her sleep, after he left, so that now she lay on her right side with her head thrown back. He studied the slim neck and the graceful line of her jaw. The pulse in her throat was visible, just above her larynx.

He reached down and touched her skin with his index

finger, exactly on that tiny regular spasm of pumped blood.

The other option. He believed that he knew what his instructions would be. But until he heard for certain, patience was needed.

Jinx lay down again by Lola's side. Pleasure deferred could be thought of as pleasure enhanced. And pleasure should not be mixed with business. This was still business.

His own pulse steadied and slowed. Within five minutes he had sunk into a dreamless and contented sleep.

Lola needed less rest than most people, and she always slept lightly. As soon as Conner left her side, she had sensed the loss of his warm presence, and when her outer door clicked shut, she had come fully awake.

She read his message on her console. It made little sense. Not even a media reporter got up and went to work in the middle of the night, unless he received a wake-up call to say that something new and urgent had come up. She had heard no call.

So why had Conner gone wandering off?

Lola lay thoughtful in the dim-lit room. One of the gifts—or curses—of being a haldane was that you could never turn off your antenna. You were sensitive, even when you sometimes wished that you weren't. It was quite obvious that Conner was not what he had said he was. She had known that for more than a week, and had ignored the fact because she wanted to. However, during the hours when she was awake and he was sleeping, she had already planted her deep verbal hooks. But would it be right to exercise them?

She was sure she could find some way to justify whatever she did. Most of the conscious mind's efforts went into an attempt to provide logical explanations and justifications, after the fact, for the perverse and nonlogical ninety-five percent of human actions dictated by the unconscious mind. Not even a haldane was exempt from that.

The idea of quizzing Conner without his knowing it had originally been justified as a game by her conscious mind. Now she suspected that it was no such thing. It was a dark suspicion derived from the underside of her brain. The haldane's basic training texts offered explicit advice: *Do not be afraid to act on your gut instincts. Psychometric tools are of great value, but they are most useful when they confirm and reinforce what you suspect to be true.*

She was awake when Conner returned, but she pretended to be still asleep. She watched through slitted eyes as he removed his clothes. The moment when he stooped to place his stiffened finger on her naked throat produced the first touch of fear. His face had changed. His movements were somehow different, too, the unpredictable actions of a stranger.

When he lay down again at her side and quickly fell asleep, she told herself that she was suffering from an attack of excess imagination. He had gone away for a few minutes to respond to a work emergency, found that he was not needed, and at once come back to her.

But why had he leaned over her with his hand at her throat, and what was that alien half-smile on his face?

Lola knew that she had to do it, or remain sleepless for the rest of the night. She did not move, but she spoke the first of the sequence of planted keys: *"Black Arrow."*

He did not respond. Apparently did not hear her; but she knew that the hook was set. Ten seconds later she had confirmation. His eyes flickered open, stared at nothing, and then closed. Lola felt her own shiver of awe. It was here, and not in the much publicized mind-reading abilities, that the haldane magic lay. Even the best theories were inadequate to explain how this worked, or why sometimes it failed.

She waited thirty seconds, then intoned softly, *"Treasure Island."*

The spoken key produced no visible reaction at all. Lola

expected none. She waited another full minute, and finally said, *"Kidnapped."*

His eyes opened, and this time they stayed open.

It was time to begin. "Conner?" That produced no re-action; so she added, "Conner Preston: Are you awake?"

His lips moved, but no sound came out.

"Can you hear me?"

"I can hear you."

"So why didn't you answer me?"

"Because I am not Conner Preston."

Lola did not know what she had been expecting. It was not this. "Then who are you?"

There were a few moments of what seemed to be an in-ternal struggle, until at last he muttered, "I am Jinx Barker."

A strange reply, far off from anything that Lola might have predicted. "So who is Conner Preston?"

"He was a media reporter for Ceres Broadcasting."

"Is that the same as United Broadcasting?"

Another pause. "Ceres Broadcasting became part of United Broadcasting, after the war."

"And do you work for United Broadcasting?"

"No."

"So who do you work for?" After a long unyielding si-lence, Lola added, "Who do you work for, Jinx Barker, and what do you do?"

His silence continued. At last it became apparent that he was not going to answer.

What was she supposed to do now? Lola rose from the bed and began to pace the room. She was naked, but she didn't even notice. Deep hooks and keys were a standard part of haldane technique. She had run through a dozen ses-sions with them during her own training, as both a subject and as a haldane questioner. She had read transcripts of scores more. Sometimes a subject would freeze, as Con-ner (or Jinx) had frozen, but it was always when the questions touched on some deeply personal or long-hidden topic. It was unheard of for a subject to tense up when asked something as simple as who he worked for, and what he did.

The worst thing that she could do now would be to act rashly. She needed time to ponder what had happened and perhaps consult references or another haldane.

And in the meantime, she needed to protect herself. It was probably quite unnecessary—but she felt again the finger on her neck, and saw the strange, almost exalted, expression on his face. She crouched naked by his side, and prepared to implant the series of haldane protection keys.

Would they work? She had never tried them before, never knew anyone who had. Conner seemed a gentle, loving man, but patients who turned violent were not uncommon. She had to prepare for the worst.

It took almost an hour—installing the verbal cues and then checking his physical responses over and over until she was satisfied. At last she gave the command that released the original triple hooks: *"Kidnapped. Treasure Island. Black Arrow."*

It was like cutting an internal string. His eyes closed and his taut body relaxed. If he had ever been awake, rather than in some induced state between sleep and waking, that had now been replaced by a deep natural slumber.

Lola lay down beside him—beside her lover, Conner Preston, who was also a stranger, Jinx Barker. She felt watchful and wary. Twenty minutes earlier she had been worried about the possibility of lying awake all night; now she was afraid that she might go to sleep.

It never occurred to her to leave. Above everything else, she was still a haldane. At her side lay a man with a deep, deep problem.

Even when she was distracted by worry and lack of sleep, work had to go on. Lola blinked at Bryce Sonnenberg, sitting in the chair opposite, and wished that she could borrow some of his bright-eyed energy. She had remained awake until Conner Preston left, early in the morning, and by that time it was too late to think of sleep.

She started slowly and easily, more for her sake than for his. "I'd like to talk to you about your mathematical work. When did you first become interested in number theory, and how old were you when you got into it?"

It was a minor trap, since it offered Bryce an easy chance to talk about parental influence. But he answered without hesitation. "I can't really answer that question. I know that I could do sums before I could read or write, almost before I could speak. When I was a child, my idea of a good time was a long, complicated calculation."

"Did anyone ask you to do calculations?"

"Why, yes." His brow wrinkled. "When I was very young, it was my father. He encouraged me, gave me harder and harder problems."

According to every instrument, and backed by Lola's own experience, he was not lying.

"During our first session," Lola said gently, "you told me that you never knew your father."

"That's true." The instruments confirmed his confusion—and still insisted that he was telling the truth. "I didn't know him," he went on. "But this is weird. If I close my eyes, I can *see* him. He's bending down and asking me something. And I know he died, when I was still very little."

"Let's take a look. Concentrate on him. Listen to him."

Lola felt disappointment as the computer feed came in. This derived-reality scene lacked the sharpness of previous sequences. The visual information was minimal, and a gruff but soft voice was saying, "All right, here's another one. What's twelve thousand and sixteen times thirty-seven?" The human shape that came with the voice was blurred in outline, its features indistinct. Only the numbers seemed real, springing into existence before her, then rapidly reshaping themselves into a new form. She rattled off the result like a machine: "four hundred and forty-four thousand, five hundred and ninety-two."

"Right!"

After that word of praise came a sudden discontinuity. She felt overwhelming fear and sadness. Another form hovered over her, and a harsher voice was in her ears: "Forget that stuff, and forget them. They're both dead and they're not coming back. You do what I say now. Understand? Exactly what I say and when I say—or you'll pay."

The image faded. Lola waited, but nothing else happened.

Memory, or imagination?

"Bryce. I'm going to ask you questions. I want you to reply as quickly as you can, or tell me if you can't answer."

"Very well." There was no alarm or tension in him. He seemed almost bored.

"What is three hundred and sixty-four times nine hundred and seventy-six?" Lola had his interior body scans, as well as the evidence of the telemetry. He had no form of augmenting implant. His reply came almost before she had finished speaking: "Three hundred and fifty-five thousand, two hundred and sixty-four."

"What is the cube root of nineteen?" Lola did not bother to check his first answer. There would be time for that after the session.

"Two-point-six-six-eight-four-zero. How many more places do you want?"

"That will be enough." She would check that answer, too, but she had little doubt as to what she would find. No one would spit out answers with such confidence and precision unless they were correct. Bryce Sonnenberg was a born calculator. His "memory" of his father asking him questions was unreliable, since his own subconscious might be feeding him those answers.

However, there was a huge difference between arithmetic and mathematics. History was full of *idiots savants,* able to do prodigious feats of mental calculation while having no idea of the nature of mathematical proof. Was he truly a mathematician, as he had claimed?

"You specialize in number *theory,* " she said. "Would you agree that theory is a long way from simple numbers and calculations?"

She expected agreement, but instead his whole face brightened and he laughed aloud. "Are you kidding? There couldn't be a closer connection. In classical number theory, everything starts and ends with the numbers." His words came bubbling out twice as fast as usual. He was more animated than he had ever been before. "You see, it's not like physics or biology, where you might do an experiment and then spend years trying to come up with a theory, or develop a theory and not be able to find a practical way to test it. All the great number theorists in history, Fermat and Euler and Gauss and Ramanujan and Deslisle, all the way back to Euclid—they found their theorems by playing with the numbers themselves. They still had to *prove* a result after they discovered it, and that can get fiendishly hard—like the Goldbach conjecture, or the infinite number of prime pairs, or the last Fermat theorem—but it helps a lot, when you're trying for a proof, if you are already convinced that the result is true. Quadratic reciprocity, the little Fermat theorem, the prime-number theorem—they all started from numerical examples. Of course, sometimes even the greatest theorists were *wrong.* Even Fermat was wrong about a particular sequence of numbers being primes. But then the numbers proved that, too. One ugly counterexample; it's enough to dispose of a beautiful conjecture. Did you ever hear of de Pulignac?"

Lola was surprised to find that he knew she was still there. "I don't think so. It's not a name that springs to mind."

"It ought to be." He grinned at her. "Poor old de Pulignac—he is an awful warning to number theorists. In 1848, he stated that every odd number can be written as a sum of a power of two and a prime number. For example, thirty-seven is thirty-two plus five, and eighty-seven is sixty-four plus twenty-three. De Pulignac said he had confirmed his theorem for every number up to three million."

"And?"

"Well, he was wrong. And in a very embarrassing way. His theorem doesn't work for one hundred and twenty-seven, and that's not what you'd call a big number. Try it for yourself and you'll see."

"I'll take your word for it." But she didn't need to. Anyone could improvise a lie. What a person could not do was display expert knowledge in a particular field where it was easy to expose a factual falsehood. "Have you ever had other memories in which you were doing mathematical calculations?"

"Not calculations, but writing numbers. I've had several sets of memories, all mixed up with each other."

"Let's take a look. This time I'd like to try for full synthesis."

"Sure." He was familiar with the protocol, and as his chair inclined backward, he was reaching for the sensor cups. Lola did the same. The other sensors were already in position. This morning the computer link was unusually slow to establish itself. She waited, wishing that her headache would go away.

The computer's difficulty in making linkage was not Bryce's fault; it was hers. Her stomach was churning, and the top of her head felt ready to blow off. *Physician, heal thyself.* She had had no sleep and no food, but who was to blame for that? She was. She had not been able to eat breakfast, could not get last night out of her mind. Who was Jinx Barker, what was he? Why had he taken on a false name? Had his move into an office close to hers been accidental, as he claimed? Or had he sought her out, stalked her, and moved effortlessly into her life and bed?

God, she had been so easy. A pushover. It hurt to think how easily she might have been deceived and used.

But her sense of logic came struggling back. Used *how?* He had given her great pleasure, and he had taken nothing from her. It was ridiculous to suggest she had been used or abused.

The computer's synthesis impatiently pulled her away from her introspection. It was almost a relief to be thrust into Bryce Sonnenberg's reality.

His hand moved in front of him, withered and marked by dark-brown spots. He was sitting in an easy chair, borne down by some crushing force. Not gravity, nor acceleration. It was the weight of years, a deadly fatigue that dragged him lower. He was painstakingly writing a long and meaningless series of numbers, in purple ink on creamy white paper: 3: 0.00463; 4: 0.01389; 5: 0.02778; 6: 0.04630; 7: 0.06944; 8: 0.09722 . . .

He ignored the numbers—they would all be recorded— and concentrated on the fingers that held the pen. He saw a strange double image. There was the skeletal hand, its joints swollen and reddened and its back marked with brown liver spots. At the same time it was a plumper, well-fleshed hand, trembling slightly, with pale digits and carefully trimmed nails.

And the field of view was also double. He was sitting at a desk, looking far out over the curved surface of a world with a pink sunset and a dusty, red landscape. And at the same time a younger version of himself was sitting in some kind of submersible, moving deep through clear water. The ports on either side showed long strands of dark-green weed, where little red-bellied silverfish were wriggling along through the trailing fronds. There was a sense of tension within him. He was waiting for something to happen, some long-planned accident that would not be an accident.

And while he waited, simply to have something to do, he was writing. The same numbers were appearing, continuing the sequence: 7: 0.06944; 8: 0.09722; 9: 0.11574; 10: 0.12500 . . . As he watched, they began to vanish, fading into a faint set of isolated spectral digits.

Lola waited, staring at nothing, until the final ghostly number had gone completely. At last she removed the sensor cups. Bryce Sonnenberg was lying in the inclined chair, eyes covered.

"Well?" he said.

"I'll be honest with you." Lola gave the signal to swing Bryce back to an upright position. "I don't have the slightest idea what all that was about. But believe it or not, we are making progress. I hate to sound overoptimistic, but I think you are close to a breakthrough point. In another couple of sessions, you'll know what all this means—and it won't come from me, it will come from *you*. You are suddenly going to find that you can make sense of everything. Meanwhile, let me work on the numbers. I'll give the sequence to the computer, and it can look for correlations with every sequence that's ever been invented."

"Oh, you don't need to do that." Sonnenberg was removing the neural contacts. "I could have told you what the numbers were before we started, but I didn't think it would help. They are just probabilities for throwing dice. If you throw three dice, then your score must be some number between three and eighteen. Suppose you want to know your chances of scoring a particular total. Well, there's just one way you can score three. But there's ten different ways you can score six, and twenty-seven ways you can score ten. That gives odds of 1 in 216 for scoring three, 10 in 216 for scoring six, 27 in 216 for scoring ten, and so on, for all the others. Convert those to decimals, and you have the numbers that I—or whoever—was writing."

He was right. It did not help. But it was curious that he would have the answer so close at hand.

"Do you gamble much?"

"Never." The session was over, and he was standing up.

"So how do you know those odds so well?"

"I don't know." He shrugged. "I just do."

Was it something that any mathematician would know? He had said that in his own field, intimate familiarity with numbers was assumed. But it was not Lola's field. She needed help. For the rest, she was convinced that the real key did not lie in numbers. It lay in that swollen, arthritic hand, seen together with the overlain doppelganger of a younger version of its own self.

There, if anywhere, was the solution to Bryce Sonnenberg's problem.

16

The announcement had been placed in the fourth access level of the *Electronic Daily*. Only a reader who was interested in knowing everything about that specific subject would dig down so far in the files, and even then there would be little reward.

The obituary was quite short, not much more than a bald statement of facts: "The death was reported today of Jeffrey Cayuga, leader of the fifth, sixth, and seventh Saturn expeditions. Mr. Cayuga was a member of a well-known family of planetary explorers, and the great nephew of Jason Cayuga, who served as a junior officer on the first Saturn expedition. Mr. Cayuga's death, of natural causes, occurred aboard the vessel *Weland*. His heir is his nephew, Joss Cayuga, who is one of the few survivors of the Ceres final battle and recently arrived in the Jovian system from his home in the Belt."

Alicia Rios was watching Cayuga as he read the announcement. They were sitting facing each other across a low table in her forty-room apartment, deep in the lowest residential levels of Ganymede. She and Cayuga both sought the safest possible place to live, but they disagreed on how that could be achieved. He favored the isolated planetoid of Lysithea, a world that could not be approached from space without alerting his defense systems. Alicia preferred to live on a busy and populated world, in a large suite with a single guarded entrance—and a dozen hidden escape tunnels that she alone knew.

"Reasonable?" she said, as soon as he had finished.

"It would have been even better to have no announcement at all. And I don't like this part." Cayuga pointed to the last sentence, and the name, *Joss Cayuga*. He appeared to be a baby-faced nineteen-year-old, with glossy, jet-black hair and smooth, pale, and unlined skin. He had been nibbling constantly at the cold snacks on a great tray that Alicia had placed in front of him, and now he was playing with a sharp-edged serving knife.

Alicia sighed. "Be reasonable. The name's in there because I was specifically asked who inherited. It was a perfectly natural question. How could I avoid answering it?"

"I guess you couldn't. Anything else from the media?"

"Nothing significant. No one asked how you died; no one seemed to care what had happened to your body."

"How *he* died. What happened to *his* body. You know the rules, Rios. Jeffrey Cayuga must be a fading memory. Past tense only, please. And if you and I meet in public, remember that we hardly know each other."

"For God's sake, Cayuga." Alicia raised sculptured, pencil-thin eyebrows. "Are you getting even more paranoid? It's hardly as though you and I have never been through this before. As for what we say here, we're completely alone, and I check for bugs every day. No one gets in here whom I don't know personally."

"If I'm paranoid, then you are irresponsible." Joss Cayuga's voice resembled Jeffrey Cayuga's, but it was softer in tone and a little lower in pitch. "Have you forgotten how close we are to success on Helene? One more month, and it will be ready to proceed. How would you like the Club to label you as the one who risked the whole project?"

"Don't try to threaten me, Cayuga," Alicia snapped back. "And don't lecture me, either. *I'm* the one who said we should do this here, in person, rather than through some communication channel that might be tapped."

"Point taken." Cayuga turned from the display. "So let's get down to business. I don't want to stay on Ganymede one minute longer than I have to. What did Jinx Barker find out?"

"Exactly what we asked him to find out." Alicia summarized Jinx's activities over the past few weeks, and what he had learned about Lola Belman and Bryce Sonnenberg. "Her patient is a strange individual," she concluded, "but anyone who goes to a haldane is likely to be that. Jinx will stake his professional reputation on the fact that Sonnenberg has no relevance to our interests. So far as he is concerned, the investigation is over. He is lying low, asking me what he ought to do next. I think I know what he *wants* to do."

"Dispose of Lola Belman?"

"Exactly. But I don't see that as a necessity. Jinx can simply tell her that he has to return to the Belt, and break off the relationship."

"If it were anyone but Lola Belman, I would probably agree." Cayuga tested the knife's edge thoughtfully on his finger. "But Jinx has been dealing with a haldane. We know what he learned about her. I'm afraid of what *she* might have learned about *him.*"

"He says, nothing—except what he wanted her to learn."

"That may reassure you, but it leaves me cold. Haldanes can't read minds, the way a lot of people think, but they are awfully good at reading everything else. I say, Why take the risk? Let Jinx do the rest of his work."

Alicia shrugged. "If you feel that way. Jinx will be delighted to oblige. Lola Belman?"

"Lola Belman, and while we're at it, Bryce Sonnenberg. That ends our worries, even if Jinx is wrong and she knows too much."

"What about the others? Jinx met Lola Belman's kid brother, and his fat friend Battachariya."

"I think so." Cayuga stabbed the knife he was holding deep into the serving tray. "Cut root and branch—that has been our philosophy. A clean sweep is safer."

"You don't have to get symbolic with me." She reached forward, plucked the knife free, and examined the gash it had made in the platter. "You just ruined my best tray. All right, I'll tell Jinx to go ahead at once."

"When you do, make something else clear to him." Cayuga gestured to the knife in her hand. "We don't want any physical evidence left behind. Tell him: no guns, no knives, nothing that might be traced back to him or to us."

"Jinx won't mind that at all. In fact, he'll be delighted." Alicia smiled. "He always finds work more exciting when he's allowed to make it what you might call highly *personal.*"

The haldane profession had its hidden dangers. Lola had heard of only two cases where a haldane had been attacked by patients, but she knew of scores where the haldane had been drawn deep into a patient's own psychoses.

It was a consequence of a natural empathy for others, reinforced by years of training. And perhaps it did not apply only to patients. Maybe it happened to lovers, too. Lola, with a dozen patients to worry about, found herself obsessed with Conner Preston.

She stared at her display screen, but she hardly knew what was showing there. After their last night together he had simply disappeared. His office was empty. His message center said that he was on special assignment and could not be reached. That sounded quite reasonable—he worked for the Belt, where secrecy and undercover work had been a way of life even before the war—but Lola's mind offered a dozen other explanations.

Suppose that Conner had been preconditioned to resist the sort of hooks that she had planted. Haldanes tended to assume that they were the keepers of the flame, guardians of a special set of secret techniques possessed by no one else. But that might not be true. There were rumors of Belt technologies, developed before the war, that affected the brain both physically and mentally. If anyone would find those techniques useful, it would surely be the media, with their obsession for scoops and exclusive stories.

Suppose Conner had been protected against her hooks and had responded with the "Jinx Barker" name as a red herring designed to keep her away from his real work. He had refused to talk about that, or reveal who he was working for, even when he appeared to be in the response state. According to conventional haldane theory, that meant either that the information was a closely guarded secret, or else the subject was protected against inquiry. Suppose Conner had been conditioned to say nothing if anyone tried to use haldane hooks and probes on him, and that, after it, he had been told to vanish without another word.

It was an enormous relief when late in the evening of the fourth day he came breezing into her office without knocking, just as though nothing at all had happened and he had never been away.

"Where have you been?" She allowed him to grab her, and hugged him just as hard.

"Now, you ought to know better than to ask that of a card-carrying media man." He was grinning down at her, apparently in high good humor.

"I've been worried about you." She did not want to say she had been able to think of little else.

"Well, you shouldn't have been. Didn't you call my message center? You ought to know that I can't talk about special assignments—you're not the only one with professional secrets, you know. I'll tell you this much: If you want to learn more about where I've been and what I've been doing, you'll have to be nice to me."

"I'm always nice to you."

He finally released her. *"Extra* nice. Starting with dinner. I'll pick you up an hour from now—all right?"

"Tonight? It's late already. Where are we going?"

"Another professional secret. Don't overdress, though. Dark shirt and slacks, no jewelry. Plain shoes—we'll be doing some walking. And be ready for a long night. Now, finish your work. I'll be back in one hour exactly."

He turned and was gone, before she could ask any more. Lola smiled to herself as she turned off her display. Good thing Conner didn't realize how little notice she had been taking of the display, or how little work she had done since he left. He had a high-enough opinion of himself already.

She followed his instructions and was wearing a plain, tight-fitting blouse of dark blue and matching pants when he arrived. He had changed to sober clothes of charcoal grey, and nodded his approval. "Perfect. Tonight you'll see how the other half lives."

He wouldn't say any more as he led them to a high-velocity transit chute and they climbed in. The little car dived at once into its evacuated tunnel and sped over two thousand kilometers vertically downward. When they emerged, Lola stared around her with genuine curiosity. In five years, she had never been anything like this deep. The residential levels lay far above them. She knew little about the middle of her adopted homeworld, except that it was supposedly all industrial.

She found herself standing on a flat platform that overlooked a curved and close horizon. The gravity was much less than on the residential levels, hardly enough to secure her footing. It meant that they must be close to the center of Ganymede. The ceiling was kilometers above them, lit with high-power sonoluminescent strips.

She looked around in vain for any sign of other people. "This is *nowhere*. Are you telling me that we'll be having dinner down here? I don't believe it."

"Wait and see. Come on, I want to show you something." He took her hand and led her to the edge of the platform, away from the transit-chute exit. They descended a long ramp, floating more than walking, and moved to a waist-high guard rail.

"I've been exploring this region. I want you to go right to the edge and look down." Conner, still holding Lola's hand, eased her forward. "This is one of the best points to see things from. What do you think of that?"

Lola followed his gesture and found she was staring down at a billowing sea of blue-green. The glassy surface moved in great, steady waves, although there was no breath of moving air.

"Stirred from below by paddles, to provide circulation," said Conner. He had moved so that he stood right behind her, his hands about her waist. "The surface tension is provided by a monomolecular layer on top of it; otherwise, the brew would be frothing about all over the place. The surface isn't very strong—if I jumped off here, I'd float down and right on through. But the layer does its job, and if it ever gets damaged or ruptured, it's self-renewing. It's slightly acid, too, underneath there. Once I went under, I'd become part of the nutrient supply in a few days."

"Is it for agriculture?" Lola eased back a little from the edge, pushing into Conner.

He laughed in her ear and moved his hands up to rest on her shoulders. "Nervous? Don't worry, I've got you. It's strange, but everyone from the upper levels who ever comes down here says, 'Agriculture.' Apparently all that you people think about is eating. This, though, is far more vital. You are looking at the main source of Ganymede's air supply: blue-green prokaryotic bacteria, busy in photosynthesis. They produce a thousand times as much oxygen as the agricultural regions near the surface. Food, too, though it's not the sort you are used to." He turned her toward him. "And speaking of that, I promised you dinner. So if you're ready, let's go. We can come back here if you want to—after the restaurant."

"A restaurant down here? Who is there to feed?"

"A very good restaurant. You'll see the clientele for yourself. I told you, you're going to see how the other half lives."

The path that they took was a narrow causeway, with the restless blue-green lake churning on either side. It went on and on for several kilometers, until Lola admitted the importance of his advising her to wear walking shoes.

"Are we ever going to get there, or do we walk all the way around the world?"

"We're nearly there. Look. See the white arch?"

From a distance it was small and sharply angled, like the open jaw of a shark. As they came closer, Lola saw that she had drawn the wrong animal from the oceans of Earth. The arch was enormous, three times as tall as she was, and a sign hung down from its apex: "The Belly of the Whale."

No one greeted them at the entrance. Given the late hour, Lola was not really surprised. They walked on through, past half a dozen curtained booths. Conner led them to an empty one with undrawn curtains.

"No human servers, of course," he said as they sat down. "If we leave the drapes open it's a breach of manners, but we'll do it for just a few minutes so that you can take a look at a couple of other customers. Don't stare at them, that's all. Here's a couple now, leaving."

Lola kept her eyes fixed firmly on her menu and stole a quick glance from the corner of her eye. She saw two men, as simply dressed as she and Conner. They seemed serious, almost dour, and as they passed the booth they offered a glare of disapproval.

"I guess we ought to close the curtain," Conner said as

soon as the men were out of earshot. "When you've seen one, you've seen them all. Everyone down here is pretty much the same."

"What's wrong with them?"

"Not a thing, in their terms. They wonder what's wrong with *you*. They would ask why we like to talk so much to other people. The big mystery to me is how they find out to come here, because it sure isn't by word of mouth. The deep interior has its own society rules, and it practices its own form of courtesy. Rule number one: Mind your own business. Rule number two: Speak only when you're spoken to. It's a wonderful place for anyone who has had it with other humans."

"But that's awful." Lola stared at the curtained booths. "These people should have treatment."

"Down, girl. Stop being a haldane for a while, and let's have dinner. From what I've seen, the people down here are as happy as people anywhere else. And if you ever want to be alone for a while, or escape from something or somebody, can you imagine a better place?"

Lola formed the sudden conviction that this was where he had spent the past four days. His comment—"If you ever want to be alone for a while"—was not lost on her. Haldane hooks and unanswered questions to one side, had she come on too strong to him? No matter how good things were physically, lots of people became uneasy if a partner hinted too soon at something permanent or even long-term. Maybe she had been doing that, without realizing it. People gave out signals at so many different levels.

"All right, I'll try not to be too much of a haldane for tonight." She waved the menu. "Even if I were, I can't read your mind, and I can't make sense of this thing. I've never heard of any of the dishes. Tell me what I ought to eat."

"I'll do better than that. I'll order for both of us. Suspend your prejudices and go with your taste buds." He began to make entries in the tabletop order panel. "Just remember that everything you eat in The Belly of the Whale is made out of single-celled organisms, and it started in the vats out there. The people down here prefer it that way. No dead animals, no complex vegetables. Prokaryotic forms are the top of the line. If there was a rule number three, it would probably be: Don't eat any cell with a nucleus."

Lola tried to do as he said and put her prejudices to one side—all of them. She wanted tonight to be as pleasant as the first night that she had spent with Conner. She didn't even want to think. It was a relief to find that yeast was a simple-enough life-form to be acceptable, which meant that wine was definitely on the menu.

He made it easy for her to forget her worries. He filled both their glasses, and across the table he kept smiling at her with a warm and possessive expression in his eyes that made her feel infinitely desirable and wanted. When each dish arrived he tasted it carefully, cocking his head to one side as he chewed the first mouthful. Only once did he frown, glance down, and say, "Sorry. This isn't what I thought it was. I suggest we skip it—unless you want to try it and give a second opinion?"

Lola shook her head. This was another evening on which she wanted to let him make the decisions. He certainly knew what he was doing. The food at The Belly of the Whale was strange to her, in flavor and even more so in texture, but his instruction to suspend her prejudices had been the right one. And so was his question—"Want to?"—asked after the last course had been served and eaten.

"I sure do. Is that too forward?" She frowned at the curtain. "You mean in here?"

"Hardly." He was laughing at her. "Just because you can't see through that doesn't make it soundproof. The clientele might not say anything, but they'd certainly think a lot." He stood up. "Come on."

"You mean we have to go all the way back?" Lola felt

warm and ready, and her apartment was at least an hour away.

"I don't see why." He was leading her out through the great arch of the door. "The restaurant is the center of civilization this far down, but you won't see anybody wandering around so late at night. We ought to be able to find a thousand quiet places outside."

"One will be enough." Lola wondered how many times he had been here before with other women. Then she decided that she didn't really want to know. He was with her, and not with them, whoever they might be, and she could tell already how excited he was—the hand holding hers felt very warm, with a definite tremor in the long fingers.

"Be patient. We have plenty of time." She tried to slow him down, but he was hurrying her along a path that branched off to the left and went around the back of The Belly of the Whale.

"I have been patient," he said, in an odd, breathless voice. "You don't know how patient."

"Well, you won't have to be patient much longer." She could see where he was taking her. They were approaching a deserted double bend in the path, shielded from above and from both sides. They would be invisible unless someone were to walk right by. The nook was equipped with a broad, resilient bench, where anyone could lounge at ease and stare at the endless sea of rolling blue-green.

Or, if they chose, do other things. She had never felt more excited.

Lola sat down, then at his gentle urging moved to lie full-length along the bench. She lay on her back, staring up at the ceiling with its glowing strips of luminescence. Conner's face suddenly loomed above, cutting off part of the light. He was smiling down at her.

"This is nice," he said dreamily. "I've looked forward to it for a long time. This is going to be really, really nice."

He leaned over and kissed her gently on both eyes, closing them, and then sensually on the mouth. As his head lifted away from hers, she felt the touch of his right thumb. It was on the pulse in her throat—exactly where he had touched her before, when he believed that she was sleeping. His other hand moved so that both thumbs touched each side of the front of her neck, while his fingers curved gently around toward the back. He was lying more heavily on top of her, pinning her down, so that she could not move her legs or trunk.

"Conner!" She opened her eyes.

"It's all right." His fingers moved up to caress her ears, then slid down and around to grip the back of her neck. "This is going to be just fine. Perfectly fine."

Lola did not have time to think, but excitement turned to instant panic. As his hands tightened, she gabbled out the haldane protection sequence. She felt a moment of absolute terror. She had left it too late—it was not working. His hands were still squeezing, twisting to one side and at the same time turning her head. It hurt terribly—another second and the vertebrae of her spinal column would snap and shear. She knew what came next, the long drop into the billowing, bacterial sea, but that would not matter. She would be already dead.

She heard a long, shuddering sigh. The pressure on her neck eased. After a moment she realized that he was lying totally immobile on top of her. Even in the low gravity, she needed an effort to release herself from his grip and wriggle free.

She stood up, shivering. Less than an hour earlier she had drunk three big glasses of wine. Now she felt as cold and chillingly sober as if she had been plunged into a bath of ice water. She could still feel those strong fingers on her throat. She had absolutely no doubt that she had escaped death by only a fraction of a second.

She stared down at him—he was lying prone with his face invisible to her. What now? She was safe enough while the haldane protection continued to work, but she had no idea how long that might be. Should she leave him here and flee? But then he could pursue her, and she would never be sure where he was or when he would catch up with her.

The conclusion, unpleasant as it might be, was obvious: She had to take him with her. She dare not, under any circumstances, allow him out of her sight until he was too heavily sedated to move. The drugs to permit that were in her office—forbidden for nonmedical use, but the hell with regulations. The rules do not apply when your life is in danger.

Meanwhile, they were an awfully long way from her office. The first question was the important one: He had resisted her earlier questions, but did she now have *physical* control over him?

And if she did not? She glanced over the edge at the blue-green sea and knew that no matter what happened, she could not do that. If she had been struggling for her life, and had found a chance to throw him over and save herself, maybe she could have done it. But in cold blood it was out of the question.

"Jinx. Can you hear me?"

Lola could not see his lips, but she heard a faint "yes."

"Sit up and face me." And, as soon as he had done so, "Are you really Jinx Barker, or are you really Conner Preston?"

"I am Jinx Barker."

"Is there a Conner Preston?"

"No."

"Was there?"

"Yes."

"Is Conner Preston dead?"

"Yes."

"How did he die?"

The impassive face frowned, and his mouth opened

without making a sound. Lola cursed her own stupidity. His block against providing some particular piece of information was still effective, and she should not be testing it here. Until she was in a position to employ psychotropic drugs, she should do nothing at all that might weaken her control.

"Stand up, Jinx." And, as he came slowly to his feet, "Everything is fine. We are going back to my apartment. Do you remember the way?"

"Yes, I remember." His face and voice lacked expression, but that should not matter—no one would be likely to speak to them, and Lola could make sure that they kept clear of other travelers.

"Good." She reached out to take his hand, then changed her mind. She did not want to touch those fingers. "I want you to take us back to my apartment. You lead the way, and I will follow you. Do you understand?"

"Yes. I understand." He began to move off, slowly, but with no hesitation.

Walking close behind him, Lola realized that her troubles were not over. They were just beginning.

There would be no sleep tonight. And maybe not tomorrow night, either. Until she found a permanent way to deal with Jinx Barker, she would have to remain close to him and hold him under her personal control—forever.

17

Lola sat in her office chair, nerving herself for the final step. She had spent the whole night getting ready and still she felt unprepared. Jinx Barker sprawled next to her, the telemetry sensors already in position on his body. All she had to do now was administer the rest of the psychotropic drugs and instruct the computer to seek synthesis.

All she had to do.

Provided that you accepted the idea of haldane infallibility, it sounded easy. A haldane was cool, nerveless, always in control of herself at the same time that she controlled others. A haldane felt no emotions of her own. She was not allowed to look down at the man beside her, remember him as a warm, tender lover, and weep for the bright future prospect that last night had turned to ashes. The heart of a haldane could not break.

Most of all, though, a haldane was not permitted to be afraid.

Yet there was good reason for fear. Before she could induce synthesis, Jinx Barker would have to be released from his mental bonds. If he were insufficiently sedated, Lola could then be within his grasp in two seconds.

She told herself again that he was not a patient, that he

did not have to be treated with the same consideration as a patient. Then she did what no self-respecting haldane would ever do: She went across to the chair and taped Jinx Barker to it, hand and foot.

That should provide physical security. Still she hesitated. There remained the fear of touching his mind, of the awful things that she might find within it. She could not forget the look on his face as he smiled down at her, just before his kisses had closed her eyes.

Lola took a deep breath. As a haldane, she should be used to meeting the unspeakable. And if she did not act soon the psychotropic drugs would pass their peak of effectiveness.

She spoke the release sequence, gave the signal for the computer to proceed at once—before she had a chance to change her mind—and lay back in her chair.

She had not been able to force herself to place the sensor cups over her own eyes. Although that omission ruled out any possibility of derived reality, she felt that she had to watch every movement of his body. If he somehow broke the tape and came toward her . . . His eyes were hidden by sensor cups, but she knew the exact moment when he became conscious. There was a brief jerk upward of his head, and before it seemed possible he was flexing his arms and legs, testing his bonds.

The most frightening thing was his silence. He did not grunt, or groan, or ask, "Where am I?," as Lola felt sure she would have done. Instead, he rapidly dipped his head down and to one side, to bring his mouth into contact with the tape holding his wrists. His teeth were already tearing the broad strip free when the rest of the drugs hit home. Lola shared his dizziness through the telemetry, and felt a sudden and disorienting burst of rage.

"Relax, Jinx Barker." She watched closely as his body came upright and he slowly leaned back in the chair. The tension went out of his muscles. So far, so good—she had physical control.

The next stage would be more difficult. If she probed too hard and drove him beyond sanity, she could share the descent into madness. "Jinx Barker, I am going to ask you a series of questions. Do not be afraid to say that you do not know an answer, or cannot answer. Do you understand?"

"Yes."

"I am Lola Belman. Were you going to kill me after we left The Belly of the Whale?"

"Yes."

"Why?" (Bad question: Even under the influence of powerful drugs, a human could offer self-serving answers. Anything that she asked should permit only a simple yes or no reply.) "Ignore that question. Did you expect to enjoy killing me?"

"Yes."

The calm certainty of the reply came with a deep, visceral rush of sensual excitement. It made Lola shudder, but she forced herself to go on. "Were you going to kill me simply because it would give you pleasure?"

"No."

"Were you *ordered* to kill me?"

"Yes."

"Tell me the name of the person who ordered you to kill me."

"Alicia Rios."

The answer threw Lola into a spin. She had expected the name of a sick and angry patient, or perhaps someone close to a patient, like the boyfriend of the man who had committed suicide. But Alicia Rios? She had to grope around inside her head before she could even identify the name. That was the person at the party, the tiny, exquisite woman with dark hair and eyes, whom Jinx Barker had identified as a member of the Saturn exploration families.

Alicia Rios had walked up to Lola and examined her closely. That had seemed odd at the time, but why would a woman who hardly knew Lola want to *kill* her? It made no more sense than that Jinx Barker would try to kill her.

Or as much sense. If Jinx were working for Alicia, then maybe Alicia . . .

"Did Alicia Rios receive her instructions to have me killed from someone else?"

"I don't know."

"Do you *think* she received her instructions from someone else?"

"Yes."

"Do you know that other person's name?"

"Yes."

"What is the name?"

"Jeffrey Cayuga."

Things had gone from perplexing to ludicrous. At least Alicia Rios had a face to go with the name. Cayuga was certainly a name—a famous name, from the first human Saturn expedition. But that had been *Jason* Cayuga. Jeffrey Cayuga, his descendant, hadn't even been at the First Family party—he had been off on some expedition, millions or billions of kilometers away. Lola felt sure that she had never met him in her whole life.

One more try.

"Did Jeffrey Cayuga receive his instructions from someone else?"

"I don't know."

"Do you *think* he received his instructions from someone else?"

"I don't know."

Dead end. She would have to abandon the yes-and-no technique, even at the risk of being misled.

"Do you know why Alicia Rios was interested in me?"

"Yes."

"Tell me why."

"Because of information that you had obtained as a haldane."

Progress. "Was it information that I had obtained from one of my patients?"

"Yes."

"Which patient?"

"Bryce Sonnenberg."

Lola had sensed the answer before it came. Sonnenberg's case had baffled and tormented her for weeks, but she knew nothing in him or his past that might explain murder.

"Were you instructed by Alicia Rios to find out about Bryce Sonnenberg?"

"Yes."

"And were you—" Lola faltered. The next step seemed so logical, yet so preposterous. "And were you instructed to kill him, also?"

"Yes."

With that answer came a terrible fear: "Have you done it?"

"No."

"Will you do it?"

"Yes."

Not *maybe,* or *If I can,* or *If I am released.* Just the bald reply, and with it the wave of total confidence from the chair next to her.

"Do you know *why* you are supposed to kill me and Bryce Sonnenberg?"

"Yes."

"Why, then?"

"To make sure that you do not speak to anyone about what you know."

"What do we know?"

"I don't know."

Lola repressed a hysterical groan. He was ready to kill her and Bryce for whatever it was that they thought she knew, while she was absolutely sure that she knew nothing that could matter to them. It was another dead end, and she was forced to rely on a murderer's answers to save herself.

"Do you know why Alicia Rios employed you for this?"

"No."

"Can you suggest a reason why she might have?"

"Yes."

"What is the reason?"

"I have done work for her before."

"Similar work?"

"Yes."

"You mean"—she had to make absolutely sure—"you have *killed* people for Alicia Rios?"

"Yes."

Lola went cold. She had slept with a professional assassin, been driven giddy with excitement by a killer's lovemaking, fallen asleep snug in a murderer's arms. The next question didn't seem to have much to do with anything, but she had to ask it.

"Do you kill people with—with your bare hands?"

"Yes." Again the surge came through the telemetry, an ecstasy so strong it was almost pain.

Physician, heal thyself. Lola fought for self-control. There was nothing in haldane training to prepare her for this. She had to bring them back to objective issues or go crazy.

"Does Alicia Rios live on Ganymede?"

"Yes."

"Is she on Ganymede at the moment?"

"Yes."

"Do you know her address, and how to get there?"

Two questions in one—something that you were taught not to do in the first haldane instruction course. But he was answering: "Yes."

"Tell me how to get there."

As he gave directions, in the clear and matter-of-fact manner that had impressed her the first time they met, Lola wondered what she was going to do with the information.

Call Alicia Rios? Hardly. How were you supposed to begin the conversation? "Hello, I understand that you gave orders for me to be killed, and I want to ask you why." That seemed like a certain way to make sure that Rios sent a second murderer, to try again where Jinx Barker had so far failed.

A knock on the outer door of her office, coming just when that thought of a possible other killer was already in her head, brought Lola rigidly upright in her chair. She heard the outer door open, then a click as it closed. It was self-locking. As soft footsteps moved through the entrance hall toward the inner office door, she stared wildly around her, wondering how to defend herself.

Someone tapped on the inner door. Lola jumped to her feet—did killers knock to announce their arrival? Who knew what killers might do, when killers could also be lovers? Her relief, when the inner door opened and Bryce Sonnenberg's face appeared, was so great that her knees buckled and dropped her back into her seat.

"Bryce!"

"I'm sorry." He did a double take at the sight of the man lying full-length in the patient's chair. "But you did say to come first thing in the morning, so I did." He noticed the tape on Barker's wrists and ankles. "I didn't mean to interrupt you, and I did knock on the door before I barged in. I'd better go now. Call me when you're ready to see me."

"No!" Lola jumped up and grabbed his arm. Since the first session she had regarded Bryce Sonnenberg as not much more than a kid—a strange and troubled one, with a changing personality that was still hardly formed, so that even though he was tall and strongly built, he seemed far

younger than she was. But now she was vastly comforted by his deep chest and the heavy muscles in the arm that she was holding.

"Don't leave, Bryce. Whatever you do, don't leave. This involves you as much as me." And, when he stared at her in open disbelief, "It does, it really does. Give me one more minute; then I'll explain."

She bent over Jinx Barker, making sure that the tapes were securely in place, then commanded the computer to end synthesis and place him into sedated-care status. The computer recordings would all be filed away, so that she could perform a later analysis of the session. Meanwhile, with nutrients provided by IVs and all body functions monitored, he should be quite safe. A patient could remain in sedated care for a long time— if need be, for weeks.

But time alone would not solve the problem of Jinx Barker.

"Sit down, Bryce, and listen closely. You're not going to believe this at first, but let me tell you everything before you start asking questions."

She read him the summary of her interaction with Jinx Barker all the way from the beginning, when "Conner Preston" had taken an office along the corridor and had first showed up in her office, to last night's realization of what was about to happen, and then to this morning's questioning.

"Does it mean anything to you?" she asked at last.

He hardly needed to answer. Although at the talk of murder his expression had changed—becoming at first startled and then somehow older and more guarded—he had shaken his head when she mentioned Jinx Barker, Alicia Rios, and Jeffrey Cayuga.

His reaction to her question came as a surprise to Lola. He rubbed at his nose for a moment, then went off in another direction completely: "He was ordered to kill you and me. Who else was he told to kill?"

It was a question she had not thought to ask, and for the moment it was too late. Jinx Barker was under deep sedation.

"What makes you think there might be somebody else involved?"

"Logic." He grinned at her, unmoved by the news that he was on a murderer's victim list. "Or maybe I should say, lack of logic. If there's no reason at all for killing you or me, there's just as much no-reason for killing someone else. *Anyone* else."

Lola thought immediately of Spook. He had tried to help her sort out Bryce's muddled and contradictory background, and she had encouraged him. But if she had exposed him or Bat to danger *("Look after Spook, don't let him get into trouble"),* then it was all her fault if . . .

"As for what we should do next," Bryce was continuing, cutting off that troubled train of thought. "I don't know. We can't leave him trussed up like that forever. On the other hand, we can't let him up to have another go at you, or me, or anyone else he chooses. So I say we visit the person who set him onto us, and find out what's really going on."

"But what about him?" She glanced down at Jinx Barker.

"You stay. When I said *we* make a visit, I actually meant *me.*"

"I can't let you."

"So give me an alternative. We have to discover what all this is about, because it's obvious that somebody thinks I'm something I'm not. The obvious person to talk to is Alicia Rios, and from what you told me, she's not that far from here. Are you willing to leave him here alone?" Lola's shiver gave the answer. "I thought so. Nor am I. And we couldn't possibly take him with us."

There was a gleam of manic excitement in his eye. Lola recalled the hurtling space scooter, skimming within inches of a mottled mountain of rock and ice. That had been his idea of *pleasure*. But these dangers were likely to be far more subtle.

"What will you say to her?"

"I don't know. Something innocent. It will depend on what she says to me."

"Be careful."

"I will." Again he seemed changed, older and more aware of himself than she had ever seen him. He was nodding his head thoughtfully. "I know how to be careful. I know it very well. And unless you have any other suggestions I ought to be on my way before Alicia Rios has time to suspect that her plans are not working out."

Joss Cayuga was still on Ganymede. The brawls of the big world made him nervous, and he would much rather be safe on Lysithea, but he had learned to follow his instincts. His last meeting with Alicia Rios had left him profoundly uneasy.

Allowing Jinx Barker direct and personal interaction with a haldane had been an act of pure folly. Worse than that, though, was Alicia's admission that Barker had been crazy enough to bring Lola Belman to a First Family party. That was Jinx's braggadocio, the very opposite of discreet behavior—and Alicia Rios had gone right along with it. According to Lenny Costas, Belman had seen both him and Dahlquist, while Alicia had actually walked right up to the haldane and done everything but talk to her. Inviting attention like that was asking for trouble. It forced the question, How much could Jinx Barker be trusted? And, since Alicia Rios apparently had infinite faith in the man, a second question: Had Alicia herself become an intolerable risk for the Ganymede Club?

Cayuga had been hiding out in a travelers' terminal on one of the upper levels, close to Ganymede's biggest spaceport. He had been there for two days. It was a perfect place to remain unnoticed, because, although food and accommodation were available around the clock, everyone else was in transit. Every few hours a different set of strangers rolled in, each preoccupied with worries of ship timetables and manifests.

Cayuga consulted his watch. He had told Alicia that he would call her at about this time. She would be in her own quarters, but she believed that he was far away on Lysithea.

He left the restaurant and made his way to a booth in the travelers' communications center. His call could not go to Alicia directly through Ganymede circuits, or she would notice the absence of signal travel time to and from Lysithea. Cayuga requested a call route via a relay station on Callisto, including a half-minute hold on signals forwarded in each direction. He waited patiently while the connection was established to Callisto and back to Alicia's home deep in Ganymede, and waited again for Alicia to pick up. He was becoming convinced that she was not there as planned when at last her face appeared within the display volume.

"Cayuga? Where have you been? I called you an hour ago, and all I got was a low-level fax. You need to change him, by the way—he's still a Jeffrey Cayuga facsimile."

"I will, as soon as I get some free time. I've been up near the surface, reviewing the defense systems. What's the status with Jinx Barker?"

While the message was beamed to Callisto and back, he decided to leave a higher-level fax in charge the next time he was away. The level-two fax that he had been using was not very smart, and a clever questioner might be able to trick it into revealing things about Lysithea that Cayuga did not care to have known.

"It's going very well," said Alicia Rios at last. "In fact, the first and most difficult part is complete. Barker took his haldane-friend on a very special date last night. No one but Barker knows where they went—not even me—and he assured me that there would be no physical evidence. She's definitely history at this point. Otherwise Jinx would have called me today and said there had been a hitch, and I have not heard from him. Next he plans to deal with the others—the patient and then the brother and the brother's friend. Jinx hardly knows them, and they don't know each other very well, so no one will connect them or suspect him when something happens to them. All right?"

"Excellent. He is sure that is enough, and there is no need to spread the net wider? Maybe there should be others."

"Be reasonable, Cayuga. He says that's everyone. We have to trust Jinx."

"I trust no one."

"Well, we have to stop somewhere—otherwise there will be no one left on Ganymede."

"No one except members of the Ganymede Club? That would be acceptable. Never forget the stakes, Rios. We have too much to lose. When will Barker complete the rest of his work?"

"Today. I am expecting him to call me when it is done, and then I will call you."

"At once, if you please. This situation is not at all to my liking."

Cayuga terminated the connection but remained seated in the booth. He ought to feel relieved, and did not. "We have to trust Jinx." There you had it, the problem with Alicia Rios. She hardly seemed to realize that Jinx Barker was not a Club member. Better if she had said, "We must check constantly on everything that Jinx does."

Almost without thinking, he consulted the Ganymede directory. The listing of licensed haldanes showed the name, Lola Belman, and the full routing. He placed a call, directly this time, and waited. He was expecting an answering service, a fax, or possibly no reply at all. There was a long delay, until he was sure that no one was there and he was ready to cancel. When his finger was already on the button, the display volume came alive, a breathless voice said, "Yes?," and a woman's face appeared.

Cayuga hit the disconnect instantly. With instinctive caution he had disabled the video link from his end, even though he had not expected a human to answer. It was remotely possible that she would be able to trace him, but only if she were already in tracking mode before the call came in. She would not have had time to enable it in the split second that they were connected. He, on the other hand, had been concentrating hard on his display. Her face, whoever she was, was clear in his memory. He returned to the directory and asked for access to information files on haldane services. It took a minute or two to locate what he wanted, but the file on every licensed haldane, as he had hoped, included an image ID.

He waited until retrieval of the image of Lola Belman was complete. His warning voices had already told him what he might see. Sure enough, here it came: Lola Belman was the woman whose worried face just two minutes earlier had filled the display. A worried woman, but certainly alive. According to Alicia Rios and Jinx Barker, she had died last night.

Cayuga did not waste time cursing. He recorded the image and then at once placed another call. This time he needed the video link. He waited impatiently until Lenny Costas's frowning face appeared in the display.

"Lenny, we have a problem. A big one."

"Another one?" The big greying head nodded slowly. "You know, I am not surprised, even though Jinx Barker and Alicia are supposed to be fixing everything."

"They are a major part of the problem." Cayuga summarized for Lenny Costas his conversation with Alicia, and what he had since learned. At the end he said, "We must seek the concurrence of the rest of the Club, but I think that you and I have to be ready to act—at once. Barker and

Rios, by their actions, are threatening everything that we have worked so hard to create."

Costas shrugged. "Again, you fail to surprise me. Are you proposing what I think you are?"

"Yes."

"For both Jinx Barker and Alicia Rios?"

"Yes."

"Barker, without question. But she is a member of the Club."

"True. And she should therefore have taken her responsibilities much more seriously. We are all bound by the same rules, Lenny. We must recognize the same consequences."

"It is easy to *say* that we must deal with Jinx Barker. But you, Cayuga, warned me long ago how difficult that might be."

"Less so if we act before he suspects. I am willing to take that responsibility if you will handle Rios."

"You give me the easy one. I know her schedule, where she is, what she does. What about Barker? We do not know that he even returned from his assignment with Lola Belman."

"Let me worry about that. As an additional action I propose to do what Jinx Barker failed to accomplish with Lola Belman. I hope that she, with suitable persuasion, will also be able to tell me the location of Jinx Barker."

"Be careful, Cayuga. This whole thing could have been set up as a Barker-Rios trap."

"I am always careful. Now I will call the other Club members. If they feel as I suspect they will feel, you must be ready to head for Alicia Rios's apartment within the hour."

"You think it is that urgent?"

"I don't know. I dare not assume that it is not. One other thing: It is imperative that no trace of Alicia Rios remain for analysis."

"I know that as well as you do."

"My apologies. But we can never be too careful." Cayuga gave the signal to transmit the file image of Lola Belman to Costas. "This is the haldane whom Barker failed to eliminate. If I succeed with Barker but do not myself survive the event, there will be an item of unfinished business. You will need to dispose of her. And if you do, let me return to you the warning that you offered me: Be careful, Costas."

18

An accidental call from another person meant nothing. Such things happened all the time. Lola had certainly made calls like that often enough herself.

But suppose that the call came when you had been the victim of a murder attempt only fourteen hours ago. Suppose that you had not slept since then, or since the previous morning, that the would-be killer was even now stretched out, unconscious at your side; and that practically all you knew about him was that he was working for someone you had never met. Did a short and aborted call still mean nothing?

Not if you were Lola Belman. Not when the unseen other person terminated the call at once, with no word of explanation or apology.

Within a few seconds of the phone signaling its disconnect her forehead was cold and clammy, and her stomach churned with tension. She glanced over at Jinx Barker, suddenly afraid that he might be awake and trying to free himself. He was still lying there, peaceful and sedated.

Had the caller, whoever it was, expected to see him and been shocked to see Lola? Worse than that, the person at the other end now knew that Lola was alive. She had even spoken to the person—only one word, but maybe one word too many.

Her old fear came rushing back. She had omitted to ask Jinx Barker a crucial question, and now that he was heavily sedated it could not be asked: Who else had he been ordered to kill? Her and Bryce, she knew that, but what about Spook? He had been involved with the Sonnenberg case. Barker had actually met Spook several times. She might even have told him that Spook was helping her.

The internal door leading from the office to her apartment was locked. All thumbs, she fumbled at the setting, until at last she managed to engage the wards and the multiple bolts slid free. She hurried along the little hallway that led to Spook's rooms.

He wouldn't be there, surely; it was early afternoon. The study was empty, but she gasped with relief when she barged into his bedroom and saw a hump in the untidy heap of the bedclothes.

"Spook!" She went across and grabbed his shoulder. "Get up. Right now."

He grunted and tried to turn his back to her. She took his arm and neck and shook as hard as she could. "Wake up!"

"Quit that." He raised a tangled head and scowled at her. "I need sleep. I was up all night."

She dragged him, bedclothes and all, onto the hard floor. "I'm not joking. Get up, or I'll pour cold water on you."

He was finally awake enough to register her tone of voice. He sat upright. "What's wrong with you? What happened?"

"You have to get dressed and out of here this minute. This place isn't safe."

He stared around him, as though expecting cracks to open in the walls or poison gas to come flooding from the ventilators. "It sure looks safe." But he was already over at the closet, grabbing at a bundle on the floor. "Get out and go where? We live here, remember?"

Where? Somewhere safe, somewhere unknown to Jinx Barker and to everyone connected with him.

"Your friend Bat. Did he or you ever tell Conner Preston where he lives?"

"Are you kidding?" Spook didn't believe in wasting time on things like folding clothes. The bundle he had grabbed was a crumpled shirt and slacks, and he was already into them and grabbing his shoes. "The Bat Cave? Bat would kill me if I even hinted at where it is. He's a real privacy freak."

"Great. You're going over to Bat's place, and you're going to stay there for a while."

"Get real, sister. You think I can just wander over to the Bat Cave, and drop myself off there as a house guest?"

"You have to." Lola made a decision. Jinx Barker would be out completely for at least a couple more hours, and his ankles and wrists were still bound by heavy tape. It would surely be safe to leave him. "I'll come with you and explain to Bat why it's really important."

"Fine. Why don't you start by explaining it to *me?*"

"I'll do it on the way. Come on. We have to leave this minute."

"At least, let me call him first."

"No. No time for that. Let's go." Lola led the way back to her office. Spook, mystified and trailing behind, suddenly caught sight of the figure of Jinx Barker, unconscious and bound at wrists and ankles.

He stopped and stared, wide-eyed. "Conner Preston—"

"Isn't Conner Preston at all." Lola bent over and checked one more time that her silent prisoner had not stirred. "This man is Jinx Barker. He's one good reason for leaving, so let's get out of here. I'll tell you everything as we go—at least, I'll tell you as much as I know."

It was two hundred kilometers to Alicia Rios's home, but the journey should not take more than an hour. Bryce Sonnenberg entered the location of her home into the Ganymede transportation guide and received a detailed list of the chutes, slides, vehicles, and rapid-transfer points that he needed to get there. Her message service indicated that she was at home. Bryce also received a note that he should have expected: Alicia Rios lived in a region of restricted access. When he got there, he was likely to find himself excluded by her security system.

That was one good reason for pausing before he entered the descent tube that formed the final stage of the journey. The other reason had nothing to do with Alicia Rios.

He halted at a travelers' transfer node, walked over to a service area with dozens of tables and scores of service machines, and sat down. He ignored the server that rolled across and stood waiting for instructions.

Something was going on, something deep inside him. During the most recent haldane sessions, Lola Belman had suggested that he was approaching a breakthrough point in his treatment. She had not said how it might be triggered or how it would show itself—in fact, she had said that she did not know what form it might take. But he had assumed that there would be an end, either sudden or gradual, to the blackouts and the bizarre "memories" that arose during them. Then he could return to the calm life that he had enjoyed on Callisto before his brain began to misbehave.

He realized now that he had been a simple-minded optimist. Changes were occurring, as predicted, but they were going in the wrong direction. False memories were no longer the stuff of dreams and blackouts. They had become a continuous part of his existence, surfacing by association during his normal waking hours.

The sight of Jinx Barker—bound and unconscious—followed by Lola's talk of deception and murder, had been the final hard jolt. He suddenly "remembered" another whole life. He had been a youth on Earth, mathematically talented as he was talented now, but raised in tough and frightening surroundings. In that other life he had been forced to turn his back on his mathematical gift in order to survive. And survive he had, to become rich, powerful—and wary.

When he assured Lola Belman as he left her that he knew how to be careful, he had spoken from experience. He knew a hundred ways that an assassin might choose, and he had learned a hundred defenses. He had learned the danger of friendships. He recognized the awful power of money. A lovely woman who shared your bed, apparently so willing, might be a purchased killer waiting for her chance. The price of life was eternal vigilance. You learned to break into locked apartments as easily as into locked data files, or to escape from danger along routes that did not seem to exist.

All of which meant—Bryce, now sitting at the table while the little serving machine stood in front of him and waited patiently to take his order, leaned far forward and placed his hands over his face—it all meant that rather than being close to a cure, he was more unbalanced than he had ever been. Other memories of other lives were beginning to creep in. He was an old man living quite alone, pottering about a huge apartment and playing his quiet statistical games. And then he was young again, lying in agony in an aseptic low-gee hospital bed, knowing that he had returned from the very edge of death and realizing that he was still years away from normal health.

As impossible memories flowered within him, his own life flickered and faded. He tried to recall his years on Hidalgo and Callisto, and could not produce a single moment of vivid memory. He tried to picture his mother's face, and it would not come into focus. When he made a more concentrated effort, the image of Miriam Sonnenberg, the cool and intellectual Von Neumann designer, vanished. In its place appeared a scowling vision of stringy brown hair and bad teeth, leaning over with arm lifted to strike. He was defiant, ducking under that brawny raised arm and running down the stairs and out into a narrow alley littered with garbage. It was late at night. He was very small. But no one came after him.

"Your order, please."

The service machine had reached the limit of its programed wait. Bryce lifted his head and stared at it. He had been far away, locked into the maze of his own impossible memories. But this world was still here, going on about its usual business.

"No order." He stood up and watched as the little machine rolled off. The worrier inside him said that what was going on in his head was happening at the very worst time. But another voice asked, When was a good time? There was another way to look at all of this: His wariness and instinct for danger had come along exactly when they were most needed. Confused memories were the price of the special knowledge he might need when he reached Alicia Rios's home.

He glanced at his watch, and was surprised to see that he had been at the travelers' transfer node less than a quarter of an hour. If he pushed his introspection behind him, in ten more minutes he could be at the entry point to the restricted complex where Alicia Rios lived.

He set out, reflecting on another curiosity. The *single* entry point to the whole complex. Odd. There were forty rooms in her sprawling apartment, but they were served by only the one access. Only one way in—that provided for maximum security. But only one way *out?*

Not if he were designing it. You always, no matter how impenetrable and well defended the castle, provided yourself with a bolt-hole. If he could not get to Alicia Rios because the way in was restricted, perhaps he could reach her through a hidden way out.

The region that he was approaching was on the deepest residential level, but it reeked of wealth. He could see it in the elegant bioluminescent inlays that lit the corridors with soft and discreet blue-white, in the custom-designed—*human*-designed—murals and statues along the walls, in the inaudible air-supply system, in the numerous and silent cleaning machines that carefully stayed a good ten meters away from him.

The entrance to Alicia Rios's home occupied the blind end of the corridor, an innocuous white screen that could be anything from a door of thin plastic to an impermeable wall of unknown thickness. Bryce walked slowly over to the query panel on the left. He had no intention of touching it, or indicating in any other way his interest in entering. He wanted time, first to observe and then to think. His arrival at the apartment entrance would certainly have been noted and recorded by the house security systems, but unless he did more than stand there it was unlikely that the information would go beyond a low-level fax.

The panel lights, to his surprise, were all switched off—every one, even the little power indicator. That suggested one of two things: Either the whole panel was a sham, and access to the apartment complex was obtained in some other way; or the security systems were not operating, and anyone who wanted to could simply walk on in.

The wary underside of his mind pointed out that there was of course a third option. This could be a trap, intended to lure him inside.

He paused to assess the odds. Lola had learned only this morning that Alicia Rios was behind the attempt to kill her, and now he knew also. But he and Lola had spoken to no one else, so no one *knew* that Bryce knew. Without that information, he would never have found his way down to this deep, exclusive level of Ganymede. Therefore, no one could possibly be expecting him.

Bryce walked over to the smooth white wall that formed the end of the corridor and paused with his fingers an inch away from it. He was making another assumption: that Alicia Rios had no other enemies she wanted to trap. If she had tried to kill Lola Belman, for whatever unknown reason, she might be just as eager to kill someone else. And he could finish up just as dead, even if he were not the intended target.

Odds, odds, odds, whispered a now-familiar voice deep inside him. *Everything in the world is odds. You can calculate and calculate, but when it's all done you still have to throw the dice.*

Bryce moved his left hand forward to meet the wall. He could see no seam where a door might be located, but as his fingertips reached the smooth white panel, they passed right on through and he felt a tingle in their ends. He jerked back. It was not a material wall at all, it was a hologram. He could walk right in—unless some other type of protective field were active. He could think of half a dozen that would offer excellent security. Something as simple and lethal as a triggered laser, able to reduce Bryce to his component elementary particles—that was a little extreme, and the Ganymede laws would not permit it. But what about something as benign but binding as a magnetic freeze field? That would lock him rigid in one position once he was completely within it, then hold him there until he died or someone came along to turn it off.

Bryce patted his pockets, looking for something ferromagnetic. He had ID cards, with their tiny metal strips, but they might not be enough to trigger a defense system. The only thing he could find was the key ring on which he kept the controls that allowed him into the Callistan spacescooter hangar.

He stared at those thoughtfully, almost wistfully. Why did any of the past few months have to happen? He had been busy and mindlessly happy, with his work in mathematics and his sport in low-gee space racing. Now here he was in unknown territory, wondering if the next few minutes would see his body blown apart or his brain scrambled.

He backed up half a dozen steps and lobbed the key ring at and through the field. There was no ringing of alarm bells, no flash of incandescent metal. After waiting another thirty seconds he approached the field and walked on through. His key ring was waiting on the floor at the other side.

He picked it up and looked around. He was at the edge of an enormous foyer, fifteen meters square and six meters high. The ceiling was elaborately decorated and was supported by pencil-thin, fluted columns. Gravity was higher here than on Callisto, but hardly a hindrance to architectural design. The corridor that led away from the far side of the foyer ramped steeply downward, while other openings, clearly intended as doors, were two or three meters up in the walls.

. Everything in the apartment foyer seemed normal, and yet something was badly wrong. It took Bryce half a minute to pin it down.

Air.

Everywhere on Ganymede, as on all worlds of the Belt or Outer System, you heard the continuous background noise of air circulators. A region without a steady breeze of pumped air was dead or dying. But here within the apartment there was total silence. The still air was breathable, although he detected in it a lung-searing whiff of ozone.

In an apartment this size he could stay for weeks without running out of oxygen, so he was in no immediate danger of asphyxiation. But he could not imagine that Alicia Rios would choose to live without circulating air. He was already feeling uneasy after just a few minutes.

There was one obvious conclusion. No matter that her message service said she was home, she was actually away and she planned to be away for some time. For some odd reason she had chosen to turn off the air circulators. He must look for her elsewhere. However, in her absence the opportunity for a thorough search of the living complex was too good to pass up.

Bryce began to prowl. It seemed completely natural to pause at the entrance of each new room and run a survey for possible traps. His subconscious mind apparently knew exactly what to look for. He identified five problems as he penetrated deeper into the complex. Two of them were nothing but hidden monitors, designed to provide an alarm to some central control room. Both of them were turned on and apparently working. The other three were more dangerous. They could be used to kill any unwanted visitor. After he negotiated the third one unscathed, he should have been breathing easier—except that something else was raising the hair on the back of his neck.

It was a smell. In the still air, another odor was diffusing through to add itself to the ozone. This one was more acrid, a lung-burning mixture of ionized atoms.

He followed his nose. He was approaching the master living room, a great chamber furnished in an old-fashioned style. The furniture, screens, and murals presumably reflected Alicia Rios's own tastes—Earth fashions that had been popular forty years ago.

The unpleasant smell was coming from this room. He halted at the threshold. At the far end stood a long, low table, with six wing-backed chairs around it. They would have been a matched set, with covers of pale blue—except that one of them had been burned to a black skeleton of metal. The thick carpet beneath it had vanished, to reveal seared metal floor panels. A wall screen, five meters behind the chair, was charred and ruined.

Bryce stepped forward carefully. From the pattern of burns on the wall and floor he could deduce the geometry of the event. The beam of heat that destroyed chair, carpet, and screen had propagated in straight lines so that the chair had partly protected the wall screen and the carpet behind it, and the screen in turn had partly protected the wall. Following the line of the beam back to its source, Bryce placed its origin at a chest-high point just in front of a chair at the other end of the table. The table itself was untouched, except for a charred few centimeters at the end closest to the chair.

That chair was not completely burned to a skeleton. He walked over and inspected it, and felt his pulse speed up. A broad region along the center line had been protected from the heat. It formed the silhouette of a human figure, seated and with one arm by its side. The other hand's outline was on a control board, whose remnant was fused into the chair's frame.

Bryce sat down on an untouched pale-blue chair facing the entrance of the room. The images were clear within his mind. A visitor had come to the apartment (and a *familiar* visitor, because the apartment defenses had not been called upon and the two people had sat down together); there had been a meeting, Alicia Rios in the chair where she could command the apartment controls; the visitor seated across from her. And then, with no more than a split-second of warning, a portable triggered laser had been produced and fired, its beam focused on Alicia.

She must have died instantly, within the first fraction of a second. But for some reason her killer had not stopped there. He (or she) had pulsed the laser again and again, until Alicia Rios was not merely dead, but her flesh, blood, and bones had been dispersed to their individual ionized atoms. It made Bryce feel sick to know that the smell that filled his nostrils, as he wandered through the apartment, came from Alicia Rios's cremation. The murder must have taken place no more than an hour ago. If Bryce had not paused to brood over his own situation, he might have arrived while Alicia Rios was still alive—and shared her fate.

But why burn her after she was dead, again and again? There must have been a terrible, deep-seated hatred to want such total destruction; or could there be another motive, some reason why the body of Alicia Rios had to be utterly destroyed, without a hair or a fingernail remaining?

Bryce could not imagine one, but he could think of a good reason for the death itself. Someone was covering his tracks. Over on the other side of the room stood the burned and melted remnant of a records center. Alicia Rios was gone, and so were her private files. This gave Bryce additional evidence that he was on the right lines. Someone knew that Jinx Barker had failed. And they were afraid that Jinx Barker, captured and willing to talk, might lead to Alicia Rios. So Alicia had to go, too, along with anything that might point to someone else in the chain. Bryce had seen that sort of thing often enough in the past to be convinced that he was right.

(The bewildering thought came: In which past? He had never in his whole life met anything like this, and yet he was sure. In that moment came the realization of who he was. He knew his life history, together with the series of accidents and designs that had brought him here. But he was in too much immediate danger to dwell on it now.)

With self-knowledge came another conviction: The people who had done this to Alicia Rios were thorough and totally ruthless. They would not stop with her. They would go back to the source and eliminate Jinx Barker, and then Lola Belman, and then Bryce Sonnenberg, and then anyone else whom they saw as a possible problem. Lola was in peril—terrible and immediate. So was he. But Bryce still did not know *why* they were in danger.

He examined the melted remains of the control panel on the arm of the ruined chair. It could no longer function, but there were half a dozen other control centers scattered through the apartment. He recalled one in the foyer through which he had entered. It might not be the closest, but it was the one that he could reach most quickly.

He retraced his steps at maximum speed, convinced now that the security systems were not a source of danger. Alicia Rios had turned them off for the sake of her visitor—and been rewarded with sudden and violent death.

Thanks to frequent haldane appointments, he knew Lola's access code by heart. He called her from the apartment foyer, as anxious for her to answer as he was to leave.

The call signal went on and on. After three endless minutes, Bryce gave up. Why didn't her fax cut in and answer for her? She must be there, but she wouldn't answer. She was scared. She was sitting and waiting for Bryce to return. She might not suspect what he now knew for sure: that Jinx Barker was not the only source of danger.

He left the apartment and ran back along the corridor. In Lola Belman's office he had decided that the trip to Alicia Rios's apartment could be done in an hour. On the return journey he had to shave that by at least ten minutes.

19

On the long journey down from the surface level, Cayuga's anger had been steadily growing—at Alicia Rios, but even more at himself. He had made a big mistake six years ago, and now he was paying for it. He should never have allowed Barker to get rid of the busybody media reporter, Conner Preston. Alicia had pressed hard, but Cayuga should have realized that when it came to Jinx, her judgment disappeared.

Cayuga could see the terrible irony. In order to make himself and the Ganymede Club completely safe, he had approved an action that was now leading him into a situation of supreme danger—he was on his way to tackle a killer for whom murder and survival from attack were a way of life.

As he neared the region of Ganymede where Barker had set up his office, Cayuga became more and more alert to his surroundings. The only way to make a successful hit on a professional assassin was to come at him from an unexpected direction. That ruled out a direct entry to Barker's office. He could expect a dozen defenses there, ranging from passive observation to instant counterattack. It would be just as bad to try to disable the air-supply system for the whole section, or to introduce poison into it. The living areas had smart sensors built into each room, and a dozen maintenance machines would be bustling onto the scene with neutralizing agents at the first lethal microgram.

The good news was that Jinx Barker had never met Cayuga. A walk along the corridor beyond Barker's office, as though he were a patient calling on Lola Belman, ought to arouse little suspicion.

Maybe a better idea was actually to go into Belman's office. Barker had been instructed to dispose of her. He had failed to do so, but he was likely to try again. The best time to eliminate an assassin might be when Jinx Barker was focused on killing someone else.

Cayuga could stake out Belman's office. He might have to get rid of her before he could do so, but that was on the agenda, anyway.

He studied the door as he was pressing the buzzer. It was a simple lock in a light frame door, easy enough to burn through if he did not mind leaving evidence. There would be a little noise, but it was a quiet time of day for business and the corridor was deserted.

There was no answer. She was apparently not in. Cayuga glanced in both directions along the corridor and then bent to his task. The tight, high-intensity beam could be focused until it was less than a millimeter wide. At that setting there was no problem with the materials of the lock, and the burn would be invisible from a couple of feet away. He cut through the bolt, slipped inside, and closed the door behind him.

The inner office was not even locked. Either Lola Belman considered the outer lock sufficient, or there was nothing in the place really worth stealing. Jinx Barker was probably the only person who had ever tried to pry into patient records, and even for those he had found no more than nominal protection.

Where was the best place for Cayuga to position himself? It would be a spot from which he would have an advantage over anyone entering the office. He also had to recognize the possibility that Lola Belman was hiding inside, afraid to respond to the buzzer.

Cayuga changed the heat-beam setting to broad-band antipersonnel and pushed at the inner door. He took a couple of steps back as it was opening.

No one was at the desk, no one was sitting at the dark table. But over *there*—Cayuga lifted his weapon and felt an overwhelming urge to fire. It was only at the last moment, as he saw the bonds at wrists and ankles, that he was able to hold back.

Of all the sights that he might have imagined, this one was the least plausible—it was Jinx Barker, stretched out horizontal and apparently helpless on an adjustable seat. Conceivably it was a trap, but it did not look like it. Cayuga held his weapon aimed straight at Barker and slowly walked forward until he was no more than a couple of feet away. Sure enough, it was Jinx. He was bound with strong tape, and he seemed unconscious. Cayuga saw empty drug vials on a metal table alongside the chair.

Here was another irony, another circumstance that defied belief. On the way here Cayuga had wondered how he was going to deal with a wily and infinitely dangerous professional. Now the man was being served up to him, trussed and sedated and ready for the kill.

It was no time for musing on the strangeness of events. Cayuga stepped forward. At the last moment, staring down at Barker's unconscious face, he paused. Jinx Barker was not a member of the Ganymede Club. It was not necessary in his case, as with Alicia Rios, to ensure that no body became available for postmortem examination. And Lola Belman remained to be disposed of. If Cayuga was to handle that, he did not want her alerted on her return to the office by the smell and smoke of a human body flash-flamed to ionized gas.

There was a simpler way. An old-fashioned, neat and quiet way. Cayuga moved across to the couch in the corner of the office and picked up one of the soft, plastic-covered cushions. He placed it over Jinx Barker's nose and mouth and pressed down firmly.

After half a minute the chest began to shudder, but there were no signs of returning consciousness. Cayuga waited, cutting off all air as the limbs heaved against their tape bindings. Soon they strained less hard, twitched, spasmed once or twice in reflex, and finally subsided. Still he waited, another two full minutes. At last he removed the cushion, leaned over, and tested Barker's pulse.

Nothing. Not a trace.

Cayuga permitted himself a long, shivering breath and stood staring down at the body. It was a frightening reminder of how quickly and easily such a change could arrive. Five minutes ago a living, breathing human, now a lifeless lump of useless flesh. If that could happen to Jinx Barker, it could happen just as easily to Joss Cayuga—and he had so much more to lose. Eternal vigilance, swift action, and no time for sentimental softness—those had to be the rules.

The buzz of the communications center in the corner of the office brought him out of his reverie and made his heart pound.

It could not be for him, since no one had any idea that he was in Lola Belman's office. Most likely it was a call from one of Belman's patients. He had no interest in them, but it reminded him of something else. He needed to speak with Lenny Costas. He had to tell Lenny that Jinx Barker was no longer a threat, and he had to learn how Costas had managed his mission with Alicia Rios. If Barker and Rios were both out of the way, the hardest part of the job was already over.

He walked across to the office communications center; but there he hesitated.

What were the chances that Lola Belman, as a matter of routine, recorded every ingoing and outgoing call?

All too likely. Haldanes were legendary for their insistence on maintaining and reviewing complete records on patient activities. With Ganymede Security sure to be called in to investigate the death of Jinx Barker, Cayuga could not afford to be associated in any way with this office. That would be even more important when he had taken care of Lola Belman.

The same problem applied to Jinx Barker's office, along the corridor. He dared not make a call to Lenny Costas from there, because that would be another focal point for investigation as soon as Barker's death became known.

It had to be some anonymous public call station, and the conversation with Lenny Costas must sound totally innocent and dull. That should not be too hard—they certainly had enough experience—but making a public call meant leaving Jinx Barker alone while he did it.

Cayuga glanced again at the body. Jinx would not be going anywhere, now or ever, but Cayuga wished that he knew who had sedated him and bound him to that chair. Chances were it was Lola Belman—she certainly had easiest access to the drugs, and this was her office.

How would she react on her return, when she discovered that Barker was dead? Suffocation left no marks. She would probably assume that Barker had died as a result of the drugs that she had administered.

As Cayuga opened the outer office door, it occurred to him that Barker's death might also be the key to the Lola Belman problem. What could be more natural than a haldane overcome with grief for the accidental death of a patient by a psychotropic drug overdose? Who would question it if she, living on the brink of insanity as the profession was obliged to do, was unable to handle that death?

With a little help from her drug supplies, Lola Belman's "suicide" would make perfect sense.

Spook always exaggerated. He had been doing it as a matter of principle since he was three years old, and Lola felt sure that he was doing it now. All the way to the place where Bat lived, along labyrinthine tunnels and across grungy fields of moth-eaten plants of a type that Lola had never seen before, Spook mumbled and muttered about how *nobody* just dropped in at the Bat Cave.

"But you've been there before," Lola objected. "When you came back, you talked my ear off about it."

"Maybe I have, and maybe I did." Spook glanced around to make sure that no one was watching them—a pretty useless act, in Lola's opinion, since no one who could avoid it would go anywhere near a hemispherical chamber that reeked of ammonia and untreated sewage. He led them down a broad ramp to yet another agricultural level. At least this one was hydroponic, and the produce looked clean and edible.

"You should have let me call him before we left," Spook grumbled, "or while we're on the way. He'll fry us."

"We had to get out of there—and I have to get back as soon as I can. All I want to do is drop you off, explain to Bat what's been happening, and leave."

Spook's silence was itself an answer. She had already explained to him about Jinx Barker and his attempt on her life, and what he had told her about Alicia Rios. It had not been well received. "And for this nonsense, you dragged me out of bed," Spook said when she finished. "Good luck when you try it on Bat."

Lola stared around her as the ramp they were walking on doubled back on itself in another three-hundred-and-sixty-degree turn. She added an item to her list of worries: She had to get back while Jinx Barker was still fully sedated, but it wasn't going to be easy to find her way. Bat apparently chose to make his home in the middle of a maze.

"For God's sake, Spook, how much farther?"

"Hey, it was your idea to come, not mine. But we're nearly there—see the door, right at the end of this corridor?"

Bat's idea of reasonable illumination did not match Lola's. As they left the bright lights of the corridor, she stumbled along behind Spook into a long and dim-lit room littered with what seemed to be random pieces of old junk. Apparently this was the fabulous Bat Cave that had so impressed Spook. She might have known. She saw no sign of Bat, and it would have been easy to believe that the whole place was empty, had it not been for the tantalizing smell of cooking that came wafting down the room to greet them. At the far end she saw a tall, black partition that ran across almost the whole width of the room. Spook made his way toward it, with Lola close behind. He peeked uneasily around the edge.

"Bat? It's me, Spook. My sister is with me."

Lola heard a grampus snort of outrage or disbelief, and then an irate voice: "This is quite inexcusable. You have violated my trust and my private sanctum. Do you wonder why I am so reluctant to divulge its location to others?"

Bat was not amused. But apparently he was at least wearing clothes, because Spook with the hand on Lola's side of the partition was beckoning her forward.

"Don't blame him," she said. "Blame me. I made him bring me." Lola, rounding the partition, saw a black apparition rising from a great padded seat. It was Bat, swathed in black robes and swollen with indignation to what seemed like twice his usual size. Or had he always been that big? Behind him a complete kitchen covered the whole of the end wall, its orderly layout in contrast to the chaos that filled the rest of the Bat Cave. Beside Bat's chair stood the most complicated communications center that Lola had ever seen, with whole panels labeled "Outer System Transport," "Local Travel," "Belt Travel," and "Inner System Connections."

"What I am going to ask you now is very important." She rattled out the words, before Bat could reach explosion point. "You met Jinx Barker. Did you ever reveal to him the location of this place?"

The question was curious enough to distract Bat's anger temporarily from their uninvited arrival. He peered at Lola from within the cowl of his robe and stood thinking hard for several seconds. At last he shook his great round head. "I met Jinx Barker three times, each of them a brief encounter, I am sure that I did not hint in any way at the location of the Bat Cave."

"Good." Lola sat down uninvited on another chair that swallowed her up in its depths. "That means we don't have to run for it right this minute."

Bat glared at her, but he gradually sank back into his own padded seat. "Since you are not a Puzzle Network member," he said, "and you do not therefore prize paradox for its own sake, I accept your statement at face value. However, I suggest that an explanation is in order."

"That's why I'm here." Lola sighed, and suddenly felt faint from hunger. She glanced across to the long stove, where three black pots simmered over a low heat. She had eaten nothing since her dinner with Jinx Barker—how long ago was that? A lifetime and a half, from the feel of it. "Do you suppose . . ."

Bat had seen her starved and longing look. It aroused his deepest sympathies. He rose and went across to the kitchen counter. "If you can eat and talk simultaneously, I can certainly eat and listen. You are most fortunate. This is my special five-cheese fondue."

"Do you have enough?" Lola saw Bat's reproving expression. "I guess you do. Yes, I can eat and talk at the same time. It will take a while to tell you everything."

"Leave out nothing." Bat brought over a low table, placed a bubbling black pot where all three of them could reach it, and gestured to Lola to help herself. "Nothing," he repeated. ";Remember, the details matter."

Lola nodded. She took a first mouthful, burned her tongue, and began to talk. It was the third time she was telling it, and she could finally distance herself a little from what she was saying. The shock of seeing a tender lover turn murderer had not faded, but now she could see how easy she had made things for Jinx Barker. With anyone else she would have asked questions. At the very least she would have made sure that she could be reached in case of emergency, before diving two thousand kilometers—for *dinner,* no less—into Ganymede's unknown interior. She had been lucky. Like Jonah, she had been into The Belly of the Whale and returned to talk about it.

Bat asked only two questions and made one comment. "You are sure of the name, Jeffrey Cayuga, for the man who supposedly gave instructions to Alicia Rios?"

"Yes. Do you know him?"

Bat shook his head. "Who was the other man, the one who talked to Alicia Rios at the First Family party?"

She ought to know that. But after a day and a half without sleep her brain could not produce a name. "He was descended from someone on the first Saturn expedition," she said. "I'm sure of that. I'll try to remember his name later."

"Do so." Bat spoke as though he were her senior and she was the teenager. Lola swallowed her exasperation. She had not yet told him that she wanted Spook to stay in the Bat Cave until she was sure of their safety.

"It seems clear that Bryce Sonnenberg is somehow at the heart of this," Bat went on, "since there is otherwise no logical reason for killing both of you. And, as Spook and I have discovered, Sonnenberg is himself an abundant source of mystery. He is not what he seems. His stated background and his recorded background do not match. Although I am beginning to have suspicions, they still lack coherence."

He subsided thoughtfully into his chair, a great mass of flesh and swaddling clothing. One of the pots had been emptied, and a second was down to the sticky residue at the bottom. Lola had eaten too much, and now she was feeling an overwhelming weariness. She told herself that she had to leave the Bat Cave in the next ten minutes, or fall asleep on the spot.

She stood up. "I have to get back home." She realized that it wasn't just weariness. She was afraid to return to her office, afraid of Jinx Barker, even when he was tightly bound. *If* he was tightly bound. "He ought to stay unconscious for another three or four hours, but I dare not risk that. If once he wakes up, I know he'll find a way to free himself."

"I am forced to agree with you." Bat was nodding. His face behind the hood of his robe seemed almost pleased. Lola had presented him with a new puzzle. "Barker awake presents a threat," he continued. "You must return to him before that threat can materialize. Meanwhile, there is work to be done here. The central banks should certainly contain information concerning Jeffrey Cayuga. Also, we must trace the name of every descendant of every member of the original Saturn expedition."

We must trace the name. He must be including Spook, rather than insisting that her brother leave with her. Lola was around the black partition before he could change his mind. She poked her head back just long enough to croak, "Thanks for the food, you're a great cook," and hurried toward the front of the Bat Cave. With her eyes adjusted to the low lighting level, she could pick her way more easily across the crowded floor, but the battered equipment and cabinets seemed no less like old junk.

War relics, said her exhausted brain. Like Spook, Bat

was obsessed with the awful war. Maybe that was a good thing. Who was it—Santayana?—who said that if you didn't remember the past, you would have to repeat it. Unfortunately, that told only half the story. When you dealt with humans, it seemed that even if you *did* remember the past, you still had to repeat it. How many "Great Wars" had there been, wars that for a few years were supposed to end all wars? And even if all-out war one day became a matter of history, there would still be the Jinx Barkers, the professional assassins. Death was no less final whether you died alone or at the same time as nine billion others.

Lola's return was a dream journey—hurrying along dimly remembered corridors, ascending hundreds of meters in high-speed lift chutes, hesitating before making a choice of a transit slideway. She needed to get there as fast as she could, but at the same time she was dreading the thought of her arrival. She had to turn Jinx Barker over to Ganymede Security, but what if they did not believe her? What had he *done,* that she could actually prove? Nothing criminal. Shown personal interest. Made love to her. Taken her out to dinner. He could claim to be the one with the right to complain. She had bound him mentally and physically, drugged him and questioned him, and then left him tied up for hours.

They would let him go. What they might do to her was another matter.

By the time that she arrived at the final corridor her stomach was tight with tension. Rather than going directly into her office she went along to the next entrance and into her apartment. The interconnecting office door was closed, and she tiptoed along to it and stood listening. She heard not a sound. Jinx Barker must still be unconscious.

The door opened away from her. She eased it open, inch by inch, and stepped inside. Barker ought to be exactly where she had left him, on the reclining chair at the other side of her desk.

She took one pace into the room, craning her neck to look for him. As she cleared the doorway, she was grabbed from behind. Before she could cry out, a hand came up to cover her mouth. She was pulled back hard into the space behind the open door.

20

Lola felt again the terror of a strong hand gripping her by the neck. She kicked backward and heard a grunt of pain.

"Ooh!" said a pained voice in her ear. She was turned—hard—and found herself staring into Bryce Sonnenberg's startled face. He took his hand away from her mouth. "Keep quiet. I didn't know who you were when I grabbed you, or I wouldn't have been so rough. Look at that."

He turned her again, this time toward her desk. Beyond it she saw Jinx Barker, exactly as he had been when she left him. She breathed a huge sigh of relief.

"Good, he's still there. My God, but you frightened me."

"You should be frightened." He took her by the arm and walked her forward to stand by the reclining chair. "Did you do this to him?"

"Do what?" And then she saw it. Barker looked different. His eyes bulged beneath half-open lids, and his face was livid. He did not seem to be breathing. "I didn't mean to—the drugs I gave him, the doses were the same—"

"Not drugs." Bryce Sonnenberg looked different, too. The puzzled young man who had walked into her office a few weeks ago had gone. The replacement was older, tougher, and far more knowing.

"He's dead but he didn't die of drugs," he went on. "He died of asphyxiation. Somebody suffocated him while he lay there."

"Were you here when it happened?"

"No. I arrived ten minutes ago. He was like this when I walked in."

"Then how do you know?"

"Trust me. I've seen this sort of thing before." Bryce did not explain, but walked them steadily toward the door. It was just as well that he kept his grip on her, because Lola's legs wanted to buckle.

"Somebody came and killed him." She felt dazed. "I didn't kill him. Yesterday he tried to kill me. It makes no sense."

"It makes excellent sense." They were at the door of the outer office and Bryce pointed to the lock, where a thin line had been burned through the metal. "That's how they got in. You are seeing somebody covering their tracks. Jinx Barker was hired to kill you by Alicia Rios, but he failed to do it. So he was killed himself. And she has been killed, too, and all her records destroyed. You and I are still in danger. The difference is that now we have no idea where the attack might come from. Until we know that, we can't possibly stay here. They could return any minute." He glanced along the corridor in both directions. "We seem to be all right for the moment. Where's Spook?"

"He's safe."

"Then let's go."

"I can't just leave here. Jinx Barker—and my patients—"

"You know how to reach them. Tell them you won't be able to treat them for a while. Give them the name of another haldane if you have to. But don't do any of that here and now—do it when we reach a safe place. Same with Jinx Barker. We don't call Security until we have a place to hide."

"Your apartment?"

"Definitely not. Remember, I was on Jinx Barker's list as well as you."

"Where, then?"

"I don't know." They had reached the end of the hallway and he turned for a last look back along the corridor. "Still seems quiet. We'll have to do a few double loops in case they use some fancy tracking gear, but we'll start that when we're a bit farther away. The big question is, Where do we go?"

Lola sighed. As the new adrenaline drained out of her she was ready to fall apart. The idea of combing Ganymede for another safe haven was quite beyond her.

"I know a place," she said. "Just don't expect the welcome mat to spread out for you when we get there."

Bat did not kick and scream and throw a fit. It was not his way. He simply looked at Bryce, then glared at Lola in stony accusation.

"As before," he said, "I suggest that an explanation is in order."

It was, but Lola didn't have the strength to provide it. She was at the absolute end of her tether. She had lost track of how long it had been since she had slept. She waved toward Bryce, slumped down into one of the Bat Cave's enormous easy chairs, and closed her eyes. Whatever had to be done would be done without her.

She was vaguely aware of Bryce Sonnenberg talking, with Bat and Spook listening and asking occasional questions. Something that Bryce had said to her earlier registered for the first time. He was convinced that Alicia Rios was dead, and that she had been murdered.

"Which brings us to Jeffrey Cayuga," said Bat. That name brought Lola to partial awareness. "After Spook arrived here, the two of us searched the data banks. Jeffrey Cayuga is in there as an entry. He is also dead."

"Cayuga, too?" Bryce Sonnenberg perched himself on

the edge of Lola's chair. "That's it, then. Every single lead we had is gone."

"But Cayuga didn't die in the last few hours," Spook added. Lola recognized that tone of voice. It was wobbly and in danger of cracking—not with fear, but with excitement.

"He's not like Jinx Barker or the Rios woman," Spook continued, "because he died weeks ago—that's why the death's already reported in the bank. See what it says."

He called for a stored file, and the brief announcement rolled into the display: *The death was reported today of Jeffrey Cayuga, leader of the fifth, sixth, and seventh Saturn expeditions* . . .

Bryce pointed to the end of the message. "What about the nephew they mention, Joss Cayuga?"

"Most unpromising," said Bat. "For one thing, he is much younger than all the other individuals we have so far encountered in this matter. For another, he is apparently a recent arrival in the Jovian system. According to the record, he was born in the Belt, was fortunate enough to survive the war, and shipped out to join the most recent Saturn expedition less than two months ago."

"So that's it. The story's over, except for one thing." Bryce pointed to Lola, completely asleep now in the chair next to him. "Someone is still out to get her and to get me. We don't know who, and we have no idea how to stop them. And I don't see why *that's* anything to look pleased about."

"My apologies." Bat did his best to appear contrite. "I am not at all unsympathetic to your plight, even if I appear to be. However, you must understand that this has all the ingredients of a complex and fascinating puzzle. One that can surely be solved, given a little more information. And might I suggest that some of that information is contained *there?"* He pointed a pudgy finger. "Right there, with an individual named Bryce Sonnenberg, who may originally have been completely honest with Lola Belman, and even with himself, but who has recently, I am now convinced, become rather less so."

"It was never good odds, you see," Bryce said, "but it was a whole lot better than no odds at all." He, Bat, and Spook had moved to a dark corner of the Bat Cave, leaving Lola to sleep where she sat. Bryce was leaning over a battered piece of metal, which had originally formed a broad, flat hoop with hundreds of tiny filaments on its top edge. "Yeah, you're quite right. This is part of one, same thing as I had."

"A brain-coring experiment?" Bat sank for a moment into his own personal war nightmare, of lumbering, sightless men and women and isolated, cored brains.

"Not like you're thinking." Bryce was rubbing his fingers thoughtfully over the tangle of thin neural filaments. "You've probably heard stories from the war-tribunal hearings, and that sort of thing did go on in some of the Belt labs. Pretty gruesome. But there was another side of it, straight commercial. If you had money—and I had plenty—you could take out a sort of life insurance. If you died with your brain intact and well preserved, it would be hustled into ultra-cold storage, and assuming they had a donor available in the Belt, you'd wake up—if you were lucky—in a new body."

"Bryce Sonnenberg," said Spook. "Died on Hidalgo of a brain hemorrhage. Natural causes, seven years ago."

"Which is a relief to me." Bryce put his hand up to his head. "I never asked, but I did sometimes wonder when I first woke up if he had been, how shall I put it, 'helped along' on the way to becoming my body-transplant donor. I'd made my plans soon after I escaped from Earth to Mars, but of course I never had any idea when I might require the service. So there was no way to make sure a donor would be available if I needed one."

"The memories that the haldane treatment tapped." Bat pointed in the direction of the sleeping Lola. "The casino, and the submersible, and the dark-haired young woman— they were of your life on Earth?"

"Those ones were. That was Danny Clay's life—my life. Being starved and beat up as a young kid is Danny, too. Dying on Mars, though—that was Julius Szabo." Bryce shook his head in a puzzled way. "Something else about Julius, before the fall. But I can't quite get to it. It's strange, bits and pieces of memory drift back in and I have no control of when or what. I guess Danny's me, and Julius is me, and I'm me, but I feel like we're still sorting out the territory. I don't know who I am any more. It didn't mention anything like this when I bought the policy."

"I am not surprised," Bat said. "It seldom does. I suspect, however, that there was a statute of limitations. You are unlikely to be eligible for a refund."

Bryce stared at Bat, not quite sure that he was joking. "That's one way to put it. But I can't blame the group that did the transplant, unless you can also prove they started the whole damn war. They told me the ground rules up front. If I got zapped on Mars but my brain came through in one piece, I'd be popped into a donor. But that would be just the beginning. No point in sitting inside a body you can't control, and nerve tissue is tricky stuff. It can be regrown with the right hormones, but it's a slow job and a delicate one. I was warned, there would be a five-year period of treatment and convalescence before I was back to normal, even if things went exactly right."

"And long before that, the war began between the Belt and the Inner System."

"Right. I'd been there only a couple of years. So I was screwed. Or I was superlucky, depending on how you look at it. Most of the other people in the transplant center with me had been there just a few months. Their brains and bodies had hardly made contact. Me, I guess I managed to get to the surface and onto one of the escape ships when Hidalgo was hit, but when I was done my lungs were ruined and my brain wasn't fit to make cabbage soup. I was sent to a place on Callisto."

"The Isobel Busby Sanctuary for War Victims," said Spook. "I went there, but they wouldn't let me in."

"That right?" Bryce stared at him in surprise. "Well, you did better than I did. They wouldn't let me *out.* And the whole place was packed with madmen. I know, because I was one of them. The staff did their best, but of course they had no idea what had happened to me—nor did I. They regrew my lungs, and they regrew my hair and toes, and they treated me for 'war psychosis,' whatever that is. But they didn't have the neural feedback equipment I needed, so for the first couple of years I got worse and worse. I only began to get better when they gave up on the treatment and left me alone. After I could walk and talk and stopped wetting my pants, they wired me up and gave me the best set of planted memories that they could conjure up from my records. Three years of that, and I knew who I was again. Of course, most of my memories were bogus, but that didn't matter as long as there was no competition inside my head. I was released, thought I knew who I was, started to live my life—and then things really went to hell. I began to get *real* memories. That's when I came to Lola and she started picking my brain apart." He stared thoughtfully back toward the partition. "She's a sexy young woman, you know. No wonder Jinx Barker liked his assignment." He saw Spook's expression, and added hastily, "The first part of it, I mean."

"She's older than you are!"

"Depends how you count. Older than Bryce Sonnenberg, a quarter of a century younger than Danny Clay. Over half a century younger than Julius Szabo's official age. But I don't see what age has to do with anything."

"She's my sister!"

"Most women are somebody's sister. All right, all right." Bryce held up his hands. "Don't get excited. I've got no designs on Lola. She and I have other more urgent things to worry about—like staying alive."

Bat had been listening to these exchanges with disgust. From his expression, it seemed that people who thought like the new Bryce Sonnenberg were hardly worth keeping alive. "In order to remain among the living," he said, "it is necessary that you learn exactly who is seeking to kill you, and why."

"Right. And we just agreed that we came to a dead end there. We have zero clues."

"Not at all. We have numerous clues. It is only a matter of pursuing them, and constructing a rational whole from what we learn." Bat sighed. Something else was becoming apparent to him. As long as the lives of Lola Belman and Bryce Sonnenberg were threatened, he could hardly expel his uninvited guests from the sanctuary of the Bat Cave—much as he might wish to do so.

"Rest, if you wish," he said. "For my part, I propose to initiate my investigations at once."

There was no point in mentioning that his own desire for a swift resolution exceeded anything that Lola or Bryce could possibly be feeling.

Five hours later the Bat Cave was still and silent. Its solid outer door was secured, its security system active. There was no safer place on Ganymede.

Lola lay curled up in the same chair, dead to the world. Bryce Sonnenberg had watched Spook and Bat for a quarter of an hour, then shook his head and stretched out on the kitchen floor. He fell asleep in a couple of minutes. For someone who had seen violent death twice in the past twenty-four hours, and who was threatened with it himself, he seemed remarkably relaxed.

Spook had worked at Bat's side for the first four hours,

until he at last yawned, said, "Wake me when it's my shift," and wandered off along the darkened Bat Cave to seek a soft place to sleep.

Bat struggled on alone, with grim concentration. All very well for Spook to snore away the rest of the night—it wasn't *his* home that had been invaded.

Progress was slow. Bat told himself that the puzzle he faced could not be nearly as complicated as some of the transportation problems that he had solved, involving, as they did, interlocked ship schedules, moving destinations, time constraints, and even the reprograming of pilotless cargo vessels that had been designed to resist all outside interference by cargo hijackers. The difference was that in this case his objective was harder to define. The obvious goal—save the people with him in the Bat Cave—felt like an incidental to the real problem.

He had been sorting questions and answers mentally, but now he felt that he needed to see them sitting in front of him. He made a list.

Who wants Bryce Sonnenberg and Lola Belman out of the way? Answer: some group or individual who believes that the two know something dangerous or damaging. It was irrelevant whether or not they did know such a thing. However, it did point out the ruthless nature of the people that Bat had to find. They were quite willing to kill on the basis of suspicion.

Why had Jinx Barker and Alicia Rios been killed? This time the answer was easy. Bat agreed with Bryce Sonnenberg: Barker and Rios had been killed to close off a trail that might lead to someone else. That suggested that whoever hired Barker and Rios did not have total trust in them. Also, that the secret being protected was so important that many lives would be sacrificed to keep it.

Did the death of Jeffrey Cayuga have anything to do with the present mystery? Bat had no answer. He collected everything that he could find about Jeffrey Cayuga from the general data banks and merged them into a file of their own.

Who else might have been involved? The only information available to Bat was a vague statement made by Lola Belman that the other man who had talked to Alicia Rios at the First Family party "was related to someone on the first Saturn expedition." Maybe she would remember his name, maybe she would not. But there was one sure way to jog her memory: Bat could present her with a list to choose from. Obtaining that list might prove tedious, but he was used to tasks that called for infinite patience. And in this case he had his special helpers.

Bat summoned *Mellifera* once more from his private directory. This time the instructions provided for the program area had to be more complex. He was not interested in the route to a particular destination, as he had been with the Hidalgo data base. Instead, he wanted to know the complete list of descendants of each member of the original Saturn expedition. He also needed to know whether each of them was now living or dead. Bat decided that this time five hundred copies of the completed version of Mellifera should be more than sufficient. He provided a different entry point for each one into the general Ganymede data banks and released them all into the network.

He expected a long delay before he had feedback. The original expedition had started from Earth, over forty years ago. In that time the descendants of the crew members were likely to have scattered all over the system. If they had stayed on Earth, or moved to the Belt, their fates might be unknown. He had to face the possibility of making another exploration of incomplete or inaccessible data bases.

He was rising from his chair—his mouth filled with naturally salted pistachios from the halophytic-plant farm two levels down from the Bat Cave—when the attention light flashed on his console. He sat down again, anticipating trouble. When a Mellifera probe returned so quickly, it was usually the sign that it had encountered an immediate dead end to the search.

It was even worse than he had feared. *All* the probes had returned, and all reported the same information. The data banks indicated that there were no living direct descendants of *any* of the original Saturn expedition members.

Bat realized that he had made an assumption, and apparently an invalid one. Lola Belman had said she saw a man "related to" someone on the first Saturn expedition. Bat had wrongly interpreted that to mean "descended from."

It would be easy, though tedious, to cast his net wider. Bat could first invert the direction of the search, ascending the family trees to seek out the parents, grandparents, and even great-grandparents of the members of the first expedition. Then he could reverse the process, descending the family trees and asking for all living descendants of each ancestor. There were two problems with that. How far back would he need to go? And how many people were likely to be on the final list?

He could calculate a plausible answer to the second question if he made a couple of assumptions. First, assume that it would be enough to go back as far as grandparents. There had been ten people on the first expedition, which would mean that there were twenty pairs of grandparents. Now, assume two children per generation, and four generations to bring you to the present day. If all those fourth-generation children were still alive, Bat could expect to see a hundred and sixty names of people who were related to the original expedition members, but not descended from them.

He could do all that, probably without much difficulty, and maybe the answer would allow Lola Belman to pick out the right name when she awoke. But Bat had worked the Puzzle Network too long to ignore minor anomalies. One of them was staring him in the face.

He returned to the information gathered by Mellifera. The probes insisted that no member of the original expedition had a living descendant. That was certainly possible, and a computer would have had no problem with it. But a human is a strange amalgam of logic and illogic, where hunches from the subconscious guide and warn conscious thought processes. Bat knew the answer he had received was possible; but it seemed somehow implausible.

He again summoned Mellifera. This time the probes went into the Ganymede data banks with a different mission: to report any known liaisons of the first expedition members, and any descendants—living or dead.

The answer, when it came, was worse than the last one. According to the data banks, no member of the first expedition had ever engaged in a long-term liaison. None had ever been the mother or the father of a child.

Implausibility was approaching impossibility. Lola Belman had seen a man "related to a member of the first expedition." Related *how?*

Bat moved away from the communications center and sought the darkest corner of the Bat Cave. He was disappointed—with himself. It was obvious that he had been delivered a fact profoundly relevant to the deaths of Jinx Barker and Alicia Rios and to the lives of Lola Belman and Bryce Sonnenberg. It was equally obvious that Bat did not understand what he had been told. The reason for his data-bank search was not really a quest for *facts;* it was for *insight.* And that insight was sadly lacking.

Bat sat alone and sleepless, through the small hours of the night, waiting for the still, small voice of enlightenment to whisper in his ear.

21

Lola woke up groggy and uneasy. It took her a few seconds to realize where she was, and to decide that she had every right to feel worried. Even the depths of the Bat Cave provided uncertain security.

She was still where she had fallen asleep, but someone had come along and thrown a thick blanket over her body and her feet, which hung over the edge of the chair. She didn't remember kicking off her shoes, but she was now barefoot.

She pushed back the cover and leaned over to scrabble on the floor, working by touch more than by sight. Once she had her shoes on, she couldn't justify lying down again. She rubbed her eyes, looked around, and saw no signs of anyone.

And no wonder. She glanced at the clock on the long kitchen range and saw that she had snored away the whole night and half the morning. Over by the communications center the display was frozen and a red attention light was blinking. She went across to it. The message said:

To Lola Belman: Spook and Bryce Sonnenberg both rose earlier than I, and they have gone off somewhere together. I, too, have occasion to be absent. I offer my apolo-

gies for providing nothing more than the food-service ma-
chine can offer. On another matter, would you kindly pe-
ruse the list that follows, and determine if any of the names
listed therein correspond to persons reported by Jinx
Barker as having been present at the First Family party
that you attended. Signed: Rustum Battachariya (land-
lord).

The last word wasn't much of a joke, but Lola was surprised to see it there at all. She, more than anyone else, recognized Bat's desire—better call it a compulsion—for
privacy. Count it as one more reason why she had to find
out who was pursuing her and liberate them all from the
Bat Cave.

The list of names, then— as soon as two more urgent
items had been taken care of. Lola used the bathroom and
found it amazingly neat and clean, considering Bat's
slovenly dress and apparent lack of interest in bathing.
She would have to have a word with Spook. Let him loose
in there for half an hour, and Bat would throw them out
and damn the consequences.

She went back to the kitchen and studied the autochef.
It was a top-of-the-line model, new to her and able to produce food that was not merely adequate but better than
what most human cooks could manage. Apparently Bat
was a real gourmet. On the other hand, you didn't get that
fat without being a pig as well. Lola itched to lure him into
the haldane's chair, then scolded herself. It was her job to
treat people whose problems were making them or others
unhappy. There was no sign that Bat was guilty of either
sin.

In other circumstances she would have had fun testing
the limits of the autochef, but today had higher priorities.
She filled a bowl with sliced fruit, smothered it with cream
and honey, and did what she had told Spook never to do
again: She set it down on the communications-center console and started to spoon sticky food into her mouth as she

examined the list that Bat had left her. The astonishing thing was that nervousness and stress and fear of deadly attack didn't destroy the desire to eat. It seemed, in her case at least, to increase it.

There were scores of names on the list. Unfortunately there was a high degree of similarity among many of them. She counted twenty-one Dahlquists, twenty Cayugas, eighteen Jing-lis, fourteen Rioses, eleven Munzers, eight Costases, and six Polks. After a long time, enough for her to empty the bowl and go back for another helping, she tagged two of the names: Lenny Costas and Ignatz Dahlquist. She added a note: *I'm not absolutely sure, but these two seem right. Can you obtain a physical description of them? I remember what they looked like.*

At that point she seemed to be at a loose end. For all her sense of urgency she had no idea of what to do next. She studied Bat's communications center for a few minutes, marveling at its complexity. He seemed to have a computer contact point in every transportation center and every ship throughout the whole Jovian system. He might never travel himself and might shudder at the thought, but he had his inorganic eyes, ears, and hands everywhere. There was no sign saying, "This is an illegal operation," but Lola was sure that Bat paid little attention to anyone's right to privacy, except his own. If he wanted to, he could have tapped her patient-data files. Maybe he had. More likely, the tampering that she had detected there had been part of Jinx Barker's efforts.

Jinx Barker. Lola sighed and did what she had not been able to face doing the previous day. She chose a message mode that could not be traced back to its origin and sent a terse note to Ganymede Security. The body of a man, Jinx Barker, would be found in the office of the haldane, Lola Belman. She provided location coordinates.

Her action made Lola's own position worse. She knew Security would go to her office at once, with a full investigating team of humans and machines. The presence of haldane drugs in Barker's body would be determined within minutes, together with the cause of death. Her own absence would suggest her guilt to them. Then the mystery employer of Jinx Barker would not be the only one interested in finding Lola. She would become a fugitive from the Ganymede government, wanted at the very least for questioning. Security had some very fancy tracking methods. There was no reason why they would keep this location a secret if they found it, so her presence in the Bat Cave endangered all the others.

She was keenly aware of her own feelings of guilt toward the other three in the Bat Cave. Jinx Barker and his employers had really been after *her*, with anyone else regarded as secondary. More than ever, she had to find out who wanted her dead, and why. And she had to get away from the Bat Cave.

She saw on one of the communication center's other units, over to her left, a fixed display. It was something she remembered vaguely that Bat had been talking about last night when she was right at the point of passing out: *The death was reported today of Jeffrey Cayuga, leader of the fifth, sixth, and seventh Saturn expeditions . . .*

That's right. Jeffrey Cayuga was dead, too, and with him went their last real lead. Lola stared hard at the final sentence of the display: *His heir is his nephew, Joss Cayuga, who is one of the few survivors of the Ceres final battle and recently arrived in the Jovian system from his home in the Belt.*

Since Joss Cayuga had inherited his uncle's estate, he also presumably had all Jeffrey Cayuga's records. Alicia Rios's files had been destroyed, but if Cayuga's were intact, they might hold the key to everything that had been going on.

Joss Cayuga had made his home in the Belt, but that was before his uncle's death. Where had Jeffrey Cayuga lived?

As a leader of Saturn expeditions, there was a good chance that he had chosen the Jovian system, perhaps even Ganymede.

Lola consulted the general data banks, not knowing she was covering ground that Bat had explored less than twelve hours ago. She had an answer inside two minutes. Jeffrey Cayuga was there all right, and was correctly identified as the late Saturn explorer. He had lived, as she hoped, in the Jovian system—but he had lived on *Lysithea*.

Lola sagged in disappointment. Lysithea was certainly in the Jovian system, *technically*. In practice, no one paid much attention to anything but the four biggest moons. Io, Europa, Ganymede, and Callisto had been known and named since the original discovery of the telescope. She had seen them herself with Spook's little refractor, back when the two of them still lived on Earth. The dozen small fragments of rock and ice that orbited closer than Io or beyond Callisto were another matter. They had been discovered and catalogued in the nineteenth and twentieth centuries, but no one had taken much notice of them, then or since. Lysithea was one of those insignificant miniworlds, along with Elara and Himalia and Pasiphaë and Sinope. Lola didn't know how big Lysithea was, or how far out, except that it was a long way from Ganymede. It was news to her that anyone made a home there.

She performed a quick check. The population file indicated that Jeffrey Cayuga had been Lysithea's only inhabitant. It must have been a strange life, alone on a world, but there was no accounting for personal tastes. Bat would probably like it just fine. Lysithea's average distance from Ganymede was close to eleven million kilometers—a good day's journey each way in a medium-performance ship. There was no guarantee that if she went there, the late Jeffrey Cayuga's files would tell her anything.

On the other hand, she was learning nothing here, and there was a lot to be said for being far from Ganymede for

the next few days. On far-off Lysithea she would be safe
from pursuers and would-be government questioners alike.

Lola hesitated for a few seconds before she took the next
step. Two questions still had to be answered: Was Joss
Cayuga on Lysithea? And if he were, would he allow her
to fly out there and review his uncle's records?

She could see no point in waiting. Lola again chose a
message mode that would not reveal her location and asked
for a connection with Joss Cayuga—wherever he might be.

Spook and Bryce Sonnenberg had awakened at about the
same time, while the other two in the Bat Cave were still
asleep. Bat was a great, snoring mound of black sheets on
a bed three times normal size, and Lola was curled up in
her chair. Spook threw a cover over his sister, then by un-
spoken consent he and Bryce tiptoed around until the autochef produced their selections.

Bryce picked up a filled mug and a covered dish and
raised his eyebrows at Spook. "Outside?" he whispered.
"We can talk better there without disturbing them."

Spook nodded. He went out of the Bat Cave with his
own loaded tray and led Bryce along the corridor. The
nearest place to sit down was on the next level up. The
scenery there wasn't the greatest, rows and rows of giant
fungi covered with grey warts, but if Bryce didn't mind
looking at them, Spook could certainly stand it—so long
as he wasn't asked to eat them, or wasn't told that he had
been eating them already.

They sat side by side in silence for a few minutes. Spook
was desperately keen to talk to Bryce, but he didn't know
how to start. A few days ago Spook thought he understood
him, one of Lola's patients not all that much older than
himself and troubled by horrible nightmares. Now Sonnenberg had become a tough, wary man, who according
to his own confusing words was either twenty-five or fifty
years older than he looked.

Spook wasn't frightened by that. In some strange way the new Sonnenberg made Spook feel more secure. But casual chatting was not easy.

"You were really there?" he said at last. "You spent all those years on Earth."

"I think I was. Odd as it sounds."

"And you remember it all?"

"Better than what happened afterwards." Bryce grimaced and tapped his forehead. "I'm getting things back, bits and pieces, but there are holes. I'm still fishing hard for a particular one."

"But all those Earth memories, about you being in a gambling place—those are true?"

That produced a glance at Spook and a raised eyebrow. "You are referring to what are supposed to be secret haldane files. You've been into them? Don't bother to answer that, because it doesn't matter. Yes, I was the boss of the biggest casino on the North American continent for more than twenty years."

"It sounds great. Really exciting."

"No. Sometimes scary, more often boring." But Bryce's tone didn't match his words.

"I wish I could go to Earth."

"Nothing to stop you, in a few more years." Bryce didn't mind the way that the conversation was going. He wanted Spook relaxed and rational, and you couldn't be either if you were thinking every minute that someone was coming along to kill you. "You mean go to Earth as a visitor?"

"I want to go back to where we used to live. I want to make sure that my parents are really dead."

"I hope my adopted ones are. I guess yours didn't find neat uses for belts and basements. Were they living in the Northern Hemisphere?"

"Yes."

Sonnenberg shrugged. "Then you know the odds as well as I do. Seven and a half billion people north of the equator before the war; eighteen thousand after it—and all those in deep shelters. I don't think you ought to go to Earth for more than a short visit."

"I can take it, no matter how bad the damage is."

"I'm not thinking of that. Earth may be only half alive, but the Southern Hemisphere is booming. No, I think you'd be bored more than horrified. Earth isn't where the action is any more. My advice to you is to head farther out in the system and live fast and hard while you're young. When you get older you want things, but not as urgently."

"You mean like you with Lola?"

"That still bugging you? I wasn't thinking of that, but it's not a bad example. I said she was attractive, and she is. When I was young—really young, I mean, and not an old brain sitting in a young body—there'd have been no stopping me."

"Do you find her less attractive now?"

"No. It's just that things get more *complicated* as you grow older. You can see reasons for doing things, and not doing things, that just don't occur to you when you're young. I tell myself that 'older' means 'smarter.' I try to look before I leap."

"You don't seem to think much of young people."

"Not at all. I think it's just self-preservation on my part. If old people went at things the way young people do, they'd drop dead the first day. Not a bad way to go, mind you, if you're doing certain things."

Bryce had moved the conversation almost to where he wanted it. "If you get in a really difficult situation," he went on, "I believe that the best possible combination is two people, one old and one young. The young one says, 'Hey, this is new and neat and it ought to work.' The old one says,

'Well, yes, it might work—but here's three ways it could kill you.' "

"I don't see how you and Lola could get into a much worse fix than you are in now."

"Could be." Bryce did not voice his immediate thought: *Not just me and Lola. You and Bat, too, if I'm any judge.*

"But if you're right," Spook said, "then the two of us ought to be able to figure out what's happening."

"I don't believe this is a figure-it-out situation. It's not like one of your Puzzle Network problems, where it seems as though you don't have enough information but you know that you really do, because whoever set the puzzle *designed* it that way. Here, you have to decide what's missing. Then you probably have to go and get it—and I don't mean from the data banks. If they had enough for an answer, Bat would have found it."

"Give him time. When I left him last night he was still digging."

"Which is good. But there are other ways to operate when you have to tackle the real world."

"Like what?"

"You are the one who is supposed to tell me that. I'm the old man who says why it can't work, why we might get blown away trying. I also saw too many things first-hand, like the shadow of Alicia Rios burned into her own chair, or Jinx Barker smothered where he lay. You might think that would help, but it doesn't."

"Like me when I fight with Lola. I can't be *objective,* and that really gets to me."

"But you can be objective about this. You're rested and fed; it ought to be prime thinking time for you. Review everything unusual that you've seen and heard for the past couple of months, and tell me what we've missed. How do we find a way to whoever killed Jinx Barker and Alicia Rios?"

Bryce was not being completely open with Spook. Nor

was he lying to him. He had an idea, and he wanted to see if Spook came to the same conclusion.

Spook was frowning. "Including you, and your own arrival on Ganymede, among the unusual things?"

"Definitely. Do not exclude anything."

"All right. Everything was quiet until you arrived. Jinx Barker showed up *after* you started haldane treatment, and he wanted to kill you and Lola. It seems to me that everything started with you, even though you say it didn't."

"I didn't quite say that. I said if it did start with me, I don't know how or why."

"But it can't be just you, because you lived for years on Callisto, with no one trying to kill you."

"Right. Except maybe myself—space-scooter racing can be pretty close to suicide."

"Doesn't count." Spook sat staring off into space, the grey fields in front of him ignored. "Before you arrived, no one was trying to kill you, and no one was trying to kill Lola. So the trigger must have been your treatment. Something that you remembered, or imagined you remembered, led to the arrival of Jinx Barker. Do you have any idea what it might have been?"

"Not a clue. Those haldane sessions with Lola are like having somebody unzip your brain bit by bit until one day the contents spill out all over the floor. I'm not sure I even know what I'll remember from one hour to the next."

"But everything will be in Lola's files." Spook gave Bryce Sonnenberg a guilty sideways glance. "I got into them, other people might have done the same. One thing to keep in mind, Barker was around for quite a while before he became interested in murder. How about this?: He fished around until he had what he wanted. He reported that. And then he was told to get rid of you two so nobody else could learn what he knew."

"Good. But it's time for me to put on my old man's hat. He might have found out something important. Or he might have learned that there was nothing important to find out."

"But then why kill you? There is no reason for that."

"Think paranoid, Spook."

"All right. Paranoia. Barker was sent to investigate you because whoever hired *him* had a big secret of their own that they wanted to protect. Something that you and Lola had done or found made them afraid that you knew it. Once they were sure you didn't have it, they killed you to make sure you would never be able to find out you had been investigated, or tell anyone else about Jinx Barker."

"And Barker and Alicia Rios?"

"Same reason. To blot out the trail completely."

"Or because they didn't trust Barker and Rios, any more than they trusted me and Lola. So here's the real question: Did they succeed in destroying the trail?"

Spook had been turning that over in his mind since the moment when Bryce had asked him what they might have missed. He shook his head. "Not quite. I see one place we haven't looked. Barker said that Jeffrey Cayuga was one of the people who ordered him to kill you. Jeffrey Cayuga is dead now, as well as Jinx Barker and Alicia Rios. But we know nothing about when Cayuga died or how he died—though I don't see how Jinx Barker could possibly have killed him. So. How did Jeffrey Cayuga die? Was he killed, too?"

Bryce stood up. "Good questions. We have to find answers."

"How?"

"Carefully. Whoever is behind all this is totally ruthless. You've arrived at the same place in your thinking as I did, but before we head back to the Bat Cave I want to mention one other oddity. Have you noticed a phrase that seems to pop up over and over, too often to be dismissed?"

"Murder?"

"That's certainly true, but it's not what I had in mind."

Seeing his eyes, it was easy to believe that the new Bryce Sonnenberg was more than half a century old. "Jeffrey Cayuga," he went on. "And the *Weland* ship, where the obituary says Cayuga died. And Alicia Rios, and the First Family party. They're all connected. And the single thing that ties them all together is the Saturn expeditions."

22

Within twelve hours it was obvious that something had gone wrong. Joss Cayuga had waited, first in Lola's office and then in her apartment. She did not appear. Either she had been and gone in his absence, leaving Jinx Barker's body as she had found it, or somehow she had sensed that it was not safe to come back.

How long could he afford to wait? Cayuga retreated along the corridor to the relative safety of Jinx Barker's rented office and considered risks. Alicia Rios was suitably disposed of, along with her records. According to Lenny Costas, she had not been looking in his direction when he had taken out his weapon and fired, and in her last millisecond she probably never even knew the manner of her death.

Jinx Barker was gone, too. He seemed to have left no office records. In this at least he had been as Alicia Rios had described him, a professional. On the other hand, his body was still lying in Lola Belman's office. If she had been back and seen him, it was surprising that she had not already reported his death. In any case, Cayuga could not rely on that situation continuing—some other haldane patient was likely to arrive and notify Security, and as soon as they examined the body, they would be all over the corridor—including the office where Cayuga was hiding.

The conclusion was obvious: It would have been nice to dispose of Lola Belman and Bryce Sonnenberg, but they represented second-level risks compared with the other two. Alicia Rios had been a core member of the Ganymede Club, and given her excessive trust in Jinx Barker he had surely been developing suspicions. Belman and Sonnenberg might have suspicions, too. Cayuga did not know how much they actually knew. The real issue, of course, was what they might be able to *prove*.

After a sleepless and vigilant night, by midmorning he could not wait any longer. The very air and gravity of Ganymede made him nervous and itchy. He longed to be back in Lysithea's safe habitat.

He checked that there was no sign of his presence in Barker's office, closed the door behind him, and walked rapidly away.

And only just in time. As he was standing before the dropchute, flashing lights and sirens along the corridor warned of the arrival of Ganymede Security. He stepped forward into free fall, not taking the time to signal his destination level.

On the way down he made his plans. A couple of kilometers of descent ought to be more than enough. Then he would proceed horizontally at that level for thirty kilometers, head up to the surface port, and use the *Weland* to carry him home safe to Lysithea. He was just ending his downward motion when his portable link unit called for attention. Someone was sending a "request-to-talk" signal to his personal ID. It had been routed all the way out to Lysithea, then back to Ganymede.

He checked the caller's ID and had his biggest shock so far. It made sense that Lenny Costas might want to talk to him, or Polk or Dahlquist or one of the other Club members.

But—Lola Belman? Talking with her might be some kind of trap. On the other hand, he dare not refuse to talk to her. He absolutely had to know what she wanted. For one thing, she was using an anonymous location for her call. That suggested she knew enough to be suspicious and careful.

He made his way to a transit node's communications center, entered a private booth, and placed his return call with a signal delay to simulate a Lysithean link. After a second's hesitation he also coded for visual connect. He had to take a look at her, even if the price were that she would also see him.

While the connection was being established, he realized that the visual link might have an advantage. Joss Cayuga had the face of a nineteen-year-old. Most people equated youth with innocence.

The image that appeared in the booth's display volume was familiar to him. He had seen her a score of times, awake and asleep, clothed and naked, in the progress reports that Jinx Barker had submitted to Alicia Rios. He must not reveal that fact to her. He waited, deliberately looking slightly puzzled, while she spoke in the long message segments that people tended to adopt whenever signal delays were significant.

"Hello. We have never met, but my name is Lola Belman. I am a haldane." (*And I'd better not forget that, now or later,* Cayuga said to himself.) "I have a practice on Ganymede. Certain questions have arisen in connection with one of my patients. As I am sure you will appreciate, I am not at liberty to divulge the patient's identity, or the nature of the problem we are exploring." (*Neat. Cut off questions from me before I have a chance to ask them.*) "However, I can say this much. There is a possibility that some of the records kept by your late uncle, Jeffrey Cayuga, might be helpful. I am seeking your consent to examine those records. Obviously, I would not ask to see anything that you might judge personal."

Lola paused. Cayuga allowed himself time to think before he answered. He could arrange to meet with her on Ganymede, but where? He felt less and less safe here. By this time, Security would be looking for Lola Belman in connection with Jinx Barker's death. There must be a better way.

He put on a worried but eager-to-please expression. "Naturally, I'd like to help you if I can, but my uncle's death came as a total shock to everyone." *(Don't overdo it—suppose she starts to ask what he died of.)* "I have not yet had the time to go through my uncle's records. I have no idea what is in them. However, I believe that they are extensive, and I do know that they are maintained at his home on Lysithea. It is not feasible to transport them to Ganymede. If you would be willing to make the trip to Lysithea, maybe we could go through the records together? I would screen them for personal materials, then provide the rest to you."

She was nodding even before his message reached its end. "When can we do it?"

The promptness of her reply suggested to Cayuga that his guess about Security looking for her was right. She saw Lysithea as safe, Ganymede as dangerous. So push her a little.

"It either has to be soon, or wait for a couple of months. My home used to be in the Belt, but with my uncle's death I propose to live where he did, in the habitat on Lysithea. I have to go back to the Belt for a few weeks, though, to sort things out there."

She was nodding again. If she felt a scrap of hesitation about her decision, it did not show on her face. "I will come to Lysithea. Immediately. Just as soon as I can find a ship to take me."

"I think I can help you with that. There might be a ship available. It's—" Cayuga started to give the name, then rejected his first idea. It should not be the *Weland,* the ship he would be using himself. Also, he must not think of disposing of Lola Belman too close to Ganymede. Better use a ship that needed no crew, was expendable, and would surprise no one if it had an unfortunate accident.

"Jeffrey Cayuga owned the *Dimbula,*" he went on. "An old ship, prewar, used originally for Belt exploration. But perfectly serviceable." *(And, like the* Weland*, it can be controlled remotely from the Lysithean center. But you don't need to know that.)* "If that sounds all right with you, I'll tell you just where you can find the *Dimbula.* And I'll look forward to meeting you on Lysithea."

As his message was passed on to Lola, Cayuga pondered the strangeness of fate. You could set a professional assassin to work. When that failed, you could undertake to do the job yourself. You took unacceptable risks, and got nowhere. And then, just when you stopped chasing, just when you had given up and were heading off for home and relative safety, your quarry might drop out of hiding—and land right in your undeserving lap.

Bat knew he was smart, knew he was different, knew that while other people seemed to love company, he hated it. He knew, however, that he was less different from others than he sometimes wished. There were things he could not do, even to protect his own privacy. For one thing, he could not tell Spook and Bryce and Lola to leave the Bat Cave and face danger outside.

That left only one alternative. Bat went out as soon as he was awake. He would stay away from the Bat Cave for as long as he could stand it. He took a deep dive to the lowest levels of Ganymede, far beyond the residential, and sought out The Belly of the Whale.

The clientele of the restaurant matched Lola Belman's

description. Even in the middle of the morning the curtains were drawn on all the occupied booths. A woman who was entering at the same time as Bat deliberately looked away from his black-clad bulk. Apparently the rules that Jinx Barker had quoted to Lola were in force at all times. Rule number one: Mind your own business. Rule number two: Speak only when you're spoken to.

These levels might be more than an interesting place to visit. They might be an acceptable alternative to the Bat Cave, or even a good new home for it. They also must have formed an excellent base of operations for a professional assassin. Jinx Barker could have come and gone with complete freedom. Even if someone happened to notice his moves, that information would not be passed on to anyone else.

Bat crossed The Belly of the Whale off his list of possible information sources about Barker and his employers, and studied the menu. Every dish on it was either unfamiliar or unpromising. But he had to eat. "Hunger sharpens the mind" was a platitude for idiots. The active brain could not operate on an empty stomach, and in his eagerness to get out of the Bat Cave he had forgone his usual breakfast.

Bat placed an order for a dozen courses. Maybe one or two of them would be edible. It was another sign of the present unsettled situation that he was obliged to voyage on such strange seas of gastronomic experiment.

As successive courses were served and tasted with minimal satisfaction, Bat reviewed his progress of the previous night. The secret of Puzzle Network success was simple: Ask the right question—and question the answer. Again and again, he came back to one fact: No member of the first Saturn expedition had any direct descendants. Could it be that exposure to intense radiation fields had induced general sterility?

He had read nothing to suggest that, but it was easily

checked. He could have an answer in fifteen minutes from any public-access node to the data banks. So why wasn't he rushing off to do it?

Bat struggled with a mouthful of gritty, fennel-laden rubber that he would have thrown away as an instant failure in his own kitchen (an "herb omelette," according to the menu), and provided an answer: He was in no hurry to check because it did not feel like the right question.

There were plenty of *indirect* descendants—too many of them. One hundred and two people were on the list that he had left for Lola Belman's evaluation. Surely they couldn't *all* be people who wanted Jinx Barker and Alicia Rios out of the way. How was Bat to winnow it down?

Location?

Consanguinity with the original Saturn expedition members?

Profession?

Absence of direct offspring?

Bat snorted to himself. Lack of fertility as an inherited characteristic did not appeal to his sense of logic. And then in midsnort, with a laden fork poised in front of his open mouth, another thought came sneaking in from nowhere.

Inherited. That was the key word. Since the original Saturn team had no offspring, someone must have inherited their estates. Who? And if those people had since died, who had inherited from *them?*

It was a question he could not answer, but at last it felt like the *right* question. A knowledge of inheritance could narrow a wide field of people to a small and meaningful subset. A few hours of work at a public-information node should provide an answer—or fifteen minutes of effort, with the specialized tools that he had developed for his own use in the Bat Cave.

Bat stared down at the plate that had just been set in front of him by the serving machine. It contained an amorphous slab of striped leather swimming in a yellow pool of slime. The menu advertised it as "sea bass in mustard sauce."

Fifteen minutes in the Bat Cave, versus several hours down here. And, if Bat hurried, time to enjoy a decent breakfast while his own programs did their work.

He pushed the offending dish away from him and stood up.

Privacy was important; but so were other things.

Bat had held a faint hope that when he got to the Bat Cave, it might be deserted, but no such luck. Bryce Sonnenberg and Spook Belman were sitting side by side at the communications center as he came in.

Spook turned at once to Bat.

"Was my sister here when you left?"

"Right there." Bat pointed to the big easy chair, with its neatly folded blanket.

"Did you speak to her?"

"No. She was sleeping." Bat did not add that he rarely initiated conversation with others, whether they were asleep or awake. "Why?"

Instead of answering, Spook gestured to one of the display regions.

A message there said: *To Spook, Bryce, and Bat. I believe that you are safe in the Bat Cave, but not when I am with you. I have reported the death of Jinx Barker to Security. They will soon be seeking me, if they are not already doing so. You know how efficient they are, and you also know that the media follow along behind them. I consider it a certainty that when I am found, my location will become generally known and even broadcast. It is much better if I remain far away from you and away from Ganymede, until this is all over."*

"Away from *Ganymede?*" said Bat. But the rest of the message was already appearing.

However, this matter cannot end until we know why

someone wants to kill Bryce and me. I may be able to find out, since I have been given an opportunity to examine the records of the late Jeffrey Cayuga. The trail from Jinx Barker seemed to stop there, but perhaps I can find a way to continue it. Since the records are all located on Cayuga's home on Lysithea, if I myself leave a trail, it will be to a place far from you. I am going to meet with young Joss Cayuga, who seems cooperative. I will be traveling to Lysithea, alone, aboard the vessel Dimbula. *I have to leave at once, or risk Security finding me and stopping me.*

I hope that the next time I talk to you, it will be with good news. Lola.

PS: Say thanks to Bat for a great breakfast. Tell him that his food machine is a genius.

Bat's grunt of outrage was ignored. Bryce Sonnenberg, busy at a terminal, spoke over his shoulder to Spook: "You know Lola a lot better than we do. Did she worry much about danger?"

"Danger to herself? Not much. But she worries all the time about danger to me. You'd think I was made of snowflakes and living on Venus. If she thinks anything might happen to me, she loses it. She's a you-can't-handle-it, leave-it-to-me, I-can-do-anything type."

"That's what I was afraid of."

"You think she might be in danger? It doesn't sound like it. According to Jeffrey Cayuga's obituary, Joss Cayuga is only nineteen."

"While sin and violence, of course, are strictly the province of the old?" Bryce had set up a series of pointers and was waiting for the data banks to hustle through them. "Lola might be fine, and Lysithea may be the safest place in the system for her. Me, I just like to be sure. Ah, here we go."

The information that he had requested was appearing in the display region. *Dimbula. Commissioned 2044, Miranda class. Employed by the fourth Saturn expedition, later mothballed at Callisto Base, 2066–2068.* ("So it missed the whole war," said Bryce. "Clever ship.") *Brought back into regular use, 2069. Currently rated spaceworthy for travel within Jovian system and for Jovian-Saturnian transfers. Restrictions: Speedwell drive places acceleration limit at 3 meters/sec². Cannot be used within a planetary atmosphere. Present owner: Jeffrey Cayuga.*

"Hope the rest of it's more accurate than that last bit," said Spook. "Data base needs updating."

"No great rush." Bryce was querying for details on the *Dimbula's* communications system. "Joss Cayuga knows he owns the ship, because he must have made it available to Lola. It all looks pretty good so far. The ship is in working order. She'll be traveling alone, which is good. This, though, I don't like. Any idea what it means?"

The display had changed to read: *Dimbula. Restricted access.*

"If I may." Bat eased past Bryce Sonnenberg, moving lightly in spite of his size. He resisted the urge to point out that he had forgotten more about system travel, communications, and communication restrictions than the other two were ever likely to learn. It pained him to see Bryce Sonnenberg struggling over trivia.

He called up a couple of his picklock query tools. They were not actually illegal, though he suspected they would be if anyone learned they existed. Results came back in a few seconds. The condensed form was gibberish to the others, but Bat had seen similar strings a hundred times. He stared at the sequence, X-58651-KY-G-ppLY, and shook his head. Suddenly he agreed with Bryce Sonnenberg. This, he did not like.

"What is it?" Sonnenberg had been watching Bat's face, rather than the display. "Do we have a problem?"

"It is not a problem, in and of itself. There are, however, possible implications." Bat pointed to the beginning of the displayed sequence. "Some of this you already know. The first symbol, X, merely indicates that *Dimbula* is a Miranda-class ship, rated for either crew or cargo. It is also capable of piloted or remotely controlled operation. The next five digits, 58651, are *Dimbula*'s unique ID within its own class of vessel. The next two, KY, define the Speedwell drive type and restrictions on ship use—in this case, no travel in the inner system, or out beyond Saturn. No problem, for travel to Lysithea. The code G shows that the ship contains life-support systems for no more than seven people. Again, no problem for one passenger. The final ppLY designator is the one that causes me concern. It says that communication with *Dimbula* is currently restricted, with signals to and from the ship proceeding via and screened by a ground-based station. However, as you might guess from the code name LY, that station is located on Lysithea."

"Try sending a message to my sister. See if it goes through. That way we'll know if she's on the *Dimbula.*"

Instead of answering or attempting data entry, Bat waved a dimpled hand at the display. He had already sent a query, and a return message was appearing: *Dimbula. Not presently accessible.*

Spook looked at Bryce. "That settles it. We have to go."

"If we can. But don't let's overreact." Bryce turned again to Bat. "Even before we knew that Lola was going to Lysithea, Spook and I had decided we needed to talk with Joss Cayuga. We didn't realize we'd find him on Lysithea. Is there any way you can tell if Lola is already on the way?"

"Lola as an individual, no. My data bases show only equipment, not people. But I can determine the flight status of the ship." Bat was entering another query as he spoke. "Here it is. The *Dimbula* is shown with spaceborne status. It lifted from the surface of Ganymede two hours ago, with Lysithea as its indicated destination."

"And you are sure you can't get a message through?"

"Given time, I can probably gain access to the ship's control center and drive. The communications center is more difficult. My message would surely be blocked when it reached Lysithea."

"Can you get us there?" asked Bryce.

"You mean, procure a ship for your travel to Lysithea? Almost certainly."

"Good. Can you get us there before Lola?"

"Almost certainly not. Most people on Ganymede regard Lysithea as a remote object, but in solar system terms it is no more than a hop. I can probably find you a faster ship. However, it is unlikely that you can make up for the *Dumbula*'s earlier departure."

"We have to try. Find me the earliest Lysithean arrival time that you can." Bryce turned to Spook. "One other thing. Better if you don't go. You stay here with Bat. I'll make the trip alone."

"Forget it!" Spook glared. "She's *my* sister, not yours. You told me, the two of us ought to work together."

"That was when I thought we would be working *here*. Bat? What do you think?"

"I am persuaded of the truth of the maxim, 'Work proceeds most rapidly in solitude.' "

"See, Spook?" Bryce stood up. "Bat agrees. You should stay here."

"Not at all." Bat had been waiting for Bryce to vacate his favorite chair, and now he sank down into it like a broody bird returning to nurse a clutch of eggs. "I believe that Spook should go with you. When I spoke of the virtues of solitude, I was thinking of my own efforts to solve our problem by more analytical means. I have had significant new thoughts. They become more difficult to pursue when others are present."

It finally dawned on Bryce why it was useless to talk with Bat and Spook. There was a fundamental difference between him and them: They might talk worried, but they weren't. Neither of them had witnessed anything at first hand, and they mainly saw an intriguing intellectual puzzle. But Bryce Sonnenberg—who was more and more Danny Clay—had a different perspective: Danny Clay sniffed death hovering in the air.

He sighed. "We don't have time for arguments. Let's go, Spook. Bat, see what sort of ship you can find us. We'll call you from the spaceport for details."

Spook followed him toward the Bat Cave exit. "You mean leave right now? This minute? Do we really have to be in so much of a hurry?"

Bryce shook his head. "I don't know. I wish I did. It's one of those bets you hate to make: If you're right, you still usually lose."

23

With Spook, Lola, and Bryce Sonnenberg on the way to Lysithea, the Bat Cave was almost back to normal. Bat was tempted to make it completely so by having a leisurely tour of his war treasures and a home-cooked meal. That he did not do so implied no concern on his part for the travelers on their way to Lysithea. He considered them moderately bright; they knew how to take care of themselves, and he suspected that Bryce was overreacting. It was only Bat's own curiosity that overruled his desire for solitary relaxation

Seated in his favorite chair, he prepared the appropriate programs. They would dive into the data banks and seek answers to his question: Who were the heirs of the first Saturn exploration team, from the time of the original expedition forty years ago down to the present day? Almost as an afterthought, Bat added a subsidiary question: What were the dates of each succession?

With the *Mellifera* probes scurrying, as needed, all over the system, feedback could be expected in bits and pieces. Bat, reluctant to leave his post by the displays, nibbled cold snacks and pondered. If Joss Cayuga was going to help Lola Belman on Lysithea, why was access to her ship cut off by the communications center? What purpose did it serve that Lola was unable to send or receive messages? More questions, with no answers.

The first response to his data search came in after only ten minutes. That meant the necessary data were stored locally in the Ganymede banks. *Simone Munzer*—she had served as anomalist for the original Saturn expedition. Born on Earth but dying in the Belt in 2050; the records indicated that her heir was her first cousin, Estelle Munzer Magritte. Estelle Magritte in turn had died in 2067, during the first weeks of the war, leaving all her possessions to her sister, Shawna Munzer Magritte. Shawna was alive today and a resident of Ganymede.

After that no reports came in for almost an hour. The delay implied that the search was running farther afield. Confirmation of that came with the next history. *Hamilton Polk*—he had been chief engineer for the first Saturn expedition. Like all the rest, he had been born on Earth, but after the first expedition he had disappeared for a few years from the data banks. He popped up again in the Earth records in 2038, lived there until 2053, then headed again for Saturn. He had been killed in 2053, while exploring the Saturn moon Iapetus. Everything that he owned had been left to a second cousin, Hayden Polk. Hayden Polk was alive and living on Ganymede.

Bat, like any high-level Puzzle Network player, marked one obvious but minor oddity about the information that he had received so far. He waited patiently for his program probes to deliver the next result.

This one, when it came, he knew a little about already. *Athene Rios*—she had been one of the junior members of the *Marklake* when that vessel left Earth orbit for Saturn-system exploration. After the expedition was over, she had returned not to Earth but to Mars. Upon her death, during the fourth Saturn expedition in 2054, everything that she owned had been handed down to her half sister, Alicia Rios.

Alicia was reported by the data banks as being alive on Ganymede. Bat had been told otherwise. What were the chances that Bryce Sonnenberg had been misled by what he had seen in Alicia's apartment? Suppose that she *were* actually alive. Bat could not dismiss that possibility, despite Bryce's confidence as to what he had found.

Data were flowing in faster now. Bat organized everything into a single table. After the eighth person he knew what to expect. The final data set confirmed it: *Jason Cayuga*—he, like Athene Rios, had been a junior crew member on the original flight to explore Saturn and its moons. He had returned to Earth with the expedition, but immediately afterward he had moved his home to the Jovian system. He had died on the fourth Saturn expedition in 2054, soon after creating the deep habitat and the communications and transportation systems for Lysithea. Jeffrey Cayuga, his heir, had relocated from Earth to continue the work. Now he, too, was dead. His heir, Joss Cayuga, in turn had given up his home in the Belt in favor of Lysithea.

The original oddity that Bat had noted was sustained all through the data: The inheritors, in every case, had the same initials as the people who had died. The one exception, Estelle Magritte, was easily explained, once you noted that a familiar and shorter form of Estelle was Stella. Did it make sense that your estate should be handed down only to individuals who shared your initials? Not in Bat's opinion. He put the fact to one side and examined the data for something more significant.

What he found at first seemed like simple bad luck. The original explorers had all been remarkably short-lived. The oldest of them had died at age fifty-eight. Was that a byproduct of a hazardous explorer's life, exposure to accidents, excessive radiation, or chemical toxins? There was no way to test that hypothesis. Instead, Bat wondered about the heirs. How long had *they* lived. If they were still alive, how old were they?

It meant another trip to the data banks, and another long wait. Bat blamed himself for that. He ought to have had the foresight to ask for more information on the first search. Fortunately his patience was well developed. He had once spent four full days and nights at his data station, cracking a Claudius puzzle. That problem had required that he pull information from the data banks of every colonized body in the solar system—including Venus and Luna, depopulated by the war, and twelve asteroids sterilized by wartime attacks. Two days had been eaten up learning how to communicate with the abandoned but still active computers and communications systems of the vanished colonies. By Puzzle Network standards, four days were a small price to pay for ascent up one rung of the Masters' ladder.

This time Bat asked for full biographical details on the heirs. When the information came streaming back in, it merely added to the mystery. The heirs were as ill-starred as the people from whom they had inherited. Everyone, living and dead, was less than fifty-eight years old.

Bat frowned at the display. They couldn't *all* be weakened by radiation or poisons—unless every one had grown up in the same killer environment.

Was that the case?

This time Bat had the information right at hand. He pulled up the records. As he went through them, one by one, a clear, cold suspicion began to bristle the stubbly hair on the back of his shaven neck. At some level, he already knew where the data would lead.

He laid out the facts as they were confirmed by the data banks:

- No member of the crew of the original Saturn expedition is alive today.

- No member of the original crew had any direct descendant.
- No one who *inherited* from a member of the original Saturn crew had any direct descendant.
- No one, original crew member or descendant, had ever lived to be more than fifty-eight years old.
- Each member of the original crew had died between 2050 and 2054—that is, sometime between eighteen and twenty-two years after the first expedition.
- Anyone who had inherited from the original crew in 2050 had died in 2067 or 2068, seventeen or eighteen years later.
- Everyone, original crew member or inheritor, had made at least one expedition to the Saturn system.
- Jeffrey Cayuga, who had inherited in 2054 from first expedition member Jason Cayuga, had died this year—just eighteen years later.
- Alicia Rios had inherited from original crew member Athene Rios in 2054. According to Bryce Sonnenberg, she was now dead.
- There was no record of an autopsy's having been performed on any expedition member or heir.
- There was no indication as to where any of the bodies had been interred. According to Bryce Sonnenberg, the body of Alicia Rios had been deliberately destroyed by extreme heat.
- There was little background history for any inheritor. They had come from the Belt, from postwar Earth, or from other regions where records were spotty or nonexistent.

And now, the implications: If you were on the original Saturn expedition, you died sometime between seventeen and twenty-two years later. If you were an *heir* of someone on the original Saturn expedition, you also died between seventeen and twenty-two years later. How long you lived depended on how long your testator had lived, after he or she returned from the first Saturn expedition. The death of Alicia Rios was anomalous, but it had been by violence, rather than natural causes. Otherwise, she would have been "scheduled" to die by 2076 at the latest, four years from now.

With those implications, Bat's original wild surmise grew to certainty. He did not wait for confirmation, and his fingers flew over the communications-center keyboard. It took less than ten seconds to set up a coded link with the *Kobold,* the ship that was carrying Spook and Bryce toward Lysithea.

"Mr. Sonnenberg, I owe you an apology." Bat started to speak even before the visual circuit was in operation. "When you left the Bat Cave, I was skeptical."

Spook's startled face appeared in the display region. "Bat? Hang on a minute, Bryce is messing around in the drive area. I'll go get him."

Bat waited impatiently, checking departure times from Ganymede and the travel schedules of the ships. Even at top speed the *Kobold* would reach Lysithea after Lola and the *Dimbula.* He suspected that was what Bryce was doing—fiddling around in the drive area, hoping he could find a way to crowd out a little more acceleration. It wasn't going to work. Bat knew what the Miranda-class ships could and couldn't do.

Bat noticed that the *Kobold* and the *Dimbula* were not the only ships to have left Ganymede in the past few hours. The *Weland,* official ship of the Saturn exploration parties, had lifted within minutes of *Dimbula.* The register showed the owner as Jeffrey Cayuga—which meant that the owner was now Joss Cayuga. Had Joss Cayuga been *here,* on Ganymede, all this time, while Lola believed he was on Lysithea?

He put the question to one side as Bryce Sonnenberg appeared in the display.

"I owe you an apology," Bat repeated. "Although you said that there might be real danger to Lola Belman, I did not believe you. I believe you now."

"Why?" Bryce was no longer the man that Bat had met in Lola Belman's office. He looked weary and wary, his eyes blinking rapidly as though the lights in the ship were too bright. "Are you all right, Bat? What's happening back there?"

"I am perfectly all right. I think that may not be true for Lola Belman."

"I've had that worry for quite a while. I thought you didn't. What changed your mind?"

Bat took a deep breath. He thought he was right—felt sure he was right. But no matter how he phrased it, this would sound strange.

He plunged right in. "Joss Cayuga is the same person as Jeffrey Cayuga. If Jeffrey Cayuga had a reason to kill you and Lola, Joss Cayuga still has that reason."

They didn't laugh. It would have been better in some ways if they had. Spook went bug-eyed, and Bryce made an odd hissing noise. "You can prove that?" he said.

"Only by circumstantial evidence."

"Jeffrey Cayuga was forty-two years old when he died. I can't believe he could pass himself off as nineteen-year-old Joss Cayuga."

"You will like what I have to say next even less. Jeffrey Cayuga is also the same person as *Jason* Cayuga, who was a crew member of the original Saturn expedition in 2032."

"That was forty years ago. He would have to be over sixty years old—and look nineteen!"

"Right." Bat ground on. No turning back now. "Also, Alicia Rios is the same person as Athene Rios, of the original Saturn expedition. Hayden Polk is the same as Hamilton Polk. Lenny Costas is the same as first-expedition member Luke Costas. Simone Munzer, the first team's anomalist, is now Estelle Munzer Magritte, living on Ganymede. The only one of the original group who died is the captain, Betty Jing-li, and apparently she never made it back from the first trip out."

There were other implications to what Bat was saying, possibilities that he was still reluctant to say out loud. Maybe one of the others would propose his idea and convince him that his brain was not spiraling out into total wildness. It was not encouraging when Spook twisted up his face and said, "You know, Bat, that's totally screwy!"

"I'll send you the data. You can go over it for yourself, convince yourself. But that's not why I called."

Bryce shook his head. "We can't go any faster. I've been checking the drive. We're already flat out on acceleration."

"Agreed. According to my schedule, there is no way that you can reach Lysithea within fifteen minutes of the *Dimbula.*"

"And Lola doesn't respond to messages from us. We've tried."

"I am not surprised. Like our earlier message, they are being blocked in the Lysithean relay point."

"So we can't catch up with her and we can't talk to her. Why did you call us?"

Bat puffed out his cheeks in frustration. Bryce Sonnenberg's question had the simplicity of genius. Why *had* he called? Surely not because he doubted the validity of his own deductions.

But Bryce was continuing, without waiting for Bat's answer. "Once we're at Lysithea, we can be useful. Until we get there, there's not a thing that Spook and I can do. It's up to you, Bat. Either you discover a way to get a message through to Lola and warn her. Or you suggest a way that we can speed up this ship. Or you dream up something completely new, something that none of us has managed to think of."

And at last Bat knew why he had called. It was to be told what he already knew—that nothing could be done unless he, the Great Bat, conjured up a way to do it. He had to accomplish the impossible. Once that burden was placed on his shoulders, every uncertainty went away. He could concentrate on finding an answer.

Of course, there might be no solution. Puzzle Network problems always *seemed* impossible when you first looked at them, but they were designed to have answers. This time the problem might actually *be* insoluble. And in any case, he had only—Bat glanced across at the display of ship schedules—seventeen hours and fifteen minutes. If he did not come up with something in that time, Lola and the *Dimbula* would be at Lysithea.

Bat sighed, feeling a tremor of excitement and challenge through the whole of his ample frame. It was going to be a long seventeen-and-a-quarter hours. Maybe it would also be too short.

24

Before the *Weland* was an hour out from Ganymede, Cayuga had decided on the best way to do it.

Lola Belman's death within the Lysithean habitat was something to avoid. It would invite prying visitors, wanting to know how and why she had died. Far better was a death before she ever reached the little moon, or at the moment of her arrival. The *Dimbula* was an old vessel. It was quite expendable. An equipment failure at a crucial moment—what could be more natural?

He had left Ganymede within an hour of Lola's departure, and in a faster ship. The *Weland* had been closing steadily on the *Dimbula,* until the older vessel was within the range of his forward scope. From ten minutes after liftoff the trajectory of the *Dimbula* had been under the control of the tracking station on Lysithea. That station, in turn, could be operated from the control center of the *Weland.* Cayuga confirmed his authority with a command for a brief burst from the drive of the *Dimbula.* After twenty seconds he saw the flare at the rear of the other ship. Lola Belman, if she noticed the boost at all, would take it for a routine midcourse correction.

So far, so good. The next step would be more difficult

because there were built-in safeguards to prevent it. He wanted the forward drive to cut out and the rear drive to go on—hard—during the crucial seconds when the *Dimbula* was on its final approach to a Lysithean docking. Say, one gee of acceleration for the final kilometer. That would do nicely. Instead of the ship slowing for a soft touchdown, it would speed up, hitting the frozen Lysithean surface at one hundred and forty meters a second. That would be more than enough to pulp any living thing inside the ship. Even if Lola Belman realized what was wrong, she would have no time to do anything. The total period from onset of thrust to final impact would be less than fifteen seconds. He, arriving later—regrettably, too late to be of assistance; lots of crocodile tears—would visit the wreck until militia After that the ship's flight recorder showed a drive-controller malfunction during the accident.

He settled in to override the safety locks, comfortable in the knowledge that he had plenty of time. Within three hours it was done. He had coded an extra firing sequence into the Lysithean master computer's approach control. When the *Dimbula* was one kilometer from final docking, the rogue boost command would be given. The ship would rush forward, missing the landing circle and smashing into the surface. Cayuga would watch it happen, because by that time the *Weland* would be no more than a couple of kilometers away from its own docking. After his own arrival he would delete the extra computer command from the system.

He took another look at the ship ahead. He was still closing slowly on the *Dimbula*. He resisted the urge to call Lola Belman and talk to her directly. Only fools ran unnecessary risks. There was always a danger that he might say something that hinted at what would happen when they reached Lysithea.

Instead, he monitored the message file. There had been four attempts to communicate with the *Dimbula*. Each had been halted, according to his instructions, by the computer at the Lysithean control center. He created a special message for Lola in case she called from the *Dimbula,* and before loading it into the Lysithean system he went over it carefully to make sure that it said nothing revealing.

He turned to the general broadcast channel from Ganymede. It was no great surprise to learn that Lola Belman was wanted for questioning in connection with a body discovered in her offices. The broadcast named Jinx Barker, but it did not go so far as to say that Lola was suspected of his murder. Cayuga had brought her away from Ganymede just in time. A few more hours, and Security would have had her where he could not reach her.

He did not need to call back to Ganymede and tell Lenny Costas and the others to lie low. The news broadcast about Jinx's death would do that for him.

He was a cautious man. It was against his nature to celebrate prematurely. However, it was difficult to resist the feeling that everything was going about as well as it could go. The Ganymede Club was once again secure.

Lola did not like going to space. It was not fear so much as memories. Every liftoff made her think of that chaotic final day, when Earth shuddered and the Moon caught fire. That had been five years ago, but still she tensed at the moment of ascent.

During the first few seconds she had stared at her own white-knuckled hand on the seat's armrest. Thank goodness there was no one to see her. A trained haldane ought to have better control. *Physician, heal thyself.* Easier said than done. She was physically and emotionally exhausted, tired to the bone by the strain of the past few days.

The flight was fully controlled by the ship's control center, leaving Lola free to look around. The Sun was a little disk of fierce white fire on her right. It was hard to believe that such a tiny ball could provide warmth and gravitational control for the whole system. Ganymede, visible on the rear screen, was already shrinking to a frosty half sphere. Its craters, plains, and mountains did not look much different from Earth's Moon as it had been *before* the war. Lola glanced at the *Dimbula*'s planned trajectory, presented for her benefit in one of the display volumes. Callisto was sweeping around from the other side of Jupiter. It would pass within a quarter of a million kilometers, and she would have a good view of its ancient, battered surface. After that there would be little to see. The outer Jovian moons, from Leda to Sinope, were all smaller than a decent-sized Belt asteroid. She might catch a glimpse of the biggest one, Himalia, but more likely there would be nothing but stars to look at until her final approach to the Lysithean docking facility.

After a while staring through the port and at the external display screens, she turned her attention to the interior of the *Dimbula*. Originally planned as an exploration vessel in the days when drives were less efficient and travel times were longer, its design was different from that of today's passenger ships. The total living space was tiny, but it was intended to provide as much privacy as possible. Soundproof partitions could be slotted into a dozen different positions, offering individual cramped cubicles in which a person could sit, work, and perhaps imagine that she was alone. The fittings were of dark metal and weathered plastic, worn and somehow weary looking. The food-production facilities were primitive and the selections limited.

Well, Joss Cayuga hadn't promised the royal yacht. And it wasn't as though she were going to be living here for the next few months. Everything seemed to be in good working order. The *Dimbula*'s certificate confirmed that the ship was spaceworthy, and that was all that mattered.

A musical chime sounded through the whole ship, and lights flickered briefly for attention. "WE ARE AT THE

CONTROL TRANSFER POINT," said a soft female voice. "YOUR ASCENT WITHIN THE GANYMEDE SPHERE OF CONTROL IS COMPLETE, AND THE NEXT PHASE OF YOUR TRAJECTORY WILL BE MANAGED BY THIS SHIP'S COMPUTER. THAT WILL CONTINUE FOR NEARLY SIXTEEN HOURS, UNTIL YOUR FINAL APPROACH IS TRANSFERRED TO THE TRANSPORTATION-CONTROL SYSTEM ON"—there was a fraction of a second's pause— "LYSITHEA."

In other words, Lola would have nothing to do for almost a whole day. She had brought nothing to occupy her time. On the mad run from the Bat Cave to the surface of Ganymede and the safety of space, boredom had seemed the least of her worries.

She moved over to the ship's communications center and studied the controls. The unit was small, cramped, and primitive. There were output speakers and microphones for voice reception and transmission, but she could see no option for vocal input to control the computer. Some points on the old-fashioned tactile keyboard were so worn by other fingers that the letters and numbers on their surface could no longer be seen. Even so, the layout was familiar. Lola should be able to use it without difficulty.

She sat down on the uncomfortable, spindly chair, and sat with her fingers poised above the entry unit. What she most wanted to do was to call the Bat Cave, to make sure that Spook and the others were all right. She dared not do it. She would assume that by this time her own flight from Ganymede had been discovered, by Security and her would-be assassins. If that were the case, they might know that she was on board the *Dimbula*. All messages from the ship to Ganymede would be monitored. A call to the Bat Cave was a good way to direct others to the very place she did not want them going.

Instead of initiating an outgoing message, she asked to receive the general Ganymede news channels. They were broadcast through the whole Jovian system, and she could pick them up without revealing anything of her own identity or position.

What came in confirmed her fears.

"... *Jinx Barker* ... *unexplained death* ... *Lola Belman* ..." (the sound of her own name in the broadcast gave her goosebumps) "... *mysterious circumstances* ... *wanted for questioning by Ganymede Security* ... *any report of her whereabouts* ..."

No mention of the others. Nothing about her present location. It was probably the best that she could hope for. And then came another confirmation.

"... *Alicia Rios* ... *homicide* ... *crime took place within her own living quarters* ... *anyone with information please report* ..."

Not surprisingly, the sophisticated tools available to Security had proved what Bryce had only been able to surmise. Although Alicia Rios had been burned and her body reduced to its component atoms, enough evidence remained to prove that she had been murdered.

The broadcast created another worry. What if Joss Cayuga was listening to the same news stories, out on Lysithea? It would be ironic to fly all the way to the edge of the Jovian system, and then be arrested the minute she stepped out of the arrival lock.

She could not safely send a message back to Ganymede. But she could place a call *outward,* with a tight enough beam that only someone in the direct line of sight between the *Dimbula* and Lysithea could pick it up. The only question was what she should say. It had to be something that would give her the feedback that all was well, without alerting Cayuga.

She set up for voice transmission and waited impatiently

for the link to be established. When the reply came from Lysithea, it seemed at first like a disappointment. It was Cayuga's voice, but Lola was not hearing a live person.

"Hello, you have reached Joss Cayuga. I am not Joss himself, but I am his third-level fax. He is not presently available. I can provide almost any factual information that you may need, or, if you want analysis, a higher-level fax can also be brought on-line. If you require a personal opinion, or wish to speak with Joss Cayuga himself, you may leave a message with me. I will make sure that he receives it as soon as he is available."

Normally Lola was not happy dealing with a fax. She thought of even the highest-level fax as a person with the juice squeezed out, including all the emotions and impulses and subterranean desires that a haldane must be in touch with before she could treat and help a troubled person. What Lola wished for in her own work was an *antifax*—a mind with all its surface logic and explanations separated out and laid away to one side. The conscious mind accounted for no more than five percent of the activity of the brain, but seeing through its misdirection and subtle false explanations took ninety percent of a haldane's time.

Today, though, she might be better off dealing with a fax. It would take Lola's statements at face value, without suspicions or questions.

"I do not need a higher-level fax," she said, "nor do I need to speak with Joss Cayuga personally. Just pass this message along to him when he becomes available. This is Lola Belman. I want to confirm to him that I am on the way to Lysithea aboard the *Dimbula*. The ship's trajectory and arrival time are already stored in your transportation computer. Tell Joss Cayuga that I appreciate his assistance in helping me to make this trip, and I am looking forward to meeting him and inspecting his uncle's records. That is all."

There was the predictable delay while the radio signals traveled to Lysithea and back.

"Thank you, Lola Belman, your message is received and recorded," said Cayuga's calm voice at last. Then to Lola's surprise it went on. "This is a recorded message from Joss Cayuga, addressed to Lola Belman specifically. I have recently learned that a small portion of Jeffrey Cayuga's effects are stored on the coorbiting moon, Elara. Rather than putting you to the trouble of a second stop, I am making a brief trip to Elara to pick up those records. I will return at once with them to Lysithea and meet you there. It may be difficult for you to reach me while we are both in transit, but our two ships are scheduled for arrival at the Lysithean dock within seconds of each other. I look forward to seeing your ship, and to meeting with you."

It was a reassuring message. From Lola's point of view, the only surprising thing about it was its maturity. For a nineteen-year-old, Joss Cayuga showed amazing poise and judgment. Spook wouldn't be like that in another four years—maybe not even in twenty. Lola smiled to herself, trying to imagine Spook at thirty-five. Would her brother still be full of random energy and wild enthusiasms? Probably. It was the way she remembered their father, rushing in to announce another project that would take them all to the ends of the Earth.

If only he had dragged them to the far-off Southern Hemisphere before war convulsed the inner system. Then the family might still be on Earth, and none of this would be happening.

Lola, emotionally exhausted and with nothing pleasant to occupy her mind, permitted herself a rare luxury. She lay on one of the compact little beds and drifted off into her own past. Just for once she wanted to return to the old days—the good old days when she was still a teenager; when she had hardly heard of the word "haldane"; when responsibility was something that other people worried about, and dreams did not turn into nightmares.

While Lola drifted and dreamed, Bat was desperately busy. He had three ships to deal with, plus a dozen computers of all kinds. He dared not talk directly with the *Weland,* which he was now convinced was carrying Joss/Jeffrey/Jason Cayuga to Lysithea. He could reach the *Kobold,* but he had nothing useful to say to Spook and Bryce because all his efforts had not advanced the arrival time of their ship at Lysithea by a single millisecond. They would be fifteen minutes too late—close enough to watch the near-simultaneous landings of both the *Weland* and the Dimbula, but unable to affect either one.

That left only the *Dimbula,* carrying Lola to what Bat now believed was her certain death on Lysithea. Here the frustration was at *i*ts maximum. All he needed was for a short and simple message to get through to Lola: *"Slow down, don't land."* That would make all the difference. But every effort at a linkage had been balked by the communications computer on Lysithea.

In his desperation Bat even placed a call to Jovian Security. Over the video link two Security officers stared at the cluttered mess of papers, empty plates, and strewn data files that surrounded Bat's massive, black-robed figure, and listened politely to his request for a maximum-acceleration Jovian Security vessel to be sent at once to Lysithea.

"We have heard no reports of trouble," the woman said at last. She turned to her partner. "Have we?"

"Nothing." The man was at his own console. "In fact, I don't think I've ever heard of a problem on Lysithea. The *Dimbula,* you say? Yes, that ship shows a destination of Lysithea. But we've had no distress calls. No messages from it of any kind. Do you have the names of the crew and passengers? They are not listed here."

Bat was stymied. If he mentioned the name of Lola Belman, there was a faint possibility that they would do as he asked and send an investigating ship out to Lysithea. However, there was the absolute certainty that they would haul Bat in for questioning in connection with the death of Jinx Barker. His own efforts to do something for Lola would be over until it was too late.

"I don't know who the crew and passengers are," he said weakly. He was not surprised when the man and woman glanced significantly at each other, and she said, "Well, thanks for the call. Why don't you try us again when you have more information."

In other words, Bat was written off as a nut case and was back to his own unaided resources. He had wasted a valuable ten minutes proving that fact. He slumped lower in his chair. It was time to forget Security forces and return to first principles.

Again he summoned information about the three ships. He had dealt with the *Kobold* many times before, and he knew its capabilities. He could not squeeze one more meter per second out of its drive. Spook and Bryce would get there too late. The *Dimbula* and the *Weland* were less familiar to him. He arrayed the data sets for the two ships side by side and studied them closely. Both were Miranda-class, both were rated for travel anywhere in the Jovian system, both were able to carry either passengers or cargo. But the *Weland* was a good deal newer. It could go much faster than the ship that carried Lola, and it could have easily beaten the *Dimbula* to Lysithea. For some reason, Joss Cayuga was not pushing the *Weland* to its maximum speed. Rather than arriving before Lola and waiting for her there, Cayuga had arranged it so that the two ships would reach the docking area at almost exactly the same time. The *Weland* would in fact be there a few seconds *after* the *Dimbula*.

If you wanted to dispose of somebody, wouldn't you

want to get there *ahead* of them, with plenty of time to make your preparations?

Bat sat silent and motionless for a long time, trying to think like an efficient murderer. Assume that Cayuga was monitoring news broadcasts from Ganymede. Then he would know that Security was searching for Lola Belman. He would know that the people from Security were thorough and patient, that eventually they would learn of Lola's departure for Lysithea. He would know they would follow her there. So he, Joss Cayuga, would have to kill Lola in a way that left him entirely blameless.

How?

Bat wasted more precious minutes, deep in thought. At last he put his final question and his own suspicions to the back of his mind and summoned more data. This time he needed information about computers.

It came quickly, a satisfying amount—or maybe, given the short time available, a depressingly large amount. There were individual but interlocked computers on both the *Weland* and the *Dimbula,* for communication, internal ship maintenance, and navigation and control. Those on the *Weland* were a generation newer and more sophisticated than the *Dimbula*'s. However, that didn't really matter since both ships during the final stages of approach would be slaved to the computers on Lysithea.

Bat turned his attention there. The Lysithean computers were new and highly advanced, not what you might expect on such a small and out-of-the-way worldlet. They had individual modules responsible for ship communication and ship control. The control modules were also linked to the general Jovian-system transportation computers on Ganymede. The Lysithean computers relied upon Ganymede for general registry information—ship class, drive, travel restrictions, and specific IDs—but they had their own stand-alone control authority for ship movements in the vicinity of Lysithea. They could not be overridden by a command from some other location.

They were also, as Bat soon discovered, impossible to infiltrate in the time available. Given a month, he might be able to gain access to the Lysithean control system, as he had gained access to almost every data bank on Ganymede. But he could not do it in just seven hours. He had already tried to crack the Lysithean communications module and send a message to Lola, and had failed miserably.

Bat was facing an impossible problem; and unlike the "impossible" problems of the Puzzle Network, this one had no solution at all.

He stood up. When your thoughts turned defeatist, it was time to do something different. He wandered the length of the Bat Cave, touching and fingering his priceless collection of war relics. Just a week ago he had heard rumors of another two relics, the fabled Palladian genome stripper and a variant on Fishel's renegade Von Neumann. Every copy of the latter had supposedly been exterminated after it ran out of control and converted the Trojan asteroids, but something very like Fishel's Von Neumann had been active in the Belt near the end of the war. Earth and Mars denied responsibility.

Bat moved on, circling past the brain-dead Seeker, the Purcell invertor, the Tolkov stimulator. The handful of war buffs who were also Puzzle Network members occasionally talked of something more exotic yet: the Mother Lode, a lost data base that contained a list of *all* forbidden technology developed in the Belt before and during the war.

Bat was skeptical. Why would anyone in his right mind make a permanent record that might later be used to incriminate him?

And yet a powerful leader had done exactly that, only a century ago in Earth's North America. Maybe the Mother Lode was real, created by some lunatic with no thought of consequences. Maybe a copy still existed. Maybe one day somebody would stumble across it.

If that happened, even more tantalizing questions would raise their heads: Would copies of the devices described by the data base still exist? If they did, where would they be? Not even the biggest optimist on the Puzzle Network suggested that those missing facts would be found in the same lost data base.

Bat, prowling the darkened Bat Cave, could see that the discovery of the Mother Lode alone would lead to endless wasted effort. There would certainly be plenty of speculation on the existence and location of the devices listed there, but no one would have reliable information. And wrong information would be worse than no information at all.

He paused. *Wrong information would be worse than no information at all.* Not necessarily. There might be situations where wrong information would be exactly what you needed.

He hurried to the Bat Cave's communications center and looked at the time. In a little more than six hours, the *Dimbula* and the *Weland* would reach Lysithea. It would be a breakneck programing effort, with no time for checking of his code. But he had no choice. He had to try.

He removed his bulky robe, flexed his fingers, and sat down without providing his usual array of snacks. Physical discomfort would serve as a spur. The good news was that even if he were wrong, what he planned to do could make matters no worse for Lola.

When Spook insisted on going to Lysithea with Bryce, the picture had seemed pretty clear. They would have an active role, maybe even a heroic one. They would make sure that Lola was all right, and they would put an end to any dangerous nonsense that Joss Cayuga might have dreamed up. Bat would sit at home, stewing in the Bat Cave.

Well, Spook didn't know what sort of stewing Bat might be engaging in at the moment, but he envied him. At least Bat would be doing *something,* while Spook and Bryce were sitting inside the *Kobold* like two lumps of canned meat, unable either to overtake Lola or to talk to her. Bryce had been over their flight path and their drive settings again and again, and all he had been able to do was confirm that they would reach Lysithea too late to do anything about Lola's arrival.

They would, however, be able to watch. Spook had installed himself in front of the forward display, where images from the main scope were now appearing. The *Dimbula* showed as a silver dot in the middle of the display volume. It grew steadily in size as the flight progressed. Even though the *Kobold* could not catch up, it was definitely gaining.

More perplexing, though, was the second ship that had appeared in the same display. There was no saying where it had come from, but another dot had drifted into the field of view and was narrowing its separation from the *Dimbula.*

Spook called to Bryce to come and take a look. "What do you make of it?"

"That's the *Weland.* Bat said it was on the way. Is it closing on *Dimbula?*"

"Slowly. If they get much closer together, the scope won't be able to separate them. But they'll still be a long way from actually touching."

"Let's hope Cayuga isn't crazy enough to try anything like a collision. A space impact would destroy both ships. Keep your eye on them and let me know if you see any unusual drive activity."

Bryce wandered aft again, leaving Spook to stare irritatedly at the display. Apparently he had been demoted to the role of ship's boy, with nothing better to do than sit and watch. On the other hand, what better was there to do? He stared as directed, hour after hour, until his eyes felt ready to drop out. Bryce stopped by occasionally to glance at the images and tell Spook what else was happening.

In two words, not much. There was nothing new on the general news channels. No success in getting through to the *Dimbula*. No further word from Bat, back on Ganymede—according to Bryce, he was not even responding to their calls. Probably asleep or feeding his face, thought Spook. Great lazy lump, couldn't wait to get us out of the Bat Cave and have the place all to himself.

The images of the two ships ahead had gradually merged into a single elongated dot. But now, as the *Kobold* slowly caught up with them and Lysithea itself became visible ahead as a tiny disk, the scope was once more able to separate the *Weland* and the *Dimbula*. Spook wasn't quite sure what the "unusual drive activity" that Bryce had talked about would look like, but so far the two ships in front were following the same boost sequence. They were preparing for final arrival at the Lysithean dock.

Spook watched the approach, filled with a strange and agonized tension. In another ten minutes Lola would be there, but they would not. Up to this point they had at least been able to see that she was all right. Once she was docked and inside Lysithea, Spook would have no idea what was happening to her.

Bryce joined him and they stared together in silence. Lysithea was an irregular lump of rock and ice, its craters smoothed away by human activity. The docking facility where all three ships would enter showed as a dark circle within the bland grey of the surface. Already, the *Kobold*'s own forward drive had come on, slowing them for rendezvous. The two ships ahead had been decelerating for some minutes. They were in final approach, only a few kilometers from the surface. Their landing could be no more than a minute away.

Spook was opening his mouth to say that so far everything seemed normal when the display in front of him lit with the intense flare of a fusion drive at full power. The observation sensors overloaded in the glare and for a few seconds the whole display went black. It came back slowly, beginning with a ghostly outline of Lysithea. As the image strengthened, Spook looked in vain for any sign of either ship.

All he saw was the dark mouth of the docking facility. A few hundred meters away from it a great cloud of white steam obscured Lysithea's frozen surface.

25

It happened fast, too fast to follow. She was in the final landing approach, the docking facility just ahead. Close behind the Dimbula *was another ship. She assumed it was Joss Cayuga, on his way home from Elara and arriving just a few seconds after her.*

Four kilometers from the landing circle. Three. And then the Dimbula's *drive went on—far stronger than expected. It caught her unprepared, and she fell back against her seat. The* Dimbula *lurched and spun. It was suddenly heading toward a different point on the opening landing circle. At the same moment the ship that had been just behind came arrowing across their bow. Its drive showed the actinic glare of a high-thrust setting and it was still accelerating when it smashed into the surface of Lysithea. There was a flash of light, a gout of white steam. She stared in horror until her ship penetrated the landing circle.*

Lola paused.

"And then?" asked the polite voice, for what felt like the hundredth time.

"I don't know." Lola sighed. She wanted an answer as

much as he did. "I told you, after my ship was in the landing circle my view was cut off from anything on the surface. I didn't see anything until I saw the other ship."

"Very good." The Security officer was tall and thin, with dark hair and eyebrows and a serious, owlish face. He glanced across to some hidden camera, to make sure that everything was still going into the record, and continued. "If you don't mind, I would like to review everything one more time. From the beginning. Your first meeting with Bryce Sonnenberg . . ."

He was always the same. Unfailingly polite, solicitous for her comfort, stopping whenever she showed the slightest sign of fatigue or discomfort; and remorseless when it came to recapturing every tiny detail of her memories.

He was only doing his job, and doing it very well, but it would have been much more tolerable for Lola if he had *answered* questions as well as asking them, giving as well as receiving. She felt as though she had been in an information vacuum for the past forty-eight hours.

After her arrival on Lysithea she had sat stunned for a few minutes, dazed and perplexed by what she had seen and felt on the final approach. When at last she put on a suit and opened the *Dimbula*'s hatch, she had no real idea what to do next. Joss Cayuga was supposed to meet her, to guide her to the Lysithean habitat. But his ship had been destroyed before it landed.

She was standing irresolute by the air lock, wondering how to reach a communication point from which she could talk to Ganymede, when the meshed plates of the landing circle opened wide above her. The stars were visible and another ship was descending. Joss Cayuga's ship? Lola waited, wondering if some accidental *trompe l'oeil* of the Lysithean docking system had made her see a ship being destroyed when no such thing had happened. She watched the vessel drift down to a soft landing and wandered over to it in a daze. She expected Joss Cayuga to come out. When not one but two suited figures emerged, it merely added to her sense of unreality.

The final touch was provided when she saw the faces behind the suit visors: Spook and Bryce Sonnenberg. They were gaping at her in disbelief, apparently as surprised to see her as she was to see them.

"Lola!" Spook said. "We thought that was you up there. I mean, we saw that ship smash into the surface—"

"What are you two doing *here?* You're supposed to be back on Ganymede."

Then they were both talking at once. "We couldn't get through to you." "We didn't like the idea that you were heading out to see Joss Cayuga." "Alicia Rios and Jinx Barker were both definitely murdered; we heard it on the news broadcast." "You're wanted for questioning."

"Now wait a minute!" Lola tried to stop them, but they flowed right on.

"Bat says Joss Cayuga is the *same* as Jeffrey Cayuga." "The very same person!" "And Alicia Rios is the same as Athene Rios—" "—the one who was on the original Saturn expedition."

What they were saying was making less and less sense to Lola, but one statement had jumped out from all the others. "Did you say I'm wanted for questioning? By Security? I hope you didn't tell them that I was out here."

Spook shook his head vigorously. "We didn't."

"Good, because once they get started on something like this—"

Lola paused. What she had been about to say had just become completely irrelevant. The plates of the landing circle were still wide open, and drifting down through the broad aperture came yet another ship. It was one of the new, high-performance pinnaces that Lola had heard about but had never seen before, capable of a continuous four-gee thrust. On its flat underside it bore the emblem of the

sun and planets sitting within a bright red guarding circle.
Security had arrived.

No one mentioned the words "accuse" or "arrest." It was
standard procedure that Lola, Spook, and Bryce would be
kept separate from each other and isolated during questioning. In spite of all that, Lola's cabin felt very much like
a prison cell as the Security vessel whipped the three of
them from Lysithea to Ganymede in less than a fourth of
the time that it had taken her to fly out. When they reached
Ganymede, the rooms that she was assigned were luxuri-
ous but there was no doubt that she was not free to leave.

But the rules had apparently changed. Her questions
could now coax information out of the man assigned to the
interview (her brain thought "interrogation").

"We're not incompetent, you know," he said mildly.
"But we are required to follow procedures. We knew from
the passenger registry, almost the minute you left
Ganymede, that you were on a ship bound to Lysithea.
Since you weren't a prime suspect in Jinx Barker's murder, there was no great hurry. It took a little while to obtain approval to follow you."

"I thought I *was* a suspect. I mean, it happened in my
office and everything. What made you decide that I didn't
do it?"

The owl eyes blinked at her. He seemed to be considering just how much Security might gain by telling her more.
"Barker was suffocated with a pillow," he said at last.
"The most recent skin microsamples on that pillow had Y
chromosomes. Barker was killed by a male. We are still
looking for his ID match."

"But if you knew I didn't do it, and you weren't in a
great hurry to get your hands on me, why did you come
out so fast to Lysithea?"

"We had a call suggesting that you might be in danger.
A very strange call, from someone we now know to be a

friend of you and of your brother. Rustum Battachariya is an interesting character." The man's expression suggested that he found Bat as curious as the call.

"What did he tell you?"

"At the time, almost nothing. If he had been less cryptic we might not have hurried out after you so promptly. He may have said more to us by now, because he was scheduled for questioning."

Good luck, thought Lola, to anyone who had the job of interviewing Bat. He tended to be a pain to deal with even when he thought he was being cooperative.

"Is he in custody?"

"With your permission, I would like to return to the mode in which I am the one asking the questions." The man smiled at Lola, taking any edge off his words. She decided that she rather liked him, and also that he was good at his job. Lots of empathy. With a little training he might even be a haldane prospect.

"One more time," he asked after a few silent moments, "how well did you know Joss Cayuga?"

He was going over the same old ground, but this time he had used the past tense. Apparently he thought it might help to pry information out of Lola if she knew that Joss Cayuga was definitely dead. She stared at him. The round eyes were hooded by heavy lids. She could read nothing from his face.

"I didn't really know Joss Cayuga at all. We talked over a video link—that was it. I saw him as a possible source of information."

"About Jeffrey Cayuga. How well did you know him?"

"We never met or talked."

"Alicia Rios?"

"I saw her once at a First Family party. We did not speak."

"Jinx Barker?"

"We were lovers. And—he tried to kill me."

"You *think* that he tried to kill you."

"He admitted it."

"Only to you. And he is dead. What do you know about the Ganymede Club?"

"To the best of my knowledge, I have never heard of such a group."

"Nor had I, until yesterday." He came to a decision, stood up, and extended a hand to Lola. "Thank you, Lola Belman. You have been very cooperative. You are free to go."

"You mean—I can go home?"

"Exactly. Assuming that is where you wish to go. Let me mention two things before you leave. First, we would appreciate it if you do not seek to leave Ganymede until we approve it."

"You mean you won't *let* me leave Ganymede."

"Phrase it that way if you wish. Second, do not be alarmed if you feel that you are being followed. You are, by us, until we are absolutely sure of your safety."

"I should have come to you people right at the beginning."

"You are not the first person to say that to me." He smiled. "Next time, maybe. Except that I hope there will not be a next time for you."

"What about my brother?"

He paused for a moment, as though he were listening. It confirmed Lola's opinion that unseen, two-way communication with others had been available to him all through her interview. At last he nodded.

"Augustus Belman was released half an hour ago."

"Spook. Call him Augustus and he'll kill you."

"I will remember that. As I said, Spook is free. Bryce Sonnenberg and Rustum Battachariya have also been released."

"Great. Do you know where each of them went? Actually, I'm quite sure you do. Will you *tell me* where each of them went?"

"They did not go anywhere. They were told that you might shortly be free to depart, and they remained here on Security premises. We have made accommodation and meeting rooms available for as long as you choose to stay."

"While you watch and listen behind the walls?"

"I said no such thing." His grey eyes gave her a secret, sideways glance. "But it is a curious fact, that even when people are told that they are being watched, within less than an hour they seem to forget it. Their conversation becomes quite open and natural."

He had said more than he was supposed to—Lola could tell by the final look that he gave her. She nodded, impulsively reached out and squeezed his thin upper arm, then dashed for the door.

She almost expected that Spook and the others would be waiting right outside, but that idea ended when she emerged into a bare, dismal corridor. She looked both ways and saw nobody.

"I would have come and showed you if you hadn't been in such a hurry," called an amused voice from the open door behind her. "To the right, then first left, and left again."

"Thanks." Brinkson? Berickson? Lola realized that she didn't even remember his name, though he had certainly told it to her when they first met. That was the problem—when they met, she had been in a total surrealistic daze.

She nodded her thanks and started out as directed, reflecting as she did so on how useful Security would find the tools employed by haldanes. The problem was, of course, that use of the psychotropic drugs and monitoring systems was voluntary. Every haldane patient had to sign off on them before they could be employed. No one with anything really worth hiding would ever agree to that.

The other three were waiting for her in silence when she got there. Bat, unable to find a chair wide enough for him, had spread out over the only couch. It was angular and sharp-cornered, and he was lying there with eyes closed and the mournful expression of a uniquely obese martyr. Spook was draped over a chair facing the door, looking casual. He nodded to Lola as though nothing out of the ordinary had been happening. Bryce Sonnenberg, unshaven, was over at a small bar mixing drinks of a virulent green.

He handed one to Lola without missing a beat, as though he had known the exact moment when she would arrive. Maybe he had. Lola took the glass and collapsed into the nearest chair. The sight of Spook and the others, obviously unharmed, cut a great knot of tension inside her. For the first time in a week she could begin to relax.

She took a big gulp and stared at each of the others in turn. "I'm sure each of you knows exactly what has been going on. But I don't have a clue. Spook?"

"Not me. I got things secondhand and I don't think I got everything. Bryce?"

"Not me, either." Bryce pointed to the couch. "Bat's the one who did it all. He knows the whole picture."

"An overstatement, regrettably." Bat finally opened his eyes. After Security's rude arrival and its insistence that he leave the Bat Cave, followed by a full day of questioning, he was ready for a little relaxation. Only the pleasure of logical exposition and a certain pride in hypotheses verified kept him awake and relatively agreeable. "What I actually *know* is very limited. What I am able to *conjecture* is rather more."

"Stop stringing us along." Spook knew Bat well enough to realize that he was savoring the moment. "Mix everything together and tell us what you *think* happened. And don't stretch it out too long. Tell it Alice-style. Begin at the beginning and go on until you come to the end."

"The beginning?" Bat sniffed the drink that Bryce had

given him, grimaced, and put it down untasted. "I am not sure that I know the beginning. The best that I can do is to go back forty years, to the first Saturn expedition: ten people from Earth, on a four-year mission to follow up on the robot probes and explore the rings and the moons. While they were out there, something peculiar and unprecedented occurred."

"An accident?" Lola, like every other school child, had been told of the early human explorations of the solar system. "I don't remember reading about that."

"It was not recorded—or rather, I now believe that it was recorded, and the records were later destroyed. I have scoured the data banks, and there are no complete files for members of *any* of the Saturn expeditions. You have already remarked on the fact that those expeditions are very much a family affair, dominated and staffed by First Family members.

"So. Was there some kind of accident? Only if we extend the meaning of the word. I do not believe that what happened was an 'accident' in the usual sense. I did at first, when I found that every member of the first expedition had died between eighteen and twenty-two years after their return from Saturn. The only exception was the leader of the expedition, who died before the party returned. The rest seemed to have been subjected to some lethal but slow-acting infection, like a slow virus. Could they all have acquired it somewhere in the unexplored reaches of the Saturn system? That idea seemed strengthened when I found that no member of the expedition had left direct descendants. I began to think of an infection that was not merely fatal in the long term, but caused rapid sterility in the sufferers. I could imagine that the victims of such a slow but eventually fatal infection would not wish to advertise their plight.

"All the expedition members departed Earth soon after the expedition's return and made their homes elsewhere.

By the time that fifteen years had passed, every survivor was living in the Jovian system—all but one of them here on Ganymede. That was curious, but understandable in a group whose illness had set them apart from most of humanity, and whose interests had always been in the outer solar system.

"But then the data-bank records began to appear stranger yet. The people who inherited from the original expedition members also died between eighteen and twenty-two years later. And so did *their* inheritors. It seemed as though any heir of the original expedition was doomed to die after forty and before sixty, and be succeeded by someone between twenty and thirty.

"Was it some sort of family taint, a hereditary curse that came down generation after generation? Hard to believe, since many different families were involved. However, I examined the backgrounds of the people who had inherited, and I found something else that defied explanation: Not one of them possessed a complete and verifiable background. They had lived on Earth, or Mars, or in the Belt; but when I looked for their original records, they were not to be found. The heirs appeared to have sprung up from nowhere.

"A fine puzzle indeed, but one that still seemed incompletely specified. I added in one other fact: Every individual in this whole affair died in circumstances leaving no body available for autopsy. Note that this includes the only case of which we have direct knowledge. Whoever killed Alicia Rios went to great pains to ensure that there would *not* be a body available for autopsy.

"Now I had the basis for a strange conjecture. The original Saturn expedition had indeed suffered an encounter with an alien entity, which we may, if we wish, still call an infection. However, it cannot fairly be called an infectious *disease,* since the affected hosts did not sicken and die. Quite the opposite. They were protected from all the usual forms of infectious disease, including the aging process. Anyone 'infected' could still die by accident or violence, but otherwise they might look forward to a very long life span. I do not know how long."

"I do." Bryce had been sitting with his hands over his eyes. Now he moved them to cup his chin. "I know."

"You mean you *believe* all this stuff?" Lola was staring at Bat and Bryce with equal skepticism.

Bryce ignored her. "What was her name, now? Lord, it feels like it's been a hundred years. Nelly? No, Neely. Neely Rinker. She came to see me seven years ago when I was Julius Szabo and living on Mars. She wanted to know how long she would live if she was immune to infectious diseases and she did not age. I told her: almost three thousand years. She died that same day." He sighed. "And so did I, dropping to my death through the thin air of Mars. So much for statistics."

"But I've never heard of anyone called Rinker," Spook protested. "That's not one of the First Family names."

"No. I don't believe her real name was Rinker. And she was scared."

"With reason." Bat was frowning, absorbing a new variable into his thought pattern. "We have seen that the group we are dealing with is totally ruthless in protecting its secret—whether dealing with an outsider or one of their own. Jinx Barker was expendable, and he was not a member of the Club; but so too was Alicia Rios, when she became unreliable. It is bizarre. You, Bryce, have apparently encountered the group not once, but twice. Each time they have sought to kill you, and each time they have failed. What are the odds of that happening?"

"The odds are certainty—because it *did* happen." Bryce straightened up in his seat and was suddenly a different person. Lola, watching the shift, wondered how long it would be before Bryce recovered his memory completely and became an integrated personality. That was her department, but she was not at all sure she was up to the challenge.

"And it's not surprising if you understand anything about probabilities," Bryce went on. "You know, when I—Danny Clay back then—ran the Indian Joe casino, we made a killing out of the gambler's belief in 'special luck.' With fair tables and no cheating, there's no such thing as a run guaranteed to last beyond the hand you just played. Of course, if there's one chance in five that you win each time, there's a one-in-twenty-five chance that you'll hit lucky two in a row, and a one-in-ten-million chance that *somebody* will win ten times in a row. It happens, it's bound to happen, the laws of chance guarantee it. But when somebody wins ten in a row, that's when they start to think they're so hot they can't lose. That's when they—and their friends—start to lay really big stakes on the *next* hand. And that's when the house cleans up."

It occurred to Lola, listening in disbelief, that males truly were an alien species. While she was struggling with the idea of a subgroup of humanity that was blessed or cursed with the gift of extreme longevity, the other three had wandered off quite happily to a completely different subject. They were mad, every one of them.

"Three thousand years!" she exploded. "Nobody lives three thousand years. It's preposterous."

Bat turned to her calmly. "It is admittedly implausible. But when you have eliminated the impossible, whatever remains, however improbable—"

"There has to be a better explanation."

"Perhaps. I invite you to provide one. And in your cerebrations, consider these additional facts. First, from certain hints provided by Security officials, I deduce that *all* living heirs of the original Saturn expedition have now suddenly vanished. Their escape routes must have long been planned, and it would not be surprising if they remain out of sight for what is—by our ephemeral standards—a very long time. Years or even decades may mean little to them."

"If they hide away, how will we find them?" asked Spook.

"We won't," said Bryce. "It's Security's job now. They have ten thousand times our resources."

"Second," Bat went on, as though no one else had spoken, "although no part of the body of Joss Cayuga remained intact after the *Weland*'s impact with the surface of Lysithea, the investigating team from Security discovered certain organic crystals in the debris. Anomalous, and not susceptible of exact reconstruction. The secret of the symbiote, if we can call it that, vanished with Joss Cayuga."

"Three thousand years." Bryce spoke in thoughtful tones. "Waiting for all of us, perhaps, somewhere near Saturn."

"That is the problem. *Somewhere.*" Bat stared up at the ceiling as though he could see through it. "The Saturn system—rings and moons and planet itself—is enormous. We have little idea where the expedition went, since I feel sure that any records we do possess have been falsified. Might I suggest, to anyone eavesdropping at this moment, that here we have a problem well suited to the members of the Puzzle Network."

"And a toughie," added Spook. "Since we don't have a place to start. Not even a toehold."

Lola sighed. Maybe they were going to get to more important matters—in their own good time. But there was nothing to stop her from trying to move them along. "I can suggest a toehold. It may not appeal to you three, because it's not so much logical as psychological."

"The battles within the Puzzle Network are mainly psychological," Bat said. "How can you make me head off along the wrong line of logic? How can I simulate your thought processes? Solution often begins with the recognition of misdirection."

"Then consider this. Your secret club, if it exists, doesn't just *want* to remain secret. It is *obsessed* with remaining secret. Do you realize that if they hadn't been fixated on death and mortality, they would be quite safe today, and Alicia Rios and Joss Cayuga would still be alive? So would Jinx Barker. No one *needed* to investigate Bryce's survival from what seemed like certain death on Mars. No one *needed* to try to kill him, or me. The Club's weak spot is its own obsessive fear of discovery."

Bat and Spook looked at each other. "Could be," said Spook at last. "Hey, Lola, what's happening to you? You're starting to have actual ideas."

"It's like a gambler," Bryce added. "An obsessive gambler is sure to lose, for one simple reason: He doesn't fold even when he knows he ought to. He keeps going when the odds are against him. He can't help himself."

Lola saw her opportunity. "But from what you said, sometimes he *does* win—that's what chance is all about. Cayuga could have won. Jinx Barker didn't kill me, but he came awfully close. Cayuga missed me by just a few hours in my office. And I still don't understand why he didn't get me on the way to Lysithea. Why am I alive, and he's dead? What happened during that final approach?"

"You still don't know?" Bryce waved his hand toward Bat. "Take a bow, maestro. You deserve it. And you, Lola, you should thank him."

"Fine. Thanks a lot, Bat. But thanks for *what?* I don't know what you did."

"From most points of view, very little." Bat ruefully rubbed the stubble on the back of his shaven head. "My opportunities to influence events were highly limited. But I can certainly offer you my logic. Consider the situation. I was convinced that Joss Cayuga planned to kill you. I could not get a message through to warn you of that danger, since any attempt was blocked by the Lysithean communications computer, presumably under orders from

Cayuga. Spook and Bryce could not catch up with you. Despite our best efforts they would arrive too late. Your ship, like Joss Cayuga's ship, was directed on its approach by a Lysithean control computer. I proved, by repeated trials, that I could not gain command of that computer—given a month or two, perhaps I might do it, but I had only hours. The computers of which I have the most knowledge and to which I have best access are naturally the ones closest to me, here on Ganymede.

"That was the framework of *facts* within which I had to operate. To them I was forced to add conjecture: If you could survive long enough for Spook and Bryce to reach you, your chances for survival would then improve considerably. In other words, my primary concern had to be to keep you alive until you had arrived at the docking facility at Lysithea.

"So far, everything is logical and straightforward. The next step was neither. I had to do what every Puzzle Network Master strives to do constantly. I had to simulate within my own mind the mental processes of my adversary. Unless I could *think* as Joss Cayuga thought, I could not hope to defeat him.

"So how would Joss Cayuga, eager to destroy Lola Belman, see the situation? I knew already that he had allowed you to leave Ganymede, without another attempt to kill you.

"Why? The obvious answer was that I, Joss Cayuga, was feeling the heat on Ganymede. Cayuga dared not run the risk of being caught doing new murder, or being associated with old murder. Much better to kill you far away, perhaps on Lysithea, where everything was under tight control. But even here, Cayuga could see a problem. The report of your death on Lysithea would certainly arouse Security interest because Jinx Barker died in your office. They would send representatives and examine the interior of Lysithea in too much detail. From his point of view, there was a far better answer: kill you when you were well away from Ganymede, but before you reached the Lysithea interior. In other words, dispose of you *on the journey*.

"And how would I, as Joss Cayuga, go about that?"

"This is where I—Rustum Battachariya—had my biggest problem. The journey from Ganymede to Lysithea seemed a time of greatest risk, but I had no information suggesting how Joss Cayuga might choose to kill you. All I could do was rule out certain ways on logical grounds. For example, he might ram your ship with his, but no one in his right mind would do that because it would kill both of you. He could plant a bomb on the *Dimbula*, but it is practically impossible to do so without leaving material evidence. He could order your drive to full acceleration, zooming you off to the far reaches of the solar system. However, if he did so, there was always a chance that Security would be able to track you and even rescue you. He had just one option that seemed to me both simple and foolproof: He could fly your ship on a collision trajectory with Lysithea.

"Given all of this, you can see why I (as Cayuga) had little choice but to do exactly what I did."

Bat paused as though he had now explained everything. Lola knew exactly why he had stopped—to make her *ask*—but she could not help herself: "But what did you *do?*"

"Why, I went to the Ganymede data banks, where all ships' registry and ID information is held. I simply swapped two files, the ship ID codes for the *Dimbula* and the *Weland*. Then I patched in a command that sent the information to the Lysithean computer, together with an urgent request that a file update be made immediately. No computer decision can ever be better than the data provided to it. Once the update was performed, so far as the control computer was concerned, the *Dimbula* would be the *We-*

land, and the *Weland* the *Dimbula.* I knew it would cause a few confused seconds when the change was installed, with the computer sending drive commands to redirect each ship to the other's landing site. But that was a small price to pay. The main thing was, if I had everything *wrong* and Joss Cayuga had no deadly notions in his head, nothing bad would happen to anyone. Your ships would simply be redirected to the landing site originally planned for the other. If on the other hand he *did* have murderous intent toward you and your ship, then that intent would instead be visited upon him. As it was. That cloud of hot vapor on the surface of Lysithea was supposed to be composed of Lola Belman."

"Pretty neat, eh?" said Spook, as Lola shuddered.

"Actually, quite masterly," added Bryce. "I finally believe you, Bat—you manipulate the outer-system transportation net better than anyone alive."

"Or dead." Bat was not strong on false modesty. "However, in this case I cannot take much credit. As I say, there was a negligible suite of options. What did I do? Regrettably, I did the only thing that I could think of."

He rose from the spidery couch and stared at it with distaste. Its lower support strut was bowed noticeably in the middle.

"You've ruined it," Spook said.

"Let us hope so. The popular view of Security as a modern inquisition is now in large part confirmed. I propose to seek a more congenial setting."

He headed for the door and squeezed on through. Spook, scurrying along five steps behind him, suddenly paused. He turned and slowly made his way back to Lola and Bryce. "You know, I get the feeling that he doesn't want company."

Lola stared at him in astonishment. Spook had read Bat's feelings for himself, without even a hint from her.

Maybe there was a possibility, just a faint one, that Spook was going to grow up and be human.

"Come on." She took him by the elbow. "I don't hold Bat's low opinion of Security, but I suggest that we all follow his lead. There has to be a more congenial setting."

26

The drugs were starting to lose their effectiveness. The patient still sat in the chair, but the telemetry feeds no longer provided inputs to the computer models. It was a perfectly ordinary ending to a haldane session.

Except that both haldane and patient knew that this one was different.

"It's the final session," Lola said. "You don't need a haldane any more. Integration of memories is going to take place at its own speed. It would be irresponsible of me to try to hurry that."

"I wondered." Danny Clay sat up in the chair and removed the electrodes and sensor cups without consulting Lola. "How long will it take?"

"I don't know. I suspect that the only people able to answer that question died in the war."

"Any suggestions as to what I ought to do while I'm waiting? I mean, I'm starting to *feel* like Danny Clay, but sometimes I still wonder who I am and where I am. Should I be back in the Sanctuary for War Victims?"

"That's the last place you want to be. You're not sick, and you're not a victim. You need to be surrounded by normal people." Lola hesitated. "I have a suggestion, but you may think it ridiculous."

"Try me. A lot of things have been ridiculous recently."

"I learned a good deal about you in our sessions together. Danny Clay had a fascination with probability and statistics, and he calculated odds as easily as other people breathe. He was channeled into gambling and crime because he saw it as the only escape from the gutter—the street-corner numbers game, and then the casino. But as Bryce Sonnenberg, you have a clean start. You have the chance to do anything you want. I think you should go back to being a mathematician. See how far you can take it."

"Lola, I'm getting on for sixty years old. Mathematics is a young man's game."

"You didn't worry about your age when you thought you were just Bryce Sonnenberg. Anyway, you didn't let me finish. Be a mathematician, but with a difference. Offer yourself to a medical facility as a test subject."

"You want me to be a guinea pig?"

"I don't think of it that way. At the moment you are a unique case, an older brain in a young body. But there will be others. The treatment you had will be repeated. You provide a unique source of valuable medical data."

"The experiments are illegal."

"Legal or illegal, people will do it. Weren't they illegal when you signed up? Do you think a detail like that is going to stop them? You saw the interest with even a *rumor* about humans living for three thousand years. No one mentions risks."

"Or side effects. You saw the coverage of the first Saturn expedition. Jason Cayuga and Athene Rios and the rest of them, so young and cheerful and full of fun. By the time they died they were cold-blooded killers without a scrap of feeling for anyone. Not even for their own kind." He hooked the electrodes he was holding onto the chair back and swung his feet around and onto the floor. "If that's what symbiosis does, you can have my share."

He did not sound quite convincing. It occurred to Lola that he was not the only one who had aged a lot in a short time. She could read the motives and actions of others as never before—and without the aid of drugs or machinery. She knew, for instance, that Danny/Bryce was not going to take her advice and return to mathematics.

"You have it wrong," she said. "It wasn't an alien invasion of their bodies that changed Jason Cayuga and Athene Rios. The change was in their *minds,* at the prospect of thousands of years of additional life. Maybe even immortality, because in another three thousand years technology may advance enough to make death an option. You or I or *anyone* would change if someone came along and offered the same package. We'd covet the prospect of all those years. Once we thought we had them, we'd do anything to keep them."

Danny Clay shrugged.

"Or to *get* them," Lola added. "If we saw the slightest chance that they might be available. You asked me what you ought to do. You didn't tell me what you want to do. But you've already made up your mind, haven't you?"

He squirmed in his seat. "I guess I have."

"You knew before you even came here for this session."

"Yes." He shrugged. "Can't fool a haldane, can I? But you know me, I've lived my whole life playing the odds. How could I stop playing them now?"

"You've lost me."

"It's that word you used: 'immortality.' It's like a bet with an infinite payout. Any gambler *has* to make it. An investment of some time now, for the possible gain of an infinite time in the future . . ."

"That's known as Pascal's wager—he used it to argue that you should live well and believe in God while you were alive, even if there was only a tiny chance that God existed. Because the payoff was an infinite time in Paradise."

"I wouldn't know about that. All I know is that out there, somewhere in the Saturn system"—he waved his hand vaguely up toward the ceiling—"we may find our own bet with an infinite payoff. I have to look for it."

"So why did you come to see me today? You knew what you were going to do, and you knew I couldn't change your mind."

"I thought I might change yours. I thought you might like to join me."

There was a moment—a brief one—of temptation, then Lola shook her head. "That's not for me. I'm a haldane. My problems are here and now. Looking for longevity at the edge of the solar system is Security's job."

"I'll be working with Security. They've seen Bat's data, and they've listened to his logic. They don't quite buy it."

"But even so, they feel they can't afford to ignore it?"

"That's right." As he stood up, Lola detected on his face a look that she thought she might be seeing a lot in the years ahead. There was a questing, yearning gleam in his eyes.

"Pascal's wager," he said. "We may find something out there, or we may not. I'm not sure. But I'm sure of one thing: I have to look."

27

Beyond Jupiter the solar system moves at a different tempo.
In the time that it takes Saturn and its attendant train of
satellites to travel once around the Sun, Earth has made a
dizzying thirty revolutions. If an Earth human lives for a
century, should not a dweller in the Saturn system endure
for millennia?

But the pulse of Saturn was changing. Its natural period
had been disturbed. The tireless and energetic mayfly humans were all ready to swarm outward, assisted by their
self-replicating machines. In another century or less they
would have overrun Saturn, colonizing every one of its
major and minor satellites.

The danger had been recognized since the time of the
first Saturn expedition. At the time, little could be done.
Now it could.

Simone Munzer stood alone on the surface of Helene.
After the violent death of Cayuga the decision of the surviving Club members had been unanimous: Long-term
safety could not be found in the inner system, or at Jupiter
or Saturn. It did not even lie at Uranus or Neptune. The
short-lived humans would be all over those outposts in the
next hundred years. It was necessary to go beyond. Far be-

yond, to where the risk of death became vanishingly small.

And they should go at once.

Every other member of the Club was already in position, lying in hibernation deep within the tunnels. The drive units were poised, ready to thrust. It was Simone's task to perform the final check and survey.

She looked sunward. If the solar furnace were diminished, compared with its brightness from Jupiter's distance, what would it look like from Helene when another fifty years had passed? Assuming that everything went as planned, Sol would be no more than one of many bright stars. Even a puny acceleration of a millionth of a gee had a huge effect when it continued for a sufficient time.

Simone turned her back on the Sun. Far beyond the planets of the solar system and the Jupiter Belt lay the Oort Cloud, extending a third of the way to the nearest star. Would that be far enough? Or would another millennium see humans at work there also?

No matter. Beyond the Oort Cloud shone the endless, quiet stars. Go far enough, with time enough, and safety was guaranteed.

She stopped stargazing and headed toward the nearest tunnel. Twenty minutes more, and the Diabelli drives, feeble but steady, would fire. Helene would begin to spiral slowly outward, away from Sol. Before that happened, Simone must be safe in the deep tunnels, along with the only others of her kind.

She took a last look around her and started down. Were they still human? She did not know. Certainly, she was not one of those humans, for whom a century was an unimaginably long time—long enough for memories to fade, for interest in an investigation to dissipate, for sometime reality to become the discredited stuff of legends. Every human now alive would be dust. But two hundred years was nothing for beings who aspired to outlive the Sun itself.

Simone reached the white membrane barrier and passed on through. The solar system would wait. When it was ready for them, and only then, the Ganymede Club would return.